ROUGH NEW PRIZES

by Mercedes-Mary McPherson

CJ McPherson-Heaney

Duluth, MN

Printed in the United States of America

First Printing, 2020

ISBN 978-1-7345812-0-1

Library of Congress Control Number: 2020906151

Printed by Bookbaby
Cover art by Julie Martin Design
Back cover photograph by Sandra Updyke, used with permission
Cabin sketch by Rosemary Guttormsson

alwaysandforevertrilogy.com
info@alwaysandforevertrilogy.com

For Lisa, who believed in me first...

I do not offer the old smooth prizes,
But offer rough new prizes;
These are the days that must happen to you...

From **Song of the Open Road**
By Walt Whitman

Content Warning:

This novel is intended for adults and contains a brief description of sexual violence.

Reader discretion is advised.

She stood before the door to the cottage, taking in for the last time the intoxicating smell of lilacs and silently cursing herself for not bringing the key. She lifted the padlock, knowing her actions were futile.

She squeezed her eyes shut and pressed her forehead against the rough exterior. This was *her* cabin – *their* retreat! No, she didn't want to let it go! She didn't want their marriage to end. She didn't want to let *HIM* go. Had her demands destroyed the life they once shared?

But she didn't know what to do. She didn't know how to make it right. All the pressures of this last year – all the visceral feelings of abandonment that she had experienced when she was just a twelve year-old girl – when her daddy, the first man she loved – died – crushed between train cars. She was like a tightly wound spring ready to explode.

He surmounted the hill and arrived at the cabin – and stood silently behind her. She spoke, but he barely heard her.

"Comfort me."

He leaned close into her body, but did not dare touch her. Her forehead was still pressed into the door.

"Comfort me!" She said it louder. And the tears came in torrents. She shouted the words. "COMFORT ME!!!"

Sebastian wrapped his arms around her.

Again she repeated her words, but they came out as a whisper. *"Comfort me..."*

He held her with every ounce of strength he had.

Now she wailed the words. ***"Comfort me!! Please! Comfort me!"***

He held her shoulders, his body absorbing her wracking heart beats. Sebastian felt he was holding onto his world. He *was* holding his world – his whole world. And he held his wife for what seemed hours. His arms were wet from the tears that spilled from her beautiful emerald eyes...

After several minutes, he spoke. "Kelly..." He said her name softly and with as much love as he could put into one name. "Kelly... what do you want?"

She took one last deep breath – still not looking at him, her husband, her Ulysses.

"I want my cabin," she breathed the words. "I want our life. I want you."

1

The End

The scowl on his face hadn't changed since filling the car a quarter of a tank ago. Whitman's *Leaves of Grass* lay open on her lap, its broken spine a memorial to the enjoyment she had found in it so many times before. Its pages had once held the odor of new. When she initially purchased the book of poems... she opened it, pressed her face against the pages and inhaled deeply, smelling the aroma of vestal paper. The first hours of reading had been like a religious experience, turning each page as a priest would, seeking the Gospel. The printed words – dark, clear, holding their treasures yet to be discovered.

Now she just looked at the familiar words, not reading them – now she merely touched the pages, the pages that no longer bore the texture of prophets...

She closed the book and snuck a peripheral glance at the man driving the car... so handsome, so strong, so... And those hazel eyes looking out from the shadows beneath heavy brows had a mesmeric quality.

What was he thinking... His financial accounting business? The conferences? The late-night meetings? What else in his life was more important than his work? Certainly not their marriage. That had gone by the wayside along with the leisure of he and she, the lingering early morning caresses, the coffee forgotten, clocks disregarded...

All that remained of the memories they had shared, whatever promises had been made, whatever vows declared before filled pews – all that remained was his work. He had finally succeeded in pushing her away.

Again she opened the book...
Again she didn't read the words...
Again she closed her eyes and remembered...

> *"Sebastian, we've had this date planned for weeks..."*
>
> *He absentmindedly turned and looked at her. She had done her hair and was wearing a new dress. She was beautiful – she was always beautiful. From the first time he saw her across that horseshoe-shaped bar he'd thought she was beautiful. And this evening was no different. And, not for the first time, he was going to disappoint her. He had to get this damn spreadsheet figured out.*
>
> *Tonight.*
> *Now.*
> *Shit.*
>
> *"I know... and I'm sorry... but this..." He didn't finish his thought. His attention was drawn back to the spreadsheets reflecting on his face from the large dual monitors. His eyes darted across the cells filled with*

numbers. He could do the calculations in his head, but there was an error in one of the formulas. He couldn't leave it alone until he solved the problem – a problem that would weigh heavily on him all night. And until he fixed the issue – until that problem was solved – he could not relax with his beautiful wife.

He was a textbook example of left brain thinking – analytical, logical and detail oriented. And now it was logical to him that he remain holed up in his office, analyzing every detail until he found the solution.

She didn't understand. She wasn't the logical one – she was the impulsive one. The one who had wanted to have sex with him the first night... The one who had wanted to move in with him, not ever staying in her own place again. And now she was wearing her pretty new dress...

He mumbled, "Just another minute..." But a minute turned into fifteen, then thirty. She tentatively moved closer to his chair – and touched his shoulder, gently combing her fingers through his long hair. At one time her touch had made him come alive. He said he would die without her touch. Now he shrugged off her life-giving touch.

She whispered, "Should I go alone... without you?"

He didn't answer. His attention was still on the spreadsheet formulas.
And he didn't hear her walk out of his office...
And he didn't hear her descend the stairs...
And he didn't hear the front door close. His attention was still drawn to those damn formulas...
And again she was alone...

She tried focusing on *Drum Taps*, but the print bled across the page. She whispered his name – *Sebastian* – its sound resonating like something new and sweet born out of darkness and confusion, captivating her very soul. She was impatient to be with him, this man who sat so close but whose thoughts she was sure were a millennium away.

She was months away from achieving her master's and the thought of graduating without him at her side was painful – so similar to those feelings of abandonment she felt after her father died. He was her hero and a giant of a man. But she was just a girl when he was killed in that horrific train accident. And now Sebastian would become just another painful memory.

Though he was driving well over the speed limit, the impulse to collapse into his body was powerful, the temptation fierce to seek his lips. Instead, she leaned into her side window, pressed her forehead against the coolness of the glass and turned her attention to the passing fields of corn, soybeans and threshing machines standing idle.

"*Kelly...*" the driver sighed her name. The way he said her name was so different from the way he'd lovingly whispered it not so long ago. Was it that long? Yesterday? Last year? She couldn't remember – her memory was like the pages of the book, well-worn and grey.

The long drive to the cabin had always been a happy trip, both he and Kelly looking forward to putting the week behind them and enjoying the solitude, the beauty of the area. The pond and the woodlands that surrounded it was their refuge against the world.

But today, this last trip out to their property was anything but happy. The bittersweet memories of their married life haunted him. While he drove the Porsche Boxster – his wrist resting across the leather-wrapped steering wheel, his body leaning against the door – he couldn't keep from thinking about the woman sitting next to him. And Sunday mornings...

His mind saw her in the diffused light of the morning as gauze over the camera lens. She in his stolen terrycloth hotel robe standing near the stove, her small breasts barely apparent behind the loose material – he sitting on a stool at the butcher-block counter reading the paper by the glow of the pendant lights. She pouring more of the rich dark brew – he warming his hands around the large stoneware mugs. She pouring thick cream into her coffee – he observing her silent motions with interest.

Sunday mornings were their time to reconnect, their quality day – time to review the week and catch up on missed opportunities to talk, listen, feel, touch, sense. Those were the mornings he loved.

With a searing pain in his heart, he remembered how happy their life had been. Her body... her soft, warm woman body... Even now he could feel her skin – taste her skin. The memories were burned into his soul...

And in the evenings when he didn't have pressing work, he helped review her students' essays – her college homework, too. He envied her knowledge of literature, and marveled at the number of books in her personal library.

Over the last eighteen months, the demands as a financial planner became greater. As owner, he alone was responsible for all aspects of his business, including schmoozing prospective clients. Many times he wouldn't see his wife for days, sometimes even an entire week if he had meetings out of town. He was overburdened but felt stimulated, and couldn't take the risk of turning down another prospective account – not yet.

His work, his drive, his dream now took up more of his time than he had originally planned, surely more than she had bargained – for better or for worse? Had they considered that in their marriage vows? Where was it written, that element which had been overlooked...

Lately, he was even forced to bow out of many of the things they used to do together on the weekends – walking along the boardwalk that edged Lake Superior, or taking his wife dancing down at the pub by the harbor. It seemed he was always either too tired or too busy. And though it would secretly kill him to see her walk out the door without him at her side, he knew she deserved a night out, a time to be free from her responsibilities. She needed her space, and the fact that she was enjoying herself justified the guilt he felt about staying behind. He needed to fine-tune a computer program, or create a spreadsheet specifically designed for a high-end account.

First and foremost, he had to keep those people happy. That's the problem when you're the CEO, he tried explaining to her. He knew she heard his voice, but assumed she had chosen not to acknowledge the words.

But always and forever, the best part of his day was at night when he came home to Kelly. Crawling into the great bed, he pressed his tired body against hers. In the dark of their bedroom, their shadows as one, their whispers the only signs of life. He had quickly gotten used to her body lying next to his – she was so warm, so soft. She was his safe haven, the one constant in his life...

> *...he felt her hand reaching for him. He moved closer to the woman who occupied the warm spot on the mattress. He lay on his side – and felt her fingers graze his chest. He wasn't used to sharing his bed. But her fingers – just the lightest touch of her fingers against his skin gave him permission to accept her comforting presence. Her face was close to his – he inhaled her sweet breath.*
>
> *"I didn't mean to wake you."*
>
> *"You didn't. I was waiting for you." Her hand touched his shoulder, softly massaging his arm.*
>
> *He closed his eyes and whispered, "I like this."*
>
> *"What do you like?" Her hand returned to his chest, touching the soft black carpet of hair that covered his chest, finding and caressing his nipples.*
>
> *"You. Your touch. You in my bed."*
>
> *"I'm glad."*
>
> *He sensed her eyes opening and wanted to turn on the bedside light, wanting to see her emerald eyes. But if he moved, her hand – her touch – might stop. He didn't want her touch to stop.*
>
> *Sebastian again whispered, "I like this."*
>
> *"Good." She moved closer to his body, pressing her warm woman body against his. He exhaled loudly – loving the feel of her... the nearness of her...*
>
> *"How was your meeting?" Her hand touched his face, caressing his beard – she pulled at the latigo tie, freeing his long hair.*
>
> *His hand stopped on her hip. "This is new..."*
>
> *"What is new, baby?"*
>
> *"I'm not used to talking about my business."*
>
> *She caressed his beard and combed her fingers through his long hair. "Confidential. I get it." Kelly smiled, knowing she was quickly learning her limitations with this man. "Sorry."*
>
> *"No, don't be sorry. It's just... new..." His hand continued moving, touching her skin – so smooth, so soft, so new. Again he whispered, "Please*

don't stop, don't stop touching." He pulled her closer to his body, his hand lightly massaged her butt and reached down between her thighs.

And she didn't stop touching...

He switched hands and sat squarely in the leather bucket seat. With his free hand, he fished around in the center console compartment until he found some tissues. Without looking at her, he proffered her a handful.

Kelly felt the soft tissue brush against her bare arm. Looking away from the speeding scenery she noticed the flower of pastel blue. She whispered "*Thank you.*" Had she lost her voice? Or hadn't need of it? She grasped the tissues, their fingers barely touching but the memory of the feel of his skin made her inhale deeply – forcing back new tears.

She pulled down the visor and opened the vanity mirror. Red and swollen eyes looked back at her, the waterproof mascara running down one cheek. Once her skin was taut, moist, glowing. We will live forever – wasn't that the promise of this generation? Have the sense to gaze only in mirrors rubbed old with age so as not to see the face – rubbed old with age.

With her tongue, she moistened the edge of the tissue and removed the mascara that clotted beneath her eyes – and inspected her face. The frown lines and crows' feet had merged with her laugh lines. She rearranged her shoulder-length auburn hair, streaked with threads of silver, bangs still falling into her eyes. Hopeless. Returning the visor to its original position, she shut her eyes, allowing her head to recline against the headrest.

Shortly after returning from their honeymoon, they had discussed her ambition to attain her master's degree in education. They both knew the sacrifices, but he had agreed that she should pursue her education. The following spring, she enrolled in the two-year program at the state university with classes that met several evenings a week. The drive was about ninety minutes one way, which meant she always returned home late.

And when she crawled into their bed chilled to the bone, Sebastian would be waiting for her, cocooning his muscular body around her – her safe haven – the one constant in her life...

Before he was so immersed in his business, before he became successful, before he lost sight of their marriage, he helped correct her students' papers. While on an out-of-town trip, he had bought bright colorful stickers, suggesting Kelly reward the better efforts with the small prizes.

But she wasn't sure shiny stars and smelly dinosaur stickers were appropriate for tenth graders. He countered by convincing her to let her students make the decision whether the stickers were appropriate – and he put a smelly dinosaur sticker on the top of a student's essay paper. Sebastian put a sticker on her college homework too, which made her audibly exhale in faux exasperation.

Thinking he had gotten this sticker-thing out of his system, she began putting the stack of student papers back into a folder. But he slyly put a sticker on her arm. She attempted to pull it off, but it stuck to the fine hairs...

"Seb! Don't waste them!"

"I'm not." He put a sticker on her leg.

"Sebastian! You're wasting them!" She was concerned she wouldn't have any left for the homework she would review over the weekend.

*"I'm **not** wasting them." And he put a sticker on her face... and on her chin... and on her neck. He lifted her – **his** – T-shirt, pulling it over her head and put a sticker on her breast... and another on her belly...*

"What are you doing?" But he didn't answer her. Instead he collected her in his arms and slowly laid her on the bed. Sebastian kissed her – she loved kissing him, loved the feel of his beard on her face, his long hair falling on her shoulders.

She needed to know. "Are we done with homework, mister?"

"No Love. We're just starting our homework..."

Oh how he made her laugh! But over the next year, her college classes became harder and his reputation as a financial adviser grew. Instead of working on one or two small assignments a week, he was now working with larger companies who had signed contracts with him. No longer did he sit by her side in the big bed – she no longer wore smelly stickers on her face.

Sometimes he literally worked through the night in his office down the hall from their bedroom. As she sat alone in the middle of their king-size bed correcting papers, she tried convincing herself she understood, though she felt him pushing her away.

Leaning back further into the leather bucket seat, her thoughts drifted... She was divorced from her first husband – a bad decision wrapped up in a not so tall and not so dark and not so handsome series of misdirected hormones. That brief marriage ended badly.

For several years she lived alone until she met *Him*. He was the companion, the soul mate she had longed for. But now he no longer wanted to return the affection, nor did he have respect for the love that she would always and forever feel for him. She sniffed once, successfully stifling the approaching tears, wondering if he was just another bad decision.

They used to go dancing. The Harbor Pub hired small R&B bands that played weekend nights. Kelly loved dancing with Sebastian. He was smooth. Oh, was he smooth! And when they slow danced, he held her close, his breath warm in her ear, his soft beard tickling her neck – making her crazy on that very small, very public dance floor.

And he knew what he was doing, because she couldn't wait to get him home and make love to her husband, her Ulysses. And when they were out on a Saturday night, their lovemaking extended into the early hours of Sunday morning.

He never seemed to tire, and after bringing her higher with his tongue than she ever had been, Sebastian always made sure he brought her to another orgasm before finding his own. He was so hard, so big, and she screamed his name or something sounding like his name as he continued pushing and thrusting into her – her body sliding on the sheets – her legs wrapped around his waist – her hands gripping his shoulders – and his face pressed against hers. Always and forever he was her Ulysses...

But now those nights were just a memory. Lately they rarely went anywhere together, and she invariably felt guilty when she went out without him. How could she have a good time knowing he was home working so hard? But she also knew that he needed his space, so she went out alone or with her girlfriends, but it was never the same without Sebastian.

She called him the one great love of her life – he was everything she had ever wanted in a man. As far as she was concerned, he still was...

Her thoughts fondly returned to the nights when he was late getting home from a meeting. She took advantage of those times lying in that great bed, catching up on her reading, listening for his car. She heard the front door in the kitchen open... close... his footsteps ascending the creaky stairs to their bedroom. She feigned sleep, but he was so deliberately noisy that he usually 'woke' her as he undressed and slipped between the covers. More times than not his body was cold – she gladly wrapped herself around him, this man who was the one constant in her life...

> *"Hi baby." She reached for him, holding him close to her chest. He enveloped her in his strong arms – pressing her warm body close to him, thawing his chilled muscles, nestling her face into his neck.*
>
> *He whispered, "I like this, woman... Please... never stop."*
>
> *She felt his breath on her face as he exhaled – and pulled him even closer to her – and continued pulling until his body rolled onto hers. She wanted his weight pressing on her body.*
>
> *"I can never get enough of you, woman..." And she let him take over her body, kissing her, making love with her, bringing her higher than she had ever been – she allowed him to love her, gave him permission to love her. Gave him permission to seduce her into his life, his heart, his mind, his soul.*
>
> *"I love you Sebastian... I love you..." She couldn't stop touching him – his beard, his long hair, his shoulders, his smooth back. She was starved for the feel of his skin under her fingers.*
>
> *"Show me, woman..."*
>
> *And she did – and she did again – and she did again... She never wanted to let him go, never wanted to not have him in her life, in her heart, in her world...*

She closed the book, securing the place with one finger held bent against the grey words embossed upon the well-worn page. Soon she would close the book on this relationship – soon enough. She secretly glanced in his direction but only saw his scowl.

Again she tried focusing on the worn pages on her lap – but her mind wandered, remembering the afternoon when she met Sebastian...

2

The Beginning

Kelly had been enjoying some quality alone time outside of her English Lit classroom. Spring break was a time for students to be rid of their studies for a few weeks – for the teachers it was a chance to get ahead on writing lesson plans. But for now, she just wanted uninterrupted time to read from her book of poems. That morning she enjoyed her first leisurely cup of coffee in several weeks. At noon she prepared a pitcher of mimosas and drew a hot bath. Of course, she had brought candles and Robert Schumann with her – a luxurious bubble bath was not complete without his Piano Concerto in A Minor, Op54.

Still in her bathrobe, she sat with her feet crossed at the ankles on the oversized coffee table. Her toes were in desperate need of a pedicure and she was overdue for a Brazilian wax. She'd make an appointment next week, but now – just rest.

A timid knock on the door rustled her out of the cobwebs of sleep. A soft voice called...

"Kelly? Are you ready?"

Oh shit! Gabriella! She had promised her friend she'd go to the pub with her this afternoon. Why couldn't she just stay right where she was – bathrobe and all! But this was her best friend, and she wasn't going to disappoint her. Kelly squeezed her eyes shut and groaned in mock anguish. She set her book down and stood, then shuffled to the door and unlocked the deadbolt.

"Come on in, Brie."

Her friend took one look at Kelly and mouthed *WTF*? "You're kidding! We're going to miss Happy Hour. Roger and his friends are going to be there!"

"I know..." Kelly wended her way into her bedroom to dress.

While she waited, Brie wandered around the efficiency apartment. Both she and Kelly were tenured teachers at the biggest high school in town. Brie was head of the foreign language department, teaching Italian and Spanish – and she knew Kelly could get a much nicer place. But as much as Brie suggested she come up in the world a little, Kelly was just as adamant in her decision to stay. 'Quaint' was how she described it when she signed her lease, and it was just that – if not terribly shabby chic also.

Brie stopped before the full-length mirror and checked her long brunette hair, self-styled in a classic chignon. Her silk turquoise-colored blouse displayed an ample cleavage. She leaned coquettishly into the mirror – and opened one more button. Just one more. After all, *that bartender* would be at the pub this evening. She touched the small gold pendant hanging from her necklace, its base becoming lost in the dark abyss between her breasts. Good.

She turned sideways, sucked in her belly and examined her profile. The white linen pants she wore together with the thin leather belt were the perfect additions to her ensemble. Oh yes. *He* would notice her tonight.

Kelly finally emerged from her bedroom having donned a plain white blouse with capped sleeves and dress blue jeans. Where Brie wore high heeled wedge sandals, Kelly chose her comfy moccasins. She took one last look in her makeup mirror and added another layer of mascara.

She glanced sideways at her friend. "I hate you, Brie."

"Why?"

"Because you're perfect without makeup and you don't need mascara!"

"Come on, Kell. You're beautiful. Let's go."

Kelly grabbed a sweater and the women exited the apartment. Brie watched as her friend pulled the door closed and locked the heavy-duty deadbolt.

"Roger installed that new deadbolt?"

Kelly nodded and slipped the key in her purse.

"He's sweet on you, Kelly. You know that."

"Brie, Roger is a friend. Come on – you said we might miss Happy Hour, right?"

The women ran down the one flight of stairs and out into the late afternoon sun. As they got into her car, Brie opened the moonroof. Kelly tuned the Sirius XM radio to the 80s on 8 channel and cranked up the volume. As the car pulled from the curb, the two friends acting like their teenage students sang *I Love Rock 'n Roll* at the top of their lungs. The drive to the harbor took only a few minutes and almost immediately they found a parking spot close to the bar.

Upon entering the pub they spotted Roger, but there were no seats near him. They claimed two open stools across the horseshoe bar and ordered their first round of drinks – ice-cold draught beer in chilled glass steins. Kelly asked for her usual large green olive in hers.

The appetizers were arranged on long tables behind them. Taking turns, the friends scooped up what would be their dinner and returned to the bar – lobster-stuffed mushrooms with Parmesan, crab cakes, and bacon-wrapped Medjool dates stuffed with Gouda. The Harbor Pub spared no expense in pleasing their steady clientele. Both women agreed not to talk shop and spent the time feeding their faces, laughing at stupid jokes and drinking beer.

Roger appeared at Kelly's side. He was a large man standing six-foot-four who had served in the USMC. He taught carpentry and woodworking in the technical school. A run-in with a band saw gave him the unfortunate ability of counting to 9-1/2. Both women had taken advantage of his skills, including building bookcases for their apartments. He was always thanked with home-cooked meals, which as a bachelor he never turned down. Roger was more of a big brother and not a lover – a line he never crossed.

"What are my two favorite ladies up to this evening?"

By the way he began his spiel, Gabriella knew right away he was up to something. Kelly was too busy enjoying her crab cake to notice any hidden agenda in Roger's query.

"Fess up, Rog? What's going on?"

Now Kelly was interested in Roger's answer too – although if this was another set-up, she wasn't interested. As sweet as he was, Roger was inept at the art of match-making and she didn't want to be included in yet another failed 'but he's a great guy' proposal. She returned to picking up crumbs from the crab cake with her fingers, trying very hard to ignore the upcoming speech.

Roger had been down this road before – always following the requests of hopeful suitors, but never stepping up himself. He couldn't take the chance that Kelly would not want him as a lover. He would rather have Kelly in his life. At least this way he had a relationship with her, though it was on her terms – as a friend.

"So Kelly... My friend Sebastian over there would like to make your acquaintance."

Oh God... 'Make my acquaintance'? Roger really was reaching this time. Both women looked in the direction of the men who were now huddled in a tight group, looking something like small boys sharing a prized marble. The association made Kelly laugh, but she did like the looks of the new guy – the one Roger was trying to pawn off on her. In the dimness of the bar, she noticed his full beard – and eyes shrouded beneath heavy brows. Would she like to meet him? Without taking her eyes off Sebastian, she nodded *Yes*.

As the small foreign car sped along the highway, Sebastian knew from experience he could not fix her tears. And trying to comfort her only exasperated her tears. Instead, while he drove, he was the silent observer as she primped, wiping the mascara from her face, fixing her hair, scrutinizing herself... *What are you thinking, Kelly? Don't you know you are the one great love of my life?* She was beautiful. Even in the mornings when she believed her auburn hair a fright, he knew she was beautiful.

He didn't compliment her very often. His actions spoke for him. Words were empty, he argued. Anyone could say 'I love you,' but so few people really meant the words – and so few people heard the words when the words were spoken. He wasn't as verbally demonstrative as she was. He was a quiet man in a world of irreverent sounds.

After his first brief marriage ended, he had lived alone for several years, dating infrequently – but this relationship seemed so good. Kelly was the one he had searched for his whole life. She was his Dulcinea! How else could he have explained his feelings to her, the joy of finding the perfect woman? When they had known each other for only three months, he knew they would spend the rest of their lives together. He remembered their meeting...

His phone rang. Damn, he forgot to turn off the ringer – he usually forgot to turn *on* the ringer. He raised his hips up from his reclining leather chair and pulled the phone from his back pocket. Looking at the time before he answered – he had only been napping for a half hour, for crying out loud – he almost declined the call. There were no tax emergencies today – this was Saturday. Squinting, he looked at the name on the caller ID. Roger McClennen. Okay.

"Rog, what's up?"

"Seb! Where are you?" Roger was shouting into the phone, trying to hear himself above the din in the background.

"Sleeping... good night."

"Come on, buddy. We're all down at the Harbor Pub. Michael. Cody. Phil's on leave. Get your shit together and get down here!"

Sebastian hadn't been very visible lately. This was, after all, tax season. After graduating college, he had been employed at a high-end accounting firm. The clients were pre-screened, their paperwork clean, in order, stapled.

After six years, he left the firm and at age thirty established SGB Financial Services. Many of his new clients were unprepared and disorganized, their paperwork ripped or stained with rings of coffee – or even worse. And some didn't show up at the appointed time, arriving at the end of a very long day with children in tow, trying his already stretched impatience and expecting him to stay later than his already twelve hour day. Only one more month.

He paused, one arm draped over his eyes. "I'll be down in five minutes, Rog." Yeah, he'd go down to the bar for a little while, have a few beers. Then return home to his La-Z-Boy and Lee Ritenour's soothing jazz guitar. "Have a cold one waiting for me."

"You got it, Seb." He added, "Oh and hey, there're some real lookers down here, too!"

He had to chuckle at Roger's euphemism for attractive ladies. His friend was trying to fix him up with a girlfriend. Sebastian was 35 years old and again a bachelor. And he wasn't in the mood to meet anyone right now – but the cold beer sounded good.

He sat up and pulling his long hair back, quickly tied it with a string of latigo. While tucking his shirt into his trousers, he saw his reflection in the tall dining room mirror. His beard needed a trim.

There was little traffic on the drive to the harbor area, but parking spaces were already dear and his usually distempered temper became shorter. Though it was further away than he wanted, he found a space and parked. He stashed his sunglasses in the passenger visor and began the walk down the hill to the bar. The late afternoon sun was high – he regretted leaving his sunglasses behind.

It took a few moments for his eyes to become accustomed to the pub's dark interior. The pool tables were to the left, the small dance floor behind that and the large horseshoe-shaped bar was off to the right.

"Seb!" He turned toward Roger's baritone voice, spotting him on the near side of the bar. Sebastian had to laugh. Roger's thick black mustache – along with his military high-and-tight were his best friend's unmistakeable characteristics. The other men gathered included Phil, home on leave from the army; Michael, president of his local IBEW; and Cody, owner of a plumbing supply store. It was Happy Hour and the beer flowed in frosty mugs – so good, so cold – and his long list of tax return clients became history as he began relaxing.

Soon his eyes rested on two women sitting on the opposite side of the horseshoe bar. Roger followed his friend's gaze. He was acquainted with both women and told Sebastian they were teachers at the high school. Sebastian knew neither, but was more than interested in the redhead. Uncharacteristically, he asked his friend to introduce her to him.

Roger was usually so inept at these schemes. However, since he was not the instigator of this meeting he was – gratefully – released from all blame if the connection failed. He walked around the bar to where the two women sat.

Sebastian watched as he spoke with the women. Before long, the redhead looked in his direction and, without taking her eyes off him, nodded. The women spoke to each other as Roger motioned at him to join them.

He made his apologies to his friends, making them promise to call him when their pool table opened, and sauntered over to the trio. Somehow Roger managed a simple introduction.

"Sebastian Bonsignore, this is Gabriella Murray and her friend Kelly Cameron."

Her friend Kelly was all he wanted to know. He briefly shook Gabriella's hand, but when he took Kelly's hand he held it longer, almost caressing it, and asked if he could sit with her for a bit. The women looked at each other, grinned and shrugged their shoulders. Brie agreed to give up her seat.

Roger helped her off the stool, and taking one last look at Kelly, escorted Gabriella back to where his friends were huddled in conversation. There, quietly and with mild interest, he and Gabriella and the others watched as Sebastian and Kelly compared notes.

He couldn't take his eyes off this red-headed beauty. He knew he was staring, but he didn't care. Her large emerald eyes were like nothing he had ever seen – and they were staring back at him. This was either a dream – *Oh, Lord, don't wake me now!* – or he was the luckiest man alive. But he knew his life wasn't based on luck, and he definitely wasn't dreaming. This was his reality and he'd better open his mouth or he was going to miss out on his future.

But before he could say anything, she made the first lob. Amidst the cacophony swirling around them, the music in the background – *which could be turned down!* – and the sound of his beating heart, her voice was that of an angel's.

"So Sebastian, did you force Roger to make that introduction?" From what she knew about Roger, no one could force him to do anything.

"No," he chuckled softly. "I just asked him nicely to make the introductions – and I slipped him a twenty." His eyes sparkled.

She laughed. Good, he's got a sense of humor. Check! She continued her interrogation. "So what inspired you? What was it about me?" Kelly looked directly into his hazel eyes.

"Inspired me?" He took a moment to think, never taking his eyes off her. Could he tell her he saw Dulcinea sitting across from him? When he first saw her, he finally understood the words that described the fictional character... 'The most beautiful of all women, my queen and lady.' Too corny? Would she laugh at him? Would she even know of *Don Quixote*? He was not a great reader of literature, but he knew that one.

And he was pleasantly – more than pleasantly surprised when her friend Gabriella, buxom and beautiful, left her stool, relinquishing it to him. Though she had many obvious charms, she wasn't *the one*. She didn't have the emerald eyes.

"Your eyes," he answered slowly. "Your eyes inspired me." Yes, he had wondered if she wore tinted contacts. Some women he knew did. But like the color that comes out at the end of the night, fitting into little white cases, so did the fantasy – and the reality was as fake as their eyes. No – he knew they were her eyes. Though when he first sat next to her and stared hard at her, he checked for the telltale halo just to confirm his instincts were right on.

And she had a delightful sense of humor. As he would on a balance sheet, Sebastian was checking off all her assets, and that column was quickly filling up. He had not brought a drink with him and her stein was almost empty.

"Kelly, may I buy you a drink?"

She gave him one of her looks. "I think you should, don't you?"

Though he was surprised by the look, he was pleased with her smart-ass attitude and responded with a crooked grin. He flagged the bartender...

His shirt was wrinkled! He had napped on his recliner in this shirt, and he still wore the same baggy chinos he had put on the day before. Why hadn't he changed clothes before he left his house? Because he didn't know he would be meeting his Dulcinea! And to top it off, his beard was in need of a trim. He knew he looked like a cave man. His liabilities were adding up. Could she see past his unkempt outward appearance and really see *HIM?*

While he waited for their order, he continued their conversation. "What made you say *yes*?"

It sounded like he was challenging her. "Yes to what, Sebastian?"

"Yes to uprooting your friend so I could sit here... close to you... here." He leaned into her, his muscular shoulder almost touching her bare arm.

"Oh, Brie? She knows I'm an easy mark for a good-looking guy." She laughed, feeling more at ease now.

The fresh, frosty beers were set before them, one with a swizzle stick stuck into a large green olive. He raised an eyebrow at the olive, but Kelly just smiled. Sebastian handed the bartender a ten and told him to keep the change.

"So now I'm a good-looking guy?" He sat up straight, striking a model's pose.

"You have potential."

He offered to get more appetizers, including more of the delicious Medjool dates, but before he could leave his stool, she tested his culinary knowledge.

"You know what they are? The Medjool dates?"

"Of course." He answered in a mocking tone. He had been a chef for many years and he knew his dates, but he played along. And the more she talked, the more he wanted her. Sebastian needed to stand and let his growing erection die.

He rose from the stool, giving his constricted penis breathing room. While he took his time plating the goodies, he felt her watching him – and felt his erection coming back to life. The bar was dark and so were his trousers. She'll never notice. Or did he want her to notice?

Kelly watched as he rose from his stool – his shirt sleeves tightened around his shoulders and biceps. There were muscles under those wrinkles. Check! Her eyes followed him as he walked over to the long tables where a few of the appetizers remained.

While he stood plating, she took stock of this man. His shoulders weren't too wide, his waist wasn't too narrow, and his long hair hung to the middle of his back. And though his trousers were baggy, his glutes filled out the seat of his pants just fine. At one point he reached across the table, bending at the waist to procure a few of the delicious mushrooms. Oh yes, he had a very nice ass.

Kelly turned back to the bar – she had been holding her breath. She smiled and exhaled through pursed lips. Oh, hell yes.

When he returned with a nice assortment, she noticed he had placed the canapés on one large plate which he put on the bar between them.

"You expect we should eat from the same plate, Sir?" Kelly was taking a playful haughty stance.

"Hogs at the trough, Miss. Hogs at the trough." And he smiled.

Oh, it was a beautiful smile, a perfect smile – and that perfect smile intrigued her. Another check in the positive column.

She was about to eat a piece of a crab cake, but to her surprise he picked up one of the bacon wrapped dates and offered it to her. She put down the uneaten tidbit. Sebastian carefully brought the delicacy up to her and held it close to her lips. She looked at him, then opened her mouth and allowed him to feed her. She took a bite out of the date – he popped the remainder in his mouth. Oh, sharing food on the first date. How hot!

But he apparently wasn't done. Sebastian offered her a piece of the stuffed mushroom, holding it between his thumb and forefinger. After Kelly accepted the morsel she quickly clutched his wrist, holding his fingers close to her lips. She bravely licked his fingers and playfully sucked on his thumb...

It was not lost on her that he got an erection when she sucked his thumb. That was the reaction she hoped for. She so wanted to see and experience what he packed in those baggy trousers. It had been so long since a man's head was trapped between her thighs... She squirmed just thinking about the possibilities, her bottom muscles pulsing kegels...

When she had sucked on his thumb, he didn't pull back. He could only think about how lucky it was he had on his baggy trousers because, like a biblical Lazarus, his erection came roaring back to life.

"Oh Lord, woman!" he breathed. "You're going to be the death of me." He was happy she had taken the initiative to show her hand, so to speak. But he wanted to reciprocate in his own special way…

He loved the feel of a woman's thighs around his head, the smell of her musk. Would she allow him to give her an orgasm with his mouth? Let her experience the ecstasy he could give her? Oh, he could fantasize, but fantasy was not satisfaction. How long would he have to woo her, date her until she let him taste her… And when she playfully sucked on his thumb…

Enough! He was going to drive himself crazy with these thoughts. He had to come back down to reality. Sebastian wanted her – he wanted her in his bed. His heart had finally quit beating out of his chest – his breathing calmed. But before he could explore her body, there was so much he wanted to know about this woman.

Kelly looked across the bar where Brie sat. The startled look on her friend's face was obviously a reaction to the way she had sucked on Sebastian's thumb. Maybe she shouldn't have been so forward with a man she hardly knew, but he was like no one she had ever met. *Could you be my Ulysses?*

Kelly turned her attention back to Sebastian, who had resumed drinking his beer. "Um, I was just thinking... " *And I wish I could tell you!* "I need to know more about you, for my friend, you know. She's going to quiz me later, so spill."

He flashed that same crooked grin. "For starters, I'm a financial planner and I own my company. I'm also a CPA. That's Certified..."

"For crying out loud, Seb!" She said in frustration. "I know what CPA means! Give me more."

"More?" He considered her request – his recently sucked-on thumb pressed to his lips. After all, she did say he had potential. "I've worked as a chef and I'm still a pretty good cook. I could prove that to you if you want." He let the last words fade, giving her a chance to take his bait.

"Well Sebastian, I think that's a possibility. What do you have in mind?" Now she waited, watching him take *her* bait. Kelly loved this playful tète-à-tète, but she wanted him to make his move. She leaned her whole body into him, resting her forearm on his shoulder and softly caressing his long hair with her fingertips.

He made his move. "I think we should make a date. What time do you usually get off work?"

"Oh, I don't work." Kelly sat up straight, causing the wet spot in her panties to be more pronounced against her skin. "I mean I do, but I'm a high school teacher and this is spring break." She suggested they could take a walk in the park before dinner.

He shook his head. "I don't do parks. Birds crap on my head."

She mockingly echoed his words. "Birds crap on your head? Seriously?"

He looked hard at her. "Seriously."

Awkward... "Um... Okay, well we could walk where there aren't any birds. Or you could wear a hat!"

"Kelly," he spoke carefully, not wanting to put a damper on this budding relationship. Sebastian took a breath and continued. "As sweet as you are, I'll let you take your walk all by yourself and your birds, and meet me at my home when you're done communing with nature." He didn't mean to sound so stern, but he wanted to set parameters. Returning to his beer, he hoped he hadn't messed up what could be a very good thing.

"Are you dismissing me?" *No no no!* She quickly regrouped. "Okay, Plan 2."

"Plan 2?" he asked. "I take it bird watching was Plan 1?"

Now she was on to Plan 2. Oh, he was falling for this woman! He hoped Plan 2 was anything but nature. Sebastian wanted her to give him something to work with here. And the symphony – definitely not the symphony.

"Plan 2," Kelly began. "Since you're not an outside kind of guy, I have season tickets to our wonderful symphony."

Of course she did! Didn't he figure she was a class woman? And didn't class women dress up and go to the symphony? From experience, he knew the symphony was a good place to take a nap.

He suggested they could listen to his music. "Give me some R&B, Marvin Gaye, Marshall Tucker... Or Jazz... Rippingtons, Boney James, George Howard... Any of those names spark an interest?"

"Um... no." This was not going well at all. Kelly would try another approach. "What do you like to read?"

She looked hopefully at him, thinking he must be a man of literature. But to her dismay, he said he read newspapers, namely the *New York Times* and *The Chicago Sun Times*. Sebastian lobbed the question back into her court.

"Since I teach literature, I read the classics – Poe, Melville, Whitman..." Her sentence quietly dropped off a cliff. Maybe he could have shared the Dulcinea comparison with her, but he wasn't sure she'd appreciate the connection.

Kelly looked down at her plate, contemplating leftover crumbs. "I think we're at a stalemate here."

He noticed her dejected look. "Do you like to eat?" He spoke so softly she almost didn't hear the question.

What?" She slowly looked at him – crinkling her nose. "Do I like to eat?"

"I cook. Do you like to eat?" He sounded each word with a staccato beat, giving her that same crooked smile.

She shook her head at the man who asked such a silly question, and answered his query with incredulity. "Of course I like to eat."

Sebastian turned and faced her. "Kelly, come to my home for dinner."

He couldn't read her. He took her hand – which made her turn back to him – and kissed the back of it. Oh she tasted sweet! *Would every part of her taste that sweet?* His erection perked up again. With his free hand he took a long drink from his empty stein, tipping it up in his mouth, buying time, waiting for his erection to die – again.

"Come to your house for dinner. Just like that?" When he kissed the back of her hand, his mustache tickled her skin. *Kelly silently wondered how his mustache would feel lightly brushing between her thighs.*

"Yes, just like that. Come to my home for dinner. I don't walk in nature, you don't listen to jazz. This is something we can agree on."

She looked over at Brie, who by now was in deep conversation with the bartender. Kelly took a deep breath and answered, "Yes, I would like that."

"Yes?" he repeated.

She loudly exhaled. "Yes."

Sebastian smiled his best smile and kissed her hand again. Oh yeah, definitely another check! Kelly gave him her number – he etched it in his heart. She entered his number into her phone. He promised to call her in a few days for the date.

From across the bar, Michael called out to him. "Sea Bass! Pool! Our table's open!"

He was reluctant to leave her side – the attraction was powerful. But he had made a promise to call her and hopefully would see her in a few days. He boldly leaned in and kissed her chastely on her lips. "I'll call you..." And he was gone.

Brie returned to the stool recently vacated by Sebastian and sat next to her friend – her friend who still had that goofy *I think I just fell in love* look on her face.

"Kelly. Earth to Kelly. Come on girlfriend. Spill!"

She turned to Brie – and rolled her eyes, exhaled and smiled.

The lost memories of that day – that first meeting with Sebastian... The passing scenery blurred behind fresh tears...

3

The Date

She wasn't surprised when she heard from him the next morning. If he hadn't called her, she would have been disappointed.

In preparation for this special night, she made an appointment for her pedicure and also a Brazilian wax. She wanted to be ready just in case... She didn't date a lot, practically never during the last several years. And it had seemed forever since a man had gone down on her. No one really interested her – no one except Sebastian. She hoped he was the one.

Kelly arrived at the address on time. His home was a huge, two-story brick mansion built on two acres. The front steps led to a large wrap-around porch resembling something from the days of southern plantations. She pulled up to the garage and parked.

One last time, she checked her hair in the car's vanity mirror. Her bangs hung in her eyes – she should have gotten a haircut. But she had chosen her wardrobe carefully, wearing her favorite pink blouse – the one with pearl buttons that unbuttoned easily. She also left her bra and unders at home, and felt wickedly naked underneath. Still looking in the mirror, Kelly whispered, *"It's showtime"* and flipped the visor closed.

Their first date had to be unforgettable. Relying on his years of culinary experience, he created a menu of pan-roasted salmon with beurre blanc, and his homemade fettuccine with Alfredo.

He heard her car drive up to the garage. Sebastian quickly went into the dining room and pressed play on the stereo. He returned to the kitchen and waited until he heard her footsteps on the porch, then opened the front door... He leaned in and kissed her on the cheek, and felt like he was meeting her for the first time.

Sebastian had only seen her in a dark bar – now he was looking at this woman in his home. Her emerald eyes in the bright light of his kitchen had the same effect on him as when he first sat next to her at the bar. And she was tall, standing just shy of six feet. Her shoulder-length auburn hair framed her beautiful face in soft waves.

Kelly listened for a moment and recognized the music. Vivaldi's Concerto No. 2 in G Minor. She smiled, knowing Sebastian had chosen that music especially for her. Upon entering the kitchen, she encountered a long narrow butcher-block breakfast bar. On it were a tall glass vase of white roses and a bottle of Cline Ancient Vines Zinfandel. Obviously, Roger had clued Sebastian in on her likes and dislikes.

She put her purse on one of the stools, and took a minute to look around the kitchen. Black soapstone countertops lined the perimeter of the vast kitchen. Stunning!

He seemed anxious, so different from the confident man who simply had to sit with her at the bar. Hopefully, having a drink would calm him. She watched as he poured the wine into two long-stemmed crystal goblets. Nice touch.

Sebastian offered one of the sparkling goblets to her and croaked, "To you, Kelly." He didn't recognize his voice. *Why was he so nervous?* It wasn't like he hadn't dated before. But the fact that she – this stunning redhead – was standing so close to him made him nervous as hell.

"Thank you, Seb," she graciously replied. "You know, Cline is my favorite label." Sebastian silently thanked Roger for cluing him in on Kelly's likes and dislikes.

This was ridiculous. He needed to relax, and knew once he started cooking he would. Sebastian was in his element in the kitchen. He had already prepped the salmon, applying a thin coat of a brown sugar and cumin rub to one side. The fettuccine that he had made earlier was drying across thin wooden dowels. And he wouldn't start the Alfredo sauce until after the pasta went into boiling water.

"Kelly, please sit." She thanked him and sat on one of the tall stools. Now she had a perfect vantage point from which to watch the former chef in action.

Sebastian almost felt self-conscious, but as soon as the thick steaks were placed in a pre-heated pan, he exhaled. He had never cooked with an audience – and this audience was the woman with the emerald eyes.

"Where did you grow up, Kelly?"

She put down her goblet, but still held the delicate stem. "I grew up in Colorado."

"What brought you to Minnesota?"

"That's kind of a long story..."

"We have time..." He gave her a crooked smile.

"My grandma – my mom's mom grew up here, up north in Grand Marais."

"That's quite a leap."

"Yeah, well, she married a man from Colorado. And when he wanted to move home, so I've been told, she didn't want to live without him. So she followed him back to his home – in Grand Junction."

"So, how does that bring you here?"

"I told you it was a long story." She sipped more of her wine. "She always talked about Lake Superior. And through her stories, I guess I fell in love with the lake, too."

"And so?"

She laughed. "So, after I graduated from college, I checked out the teaching opportunities here and..."

"And here you are."

"Yes... In your kitchen."

"How long have you lived here?"

"I've taught for ten years, so I guess a little over ten years."

"Do you own a home?"

"No, never wanted to be tied down with a mortgage... I live in an efficiency." She again looked around his kitchen. "Not anything like your impressive home."

"What grades do you teach?"

"Grades 9-12." Kelly knew she was causing this big man much discomfort – she hid a smile behind her crystal goblet. Sebastian carefully turned the steaks and placed the pan in the preheated oven.

Kelly was intrigued as she watched her personal chef pour Jack Daniels Whiskey into a small pot. He added crushed pineapple with juice, minced chipotles in adobo and garlic, bringing the mixture to a boil.

"This all looks so good..." Kelly sat up a little straighter and inhaled deeply. "And the smell is fantastic!" She wanted to know more about him – the man who was so comfortable in his kitchen. "So what brought you here?"

He wiped his hands on a terrycloth hand towel. "My folks immigrated to the United States – they were born in Italy, so that makes me and my brother first-generation Americans." He stirred the Jack Daniels mixture. "When they came here, they settled on the Iron Range – mining was big. But before I was born my folks moved a lot, mostly my dad finding better jobs." He looked at Kelly. "By the time I started kindergarten, they had settled in St. Paul."

"And so?"

He laughed. "And so... we'd vacation up here. My folks would pack us up and rent out one of those cabins along the North Shore. I guess I fell in love with the lake, too. After leaving the accounting firm, I moved up here and established SGR Financial."

"That's a pretty involved story."

"I told you the Cliff Notes version." He looked over at the beautiful woman who sat in his kitchen – and smiled. "Dinner's almost ready..."

After removing the small pot from the heat, he stirred in cubes of cold Plugra butter. He opened the oven door, retrieved the large pan containing the salmon steaks and quickly put a small hot pad caddy around the pan's handle.

While the steaks rested, he pulled dried strands of the pasta off the wooden dowels and gingerly dipped them into the boiling salted water. Next, he poured heavy cream into a small heated sauté pan. Using a flat whisk, he stirred in a thick slice of Plugra butter.

Sebastian gracefully took a step and, opening the large refrigerator, retrieved a brick of Parmesan, setting it on the counter next to a large nutmeg seed. He picked up the cheese and grated quite a bit over the sauce. Using a smaller grater, he also added nutmeg.

"I hope you're hungry, Kelly."

"Very... I'm very hungry." And if he only knew what else she was hungry for. Kelly was fascinated with this man, who promised her a wonderful meal – and from what she saw this was indeed going to be delicious. All week she had been imagining what she wanted to do to this man – this man with hazel eyes shrouded beneath heavy brows. And now that she was in his kitchen, she wondered if she had the nerve. Hopefully later this evening, the date would become unforgettable...

After sprinkling kosher salt and freshly grated pepper into the sauce, Sebastian turned off the burner under the boiling pasta. Kelly watched as he picked up strands of pasta with the grabber utensil and, with water dripping, added the fettuccine to the Alfredo. He repeated this process several times, stirring the pasta into the sauce with the flat whisk. Finally, he covered the small pan and turned off the burner.

"Almost ready..." Sebastian looked at Kelly. My God she was beautiful – and she still hadn't taken her eyes off him. He usually wasn't unnerved by a look, but this was more than a look.

He opened the refrigerator and put a prepared bowl of chopped Romaine and baby arugula on the counter. He lifted the salmon steaks out of the large pan and placed them on two plates – and spooned the wonderful smelling sauce over each steak. Using the tongs, he placed portions of the salad on their plates. Lastly, Sebastian added the Alfredo fettuccine, sprinkling it with freshly chopped parsley – completing the lovely presentation.

"That's it!" He walked over to the butcher-block counter, leaned over and kissed the woman who sat so comfortably in his kitchen. "Are you ready?"

Kelly bravely reached across the narrow counter and, with tender fingertips, caressed his beard. "Your beard is so soft..."

Sebastian closed his eyes – loving her touch, wanting her to touch him again...

Kelly took another sip of her wine and looked into his hazel eyes. "I'm sure the meal you prepared will be wonderful, but..."

"But what, Kelly?" He kissed her lips again – he never wanted to not kiss her lips. *Oh this woman...* He picked up his wine goblet and took a sip.

"... why don't we have sex first, then eat..."

He choked on his wine, spitting some of the burgundy liquid back into his goblet. Did this beautiful woman really just say she wanted to have sex with him? Now? *Oh, God in heaven.* Sebastian looked into her eyes, feeling as if they were looking right through him. He hadn't expected her to be so forward! His brain was stuttering – he didn't know what to say. Dinner was ready... He placed his goblet back on the counter.

Kelly misunderstood the look on his face. Was she being too forward? Did she misinterpret his physical language at the bar? Was this *not* what he wanted? Glancing toward the door – she had a chance to turn and run. Her car was parked right outside.

Silently praying for courage, Kelly slid off the stool and walked around the counter and tentatively took a step toward him. She stood so close to this big sexy man – feeling his breath on her face, close enough to feel his heart beating in his chest.

“What?" She breathed her words. "You don't want to have sex with me?” *Oh, please say something..*

With that, he had the presence of mind to open his mouth. “No... I mean yes...” He took one last look at the meal he had just prepared – it could wait.... He led Kelly by the hand and escorted her through the doorway, holding the heavy swinging door open for her. Sebastian brought her through the dining room, up the stairs, down the hallway and into the master bedroom – his bedroom. He stopped short of throwing her on the bed – instead he tried playing the gentleman card.

He looked at the beautiful redhead standing in his bedroom and asked, “What would you like to do first?” *She must think I'm an idiot!* He felt like a man about to have his first sexual encounter. It had been a few years, but he seemed to remember what to do. While removing his shirt, Kelly spoke in a voice so soft he barely heard her.

“Seb, why don't you take off your pants...” She unbuttoned her blouse, taking care to slowly push each pearl button through its slit in the pink fabric – finally pulling the blouse off her shoulders.

He watched as Kelly unbuttoned and removed her blouse – *she wasn't wearing a bra and her small breasts were beautiful!* This moment was real and he frantically tugged at his belt – it wouldn't work and his zipper was stuck.

Kelly stood before him and reaching around his head, untied the leather string that held back his long hair. Lowering her arms, she gently pushed his hands away from his waist and lightly combed her fingers through the soft, thick black hair that covered his chest and belly. Never taking her eyes off his face, she opened his belt, unzipped his pants and let them fall around his ankles.

But much to his embarrassment, his very large, very hard erection saluted her through the slit in his boxers. He looked at Kelly. She was thankfully smiling broadly at him.

Oh thank God! Kelly wanted to drop to her knees. This is what she had been thinking of and hoping for all week. Now it was literally within her grasp.

But Sebastian panicked. He quickly backed away and whispered, “*We need to do this... Now.*”

“*Yes.*” She spoke softly, echoing his words. “*Yes, right now.*” She knew he was like a volcano about to erupt, and she wanted that eruption in her!

He watched as she kicked off her moccasins, and since her trousers had an elastic waist band slipped them off, letting them fall around her bare ankles – *she wasn't wearing underwear!* Kelly gracefully sat on the edge of the bed and waited patiently for him.

Time stopped. Sebastian stared at her beautiful face. This was his fantasy and it was real. *God, I'm going to die right now!* But he was still arguing with his boxers – his cock still caught in the slit, impeding a graceful attempt at ridding himself of the garment. After finally kicking them off his feet, he mounted the bed and, pulling her under him, flattened her to the mattress, nestling his body between her legs.

She couldn't move and could hardly breathe. He was very muscular and his full weight lay on her. Their faces were but inches apart.

"We should kiss..." he suggested in a small voice.

"Yes Seb," her breath smelling so sweet. "We can kiss..." With her warm hands holding his face, she brought his mouth down to hers.

Her lips were so soft – he groaned as he let her tongue taste his. He could stay here forever, lying on her soft woman body, kissing her soft woman mouth. Oh she smelled so good...

"Sebastian..." She spoke his name in a way he had never heard, her voice sounding like an angel's. "Make love to me, silly..." And she kissed his lips again – and again.

But he had barely touched her when he came with the suddenness only a prepubescent boy could appreciate. *Oh shit!* He closed his eyes and groaned, collapsing back onto her body.

Kelly gazed into his face. He looked so forlorn. Though their faces were barely touching, he wouldn't look at her. She drew her arms around him, encircled his body with her legs, crushing him to her and held on tight. She wasn't about to let him go!

She held his face, feeling his soft beard under her hands. Pulling him closer to her mouth, she tenderly kissed his lips... and again... and again... and finally kissing him hard, forcing her tongue past his lips, sucking on his tongue the way she had sucked on his thumb at the bar.

As his breathing calmed, Sebastian opened his eyes and saw emeralds staring back at him. He chastely kissed her lips and began the slow journey down her body, kissing her neck, her breasts, caressing her beautiful small breasts – his hands totally covering them. He slowly continued the journey down across her soft belly until he was lying between her thighs – and tasted her silky skin...

And the way he touched her – the softness of his beard and mustache almost tickling her sensitive skin was like nothing she had ever felt before.

Kelly reached down between her legs and grabbing his long hair, pulled a handful into her fists and held on with a death grip. She felt the onset of the electricity flowing from her groin down her legs. She arched her back and held on to the bed covers with her toes – and *EXPLODED*! In a voice that came from deep within her, she growled, "*Oh God Sebastian...*" Her whole body stiffened. Her orgasm – so deep, so hard and seeming to go on forever.

He kissed the inside of her thighs and reclaimed her body, climbing between her bent knees, kissing her belly, her breasts, her neck, her face...

"I'm going to make love to you now. Please woman, I want to make love to you..." Sebastian kissed her face. "You are so sweet..."

Kelly had been holding her breath... and she exhaled when his soft beard touched her face, smelling herself on his mustache, his warm breath on her eyes. God she wanted this man, this big muscular man who practically suffocated her with his weight.

He reached back and grasping her legs under her knees, pulled them up and locked her ankles behind his neck, her back barely touching the mattress. And he struck pay dirt! Holding himself up with his hands on the mattress, Sebastian plunged deep into her, rocking his bed with every thrust – beads of sweat from his brow dripping on her face.

She held on to his arms for dear life – her body violently sliding on the sheets. And her body exploded again. Kelly growled his name out loud. And he thrust one last time and pressed on her, almost bending her in half with his weight. She knew he came at the same time she achieved her second orgasm. Never had she experienced mutual orgasm with anyone. Ever!

Sebastian rose up and kissed her mouth and whispered, *"I can't get enough of you, woman..."* He let her legs slowly drop from his shoulders onto the mattress and collapsed next to her – one leg partially lay across her legs, one arm draped across her chest and his other arm high above him resting on the pillows.

When she caught her breath, Kelly raised herself on one elbow, kissed his eyes, his bearded face, his mouth and sighed, "You have *GOT* to be fucking kidding me!" She saw him smile, obviously very proud of his big self. She tugged on his chest hair. He put his hand on hers, caressing her hand.

This was the man she had been waiting for. And she didn't want to let him go – ever. Again she kissed his face and asked Sebastian if he'd like to do this every night – for the rest of his life.

Without missing a beat, he surprised her by answering, "Yes, every night."

Silently, she recited a favorite Whitman poem, *"I am he that aches with amorous love..."* Sharing one pillow, she cuddled close in his arms while Vivaldi's Concerto No. 4 in F Minor lulled them into a sound sleep.

The rising sun shone through the tall bedroom windows, blessing the lovers with its early morning glow. Kelly opened her eyes and rose up on one elbow. She looked at the man who lay so peacefully next to her – his long hair wild on the pillow, his beard and mustache framing the lips she loved to kiss. She whispered, *"Are you awake?"*

He exhaled and nodded once.

"Seb... I don't want to leave."

Without opening his eyes, he whispered, *"Then don't."*

She lay back down, snuggling against his chest. "I mean, I don't want to leave. Really. I don't want to leave..."

He slowly opened his hazel eyes and, turning his head, looked at her. "What are you saying?" He kissed her forehead.

"I mean, I don't want to sleep alone... Ever. I want to sleep with you. Tonight..."

Sebastian again closed his eyes and pulled her closer to his chest. "Okay..."

"Just like that?"

"Just like that..."

Again they were silent for several minutes.

"I mean it." Kelly closed her eyes and stroked the soft black carpet of hair that covered his chest, finding his nipples, caressing his nipples. "I don't want to sleep alone, without you next to me... forever..."

He pressed his bearded face against her face, loving her touch, savoring her touch... Again he looked at her. "Just like that?"

Without opening her eyes, she smiled. "Just like that..."

Sebastian broke the serenity of the moment. "I have to make a bathroom run." He kissed her face. "Use this bathroom. I'll use the one downstairs."

They both rolled out of opposite sides of the bed. In the light of the day he looked at her – really looked at her. She was a beautiful woman... and she wanted to be with him again.

As he walked out of the bedroom, she looked at him. He was a beautiful man. Can you call a man beautiful? Yes...

He had taken a quick shower and returned to the bedroom first, dropping his towel on the floor. As he straightened the sheets and pillows, he heard the shower in the en suite bathroom shut off. Sebastian sat on his side of the bed and waited for her. The bathroom door opened – she wore his robe.

"Please wear my robe..."

Kelly smirked. "Okay!" She sat on her side of the bed. As she towel-dried her hair, she looked at the man who sat on the other side of the bed – the man who made her body explode last night. The man whom she didn't want to live without.

"Seb..." She put down the towel and reaching across the queen-size bed, touched his arm. "Sorry about your lovely dinner..."

He smiled. "So... sleep or breakfast?"

She smiled back at him and whispered, *"Neither..."*

Kelly never spent another night in her own apartment. Within days she broke her lease, and the next week moved in with him. *Him.*

While he navigated the narrow two-lane road, a groan escaped from deep in his chest as he remembered those first nights she shared his bed... remembering the feel of her hips rising to meet his, her legs entwining around his body, her soft, wet warmth welcoming him home...

He was not used to her sleeping next to him, but he learned quickly to let himself drown in the warmth of her body, allowing her sweet musk to stir his tired senses into blazing desire, kissing her lips, her shoulders, her breasts – her beautiful small breasts – the softness of her thighs... And the memory of their erotic lovemaking swept over him, causing a catch in his breathing.

Though the car traveled over the speed limit of the road, he longed to reach out to her. The impulse to pull her to him was powerful, the temptation fierce to seek her lips. He loved her so very much. His thick mustache masked a silent smile.

Kelly was the companion he had longed for. But now she no longer wanted to return the affection nor did she have respect for the love which he would always and forever feel for her. Had he pushed her away? Did she just not understand?

His hidden smile morphed into a scowl...

4

Proposal

She had gotten used to sleeping in his bed, his dark muscular body lying next to her. She loved talking with him at night, combing her fingers through the thick black hair that covered his chest and belly, the room so dark she couldn't see his face, their shadows as one, melting into the blackness. They drifted to sleep in each other's arms, sharing one pillow...

Though his work and her summer school tutoring kept the lovers apart during the day, they reconnected in the evenings and were inseparable on weekends.

She accompanied him on that humid July afternoon in his Porsche convertible. They had bought ice cream cones from the Portland Malt Shoppe, and had just crossed over the Aerial Lift Bridge to the end of the Point.

While he shifted gears, she held his cone, but the cone became quite soggy – and she held the melting ice cream too close to his lips, pushing the dissolving strawberry mint swirl into his face. The once frozen concoction melted in sheets upon her hand, rivers of pink and chocolate chips meandering down her arm. The sight had titillated him though the sticky mess had caused her much distress.

With strawberry sludge in his beard and mustache, Sebastian pulled over to the curb and slammed on the brakes. "Woman, you are going to be the death of me yet!"

He dragged her over the center console and held her tightly in his arms, trying to catch his breath. "Marry me..." He kissed her face, her eyes, her lips – and looked into her eyes. Sebastian repeated his words. "Marry me..."

"Marry you? Just like that?" Kelly laughed, sputtering through the ice cream that had transferred onto her face from his beard. She looked into his hazel eyes. This was her Ulysses and he wanted to spend the rest of his life with her.

"Yes, marry me. Just like that." He kissed her lips. "Marry me, Kelly... Please marry me."

He didn't wait for an answer. Sebastian opened the car door and, in one movement, stood with her safe in his arms. As she fought kicking and laughing, he carried her down to the beach and threw her into the chilly shallows of the big lake. In spite of almost drowning, she had somehow answered *YES!* – their kisses following them under the gentle surf.

He pulled her by the hand as they skipped across the hot sand back into his car, but she was concerned that her wet clothes would ruin the leather seats.

"Sebastian! I'm wet!"

"And you're beautiful!" He laughed at the woman who sat next to him as they drove home. He was grateful she was in his life, and now she would never leave. "Are you hungry?" Sebastian knew her happiness barometer. If she was hungry, she was happy.

"Yes!"

Good! She was happy! "Let's get sub sandwiches..." He picked up his phone, called the New London Grille and put in his order. He knew to order tuna with provolone for her.

"And chips!"

Again he laughed and speaking into the phone added, "And chips!" He ended the call, leaned over and kissed her mouth...

That night no words were needed to express his intentions to which she gladly surrendered her body, her passions, her mind, her senses. But she took charge, forcing him back onto the mattress and climbing aboard his body, his wonderful warm muscular body, held him tight between her knees.

She kissed his chest, searching through the soft thick hair, finding first one nipple, then the other. Her hands glided across his six-pack belly and down across his hips. Repositioning herself between his legs, she touched his full erection.

He caressed her auburn curls – and softly groaned... Kelly took pity on him and made love to him with her tongue – all the time holding the shaft tightly, gently, firmly...

Sebastian pulled her up so she lay beside him. He stroked her face – her beautiful face. "I'm going to marry you, woman..."

"I know. Thank God..." Kelly held his face between her hands and, looking into hazel eyes, kissed him.

He got to his knees and easily turning her over on her belly, raised her hips. Slowly he pressed into her, but just as slowly pulled out, repeating this sensual rhythmic torture. She pushed back into him, causing him to plunge deep within her.

She growled his name, announcing with quick gasps that she was close. She felt him tense, felt his fingers digging into her hips. And they shared in their passion again...

They collapsed on the mattress. Sebastian held her, his breath hot against her ear – never wanting to let her go...

As she remembered that lovely day, her body reluctantly responded at the memory of their passion. Now this life was over – he didn't want to be with her anymore. She turned away from the passing fields and through fresh tears, silently watched the scowl on his bearded face.

5

Planning

Sebastian didn't want to wait – he had wanted to get married now. And though they really hadn't talked about it, he hoped Kelly would like a small ceremony, maybe in the chapel near his home. He was not a fan of the full-blown bells and whistles program he had seen in the past. It was not about the cost – that was inconsequential. Rather, it was all about the tone that would be set for the rest of their married lives.

Shortly after his ice cream proposal, he called his brother. There wasn't anyone else he wanted as his best man. He idealized his big brother. It had been six years since they had seen each other and Sebastian was anxious to reconnect with him.

From his earliest memory he always looked up to his big brother. As children he followed Raffe everywhere, from the innocence of playing with the neighborhood boys to the foolhardy and destructive pranks that young men played. And when Raffe received the verbal lashing from his parents, Sebastian was always behind him to take his comeuppance too.

Raffaele was one of the finest operatic tenors in the world. During the time Sebastian was in college, his brother traveled throughout Europe, playing at the most celebrated opera houses. His reputation grew and soon he was singing alongside the very men and women he had idolized.

While living in Italy, Raffaele met Annalisa – a beautiful woman who shared his love of the opera. But they had been married less than a year when she was involved in an unspeakable auto accident. She was pregnant – she and her unborn child were killed.

He had been devastated. Though his family and close friends reached out to him, Raffaele retreated into his work. It was said that the years after Annalisa's death were the most productive in his professional life. His voice became richer, stronger – his passion deeper. He sang like a man possessed – his presence on the stage unequaled. But there was no life – there was no soul. The death of his beloved wife had thrown his life into turmoil, ripping the very heart and soul out of him...

Sebastian assumed his brother could be booked a year in advance and if he was on tour it could be difficult to coordinate dates. So before he and Kelly made plans, he needed to lock down a date.

He checked the time. Kelly and her friend Gabriella were dress shopping – he knew he had several hours at least. He hoped the call wouldn't go to voicemail.

"Buongiorno, piccolo fratello!" When Sebastian heard his brother's booming voice through the phone, he couldn't help laughing.

"Hello, Raffaele. Where are you today?" He expected his brother would be in Italy or Australia or some part of the world where opera houses book only the best of the best.

Raffaele's answer surprised him. "This weekend, I sing at the Harpa Opera House in Reykjavik, Iceland! *Cosa ne pensi di questo!*"

Though Sebastian was lost, he joined his brother in laughter. Raffaele easily slipped in and out of Italian, much to the amusement – and consternation – of those with whom he was speaking. But he pressed on, praying his brother would come to his wedding – what a wonderful excuse to get together.

"It's been too long since we've seen each other."

"I agree little brother. I agree. Do I sense you have a plan for this reunion?"

"Yes actually. I'm getting married..." *Oh no*. Raffaele set off into what could only be described as pure Italian words of joy. Sebastian waited, smiling at the phone until his brother finally ran out of gas. "Does that mean you're happy for me?"

"Seb, I know your life has been empty for many years without a partner."

He wondered if his brother was talking about his own life, so lonely since the death of his first wife and their unborn child – but he wasn't going to ask. That subject was off limits.

Raffaele continued his questioning. "Is this person a woman?"

In his brother's world, 'partners in life' could mean opposite sex or same sex – it would have made no difference to him who his brother married, as long as he was happy.

"Yes, she is a woman." The smile never leaving his lips. "A beautiful woman with emerald eyes."

"Favoloso! Gli occhi verdi! Lei è una tentatrice!

Though he couldn't speak the language, Sebastian could understand some of the words, and he knew *tentatrice* meant temptress. His brother was right – Kelly was a temptress, a beautiful green-eyed temptress!

"When's the big day, little brother?"

"That's why I'm calling. When are you free?" He could hear the *dit dit dit* on Raffaele's phone as he moved through tour dates on his calendar.

"I'm open the first full week of November. I have nothing pending either."

Sebastian knew he had to confer with Kelly first, but if he didn't make a firm date his brother might be booked and that window would close. "Can you pencil in the dates for November 2nd and the 9th? Both are Saturdays. I'll talk with Kelly tonight and get back to you right away."

"You've got it, little brother."

Sebastian smiled. For as long as he could remember Raffaele had called him 'little brother,' a term of endearment of which he had always been proud. He took a big breath and asked the more important question. "Raffe, would you stand up for me? Be my Best Man?"

Oh no... Raffe again launched into a string of Italian – though he spoke so quickly Sebastian couldn't pick up any recognizable words. But he knew they were words of happiness and just smiled at the phone, listening to his big brother's joyous tirade.

"Seb," he paused, finally taking a breath. "Yes, it would be my greatest honor to stand at your side. You have truly made my heart full this day."

"Thank you, big brother."

Almost immediately, his phone vibrated. Sebastian checked the caller ID. "Hello Bride!" He was in such a perfect mood and it was all because of Kelly.

"Hello almost husband," Kelly chimed, sounding like she was also in a good mood. "We're done!"

"You're done? You and Gabriella are done already?" He looked at the time. They had only been shopping for a little over an hour. "I thought you girls made a day of dress shopping?" He heard her chattering with the sales person. She was either ignoring his comment or didn't hear it.

"Do you want to take me out to dinner? I'm famished!"

He grinned into the phone. This was not news to him. If Kelly was feeling good, she was hungry – especially after an hour of hard shopping. "Where do you want to meet?"

"What about the Brew Haus, that new hamburger place by the mall? 5:30?"

Considering he once worked for an executive chef, Sebastian was leery about shelling out $100 for a meal when he could make it better at home for a lot less. Still a hamburger sounded good. He didn't know much about this place except that they brewed their own micro beers. And if Kelly wanted to try it he was game.

"Will Gabriella drop you off?" It wasn't that he didn't like Gabriella, because he did. She was full of life and energy, but he wanted Kelly all to himself.

"Yes." Again Kelly was having a conversation with him and at least two other people. *How did she do that?* "See you then, Seb!"

There were only a few more weeks of summer left before school began in September and the free time with Kelly would end. Oh how he enjoyed this time with her.

He arrived at the Brew Haus early. He could already see a line waiting to enter the restaurant. Sebastian parked but didn't get out. When he saw her, she was just getting out of Gabriella's car. He hailed her – Kelly saw him and walked to his car.

"There's a line." He didn't sound happy. He hated lines. He had no patience. "Let's order a pizza and spend the evening in the hot tub."

Her eyes lit up. The last time they used the hot tub things had gotten very hot indeed. She got into his car, leaned over and kissed him.

"Hot tub!" They laughed as he put his Porsche Boxster in gear and hurried home.

While he put in the order for the pizza, Kelly put on her skimpiest swimsuit. She came into the kitchen just as Sebastian was giving his address.

"Pizza will be here in about a half hour." He reached for her but she evaded him and trotted outside through the French patio doors to the hot tub. He ran up to their bedroom and changed into his swim trunks.

The deck was massive with flower boxes built onto the railings and a gazebo erected over on one side. In the middle of the deck was a one-of-a-kind cypress wood picnic table hand-crafted by his friend Roger.

But Kelly's favorite item was the bench swing. It had a cushion and a green and white striped awning. On sunny mornings she loved having her first cup of coffee while sitting on the swing.

The hot tub which seated eight was located further away from the general area. Many times at night Kelly and Sebastian went down to the tub in the nude. Tea light candles scattered around the deck created a romantic setting for the lovers. And tonight they hoped it would be again.

Sebastian came out and sat in a chair next to the hot tub. Kelly had turned on the air jets – tiny bubbles swarmed around her body. He watched her leisurely swishing her hands through the warm water.

"Come on in, Seb!" She playfully splashed water in his direction and hit him on his legs. "Take off your trunks and join me!"

"I'm waiting for the pizza and then I will." Looking at his watch, he realized it would be another fifteen minutes before it arrived. He reconsidered and removing his trunks, stepped down into the tub. Sebastian sat next to her and untied her top. What little material there was dropped off from her shoulders, exposing her breasts. He loved caressing her breasts – his hands totally covered them.

"When's the pizza coming?" she asked. "Do we have time..." But her words were smudged by his kiss.

"We have time," he gave her his crooked smile. She loved that smile. "Turn over, Love."

Kelly rolled over and held on to the edge of the tub. He removed her swimsuit bottoms, exposing her beautiful ass. And he made love to her, not holding back, thrusting hard – his movements in the small pool creating miniature tsunamis splashing against the sides. He knew he had to finish – time was not on his side. He braced himself and plunged deep into her. He heard Kelly cry out and felt her body stiffen. One, two, three more thrusts and – Oh, God! How he loved this woman!

The doorbell rang. They couldn't help but laugh – talk about timing! He kissed her, and finding his trunks and a towel, exited the tub. While he was retrieving the pizza, Kelly turned around and sat in the tub again. Her arms rested on the edge, her head leaned back – and she exhaled with a satisfied smile.

By the time he returned she had put on her swimsuit bottoms. Sebastian placed the pizza box on the wooden table along with Corona beers in a bucket of ice and doled out the little square-cut pieces on paper plates. Cheap, greasy pizza really hit the spot after good sex – even if it was a quickie!

They talked while they ate the pizza. He was excited about giving Kelly two dates to choose from for their wedding. Wiping his hands on a napkin, he told her he had talked to his brother. Kelly didn't know much about Raffaele other than he was Sebastian's older brother and his work had him traveling all over the world.

"What's my favorite almost brother-in-law up to these days?" She licked her fingers - slowly, sensually...

God how he loved her – especially since she hadn't put on her swimsuit top. He loved looking at her beautiful breasts. "I asked Raffe to be my Best Man."

She stopped licking. "Oh my goodness! I'm actually going to meet your brother?"

"He gave me dates he could be in town – for our wedding." He knew she wanted to talk about it, but he had been slow to set a date.

"What are his dates?"

"November 2nd or 9th. Both Saturdays. What do you think?" He saw the proverbial wheels turning as she thought.

"Well," she said, contemplating the enormity of planning a wedding. "The 2nd works best for me. There's always tests before the Thanksgiving break."

"So," echoing her choice, "November 2nd?"

"Yes!" Kelly put the small pizza crust on her plate, stood and straddled Sebastian's lap. She wrapped her arms around his neck and exhaled in his ear. *"You're marrying me..."*

Sebastian closed his eyes and nuzzled her damp auburn curls. "I'm marrying you..."

She laid her head on his shoulder and cried. He held her – he knew not to fix tears.

"November 2nd..." She sighed through her tears.

He held her closer. "November 2nd... I love you."

"I know... thank God..."

6

Groom's Dinner

Because his mind wandered – he would not soon forget the memory of Kelly in the hot tub – Sebastian almost missed his turn-off from the highway. It was a poorly marked county road, and he had missed the turn completely the first time driving to the cabin. He pushed the brake pedal harder than he intended and, as he down shifted, turned sharply. He knew Kelly felt the lurch of the car as the tires grabbed the pavement, but she was lost in her thoughts, looking up through the open moonroof.

She had noticed something and it was taking her full attention. The vision of the sun shining down on her upturned face took his breath away. There was no doubt she was beautiful, and the decision to marry her would always be one of the best decisions of his life. They were so happy back then – back when? And they wanted to share their happiness with their families...

When Kelly shared the news with Gabriella, she was ecstatic. And without waiting for her to ask, announced she would be her Maid of Honor. But Kelly also wanted her friend to sing during the processional. Together they chose *Lullaby*, a Dixie Chicks song. Brie promised to put a romantic spin on the song.

Then she had to call her mom. Ruth was an ordained Methodist minister. Because her mom was heavily involved in her church in Colorado, Kelly wasn't sure she could find time to attend the wedding. She wasn't even sure she could get ahold of her mom as busy as she was.

When she married the first time, it was such a non-event. They had gone to a Justice of the Peace – no fanfare, no ceremony. And since it only lasted a few months, it almost wasn't real anyway. She had told her mom she was getting married – no, she had told her mom *after* she got married. Her mom was smart – she must have known it wouldn't last. And when Kelly let her know she got a divorce, her mom was happy for her. But this was the real thing – Sebastian was the real thing!

Making herself comfortable on the bench swing out on the deck, she called her mom...

"Hello, my girl!"

"Hi, Mom!" Kelly was surprised her mom picked up on the first ring. "I didn't think you answered your own phone!"

"I usually don't, but my secretary is out this afternoon. What's up?"

"Um... I'm getting married..." She hated blurting out news like that without a follow-up statement. She knew her mom would have questions. But to her surprise there was only silence on the other end. "Mom, say something..."

"Kelly, of course I'm happy for you honey." There was that pause again. "I want only what is best for you..."

"Mom, this man... Sebastian... he is the best for me." Kelly so wanted her mom to be a part of this day and share her joy for falling in love with a man who would not leave her – who would not break her heart by going to work and not coming home forever.

"My girl, if you love this man, then I'm happy for you." Kelly's mom didn't pull punches, and she knew her mom wouldn't say something if it wasn't true. The fact that her mom said she was happy for her was enough.

"Mom, I have a favor to ask."

"Anything..."

Kelly took a deep breath. This was important. "Mom, would you officiate at the wedding? Would you marry us?" Again, there was only silence on the other end. It was important that her mom be present for her big day. Kelly silently prayed her mom would say yes.

"Honey, is this man that important to you?"

Kelly exhaled loudly. She was slowly getting her mom on her side. "Yes Mom. He's that important to me. He loves me like no one else."

"Will the ceremony be in a church?"

"Yes. There's a lovely chapel near his home – St. Catherine's. It's just perfect for us." *Oh please say yes...*

"Have you decided on a date?" Kelly knew her mom was looking at her calendar. This was huge!

"Saturday, the second of November." She heard the sound of turning pages – her mom must be finding the date in her appointment book.

"Honey, I am very pleased that you're getting married. And I would be honored to be part of the ceremony."

"Oh, thank you, Mom." She jumped off the bench swing and stood on the deck, bouncing on her heels. "I know you'll love Sebastian as much as I do." As Kelly ended the call, she realized this marriage thing was becoming real. She trotted back into the house.

They drove to the airport and picked up her mom. It had been forever since she had seen her mom – and the tears started.

Sebastian hugged her tight. "What are you going to do when you see your mom?"

She leaned into his arm and hugged him back. When she saw her mom come down the jet bridge, Kelly ran to her, almost knocking the diminutive woman off her feet. Sebastian stood patiently until Kelly turned and made the introductions.

"Mama, I would like you to meet Sebastian Bonsignore." Kelly took a step back and let her mom take a good look at the man she loved. She knew Sebastian was not a patient man. Kelly was proud of him now as he let his future mother-in-law take in the man standing before her. Again time stood still – and Kelly couldn't breathe.

"Sebastian," her mom held out her hand to him. "It's very nice to meet you."

"Reverend Cameron, it's a pleasure to meet you, too."

She looked at her daughter, and then back at Sebastian. "You're going to have to get used to calling me Ruth. Do you think you can do that, young man?"

"Yes ma'am! I mean, yes Ruth. I can definitely do that!" And finally Kelly exhaled.

While Sebastian drove, the women sat in the back seat of the SUV and talked. Kelly shared how she met Sebastian, with the exception of the lovemaking on the first date. She didn't think her mom would have approved.

She also told her mom about the plans for the wedding including the music, the catering at the reception and the decorating. Ruth couldn't believe that everything had been planned in only a few months. And if history was repeating itself – if they *had* to get married like she and Kelly's father did – she didn't let on.

Upon arriving home, Kelly showed her mom the location of the main floor powder room, on the way taking her on an impromptu tour of the house. Sebastian busied himself getting ingredients out of the refrigerator that would be prepped for dinner.

Raffaele knocked on the front door and slowly pushed it open. Sebastian met him with a huge hug, kissing his big brother on both cheeks. The women returned, entering the kitchen through the heavy swinging door. Raffaele noticed the beautiful redhead and asked his brother, "Is this your fiancée?"

Kelly laughed and answered, "Yes!"

Raffaele immediately seized her around her waist, lifting her off the floor and hugged her tight. He kissed her on the mouth and on both cheeks before putting her back on her feet. Ruth watched the whole welcoming scenario and clasped her hands.

"My girl, if I had any concerns about you marrying into this family, they are gone! I am so pleased to see you boys with my daughter."

Sebastian walked to her side and bending slightly, put his arm around her shoulder and hugged her.

Ruth looked up at him. "You obviously love each other, and I know my daughter is in very good hands!"

"But Ruth," Sebastian winked at his brother, "I know *she's* safe, but what about *me*?"

Eyeing him with playful shock, she elbowed him. They all laughed and hugged again, Ruth getting lost in the middle of the tall people.

Sebastian suggested Kelly and Raffe go in the dining room and set the table for dinner. He took an extra apron out of the drawer and, setting it on the counter, turned to Ruth.

"Your daughter tells me you're a good cook."

"Yes, I'm a closet chef!" They laughed, and he asked if she'd like to help him roll the fettuccine. She pulled the apron over her head, and as she was tying it said she'd like to help.

Sebastian and Ruth hit it off immediately. The pair worked most of the afternoon, Ruth playing the part of the capable sous chef, helping prepare his delicious shrimp scampi. He had made pasta dough that morning, and now the two rolled out fresh fettuccine, hanging the delicate strands on a tree of thin wooden dowels.

While the cooks toiled in the kitchen, Kelly and Raffaele set the large dining room table. Suspended above was an antique chandelier with many glass prisms. On the wall to the left, above the side table hung a tall ornate mirror extending to the ceiling. Facing that wall and between tall bookcases was a set of French doors that opened out onto the massive deck.

Kelly took stock of Raffaele. Like his brother he was dark, but appeared as the epitome of a successful businessman – clean-shaven, and his wavy salt-and-pepper hair cut conservatively short. He was also taller and leaner than Sebastian – must be an older brother thing. She tried chatting with him, but soon found engaging him in lengthy conversation proved difficult, much like Sebastian she mused. Instead, she and Raffe busied themselves bringing out and setting up the appetizers and wine on the side table.

Kelly poked her head in through the heavy swinging door to spy on the cooks' progress, but she was quickly shooed away. She retreated back into the dining room where Raffaele was now perusing through her and Sebastian's combined music library on the tall bookcases.

"We need music." Kelly suggested. "Pick out what you want to hear and put it in the stereo."

He slowly nodded – seemingly deep in thought, but soon chose a CD. "I could play this one?" He held up the plastic case.

She looked at the familiar artwork. Operatic overtures. *Really?* Although she was impressed with his choice, she didn't think Raffaele was an opera kind of guy. Kelly heard Brie at the front door and hurriedly excused herself, leaving him standing with the unopened CD case in his hands.

She greeted Gabriella and made quick introductions to her mom. Brie had made one of her famous three-tier chocolate cakes, and now held the prized dessert in her arms. Kelly took the covered dessert while her friend removed her coat and scarf.

For her friend's special night, Brie chose a low cut peasant-style blouse – her sheer lace bra barely eclipsing her dark areolas – and had styled her long hair in a tightly braided bun. She retrieved the dessert and set it on the counter, making the cooks promise not to lift the lid.

Appearing stoic, Sebastian and Ruth raised their flour-covered hands in unison, pledging not to sneak a peek. Returning to his pasta, he told the women to join his brother in the dining room.

Kelly returned to the dining room first, closing the swinging door behind her. Before joining her friend, Gabriella took a minute to check her hair, smoothing uncooperative wisps off her face with practiced fingers. When she pushed through the heavy door, she stopped dead in her tracks – the look on her face filled with astonishment.

Gabriella loudly exclaimed, "Oh my Lord in heaven..." She quickly composed herself and looking directly at Raffaele whispered, *"Dominicci..."*

Puzzled by her friend's uncharacteristic outburst, Kelly responded, "No Brie, this is Raffaele – Sebastian's brother."

"No Kelly..." Brie insisted. She held one hand over her beating heart. "This man... He is Dominicci!"

Raffaele looked over at the woman. His heart stopped. Was this a ghost? Was this a caricature, a jokester spectrum sent to haunt his dreams? He closed his eyes, praying to vanquish this gross mimicry of a woman he had loved so long ago... He opened his eyes. The woman was not an evil specter – she was real. Flesh and blood real. *Oh my God...* He deliberately took a step forward and reintroduced himself.

"I am Raffaele Dominicci Bonsignore. My professional name is Dominicci."

Professional name? Suddenly Kelly's dim light bulb shone clear and bright. "Dominicci? The famous Tenor?"

"Yes Kelly," he began, not taking his eyes from Gabriella – and remembered his manners. "I wanted to be, how do you say, incognito. This is my brother's special day, and I didn't want to overshadow it with my celebrity."

Brie stood frozen by the door, her mouth agape, her hand still covering her deep cleavage. Taking her stunned friend by the elbow, Kelly pulled her further into the room.

"Raffaele, may I introduce Gabriella Murray, my best friend and Maid of Honor..."

He dropped the empty CD case on the table and hesitantly grasped Brie's hand, his fingers lightly grazing her heaving breasts. Still not believing she was real, Raffe bowed low and kissed the back of her hand. *"Gabriella, è un sincero onore fare la conoscenza di una donna cosi bella!"*

In response to his chivalrous gesture, Gabriella whispered in perfect Italian, *"Il piacere è mio."*

Kelly had never seen her friend swoon – this was a first. She felt as an interloper watching two strangers making love with their words. Holy crap! She quietly retreated through the doorway into the kitchen.

Dinner was almost ready. Ruth was grating parmesan cheese onto a Caesar salad, and the shrimp in its thick wine sauce was slowly bubbling on a back burner. The cooks looked up from their toils and stared at Kelly, who stood with her back against the heavy door. She quickly brought them up to date on the love-making in the other room. Soon the melodic strains of an orchestra filled the house. And softly, in his deep tenor voice – Dominicci! – began singing. Sebastian, Ruth and Kelly stopped everything and just listened.

Sebastian was the first to speak. "Um, I probably should have said something..."

Probably? Kelly gave him her best *No Shit, Sherlock* look. Ruth, with her eyes closed and her folded hands leaning on the flour-covered counter seemed captivated by the singing. Sebastian knew if they didn't get dinner on the table immediately there was going to be real love-making in that room!

Using a plastic spoon, he test-tasted the aromatic wine sauce. "I hate to interrupt them but there are appetizers waiting for us in the other room." He threw his spoon in the sink and winked at Ruth.

"I know this is part of the social hour," Ruth winked back at him. "But I think some of us have already meeted and greeted!"

Kelly gave her mom a flabbergasted look and joined in the laughter.

Sebastian and Ruth took off their aprons and, with Kelly escorting her mom, marched into the dining room where the trio was met with an amazing sight. Gabriella and Raffaele held each other close, their faces inches apart and softly singing an operatic duet. Oblivious of their audience they sang the last bars – and kissed.

Sebastian cleared his throat. "Would you two like a room?" His question may have broken the ambience but not the connection. Raffe and Brie parted but still held hands.

Ruth approached them and touching Raffaele's arm remarked, "Your singing was wonderful! I truly have never heard anything like it!"

Never taking his eyes off Brie, Raffaele replied, "Gabriella's voice is like... Her voice is truly that of an angel's..."

Kelly tapped her friend on the arm and asked if she would like to get a glass of wine. Raffaele kissed Brie's palm before letting her hand gracefully drop. She escorted Brie over to the side table, reminding her that this evening was supposed to have been a celebration for herself and Sebastian – but it appeared it was turning into a celebration for her and Raffaele.

While she poured wine into Brie's goblet, Kelly whispered, *"That blouse certainly didn't hurt!"*

Brie blushed and whispered back, *"I know! He loves my blouse!"*

Kelly laughed. "Um... it's not your blouse he loves!"

Raffaele came up behind Brie and pulling her close, whispered, *"Mia bellissima Gabriella, what do you have for me, my angel..."* His lips lightly grazed her neck as he spoke. While holding her crystal wine goblet in one hand, Brie's fingers walked back along the waistband of his trousers and captured a belt loop.

Kelly rolled her eyes and walked back to where Sebastian and her mom stood. "Mama, have you seen the deck?" As they walked through the double French doors, she whispered to Sebastian that his brother and her best friend might find a secluded spot and consummate their relationship this evening.

While Ruth inspected the gazebo, he leaned into Kelly. "Maybe you and I should do that too."

She felt his growing erection and pressing her body into his groin whispered, *"Maybe later tonight you might get lucky."* She kissed his lips.

Ruth exited the gazebo. "A woman could get used to this." She winked at her daughter. Sebastian quickly turned Kelly around and held her close – her back pressed against his front.

When they walked back into the house, Kelly saw Raffaele and Brie standing at the side table – her long hair now flowed loose down her back. And Raffe was feeding her a small canapé.

"Oh no!" Kelly whispered in Sebastian's ear. *"That's how we began."* He saw it too and lovingly squeezed her hand.

Ruth raised a single eyebrow. "I think it's time to eat!"

Sebastian opened the heavy swinging door – the smell of garlic pleasantly overwhelmed the diners who sat around the table. He came out with the drained fettuccine in a five quart sauteuse pan, setting the heavy pan on a trivet near his place setting. Again returning to the kitchen, he brought out the shrimp in its delectable garlic sauce, carefully pouring it onto the pasta. He added freshly chopped parsley and, with large tongs, mixed all into the pasta. He plated the shrimp scampi onto individual portions and passed them to his guests. Finally he dished up his own plate and sat down.

Ruth cleared her throat. "Let's say grace..."

Kelly glanced at Sebastian. She certainly hadn't expected her mom would impose her religious rituals on this celebratory meal.

But Sebastian graciously agreed. "That's... Yes. Let's." He raised Kelly's hand to his mouth and kissed her fingers.

Raffaele turned to the woman who sat next to him. Gabriella could feel the electricity even before *his* hand touched hers. Following his brother's example, Raffaele raised her hand to his mouth and lovingly kissed her fingers.

Satisfied that the diners were receptive to her prayer, Ruth began... "Thank you, Lord, for bringing this family together tonight. And bless the marriage between my daughter and this fine man. Amen." She winked at Kelly. "That wasn't too much, was it?"

Kelly squeezed Sebastian's hand and laughed. "No Mama... It was perfect."

He turned to Ruth. "Would you have some wine?"

"Yes Sebastian... thank you... I have to ask, Raffaele..."

"Please, Ruth. Call me Raffe."

"Alright. Thank you." She sipped her wine. "Your parents lived in Italy?"

"Yes. In Medina, a village in the Piedmont region." He motioned to the framed painting above the fireplace. "My grandmother was an accomplished watercolourist, and when my parents made the decision to come to America, she painted that scene."

"It's lovely – and so personal. You must treasure it."

"Right now, Sebastian does." He looked fondly at the painting. "My brother was the stable one, the one who settled down. And I entrusted our inheritance to him."

"This beautiful dinnerware... Was it your parents' also?"

"Yes..." Raffe touched the edge of the colorful plate.

Gabriella could sense that the exquisite place settings held bittersweet memories for him. He turned to her – the woman who sat so close to him. His eyes glistened. She assumed he was thinking of his parents. She could not have dreamt he saw another woman in her eyes...

Raffaele finished his salad, moving the bowl aside. "Kelly, are you an only child?"

Kelly looked over at her mom and smiled. "Yes..."

"Since she was an only child," Sebastian teased, "Kelly had no one to blame if she got into trouble."

"I suppose you're going to blame me for the trouble you got into little brother?"

"That's exactly what I'm saying, Raffe." Sebastian had missed his brother, and enjoyed the banter between them.

"You see, Ruth, Seb is three years my junior, and he literally followed me everywhere..."

"And when you got into trouble, I got into trouble!"

"I'm hurt! When did I ever get you into trouble?"

"Are you kidding me?" Sebastian smiled his crooked smile. "You always got me into trouble."

"Name one time, little brother!"

He winked at Ruth. "Skipping Mass?"

Ruth raised an eyebrow.

Raffe noted her surprised reaction. "We were raised in St. Paul's east side."

Sebastian held up his glass. "The Italian neighborhood, Ruth."

Raffe winked at his brother. "Our parents kept us on a tight rein, didn't they?"

"But," Ruth countered. "You still managed to skip Sunday Mass?"

"No..." Raffe understood her concern. "The Jesuit Priests were strict. It was mandatory that we attend Mass every day before school."

With his empty glass, Sebastian pointed to his brother. "And Raffe here figured a way to skip out."

"How?" Now Ruth was very interested in the shenanigans of these two grown men as young boys.

Sebastian filled his glass, finishing the bottle. "We'd walk into the church with our class so the priests could do a head count." He stood and put the empty bottle on the side table, then opening another bottle, handed it to Raffe.

"Thanks, Seb." Raffe filled his glass. "And when the Jesuits weren't looking..."

Sebastian again took his seat. "Raffe and I would sneak out the side door."

"How, pray tell did you spend your time?" Ruth chuckled. "I can only imagine..."

Sebastian flashed a mischievous grin. "My older brother here taught me how to throw dice."

"You were an eager student, Seb."

Kelly tried imagining her future husband as one of her high school students, playing such foolhardy games. "Were you ever caught?"

Sebastian winked at her. "Oh yeah..."

"Then we had to do our penance."

"Did they make you say the rosary?"

"Nothing that easy, Ruth." Sebastian smiled at his future mother-in-law. "They gave us math problems..." He took another bite of the delicious meal, cleaning his plate.

Raffaele explained. "Like nine or ten numbers multiplied by another row of numbers." He looked sideways at his brother. "Easy for Seb, but I couldn't do it."

"So each time we skipped Mass and got caught," Sebastian wiped his mouth with a napkin. "I'd do his problems for him."

"He even proved his work with long division." Raffe nodded at his brother. "Show-off."

But Ruth had more questions. "The priests didn't tell your parents?"

"The priests," Seb looked over at his brother. "They gave us a choice – either inform our parents of our truancy or solve the multiplication problem."

Raffe agreed. "It was a justified punishment to be sure... Ruth? May I pour more wine for you?"

"Thank you, Raffe. You two are very close..."

"Yes... But we haven't seen each other since our widowed mother's funeral. And I've missed my little brother." Raffe raised his glass. "A toast... To a new chapter in our lives..."

In response, Sebastian raised his glass. "Yes, one that includes my wife." He winked at Kelly. "My wife..."

"Thank you, baby." Kelly's eyes glistened as she raised her glass. She looked at her mom. "And I'm so grateful you wanted to be included in this celebration, Mama."

"I'm glad you asked me..." Ruth also raised her glass and the clinking continued.

Ruth wiped her mouth and set her napkin down next to her empty plate. "What about high school?"

"I went to a public school, but Raffe transferred to The Center for Arts Education."

"It's a performing arts high school south of Minneapolis."

"What made you want to transfer to that school?"

"My big brother was accomplished in both piano and voice."

Ruth sat back in her chair and exhaled. "This meal was delicious, Sebastian."

"Right back at you, Ruth, thank you for helping."

Raffe pushed away from the table, stealthily moving his chair closer to Gabriella. "At the end of my sophomore year, my foreign language teacher had introduced me to the opera and as they say, my life changed forever." He put his hand on hers...

"Wasn't it expensive?" Kelly again thought of her more talented students. "I mean, that's a special school. Did you have any kind of scholarship?"

"No... Our parents sacrificed a lot for us..." He looked attentively at the woman whose hand he held. "Somehow they made it possible..."

"I have to say," Ruth confessed. "I've never really been a fan of opera. However, I think I will definitely become one now."

"Thank you, Ruth. That's very kind of you." Raffe raised Gabriella's hand and lightly kissed it. She closed her eyes and slowly blew through pursed lips. She pressed her knee against his – the man who was making love to her with his kiss...

"What about you, Sebastian?" Ruth tried ignoring the subtle attraction at the end of the table, knowing the sparks between Raffe and Brie were about to ignite into a flaming torch.

"I applied to Macalester College with perfect SAT scores in math and received a scholarship." He pushed his plate to the side. "Then, during that first semester at Macalester, I found employment as a prep cook at an upscale restaurant in Stillwater. And within a year, I was promoted to sous chef." He lowered his head, and speaking to no one, added, "I loved working at that restaurant." He finished his wine and put the empty glass on the table...

"Honey, I've never seen your diploma. What was your degree in?"

Appearing chagrined, Sebastian answered her. "I graduated with two degrees... Statistics and economics with a minor in the computer sciences."

Kelly laughed. "Of course you did!"

Raffaele and Gabriella were becoming more intimate and had gradually migrated to the far corner of the table. If he could have gotten any closer to her, she would have been sitting on his lap.

Ruth slyly touched her daughter's hand. "Kelly, shall we have Gabriella's beautiful dessert?"

Sebastian heartily agreed, but when he tried getting Raffaele's attention, he realized his efforts were futile. He surprised Kelly when he threw his napkin across the table at his brother, accidently hitting Brie squarely in the face.

Though she was unhurt, Raffaele quickly became her Knight in Shining Armor – coming to her rescue, caressing her 'injured' face with his hand and kissing the area where the errant napkin landed. Brie's large brown eyes shone brightly as she looked tenderly at Raffaele. Clearly they were in their own little world, oblivious of their audience.

Kelly broke the magic by loudly clearing her throat. "Brie! Dessert!"

To no one's surprise, Brie and Raffaele announced they would leave together, promising to see everyone at the wedding. Kelly and Gabriella hugged each other, both shedding tears. Brie was so happy that her best friend had found the love of her life – and Kelly hoping Brie had also found the love of her life.

Tears turned to laughter as the friends parted, still holding hands. Brie assured Kelly she would be at the chapel early and that everything would be perfect for the bride.

After releasing her friend and watching her leave with Raffaele, Kelly turned and kissed Sebastian. Her mom was taking her to a hotel for the night. Tradition, Ruth called it.

Sebastian wasn't sure about this 'tradition' thing, but he wasn't about to question Ruth's authority. He made quite the scene with his impassioned kiss, silently praying Kelly would change her mind.

Ruth broke up the lovers and good-naturedly bid goodbye to Sebastian. Kelly picked up her overnight bag, hurriedly donned her coat and walked out with her mom into the frosty November night.

7

Penultimate Minutes

The next morning, Sebastian woke and reached across his bed to cuddle with Kelly. She wasn't there – Kelly's always there! The fog lifted. She didn't stay with him last night. This was the first time she didn't share his bed since their date night...

She was so forward, so funny, so responsive. She stayed overnight every night from then on. For the first week at least, he went to bed with an aching hard-on. He couldn't wait to pull her close, feel her wonderful soft woman body pressed against his own...

She had crawled up on him. He held her tight against his chest. She kissed his mouth, his eyes, his face... Oh, he loved her sweet kisses. And she kissed him harder, making love to him with her tongue.

Sebastian opened his eyes and looking into emeralds asked, "Why did you come into my life, woman?"

"Because I wanted you to be the one... My Ulysses." Kelly kissed him. "And you are."

"Kelly, I didn't know if you would have understood... I was hoping you would be my Dulcinea – from Don Quixote..."

"I know the story well." She kissed his face. "Dulcinea was a tough peasant girl whom Don Quixote described as his queen and his lady." She closed her eyes and caressed his soft beard – and began crying.

At this point in their relationship, he didn't yet understand tears, but she smiled through her tears. He wrapped his arms around her and held her against him as he rolled over – and began the now well-traveled journey down her body. He could never get enough of this woman, inhaling her musk, tasting her silky skin – and again bringing her to an amazing orgasm with his mouth.

She pulled at his long hair. Sebastian obeyed her silent command and nestled between her open legs – and ever so slowly pushed into her, barely rocking the bed with his long, slow thrusts.

She locked her legs around his waist, becoming like a vise around his body, taking his breath away... Kelly grabbed his hair in her fists and, pulling his face down to hers, kissed him, feeling his soft beard against her face...

He slowly rolled on his side, still deep within her, her legs still around his waist. He held her close, their foreheads touching and pulled the quilt up over their bodies. They slept, sharing one pillow...

> *Sebastian woke a few hours later and gently unlocked her legs from around him, straightening them out on the bed. She murmured something unintelligible as he turned her onto her back. Slipping one arm under her neck, supporting her head on his shoulder, he pulled her next to him – and that's how they woke in the morning...*
>
> *He watched as she opened her eyes and looked at him. "Seb, would you want to do this for the rest of your life?"*
>
> *"Yes..." And because it was Sunday, they slept well into the morning.*

And now he was going to marry her...

He rose from his bed and looking at his watch knew he had several hours – he was not a patient man.

He wanted to call her...
He didn't sleep with her last night...
He didn't make love with her last night...
He didn't wake with her this morning...
He couldn't call her.

He sat back down on the bed, hung his head and resting his forearms on his knees, clasped his hands – and waited. His phone rang. It was Raffaele.

"Seb, how are you doing?"

"Not good. I'm not good at waiting." He shared his pity party story with his brother.

"Gabriella is with Kelly and her mom. Let's do brunch."

He quickly dressed in sweats and met his brother outside. They drove to a restaurant where they served bloody marys. Sebastian relished the time he was spending with his brother, knowing it would be a while until they crossed paths again.

Their conversation was light, laughing at memories, talking about Kelly – and Raffaele admitting he was falling for Gabriella. He had spent the night with her. He confessed she was everything he had ever wanted in a woman – intelligent, beautiful, funny, sensual, and her large full breasts completed the perfect package.

Sebastian looked hard at his brother and asked if he was in love with Brie, thinking how much he and his brother were so alike.

"Mi scusi, piccolo fratello," Raffaele playfully shot back. "But didn't you meet Kelly just about six or seven months ago?"

Sebastian smiled. He wasn't going to share the details of their first date, that first incredible night spent together only days after they met.

"Are we done? Let's get you married." Raffaele asked for the check – Sebastian left the tip. As he was getting up, he pulled the celery stalk out of his big brother's glass and ate it as they exited the restaurant.

Sebastian entered his home and made his way up to the bedroom. He showered and trimmed his beard the way Kelly liked it. With a towel wrapped around his waist, he opened the closet door. The tie he chose to wear for his wedding was of course the one Kelly bought for him. He felt the rich fabric between his fingers, knowing this would forever be his favorite tie.

Dropping the towel, Sebastian stood naked in front of the full-length closet mirror. His first wife had wanted his chest and belly hair waxed – her last request before he divorced her. Kelly loved the feel of his body hair. More than once, while they talked late at night in their bed, she played with his carpet as she called it.

He could almost feel her now... drawing her fingers through the thick hair, fondling it, finding his nipples with her tongue... Looking down he saw his erection – fully engorged. *Oh, God.* This was going to be a long day...

Sebastian dressed and expertly tied a perfect Windsor knot between stiff collar points. Raffaele had said the boutonnières would be at the chapel. After putting on his suit coat and slipping on his shoes, he took one last look in the mirror as a single man. Picking up the ring box he had kept hidden from Kelly, he stuffed it in his suit coat pocket and descended the stairs.

He arrived at the chapel and thought he had entered a fantasy land. Above him, twinkling lights made the large room appear magical, more intimate. Cody and his friends had done a wonderful job decorating. Kelly would love it.

He walked to the front pew and sat. The pianist was practicing from the pages of sheet music propped up against the music rack. On the side off from the pews, Raffaele and Brie were quietly singing while holding sheet music. He crossed his arms, closed his eyes and enjoyed his last minutes of bachelorhood.

Kelly woke. She reached out to cuddle with Sebastian but only touched an empty mattress. This was the day she was going to marry *him*. Kelly stretched her arms high above her and yawned.

"Kelly?" It was her mom calling through the doorway from the adjoining room. "Are you up, honey?"

"Yes, Mama." How long had it been since she called her that name? Her mom's name went from Mama to Mommy to *MOM!* Oh, they fought when she was a headstrong twelve-year old. Why do mothers and daughters have to go through that awful rite of passage? But during those times when her mother didn't understand, Kelly's father was her champion. And when her father died, Kelly felt like her world collapsed. He had adored his Kelly-Belly...

For years after his untimely death, Kelly hardly spoke to her mother. It wasn't until she had moved out and started college that she finally talked to her mom again. She felt blessed that her mom had waited patiently for her to get her brains back. Now they were so close and she was overjoyed that her mom was with her on this special day.

"Should we do coffee?" That sounded good. Kelly said she'd meet her in the hotel cafe. Rising, she pushed her feet into her slippers and padded on the plush carpet over to the bathroom. She looked in the mirror. Why was her hair always a fright in the morning? She quickly dressed in comfortable sweats.

Her mom had already ordered coffee and was reading the morning paper. No wonder Sebastian and her mom got along so well.

"Good morning, Mama." She kissed her mom on the cheek and sat across from her. They ordered a light breakfast and spoke of the wonderful dinner at Sebastian's. Her mom also talked about Gabriella and Raffaele. What were the odds, she mused, that two people could fall in love so suddenly. Kelly hid a smile from her – oh, it's possible.

"Mama, didn't you ever find someone after daddy... after daddy died?"

"Oh my girl, your father was the one. I know it's a cliché to say it, but there was only one man for me – and that was your father."

Kelly poured more coffee into their mugs from the carafe. "Aren't you dating anyone? Isn't there anyone you like?"

"Oh, there's one man... His name is Matthew... and I like spending time with him sometimes. He's tall like your father – and yes he's nice looking. But he reminds me too much of your daddy." Ruth didn't look up at her daughter as she stirred more of the creamer into her coffee. Her spoon stopped. "But that's all he is – company."

"I'm sorry Mama..."

"Oh heavens, don't be sorry." Ruth put down her spoon and lightly patted her daughter's hand. "Like I said, there was no one to compare with your father. And he gave me a lifetime of beautiful memories..."

"Am I one of your beautiful memories, Mama?"

"Yes honey..." Ruth smiled at her daughter – her miracle baby. She looked at her watch. "When is your hair appointment?"

"In about an hour. We still have time." Kelly finished her eggs, sopping up the runny yolk with the last of her English muffin.

"I can always tell when you're feeling happy."

"Why is that Mama?" Kelly licked jam off her thumb.

"Because, my girl, you're eating. That's your happiness barometer."

After Kelly showered, Ruth drove her daughter's car and dropped her off at the salon. She returned to the hotel where she showered and dressed. Before leaving the room, Ruth put on her gold wedding band. Frederick Cameron was the only man she would ever love... always and forever...

When Ruth entered the chapel, she spotted Sebastian sitting alone in a front pew. The pianist was playing on an electronic piano. An acoustic guitar leaned at his side. Gabriella and Raffaele sat off to the side softly singing while reading sheet music.

As a surprise for the newlyweds during the recessional, they would sing *Vivo Por Ella*. They had practiced it in Brie's living room, accompanied by Raffaele playing the score on her baby grand. The other part of the night – when not sleeping – was spent getting to know each other in the most sensual ways possible...

Raffaele kissed Gabriella on the lips and sent her off to meet Kelly at the hairdresser's. He walked up to where Sebastian sat and tapped his brother on the shoulder, suggesting they retire to one of the rooms off from the chapel and relax until it was time to stand at the altar.

Kelly and Brie walked into the little chapel carrying their dresses in garment bags. The decorations were extraordinary. Long stemmed white roses in tall glass vases were arranged on the small altar. Tiny lights on thin wires were tastefully strung criss-crossed high above the pews. As Kelly passed beneath them, they seemed to twinkle just for her. It was truly magical. Cody and his friends had outdone themselves.

Ruth spotted the girls and quietly suggested they all retire to one of the rooms to get ready. Brie had helped Kelly find a demure pale pink dress with a scarf hem – perfect for the afternoon wedding. Kelly actually loved her hair. The stylist gave her shoulder-length hair a French Twist – with lots of bobby pins and hairspray.

For her role as Maid of Honor, Brie chose a tea length coral chiffon dress with a plunging keyhole neckline exposing her cleavage. Her hair flowed down her back in soft waves, the chestnut highlights accenting her beautiful dark brunette hair. A simple pearl headband kept the flowing locks back off from her face.

Kelly asked Brie if she needed time to fix her hair, since she always wore it in a twist or chignon. Brie smiled and, brushing one side of her long hair with her fingers, pulled the tresses down across her ample breast.

"Um... no. Dominicci likes my hair like this..." Brie blushed a deeper scarlet than Kelly had ever seen. Her intuition was right on! Kelly smiled at her friend but didn't say anything. Better to keep her mom in the dark regarding last night's extracurricular activities.

Ruth interrupted the girls. Since she was going to officiate she had to take her position at the altar. Her mother looked so polished, wearing a navy blue pencil skirt, white silk shell and matching matador-style jacket. The color was so attractive with her short, silver white hair.

She had a cowlick just off from the center of her hairline. Kelly remembered her mother trying so many hair styles trying to cope with this 'abomination of nature.' As a last resort she almost shaved off her hair – but this short style suited her, especially after she had been ordained a minister. Ruth kissed her daughter and quickly exited the room.

After putting on their dresses, Brie kissed Kelly on her cheek. “You look beautiful! Sebastian won't know what hit him!”

She pulled Brie close and hugged her – and started crying. Brie pulled a handful of tissues from a box and dabbed the torrent of tears. She knew Kelly's tears. Though she couldn't stop them, she was bound and determined to at least ebb the flow before she had to leave the room. Kelly smiled at her best friend – and the tears started again.

“You are hopeless!” Brie laughed. “You are hopeless and I love you!” She dabbed Kelly's face again and checked her watch. She picked up Kelly's bouquet and handed it to her.

Kelly pulled a small black ring box out of her bag and opened it, exposing a stunning man's ring she had created especially for the love of her life. “This is Sebastian's ring. Please hold it until the exchange of rings...” Suddenly her face fell. “Oh no!”

“What, Kelly? What could possibly be wrong *now*?” Brie was about to dab her tears but Kelly pushed her away and sat heavily onto a folding metal chair.

“Brie... *I* don't have a ring. Sebastian never gave me a ring. We never talked about rings!” And Kelly's tears gushed down her face. “This is all wrong!” She held up her left hand with a conspicuously bare ring finger. “We're not getting married...” She clutched the mass of soft tissues she had accumulated and pressed them onto her eyes.

She looked up just as Brie walked out of the little room, closing the door behind her. “What the hell...” Kelly sat back in the chair.

It wasn't but a few minutes before Brie came back in the room – grinning. “Kelly, get up. You're getting married, girl!” Gabriella pulled on Kelly's arm and helped her stand. “Dry your tears. Everything's good. You're getting married.”

She pulled more tissues out of the box, pushing a fresh handful into her friend's hand. “I'll see you in a few minutes, Mrs. Bonsignore.” Brie left the room leaving Kelly pressing the soft tissues against her face.

Kelly choked back more tears, finally composing herself. She threw the used tissues into the wastebasket and looked in the mirror. Her eyes were red. Great...

While waiting for the man who would walk her down the aisle, Kelly thought of her dad – and the tears came again. How she wished he could have been with her today, this special day. Somehow she hoped – maybe he was here in spirit. But she had chosen someone who was dear to her – someone who cared for her deeply, who protected her and had always shown a brotherly affection toward her. And her tears stopped...

Shortly after Sebastian had proposed, Kelly reviewed in her mind the short list of people who she wanted escorting her down the aisle. She took a bottle of Corona from the refrigerator and walked barefoot out on the deck. She sat on the bench swing – this would be an important call. And she hoped he would come through for her. She pressed his speed dial number, but the call went to voicemail.

“Hi, Roger. This is Kelly. Call me please. I have something very important to ask you... Thank you.”

She took a long drink of her cold beer. With one foot she pushed against the deck floor. Then sitting cross-legged on the cushion enjoyed the lazy back and forth movement of the swing. Before she could take another drink of her beer, her phone buzzed. She looked at the caller ID. It was him.

"Hey, gal. What's up?"

"Um, I have a favor to ask you."

"Anything, you know that."

She loved the resonance – a certain gentleness of his baritone voice. From the first time she heard him speak, it reminded her of a line from *The Voice of the Rain*, a favorite Whitman poem:

> *And who art thou? Said I to the soft-falling shower, which, strange to tell, gave me an answer, as here translated: I am the Poem of Earth, said the voice of the rain...*

She took a deep breath. "Roger, would you walk me down the aisle?"

"Oh, Kelly..." Roger breathed into the phone. "Oh, Kelly..." There was a long pause as he composed his emotions. "It would be my honor to walk you down that aisle. But why me?"

"Because... You introduced us. You introduced me to my husband."

"I don't know what to say." He almost whispered his words. "You are so special... You and Sebastian are special people. I'd be glad to walk you down the aisle, gal."

"Thank you, Roger. Really, thank you."

8

The Wedding Ceremony

Brie approached her place near the piano. Sebastian and Raffaele arrived and stood near the altar, looking so handsome in their suits with their tiny burgundy boutonnières. Raffaele did an overt once-over on Sebastian's suit, playfully brushing non-existent dandruff from his brother's shoulders. Ruth, who was reviewing the invocation she had written especially for her daughter, saw the interplay between the brothers and winked at Sebastian.

The guests had taken their seats in the pews under the twinkling lights. Michael's sister Connie was tapped to take the wedding photos. Everyone was excited for the two wonderful people who were entering this new chapter in their lives.

The musician stood, picked up his guitar and played the intro to *Lullaby*. This was Roger's cue. He left his seat and walked to the room where Kelly waited.

"You look beautiful, Kelly." He looked down at her and affectionately touched her face with the back of his fingers.

Her tears started again. "Roger, you know I wish my dad was here to walk me..."

He knew her tears and quickly pulled out a handful of tissues. "Here gal." He spoke softly as he gave her the tissues. "Quit your crying. This is a good day."

Holding her bouquet in one hand, she smiled up at the big man and took his arm. Standing on tiptoe, she kissed his cheek – her mouth touching his full mustache. She whispered, "*Thank you, Roger...*"

He closed his eyes and exhaled loudly...

He looked at the woman standing next to him...

He looked at the woman who he introduced to his best friend...

He looked at the woman...

Roger put on a smile and escorted Kelly out of the room and into the chapel.

Brie began singing when she saw Roger and Kelly. "*They didn't have you where I come from...*" Her voice sounded angelic, especially when she sang the chorus in Italian. Connie surreptitiously took pictures as the two walked down the aisle.

Kelly looked up to the altar to where the love of her life stood – and time stopped. Tears filled her eyes. Oh please, she prayed, don't let my dam burst! Not again! Roger lightly put his hand over hers – that helped. She walked up the steps and took Sebastian's hand – and saw tears in his eyes.

Roger nodded to his friend and silently turning, walked back to his seat, sat heavily on the wooden pew – and for a brief moment, hung his head.

Brie finished the final bars of the song and returned to stand at Kelly's side.

Ruth looked over at Brie. “Gabriella, that was beautiful. Thank you.” And she began the invocation.

“I’d like to welcome you to St. Catherine’s Chapel as we witness the marriage of two very special people. One, my daughter Kelly who I know is special – and Sebastian, who by the very fact my daughter loves him is very special. Let us begin.”

She looked out at the small gathering and asked them to bow their heads.

> “Loving God. Thank you for Your many blessings. We come today to celebrate in Your name the union of these two fine people. May they continue to honor You with their commitment to each other. We beseech You to guide them as they travel their journey together on this earth, the beautiful world You have created. In Jesus’ name, amen.”

Ruth asked the couple to face each other. Kelly turned and handed her bouquet to Brie. The faint clicks of Connie’s camera could be heard. She saw her mom wink at her, which instantly relaxed her *and* the grip she had on Sebastian’s arm.

“Let’s get started, shall we? Kelly Isabella Cameron, do you take this man Sebastian Giordano Bonsignore as your lawful husband and partner, to respect him, trust him, never taking him or his love for granted... Caring for him, supporting him and loving him all the days of your life – and giving him the kind of life of which dreams are made?”

Kelly’s voice never sounded so confident and clear when she responded, “I do.”

Ruth turned her attention to Sebastian. “Sebastian Giordano Bonsignore, do you take this woman Kelly Isabella Cameron as your lawful wife and partner, to respect her, trust her, never taking her or her love for granted... Caring for her, supporting her and loving her all the days of your life – and giving her the kind of life of which dreams are made?”

In a loud voice Sebastian answered, “Oh yes, I do!” There was laughter from the pews.

Ruth continued. “In honor of this day, Sebastian’s brother Raffaele, known in the professional operatic world as Dominicci, has graciously offered to sing *L’Ultima Canzone*, composed by Paolo Tosti.”

Raffaele walked over to the pianist who was already playing the intro. His booming tenor voice shook the little chapel. *“Foglia di rosa, o fiore d’amaranto...”*

From the look on Sebastian’s face, Kelly realized he never heard his brother sing professionally. While she watched her husband-to-be, he slyly pulled a small blue velvet box from his suit coat pocket. He hadn’t forgotten about the ring after all! They simply never talked about a ring and it wasn’t on her list of priorities.

In a soft voice, Ruth prompted. “Open it, Sebastian.”

Kelly let out a gasp that could be heard above Raffe’s singing. The ring was exquisite – an emerald diamond halo ring in 14K gold. *Oh my goodness!* She looked at Sebastian, who was now beaming with pride. She knew it was very hard for him to keep such a splendid secret from her. The combination of Raffaele’s tenor voice plus the sight of this ring made Kelly’s dam burst. Her tears flowed down her face in sheets. *Oh bloody hell!*

But Gabriella, ever the prepared Maid of Honor pushed a white lace-edged hanky to her at her elbow. Kelly felt the cloth and grasping the small hanky, hurriedly wiped the unending cascade.

Brie touched Kelly's back. When she turned around, Brie placed the small black ring box in her hand. Kelly turned back to face Sebastian and opened the box, revealing a very plain, very masculine ring – a Damascus black stainless steel ring with swirls of birch leaves embossed across the band. Sebastian's reaction spoke volumes as he loudly exhaled.

Raffaele concluded singing and, as if in concert, bowed low. The small audience in the pews erupted in a standing ovation with Cody shouting *Bravo!* As Raffaele returned to his place behind Sebastian, he affectionately squeezed his little brother's shoulder.

"The circle of the ring," Ruth began, "symbolizes the unending love between a man and a woman. As you give these rings to each other, wear them proudly, wear them with respect – wear them as an eternal statement to the world that you have professed your love to your life partner."

She turned to Sebastian. "Repeat after me. 'I give you this ring as a reminder of our wedding vows.'" He repeated the vow as he took the delicate ring from the box and placed it on Kelly's trembling finger. *Oh my...*

Ruth then addressing her daughter... "Repeat after me. 'I give you this ring as a reminder of our wedding vows.'" Kelly repeated the vow and taking the heavy ring out of the box, placed it on Sebastian's finger.

Turning her attention to the congregation, Ruth announced, "I think Kelly and Sebastian have prepared some readings." She stepped back and let the couple take the spotlight. Sebastian spoke first.

"Kelly, you are my Dulcinea. I wanted to find the words that perfectly describe how I feel. It's a poem written by Ralph Sergi. Sorry about not finding one from your man Walt." He pulled a small paper out of his breast pocket and read...

> "Te amo, Dulcinea... It's not a physical love but a love borne out of memories past ... surrounded by darkness save for one candle light... coming together as one through gaze and touch... Te Amo, Dulcinea."

He folded the paper and stuffed it in his back pocket.

Kelly was deeply touched. He must have searched many days to find those perfect words. Now it was her turn. She pulled a card from her bodice and slowly looked up at the man who stood before her.

"I guess it's no surprise I chose Whitman to speak for me... These lines are from his poem *When I Heard at the Close of Day.*" Then taking a deep breath, she read...

> "When I saw the full moon in the west grow pale... and saw my lover was on his way coming, O then I was happy... For the one I love most lay sleeping by me... and that night I was happy."

Kelly looked at Sebastian. *Oh my.* He had tears in his eyes.

Ruth once again took her place near the couple. "This is going to be a tough act to follow, but let's get these kids married, shall we?" The gathering in the pews laughed softly. She looked at them both and held their hands.

"Kelly and Sebastian, before this company of your friends, you have made promises to each other. Be kind to each other. Love one another. May the Lord bless you, bestowing His riches on you, keeping you faithful in body and soul. In the name of the Father, and the Son and the Holy Spirit. I now declare you to be husband and wife. Sebastian, kiss that girl!"

With a glint in his eye, Sebastian dipped Kelly to the floor in a passionate kiss – and the audience erupted in another standing ovation, clapping and shouting their approval. Loudly clearing her throat, Ruth gave the newlywed couple a raised eyebrow.

When the ruckus died down, Ruth continued. "I think we have a surprise now for our newlyweds. Raffaele and Gabriella have prepared a special song for you. The English translation is, "I Live for Her." I understand they worked on this most of last night..."

Brie and Raffaele walked over to the piano. Kelly and Sebastian stood transfixed as his brother and her best friend sang the beautiful duet. At the conclusion, and as husband and wife, Mr. and Mrs. Bonsignore walked down the three steps from the altar to begin their new life together – hand in hand, always and forever.

9

The Reception

After the guests had left for the festivities, Connie shot additional photos of the wedding party. During one of the family poses, Kelly turned to her mom and whispered, *"I wish my daddy was here..."*

Ruth looked up at her daughter and whispered, *"He is Kelly-Belly..."*

Connie noticed Kelly's sudden outburst of tears and looked up from her camera. She judiciously waited until Kelly composed herself before continuing.

Sebastian could see Kelly was visibly exhausted. He hugged his wife close – not wanting to ever let her go.

The drive to the Harbor Pub took less than ten minutes. After Sebastian helped Kelly and her mom exit the limo, he escorted the women through the back door. Ruth excused herself and went into the ladies' room.

Sebastian had rented one of the larger private party rooms at the Harbor Pub, and asked Tony, his former mentor, to cater the reception. Tony said he was honored to take the helm and would create a traditional menu.

Cody's partner Tom, who had decorated the chapel, also helped design and decorate the reception room. While Sebastian was hosting the pre-wedding dinner in his home, the friends worked all night on the chapel and the reception room.

As Kelly and Sebastian approached the room, they stopped – and tried taking it all in. Ivory-colored linens, tea light candles and floral centerpieces covered the round guests' tables as well as the long bridal party table. Bottles of Carpenè Malvoti Prosecco and long-stemmed crystal champagne flutes had been set at each table. And as in the chapel, strings of small twinkling lights hung above the tables and the dance floor.

In the four corners of the room, two-sided wooden structures resembling pergolas were draped with ivory gossamer fabric, giving the room a romantic ambiance. To the left of the entrance, Chef Tony stood behind the buffet-style food table.

Though Sebastian and Kelly couldn't see the DJ, they could hear the music. Kelly didn't recognize the soothing saxophone melody. Sebastian pulled her closer to him and spoke softly in her ear, "My man Boney James."

"Oh," Kelly crooned. "I love Boney James!"

"And I love you." Sebastian became serious. "And I am so sorry about not giving you the ring earlier. But the jeweler had a difficult time matching the perfect emerald to the color of your eyes." He kissed her forehead. "Brie told me how upset you were before the ceremony. I am so sorry." He pulled Kelly into his arms and kissed her hair. "I am so sorry. Forgive me?"

"Sebastian – I love you. I forgive you. But don't you ever do that to me again!" Kelly playfully slapped his arm – and gave him her best smile.

"I promise, next time we get married I'll get it right." He was about to plant one on her when he was poked from behind. Turning, he saw his brother standing next to Gabriella, whose hair appeared disheveled, compared to the sleek coif she wore only a half hour ago. Looking at Raffaele, he said in a stage whisper, *"You couldn't wait?"*

Kelly wondered what the commotion was about and turned. Brie held the pearl headband in her hand. *Really?* Gabriella blushed and clutched tighter on Raffaele's arm. Kelly noticed her mom standing behind the sexually sated couple. Thank goodness she didn't know what truly went on behind closed doors – or in the back of a limo! She rolled her eyes, looked at Sebastian and whispered, *"Let's do this."*

The guests had arrived earlier and now with the appearance of the wedding party, stood and applauded as the little group paraded into the room and took their seats. When everyone at the Bride and Groom table had been seated, Raffaele stood. He filled his champagne flute with Prosecco and raised it up. The room became silent.

"It is customary," his voice soft but strong, "that the Best Man toasts the Groom – and in this case," he looked down at Sebastian, "the Groom is my little brother." The gathering in the room clapped and cheered, some shouting "Here! Here!"

"So I will begin." Raffaele put his left hand on his brother's shoulder. "Thank you everyone for coming to honor Sebastian as he weds the beautiful Kelly. Your friendship and love for my brother touches me deeply." Many in the gathering wistfully sighed – Kelly and Ruth began crying. Raffaele took a breath and continued.

"What you may not realize... my brother literally saved my life. My former manager had embezzled my money and I was left bankrupt and humiliated – and my brother saved my life." Raffaele took a drink and paused to hold it together.

"I owe him so much, yet he has never asked for anything in return – except when he asked me to be the Best Man at his wedding." Again sighs could be heard among the friends gathered in the room.

"I can't tell you how much joy is in my heart for Sebastian and also now for his wife Kelly." The gathering was becoming more vocal and some cheering and clapping were heard. He looked again at Sebastian, then back to the people patiently holding their champagne flutes.

"May I offer a toast to my little brother Sebastian and his wife Kelly." Holding back his tears, he inhaled deeply and shouted, "Salute!"

The guests stood and joined in echoing, "Salute!" and drank from their fluted glasses. Sebastian stood and kissed his brother on both cheeks and hugged him tight. After Raffaele sat down, Sebastian addressed the guests.

"Ladies and gentlemen, my dear friends... While in college, I worked at the River View Restaurant in Stillwater under the watchful guidance of Head Chef Tony Stanbrook. He graciously agreed to cater this reception and has created a wonderful meal for us. The halibut was a Friday and Lenten staple in our home. The pasta for the ravioli was handmade this morning." He nodded in Chef Tony's direction. "The stuffing is our mother's recipe, as is the Bolognese sauce. And last but definitely not least, the Risotto Alfredo is a specialty entrée from his restaurant."

Sebastian asked Kelly to stand. He kissed her forehead and held her close as he continued. "Thank you for allowing us to share our memories with you."

The wedding party began walking to the banquet tables. Sebastian shook the Chef's hand.

"Thank you again, Chef Tony. May I present my wife Kelly?"

The chef with Nordic good looks and a genuine smile bowed his tall frame low and remarked, "It is my pleasure to cook for you tonight."

"Seb!" Raffaele broke the magic of the moment. "Food, little brother! We need sustenance!" Sebastian turned and smiled – and affectionately ruffled his brother's short-cropped hair. With full plates, Sebastian and Kelly walked back to their table and sat.

From Kelly's vantage point she noticed her mom, who was obviously enjoying her time with Chef Tony. He even kissed her hand. *Oh, my mom will be talking about this for years!* When her mom returned to the table, Kelly asked when she and Chef Tony were going to elope. Ruth blushed – Kelly had never seen her mom blush! This day was only getting better!

The clink of silverware on crystal echoed through the room followed by a chorus of clinks. Kelly turned to Sebastian, who obediently kissed his bride. The guests hooted and clapped. During the meal, they were obligated to repeat the annoying tradition many more times, but each time she kissed her husband, his kisses became more passionate. Holy Hell! This could get interesting!

Most of the guests were finished with their meals. Before the cake would be served, it was time for Sebastian to take his wife out on the dance floor. As they walked to the center of the designated area, the guests applauded. The lights dimmed, making the tiny twinkling lights above resemble stars in the night sky. The DJ played *Come Away with Me.*

She had never danced like this before. Kelly felt safe in Sebastian's strong arms as he gracefully guided her around the small dance floor. What began as a respectable waltz slowly morphed into a sultry rumba. He touched her body, tenderly pushing her hips that way, pulling her body this way. She was in heaven.

At the conclusion of their first dance he finished with a huge dip – and felt his erection grow. *Oh no, not here!* He quickly raised her up and held her close to him. The look in her eyes told him she felt his erection, too. She smiled and licked her lips. Clutching each other close, they somehow managed to shuffle back to the safety of their cloth-covered table.

Raffaele and Gabriella took to the dance floor as the sensual tones of Diego Garcia's *Stay* began. They danced a perfectly executed tango. Even as they were performing the intricate steps, Raffaele whispered into Gabriella's ear, helping her follow the steps, and she responding to his delicate touch.

Everyone in the party room was mesmerized by the dancers and Connie confessed to Kelly that she didn't know what to photograph, if indeed she should photograph their steamy exhibition. Raffaele's final move was to dip Gabriella low – so low her hair brushed the floor. As he held her, he buried his face in her full cleavage. It was obvious to everyone that Raffaele and Gabriella were totally unaware of their audience. Kelly quickly left her chair to go greet the passionate couple and escort them off the dance floor.

Sebastian felt a hand on his shoulder. He looked up and saw his friend Roger, who was looking as nervous as he'd ever seen him.

"Seb," he sat down beside him. "I walked Kelly down the aisle. Would you let me dance with her?"

Sebastian knew his friend's heartfelt plea was genuine and he also knew not to laugh – that would have crushed the former Marine. He gave Roger his blessing. "Kelly would love to dance with you."

Roger patted his friend's arm and walked over to the DJ. Then taking a deep breath and mustering all the strength he possessed, approached Kelly. She had been talking with Brie when she noticed him. She turned and smiled.

"Kelly..."

"Yes Roger?"

"Kelly, would you do me the honor... would you dance with me?"

"Of course. I'd love to."

The Commodores' *Three Times a Lady* began. Roger took Kelly by the hand out onto the dance floor. He carefully put his four-and-a-half on her back, and as a teenage boy at the prom held her hand high with the other.

From where he sat, Sebastian hid a chuckle as he watched Roger move more like a drill sergeant, dancing a precise if not stiff box step. But Kelly smiled at the big man the whole time, which only made Sebastian love her more.

When the song concluded, Roger lowered his tall frame and holding Kelly's shoulders, chastely kissed her on the cheek. Kelly returned the kiss, feeling his mustache against her face. Even in the dim light of the room, Sebastian could tell Roger was affected. Kelly hugged him and let him escort her back to her chair.

"Thank you, Kelly..."

Sebastian suspected Roger wanted to say more. Avoiding any potential embarrassment, he put his arm around his wife and kissed her neck. But Roger only smiled down at Kelly and walked away. Sebastian assumed she would be angry with him for making that outward show of affection in front of their friend. Instead she pulled his face to hers and, while kissing him, whispered, *"I want to fuck my husband!"*

Holy Crap! He hardly ever heard her throw the F-bomb. He had to wrap up this shindig and get her out of here. But by then, their guests had finished eating and began dancing. He knew they couldn't leave yet.

The rest of the evening was full of laughter, music and reminiscing. Sebastian and Raffaele and even Tony filled Ruth's dance card. Every so often the guests clinked their silverware against crystal champagne flutes, forcing the newlyweds to drop everything and kiss. But after many times obeying that request, Kelly was going to give their guests a kiss to end all kisses.

Kelly slid an empty chair into the middle of the dance floor. She beckoned Sebastian, who quickly obeyed and walked out to meet her. She pushed him down on the chair, hoisted her dress thigh high and straddled his legs. Holding his bearded face, she gave him the deepest tongue she could. He clutched her ass with open fingers and their friends cheered. She stood, turned and curtsied in triumph, while Sebastian sat all bedraggled – pretending to fan his face. That did it. No more kissing requests and everyone applauded.

They returned to their seats, but Kelly chose to sit on his lap. She noticed he had been keeping a watchful eye on Raffaele and Gabriella. He shared his concerns with his wife.

"I know Raffaele is smitten with Brie, but I also know she just couldn't leave her job to hobnob around the world with him."

"They are adults, after all," Kelly kissed her husband's cheek. "I can only assume they'll work it out."

"I don't want to see either of them getting hurt..." He remembered watching Raffe and Brie dance, appearing as if they were the only two people left on earth. "I just hope your friend won't hurt my brother."

"And I hope your brother won't hurt my friend."

Sebastian pressed his head against hers and kissed her forehead. They both agreed they couldn't spend any more time contemplating another couple's future – they had their own lives, and right now Sebastian wanted to make love to *his* future.

Chef Tony announced it was time to cut the cake. To honor this special day, his sous chefs made a two-tier carrot cake with a thick cream-cheese frosting. Connie took her position near the couple as they cut into the cake.

Kelly picked up a little piece and delicately fed it to her husband. Sebastian sucked on her fingers as he took the portion into his mouth. She whispered, *"You are so bad!"*

Sebastian picked up a piece that was more frosting than cake and fed it to his wife, but he smudged some on her nose. She laughed as he kissed the frosting off her face. They walked back to their table as Chef Tony took over cutting the cake for the rest of the wedding party and the guests.

Kelly caught sight of Cody and his date Tom, the decorator. She wanted to thank Tom for the beautiful twinkling lights and white roses in the chapel, and for the exquisite decorations in the Harbor Pub private party room. Sebastian flagged Cody. The pair came over and sat with them.

Cody introduced his partner Tom to Sebastian and Kelly, who immediately gushed about how magical it all felt. Sebastian shook Tom's hand and winked at Cody.

"Cody, I've known you about five years and I never knew you were gay!"

Cody loved Sebastian's humor, so he stuck it back on his friend. "It just never came up in conversation. And if I may remind you Sebastian, you never talked about girls either!" Cody winked at Kelly, who enjoyed the repartee.

Tom let Sebastian know it was his pleasure to decorate the chapel and the reception room, and he'd be insulted if his friend asked for the bill. Enough said.

It was getting late. Kelly looked around for Roger, but didn't see him. "I wanted to thank him for walking me down the aisle – and the dance..."

Sebastian didn't see him either. "I think he bugged out after he danced with you."

Ruth came by and said her goodbyes to her daughter and her new son-in-law. She'd be leaving early in the morning. Sebastian rose and kissed her cheek, and enfolded her small frame in a bear hug. Ruth hugged him back, then turned to Kelly and hugged her, too. He saw tears stream down Kelly's face as she hugged her mom tight.

"Thank you, Mama! I love you so much!"

"I know you do, my girl." Michael came up behind Ruth and told her he'd drive her back to the hotel and to the airport in the morning. Ruth said she felt blessed to be among so many lovely people – and she started crying. *So that's where Kelly gets it.*

Above all the commotion, Brie shouted, "Kelly! Your bouquet!!"

Kelly laughed and asked her if she was ready and tossed the bouquet in her arms. She had a feeling Brie would be the next one to get married and accelerated the process.

Brie clutched the bouquet in her hands, but Raffaele took it from her and as they walked out together, carried it high as a conquering hero holding a scepter.

Michael held out his arm and Ruth took it. Soon the rest of the guests also said their goodbyes, congratulating the couple again. The only people remaining were Chef Tony and the DJ, and since Sebastian had settled with them in advance there was nothing left to do but go home.

"But we're not going to my house," Sebastian announced to Kelly. He held her hand and continued. "We're not going to my house. We're going to *our* house. I changed the names on the deed yesterday. Man, am I glad you didn't get cold feet, woman!"

She laughed, but then the tears came again. He quickly sat and pulled her onto his lap, holding her tight. It was a good thing he had been subjected to her tears already – he knew not to fix tears. She held his head lightly in her arms. "Let's go home, mister."

"Good idea, Love." He helped her stand, escorted her out of the reception room and into their waiting limo. Sebastian knocked on the panel that separated the driver from the very private passenger area. As he dimmed the lights, he turned on the pre programmed music... Mark Isham's *My Wife with Champagne Shoulders*. The limo began moving. Kelly rested her head against her husband's shoulder – and listened to the soothing music.

"I love you, mister..."

Sebastian kissed his wife's face. "I love you too, Mrs. Bonsignore." He kissed the top of her head. "Mrs. Bonsignore... I certainly do love that name..."

She felt his grin. "I do, too..." Kelly kicked off her dancing shoes and rubbed her feet with her toes.

"Sit back, Love and put your feet on my lap."

She didn't need any further encouragement. The seats were wide enough that she could lean against the back comfortably. Kelly put her feet on her husband's lap. Sebastian began massaging them – he heard his wife purr...

"Don't stop... please..."

While he rubbed her feet, he spoke in hushed tones. "Did you have a good time, Love?"

"Sebastian, it was the best time of my life... Ooh... right there..." He obeyed her command and dug a little deeper in the arch of her left foot. He hit the right spot. "Oh yeah..."

"I can't wait to get you home, Mrs. B..."

"Oh really? So tell me, mister, what plans have you made for our wedding night? I mean, other than the obvious?"

"What do you mean 'obvious'?"

"Sebastian," she smiled. "I know you. I love you and I know you..."

He looked at his wife. Her eyes were closed – she was out. Her body had slowly meandered down the back of the seat, lying across the seat with her feet still in his lap.

And Mark Isham's music played on...

The limo pulled up to the garage. Sebastian swept his wife up in his strong arms and gingerly carried her up the steps and across the threshold of *their* home. He carried her through the house, up the stairs and into their bedroom. Before he put her down he kissed her... his wife...

Kelly wanted a bath before going to bed. While she changed out of her clothes, he turned on the water in the large Jacuzzi tub. Soon it was overflowing with foamy suds.

He helped her into the tub and joined her, sitting behind her. Sebastian put his arms around his wife's body – they lay quietly for several minutes. Kelly put her hands on her husband's arms.

"Seb..."

"Yes, Love..."

"Thank you for making this night the best ever..." And the tears started. He held her closer in his arms, not trying to fix tears – just holding her close to his chest.

"Thank you for marrying me..." He asked her to sit up and began picking out the bobby pins that held her hair in the twist, loosening her hair, letting the auburn waves fall on her shoulders. Then picking up the large sea sponge he washed her back. He brought the sponge around her shoulders and squeezed warm water down across her chest.

Kelly leaned her head against his shoulder as he continued washing her body, her belly and down to her legs. Sebastian briefly held the sponge between her legs. With his other hand, Sebastian caressed her breasts – his hand totally covering her breasts – and felt her nipples harden under his touch. Her breathing quickened...

Kelly turned and kissed his lips. "You're my husband – I don't think I've ever loved anyone this much..."

Sebastian kissed her face and again pulled her body against his. She could feel his erection at her hip.

"Make love to me, Sebastian... make love with me... but not here. In our bed." She kissed his lips, feeling his soft beard against her face. "Not here..."

Sebastian rose and stepped out of the tub and helped his wife step out onto the heated tile floor. He wrapped her in his stolen hotel robe. He quickly toweled off and lifting his wife carried her to the bed. But in the time it took to walk those few steps she had fallen asleep, her head heavy on his shoulder. He lay her on the mattress – bathrobe and all – and joined her in their bed. He pulled her close – her back to his front – and slept.

And as on that first magical night they spent together, they shared one pillow...

10

A Change of Plans

Sunday morning came too early. Sebastian's cell phone vibrated. Though he tried ignoring it, Kelly mumbled that it might be important considering the time. As he reached for the phone on his wife's side of the bed, he kissed her face. Looking at the caller ID, he whispered, *"Shit... It's Raffaele!"*

"Raffe, what's up? You okay?" Kelly couldn't see his face but she heard the concern in his voice – and hugged him.

"Seb, there's been a slight change of plans. How soon can you and your lovely bride get out to the airport?"

Sebastian turned and looked at Kelly. God, but she was beautiful! "How soon can you get ready? We're taking a little road trip."

They got out of bed, dressed quickly and soon were on their way to the airport. While driving, he called Raffaele and found out where he would be waiting. Sebastian took Kelly's hand as they ran through the airport.

When they arrived at the security gate, she saw Gabriella who was here to see Raffaele depart. But behind Brie, she saw her mom. *What?* The flights to Colorado and New York would not be leaving from the same gate.

"Mom, are you okay?" Kelly was concerned for her mom and hugged her.

Ruth hugged her back and smiled broadly. "I'm actually very fine." Then turning to Brie, she said, "Gabriella, would you like to let Kelly in on your plans?"

Without hearing the reason, Kelly knew exactly what was going on. *Oh no she's not!*

"Kelly," Brie was crying – Brie never cried! Between choking breaths, she continued. "Raffaele asked me to marry him." Proverbial crickets could be heard – the silence that followed her announcement was palpable.

Sebastian was the first to break the tension. "Raffe, are you sure?" Then looking at Brie, he asked, "What about your job? I know you're tenured..."

"But I'm not quitting," she clarified for everyone. Though her tears flowed, her breathing had calmed. "I'm taking an extended leave of absence." She sounded more confident. "I emailed my request this morning... right after Raffaele proposed."

She turned to Kelly. "You know my assistant Bastien... He's very capable." Brie wiped more tears from her face. "And my classes and the foreign language department will be fine without me for the rest of the school year."

Raffaele hugged his little brother's shoulders. "I guess our lives aren't so different after all." He looked at Kelly, then back at Sebastian. "We both found love in only a few days." His gaze fell on Brie, who was looking back at him while she quietly shed fresh tears.

"I truly love Gabriella, and she has committed herself to me. We're going to fly to New York first. I have a prior obligation to perform, and then we'll fly out to Colorado."

Ruth, whose flight would depart first, spoke up. "If it's all the same to you folks, I'd like to share my plan." She addressed Sebastian and Kelly. "With your blessing I'm going to marry these two nice people – unofficially of course. They would like you as their witnesses."

Ruth turned to Brie and Raffe. "But when they arrive back in Colorado and with the proper marriage license, I'll marry them again..." She raised one eyebrow and added, "...formally."

Kelly couldn't stop crying. "Really? Really, Brie?" She was sad to say goodbye to her best friend. "Brie, we've taught together forever... but I'm also so happy for you." Kelly clutched her friend's hand.

"Before these ladies shed too many more tears," Raffaele interrupted. "May we have your blessing, little brother?"

Sebastian got misty. "Of course!" He put his brother in a bear hug and kissed him on both cheeks. "How can I not be happy for you! I love you!" Everyone including Ruth was crying.

An airport official escorted the little party to a private room not far from the checkpoint. "Let us know when you've concluded your meeting. We'll expedite your passage through security." He closed the door behind them.

Ruth stood at the front of the room near an empty easel, Raffaele and Gabriella stood facing her. Sebastian and Kelly stood off to one side near a row of stacked chairs.

Ruth smiled. "Let's be quick, shall we?"

Raffaele looked lovingly at Gabriella, grasped her hands and held them on his chest. "From the moment I saw your beautiful face I knew I would love you forever." He unceremoniously wiped a tear from his eye, then clasping her hands tighter he continued.

"You are my future. You are my second chance, *mia bellissima Gabriella*. My heart is full again. I no longer weep at night. You have restored my heart, you have healed my soul."

Brie leaned forward, closed her eyes and pressed her trembling lips to Raffaele's. He pulled her into his arms and responded with his own deep kiss. She opened her large brown eyes and looking up at him, whispered, *"I really do love you."*

Raffaele kissed her eyes and again her lips, and breathed the words, "I know you do *mia bellissima Gabriella. E ti amo.*"

"Dominicci... Raffaele..," Gabriella began, sounding so confident, "I was not looking for you but I knew my life was not complete. My days were filled with work and friends, but my nights were empty." She swallowed hard, looked at Kelly – who was shedding copious amounts of tears – and then returned to the love of her life. She put her hands on his handsome face and continued softly.

"I would press my pillow to my face, feeling the dampness of my tears. I did not know you would come into my dreams and kiss my tears away." Raffaele grasped her hands in his own and pressed them to his chest. She continued.

"I was not looking for you, but you found me. You told me you were not looking for me, but I found you – and for that I am eternally grateful! You are my present and my future. My life will never be the same, and I cannot wait to embark on our journey together."

Raffaele raised her hands to his mouth and tenderly kissed her fingers...

Ruth politely cleared her throat and asked Raffaele and Gabriella to face her.

"This is a dry run. We'll do the legal wedding back home. Are you ready, Raffaele?" Without taking his eyes from Brie, he answered, "Yes."

"Raffaele Dominicci Bonsignore," the Reverend Ruth Cameron began, "do you take Gabriella Bridget Murray as your wife, to love her, respect her and honor her in all you do?"

Sebastian squeezed Kelly to his side. She whispered in his ear, *"You have me Seb! I'm not going anywhere!"* He smiled at his wife and eased up on the grip he had on her body.

Raffaele answered, "I will, I do!" He kissed Brie on the lips again.

Ruth turned to Gabriella. "Gabriella Bridget Murray, do you take Raffaele Dominicci Bonsignore as your husband, to love him, respect him and honor him in all you do?"

Gabriella couldn't contain her tears. Sebastian noticed her waterworks, looked at Kelly and rolled his eyes. She laughed through her own tears.

Brie calmed down long enough to answer, "Yes, Yes, Yes. Always! I do!"

Ruth continued. "Normally at this point, I would say 'You may kiss the bride,' but you two have already done that!" That was the comic relief everyone needed, and the little group laughed. Brie exhaled loudly and Raffaele pulled her into his arms, squeezing her tight.

A knock on the door disrupted the celebration. The airport official, who had directed them to the private room, opened the door and apologetically asked them to wrap up their meeting. It was almost time to board.

Everyone said their goodbyes at once. Gabriella and Raffe picked up their carry-on bags. Raffe pulled Sebastian into a one-armed bear hug. "We will keep in touch – better than we have in the past." He kissed his brother's cheeks. "Better than we have little brother."

Kelly hugged Brie, whispering that this would be the last time they would see each other for who knows how long. Both girls' tears started anew. Raffaele and Sebastian could only look at the women, then at each other and shrugged their shoulders.

Ruth picked up her carry-on bag. "Come on..." And taking the lead, walked to Raffaele and Brie's gate. Sebastian and Kelly hung on to each other as they watched their brother and friend enter the jet bridge. The almost newlyweds turned and waved, and then they were gone. Kelly's tears flowed again – Sebastian just held her close. He was now an expert on tears.

Ruth came up to Kelly. "They're going to drive me to my gate in the terminal shuttle. I'm going to say goodbye, my girl." Kelly hugged her mom, whispering in her ear that she and Sebastian would come visit her soon. Ruth kissed her on the lips and whispered back, *"Promise?"*

Sebastian helped Ruth step onto the shuttle, placed her carry-on bag on the seat at her side and kissed her cheek. She patted him on his shoulder and mouthed *Love you!* And then she was gone.

Kelly watched as her mom sped away, then turned to Sebastian and hugged him. But he had such a strange look on his face. *What?*

"So wife," he began. "How would you like to honeymoon in Colorado?" Kelly thought she was hearing things. She looked hard at her husband, who she noticed was giving her that *I've got a great idea* smile.

"Really?" She didn't mean to shout.

Sebastian only laughed and echoed her word. "Really!"

"We were counting on white sand beaches on the ocean, but white-capped snow on the mountains? What about our reservations in the British Virgin Islands?"

"I thought Cody and Tom would like a little vacation."

Kelly hugged him hard. "You would do this for me? For us?" Kelly was about to burst into tears – this day may have been her record for tears.

"Yes Love, I would, and I will – and we will!" He wiped her tears with his thumbs.

"Okay mister. Let's go..." Kelly put her arm through his and began walking out toward their car. She yawned. "So... sleep or breakfast?"

Sebastian stopped and pulled her close, so close she could feel his growing erection. "Neither..."

11

The Honeymoon

When she thought of those memories – those awful, wonderful memories her tears started again. Watching as he drove the car, his thoughts so far away, she knew he would not comfort her. Giving her comfort when she cried never fixed tears – comforting her could only exacerbate her tears, though a touch of his hand right now wouldn't hurt.

Her mind raced. Could she ask him to pull over? Tell him she changed her mind about giving up the cabin? Or would that only start another argument? She knew she couldn't ask him for comfort for fear he'd deny that request, too. Would he not want to pull the car over and reach out to her if she asked? Wouldn't he kiss away her tears if she asked? She was so afraid he'd say no – she didn't want to risk it. She'd rather be silent than be rejected by his love.

His Love. He called her *Love*. The term meant so much, especially coming from his lips – those lips that could stop her tears if only she asked...

She felt the car lurch. She knew Sebastian had almost missed the turn-off onto the county road that led to their cabin. He must have braked hard, but her attention was drawn to the passenger jet that flew overhead, bringing people to destinations unknown. Through the open moonroof, she watched as the jet trail faded out of sight. She closed her eyes against the bright sun, remembering their impulsive trip to New York and their honeymoon in Grand Junction. She loved that trip to New York, loved their honeymoon, loved him...

Sebastian had changed their original honeymoon destination from the British Virgin Isles to Colorado. But first they flew to New York. Raffaele was substituting for a fellow Tenor who was down with laryngitis. He would be playing the part of The Duke in Verdi's *Rigoletto* for three performances. He was familiar with the role. Gabriella had never seen him perform and she was so excited that Kelly and Sebastian would also be there.

While in New York, Kelly and Brie went shopping, then met up with Sebastian and Raffaele at the theatre. Kelly knew it was important that her husband see his brother in action. And they were not disappointed. As Dominicci sang his show-stopping aria, Kelly couldn't help noticing the look on Sebastian's face was like that of a young boy realizing Santa Claus was real.

After his final performance, they left for Colorado on a private jet flying directly into the Grand Junction airport. Sebastian had arranged for the couples to have their own rental cars. Kelly and Sebastian would stay at the Castle Creek Bed & Breakfast, and Raffaele and Brie had booked a room at the Two Rivers Winery and Chateau.

He and Kelly couldn't wait to consummate their marriage properly in their honeymoon bed, and Raffaele and Brie just wanted to continue their love making. Evidently according to Sebastian, Raffe and Brie had been humping like rabbits since the night of the groom's dinner.

Kelly was offended with the metaphor. "That's an awful thing to say about your brother and my best friend!"

He lobbed it back at her. "What have we been doing since our date night?"

"Humping like rabbits!" She laughed so hard she snorted. He took her in his arms and held her tight, already feeling his erection pressing against her.

They stopped off at Ruth's home where Sebastian and Kelly picked her up, then drove to a restaurant she had recommended – *il Bistro Italiano*. Sebastian was skeptical at first but Ruth said the food was wonderful. Since the menu was written in Italian, the whole table insisted that Raffaele order for everyone just to hear his impeccable pronunciation. The food was just as Kelly's mom promised – wonderful!

As the group was preparing to leave the restaurant, Ruth took Gabriella's arm. "You *are* staying with me at my home tonight."

The shocked look on Brie's face made Kelly hide a smile. Then putting on her best serious look, she reminded her friend, "It's tradition. You remember I couldn't stay with Sebastian the night before our wedding?"

Ruth couldn't hold her laughter any longer. "Brie honey, do what you want with your man." She shook her head and chuckled as she walked out of the restaurant.

"She's kidding, right?" Brie held Raffaele's arm so tight her fingernails dug into his skin through his shirt.

Kelly laughed. "Yes Brie, she's kidding!"

Raffaele raised his sleeve, showing everyone the marks Brie's nails had made on his forearm. He tenderly rubbed the area. "I'm injured, woman! *Ow!*"

Sebastian patted his brother's face and joined in the good natured kidding. "Go hump yourself silly, big brother. We'll see you in the morning." He took Kelly's hand and walked out after Ruth.

"I'm injured..." Raffaele whimpered as he walked out with Brie at his side, holding his arm and whispering her apologies.

Before Brie got into their vehicle, Kelly hugged her tight. Sebastian could tell Kelly was about to burst her tear dam. He quickly turned her around and, kissing her hard, loudly whispered, "I guess we're not the only ones humping tonight."

"Shhhh!" Kelly looked around for her mom, hoping she didn't hear that remark.

Brie rolled down her window. "Matron of Honor?"

"Wouldn't miss it for the world!"

They drove Ruth back to her home. Sebastian escorted her to the front door and kissed her on the cheek. All she could do was smile. Ruth was about to burst her own tear dam.

After returning to the SUV, Sebastian touched his wife's thigh, leaned over and kissed her. "I love you..."

"Show me, mister..."

Sebastian drove directly to the B&B. They were quietly greeted by the night innkeeper and shown directly up the stairs to their room. She wished them a goodnight, handed them their key and padded off back downstairs.

Sebastian opened the door and, lifting Kelly in his arms, walked into the room. He kissed her – and kissed her again. He didn't want to put her down. She closed her eyes, folded her arms around his head and pressed her face against his beard. He felt her tears.

He held her tighter, which only made her cry harder. Through small gasps, she whispered, *"I love you so much!"* He squeezed her body against his chest.

When he lightly set her down, he kissed her eyes, her face, her lips... He removed her blouse and kissed her breasts... Kneeling before her, Sebastian opened the waistband of her skirt and slowly undressed her. Kelly placed her hands on his shoulders as she stepped out of her clothing. She asked him to stand.

Kelly unbuttoned her husband's shirt, opened his belt and unzipped his pants, letting them fall to the floor. She slowly combed through his chest hair – feeling the soft hair with her fingers, finding his nipples, caressing his nipples... and forced his shirt off from his shoulders.

His erection was pushing against her belly. She kissed his lips, making love to him with her tongue. His erection grew and found its way through the slit in his underwear – again. Looking down Kelly couldn't help but laugh at the memory of their first night together.

After kicking away his discarded clothing, Sebastian effortlessly lifted his wife into his arms and walked backwards until his legs found the bed. Lying back on the mattress, he pulled her on top of him.

Kelly reveled in his body, loving his muscular shape beneath her – and held onto his shoulders as he rolled over on her. She cocooned herself around him, wrapping her legs like a vise around his waist. He almost smothered her as his full weight pressed on her chest.

Propping himself up on one elbow, he put his hand under her knee and pulled her leg up, holding it close to him. And ever so slowly pushed into her... and lay that way for a few moments, letting her feel the fullness of his erection.

He whispered, *"Are you ready Love?"*

"Always and forever..."

Sebastian slightly pulled out, then rammed into her so hard the ornate headboard banged against the wall. But they heard nothing except their beating hearts, their deep breaths and Sebastian's grunting as he continued forcing himself into her, thrusting deeper, harder...

Knock... Knock... Knock...

Sebastian was in mid-thrust and stopped at the first sound of the knocking – stopped like a statue. He didn't dare breathe.

Again they heard the soft ***knock... knock... knock*** on their door.

Kelly tried muffling her giggles.

A faint, disembodied voice called to them. "Could you keep it down, just a little, please?"

"Sure..." Kelly whispered between giggles. Sebastian smothered her mouth with his and whispered *sure* into her open mouth. She giggled again and couldn't stop. Sebastian let her leg drop, held her head with both hands, his forehead against her face.

Sebastian whispered into her mouth, *"You're killing me, here!"*

"Sorry... I'll be serious..." But those words only brought on more laughter from both of them.

"I think I've lost..." Sebastian began...

Kelly answered, "... that loving feeling..."

Their laughter consumed them, his erection died and he rolled off her body. He held her in his arms, her back to his front. And they slept, she in his arms, sharing one pillow, the way they had since that first magical night...

12
The Cabin

He knew he could not comfort her. Giving her comfort when she cried never fixed tears – instead, comforting her could only exacerbate her tears.

His mind raced. Would she accept a touch of his hand right now? Could he tell her he had changed his mind about giving up their cabin? Or would that only start another argument? He knew he couldn't ask her if he could comfort her because she might deny that request. Would she not want him to pull the car over and reach out to her if he asked? Wouldn't she let him kiss away her tears if he asked? He was so afraid she'd say no – he didn't want to risk it.

The better part of valor right now would be keeping silent rather than be rejected by her love. He continued driving on for another hour before turning off onto the South Lake Shore Road, which led to an unmarked gravel road and to their cabin. With a sigh of bitter sweetness, he remembered how the cabin came to be theirs...

Morning had come too soon. Sebastian had been holed up in his office with his nose in a spreadsheet and hadn't realized how late it was. When he eventually crawled into their bed he nuzzled Kelly, who wrapped her body around him. Sleep came immediately.

He woke to sweet kisses on his face. They had only been married not half a year, but oh, yes, he could do this forever. Opening his eyes, he turned his head to face the face lying next to his, sharing one pillow.

She propped herself up on one elbow, supporting her head with her hand, while with the other hand lovingly tugged at the carpet of black hair that covered his chest.

"We need to get away."

He knew what was coming. This was not the first time she alluded to wanting a cabin in the woods. "We can get away any time you want." And quickly suggested the bed and breakfast where they stayed on their honeymoon. He was trying to steer her away from talk of 'nature.'

"It was nice... mmmm... very nice..." Her hand roamed from his chest to his belly, where he stopped it with his own hand. "But I want someplace more private. We had to control ourselves in that room, remember?"

He considered the memory for a few moments. "Yeah, that's right..." And smiled sheepishly.

Still holding her hand with his, he helped her hand move lower on his body. Now she was the one who stopped the southerly progress.

"No really! We need a place out of the city – in the country. A place all to ourselves, where we can do anything we want, where we want..." Her hand broke free of his grip and playfully touched his growing erection, holding it, stroking it. He opened his legs.

"You know this isn't helping. You want to talk and this," looking down at the growing tent over his crotch, *"ain't helping!"*

Ignoring his protests, Kelly continued. "I want a cabin in the country..." She kissed his cheek. "Out in the woods..." She kissed his neck, his chest. "Where we can do anything we want..." She kissed his belly. "Any time we want..." She threw back the sheet and slid down between his open legs. "To anyone we want..."

She gave him one of her looks and unceremoniously put the head of his full erection in her mouth, silently challenging him to object.

Conversation over.

Early the next morning, Sebastian began looking for that elusive cabin. He viewed several properties on the internet and settled on acreage near a lake with many birch trees, extensive woodlands, a creek that ran into a pond... *And* located at least a mile back from the main road.

He purchased the little cabin unseen – the realtor assuring him the property was clean. The first time he drove this road was via directions drafted by the agent on a luncheon napkin. The map was crude, the ink had bled, the road impossible to find, his temper short. When he eventually arrived at the site and viewed the pristine condition of the property, he applauded himself for his intuition. However, the interior of the little cabin was in deplorable condition.

Over the next two weekends Sebastian called in his debts. He and his friends Michael, Cody and Roger converged upon the cabin to clean and make major repairs on the three-room cottage. Kelly had longed for a cabin in the woods since shortly after they met, saying she was bound and determined to introduce her city man to nature. She still talked about the cabin every so often, but he was sure she had lost all hope. Wouldn't she be surprised – especially after getting so upset with him when he was gone two consecutive weekends *on business*!

He remembered the first time they drove out to the property. Sebastian had let her think they were borrowing a friend's cabin for the weekend. He didn't immediately tell her the cabin was theirs – instead, he waited until the next morning to break the news. That morning, he had showered first. When the hot water refreshed, she took her shower.

While she was absent, Sebastian put his plan into motion. He programmed his iPod to play Vivaldi's *The Four Seasons* – somehow it seemed appropriate – and waited in bed with two wine goblets of mimosas. After Kelly came out from her shower wrapped in one of the luxurious towels, her hair dripping, he told her that he had bought the cabin. This was their place! He held out one of the wine goblets to her so they could toast to their cabin.

She screamed, "Oh hell yes!" Her towel crumpled to the floor as she propelled herself at him, causing the mimosas to spill. He dropped the goblets next to his naked lap and caught her body in mid air, holding her close as he rolled over.

She clung to his neck and whispered, *"I knew it."*

"What did you know?" He kissed her face. "What did you know, Love?"

"I knew you wouldn't let me down. I knew you were planning something..." Kelly closed her eyes and kissed his lips – she loved the feel of his mustache and beard on her face.

Sebastian closed his eyes, loving his wife's kisses, never wanting her sweet kisses to stop. "When did you figure it out?"

She stopped kissing him. "Seriously? Two weekends in a row when you were at your so-called meetings? Roger and Michael and Cody were all out of town, too."

"I didn't think you'd notice."

Again she kissed his face – never wanting to stop kissing this man, her husband, her Ulysses. "I had gone with the teachers to the Harbor Pub that first weekend when you were at your supposed conference. I thought we'd meet up with Roger, but he and your friends were all absent. And then when I stopped in at the pub again last Saturday night... I figured something was going on..."

"You're too smart for your own good, woman." He pulled her face against his. "Just too damn smart."

She kissed his lips – loving his soft lips. "I know..."

"I love you, Kelly..." He stroked her wet hair with his hand, brushing her bangs from her eyes.

Pressing her forehead against his, she whispered, *"I love my cabin..."* And again she surrendered herself – her body, her mind, her soul, her heart to the man she loved... always and forever. And she didn't mind that the sheets were saturated with the spilled mimosas – he had given her the greatest gift – his love in the form of a funny little cabin in the middle of nowhere... a place where they could do anything they wanted... any time they wanted... to anyone they wanted...

He lay on his side and pulling her into his arms, held her tight. And like that first magical night together, Vivaldi's *Winter* played on as they slept.

He woke before her and kissed her forehead, his hand caressing her damp hair. He let her sleep for a while longer – and not for the first time realizing how easy it was to make her so happy...

But what had once made her so happy was now making her so sad. They were on their way to close up the cabin, sell the property, divest their assets. They wouldn't need it anymore – no more retreats, no more long weekends to catch up with each other. The cabin was now a liability. God, how he hated that it was over!

God, how she wished it wasn't over! This road leading to their cabin held such memories. She remembered the first time they drove down the narrow road. She had teased him many times about getting a cabin – a private retreat. She was determined to introduce her husband to nature!

The first time he drove her out here, it seemed he had a hard time finding the property – she wondered if this had been such a good idea after all. But after spending many lost weekends at the little cabin together – regrouping, catching up on missed opportunities to talk, listen, feel, touch, sense – both were glad the cabin was secluded.

They used the cabin many times, but never shared it with anyone. This was their special place. When his work became too intense, when she was between semesters and could take some time off from her teaching and studies, they would gather up enough food for the weekend – Kelly bringing her Whitman, Sebastian bringing his week's worth of newspapers and the customary bottles of wine and beer – and leave town. Upon arrival, Kelly would jump from the car with her book in tow.

In the summertime, she couldn't wait to kick off her moccasins and pad around in her bare feet on the rich mossy grass. She loved the many birch trees that encircled the little cottage.

Sometimes they stayed in the big dark bed, taking turns reading to each other – one finding solace in the poet's rhymes, the other helping complete the more obscure literary clues in *New York Times* crossword puzzles. Other times, when their passions grew, they would quietly satisfy their needs – slowly, tenderly, finally falling asleep in each other's arms. Or they would simply relish the quiet, barely talking.

But always there was that bond, that special bond of love, serenity, commitment, the one constant in each other's lives – the bond that united them.

And now they were closing up the cabin. She was against it, but he was so determined she had reluctantly agreed.

13

The Beginning of the End

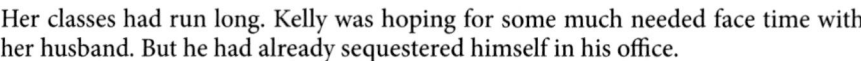

Her classes had run long. Kelly was hoping for some much needed face time with her husband. But he had already sequestered himself in his office.

Now that they were in the midst of tax season – from January through April – he and Kelly were living more like roommates than lovers. He was also taking more out-of-town meetings. She would have felt his absence more if her graduate studies hadn't taken up most of her time.

She ate dinner alone – she knew not to bother him. Let him get his work done and maybe he'd join her later. But as Kelly lay in their great bed reading, she couldn't concentrate. All she could hear was the incessant tap-tap-tapping of Sebastian's keyboard. This was ridiculous!

She rose from the bed and tiptoed down the hall – and silently pushed open the door. He was hunched over his desk – the dual monitors flickering their light on the walls in the dimly lit room.

He didn't hear her as she crept closer to his chair. She startled him. "Sorry. I was tired of waiting for you – so the mountain came to Mohammed..."

"I got caught up in this program..."

"I know..."

"What do you want Kelly?"

"You..."

He stopped typing and put his head down. "I know... sorry..."

Kelly leaned against his desk, facing him. "Don't be sorry." She reached out and caressed his hair. "I miss you..." She pushed at his shoulder, making him sit up straight and sat across his lap. He rolled his chair back from his desk.

"What do you want?" He put his hands on her back, pushing her T-shirt up to her shoulders.

"You..." She pulled at the leather tie, releasing his hair, pulling his long hair forward in her fists – and kissed him. "I want you..."

Sebastian slid his fingers under the waistband of her panties, exposing and caressing her beautiful ass. She stood. He pressed his face into her belly and pulled at her naked butt cheeks – and exhaled. "I've missed you..." He pushed his chair back further from his desk.

"So what are you going to do about it, mister?" She stepped out of her panties.

"This..." Sebastian pulled her to him – again she straddled his lap. Kelly pressed down on his erection, swearing it would burst through his pants. She kissed her husband's lips, loving her husband's lips.

"Kelly... Stand please..." He kicked off his tennis shoes and stood, letting his pants fall around his ankles, stepping out of one leg. He sat back on his chair and pulled her to him, making her sit across his lap.

She put her hands on his shoulders and slowly came down on him. He was so hard and so large – and they hadn't made love in weeks. "Oh... I've missed this..."

He held her around her waist, pulling her close to his chest, inhaling her scent, loving her, his wife. "Don't move... please."

Kelly caressed his hair and kissed his forehead, and tried very hard not to move – but she did and it was over.

He pressed his forehead against her chest. "Sorry Love..."

Again Kelly kissed his face. "I know."

His cell phone alerted him to an incoming call. She rose from his thighs and took a step back as he picked up his phone.

"Seb here." He looked up at his wife and whispered, *"Sorry..."*

But she didn't look at him. Instead, she retrieved her clothes and walked out of the room. If the caller only knew that his knowledgeable financial adviser was sitting at his desk with no pants on.

She had been dozing. Kelly woke when she felt Sebastian's body lay on the mattress. He pulled her to him. She kissed his face. "Don't forget. Tomorrow is the last day of classes."

"What am I not supposed to not forget?"

"We're going to the cabin, silly. We've talked about this. After I'm done with school we take a few days off and..." Kelly tugged at his thick chest hair. "...do nothing for a few days. Remember?"

Sebastian pulled his wife closer to his chest – he kissed her forehead. She put her head on his shoulder and tenderly combed through his belly hair, slowly moving her hand down his body, still feeling the effects of her afterglow. He took her hand and rolled on his side facing her.

Kelly nudged him with her words. "Remember...?"

Sebastian kissed her fingers and exhaled. "We can't stay long. You know that." He closed his eyes and kissed her face. "You remember that, right? We'll go, but we can't stay long."

"Maybe a few days?" She pulled her hand free of his grip and pulled his body closer.

"Maybe..." He looked at his watch. "We need to sleep. Turn over."

She rolled on her side, her back to his front. He put his arm around her. She loved the feel of his body pressing against hers...

Kelly woke and reached for him, but only felt an empty sheet. This was not unusual. Many times he would be out the door and at his office in the converted library building before she woke. She used to love cuddling with him in the mornings. She treasured those mornings. Maybe at the cabin...

She put on his robe and padded downstairs into the kitchen. Sebastian hadn't made coffee. Kelly quickly showered and dressed – she'd have her coffee at school.

The final day of school was always bittersweet. She made her end-of-the year speech to her sophomore and junior students, cautioning them to keep up with their summer reading lists. For her graduating seniors, it was time to say goodbye. She had 'raised' most of them since they were in junior high and hoped many of them would sign up for her summer classes.

Kelly kept looking at the hands on the classroom wall clock. Would this morning ever end? It seemed it had been 11:30 forever. Her students were blatantly ignoring her and exchanging summer plans. Not a lot for her to do these last few minutes.

11:35 She made a mental list of the food she'd pack for the week.

11:40 Clothing – extra clothing. The last time they were at the cabin, they got caught in the rain. They had been walking deep in the woods and were surprised by a mid-summer thunderstorm. They were soaked through – and even before getting to the cabin, they had stripped out of their wet clothing. But they never made it into the cabin. Sebastian had thrown her over his shoulder and ran down to the edge of the pond – almost slipping on the wet mossy grass. They had made love in the rain – on the shoreline next to the reeds that protected the wildlife. They were muddy – muddy and wet and making love in the rain...

11:45 Beer and wine.

11:50 Seriously? Wouldn't this day end?

11:55 "Goodbye! Have a great summer!" She knew every student by name. Her kids. She called them her kids. She and Sebastian were too old to start a family. These were her kids. Four periods of them every day from September through June.

She left her empty classroom. Yes, she would miss her kids.

While she was at the grocery store stocking up for the week, Kelly called Sebastian, but it went to voicemail. She had called earlier and left a message. She wouldn't leave another message.

His car wasn't in the garage. He knew she was anxious to leave early. If they left this evening, they'd wake in their great bed – and make love all morning... She tried calling him again – again the call went to voicemail. Oh well, now she had time to pack clothes and food and beer and wine and her large Spanish Queen olives.

It was getting late – he knew she wanted to get out of town tonight. He knew that...

Her phone woke her. How long had she been sleeping?

"I'm running late."

"No shit." She looked at the time. "When are you coming home?"

"It won't be much longer. Do you still want to leave tonight?"

"Only if you feel up to it." Kelly pulled the comforter up over her shoulder and rolled on her side, facing his side of the bed.

"I'm too wound up to sleep. I'll be home shortly."

"How long is 'shortly'?"

He exhaled into the phone. "Kelly, I'll be there when I can – as soon as I can."

"I'd really like to leave tonight."

"I know what you'd like to do. I'll try to be home soon. Okay?"

She sighed and turned on her back. "... Okay..."

The mattress compressed under his weight. Sebastian moved to her side of the bed and pulled her body to his.

"What time is it?"

"It's late... after midnight. I'm sorry."

"I love you..." She pressed her body into his, but he was already sleeping.

They left for the cabin early the next morning. But what had usually been an enjoyable drive had turned into a long lonely journey. He was on conference calls throughout the almost three hour trip. Kelly sat quietly, pretending to read from her book of poems.

He ended his call – but immediately another call came in. Absentmindedly he touched her knee, squeezing her knee – then returned to the urgent matter at hand. A new client no doubt wanting to be handled.

She laid her head against the headrest and closed her eyes. After maybe an hour she woke – and inhaled deeply. He was driving on the poorly marked county road that wound around the many bucolic pasturelands. She had memorized the smells... the dairy farms, the beef cattle farms, the horse farms. She knew them all. And she knew the smells of the harvest, especially the fields of alfalfa – that aroma of freshly mowed grass. She knew that smell too.

And she had memorized the various sounds of the roads. The smooth interstate had a monotonous hum, the two-lane paved road with its repair lines of tar held a hypnotic cadence. But her favorite sound was that of her road. The crunching sound the tires made along this narrow road of dirt and gravel that had been carved through the woods.

"Kelly. We're here." He parked and lifted the box of wine and beer out of the trunk. She followed behind with the canvas grocery bags.

He opened the cabin door and set the box on the counter. "I'll be right back."

Kelly unpacked the grocery bags, putting the meats and cheese in the refrigerator. Soon Sebastian returned with his briefcase. Without saying a word, he walked into the den and set his computer on the coffee table.

She stood in the doorway. "It's a nice day. Let's take a walk."

"I'll be out in a few minutes. I've got to check something."

She turned back into the kitchen and heard him swear. *What?*

"I don't know what I was thinking. We have no fucking Wi-Fi out here."

Again she stood in the doorway. "Isn't there Wi-Fi at the motel on the other side of the lake? At the guest cabins?"

He looked at her – she was beautiful. He should walk with her a while and clear his mind. Then head off to the motel. He rose from the loveseat.

"Come." Sebastian took her hand and together they walked out of the little cabin.

"I wish we had come out last fall and spread straw. I don't know if all my spring bulbs will bloom." Kelly looked at him. She could tell he wasn't listening – or did he just not hear her. She squeezed his hand.

"What? I wasn't listening. Sorry."

"I know. You haven't been listening for a while." They walked in silence down their road, this road bordered by a thick growth of tall old sugar maples.

His phone vibrated – he had turned off the ringer.

"You brought your phone??"

Sebastian ignored her words. "Seb here. Sure, I can talk." He put the phone to his chest and whispered, *"This will only be a minute..."* He dropped her hand and took a few steps away from her. But as he talked into the phone, he began walking back toward the cabin. She turned and continued down her road – alone. She was alone again.

She knew this road... During the summer, the dense foliage above allowed only dappled sunlight on their faces as they passed beneath. This road led to her cabin – their cabin. But now they were walking in opposite directions. They had been walking in opposite directions for months.

Sebastian was never a great talker. Getting him into any lengthy conversation had always been a struggle. But he'd listen. She'd talk and he'd listen. At least he'd listen. And now he was listening, but not to her. He was listening to whoever was talking to him on his phone. Not to her. She continued walking down her road.

This call was important. He'd listen to this caller – a new client. An important client. He had courted this guy – wined and dined him. The commission from his portfolio would be huge. He had considered charging a fee, but this client held real estate and art investments. He'd be a fool to charge his fee.

At their last meeting, Sebastian sold him on aggressive investment strategies, shooting for the highest return. And to date those investments had paid off – very well. He could not afford to let this man down. But he needed that motel's Wi-Fi.

Sebastian turned. Kelly wasn't behind him. She must have continued walking down the road. He couldn't wait – he'd leave a note in the cabin. He wouldn't stay at the motel very long.

Kelly got to the end of her road. She had never walked this far by herself. The early afternoon sun was bright – barely a cloud in the sky on this lovely day. Of course it would be lovelier with Sebastian by her side. But even if he was, he wouldn't have appreciated the various melodies of the birds or the rat-a-tat pounding of the red-bellied woodpecker.

She listened to the woodpeckers' drumming as they claimed their territories, the rhythmic sounds echoing throughout the woods. How often had she tried opening his ears and eyes – and his heart – to her world. When she had tried teaching him, he appeared... What? Uninterested? Bored? A few times she thought she had broken through that tough exterior – was he actually paying attention? But she had finally given up. His work was always paramount in his mind. She just didn't have the energy to share her knowledge with someone who wasn't receptive.

Kelly crouched down and tightened a loose shoelace. She put her forehead on her knee and wept – out of frustration? Out of loneliness? These tears had no title...

She returned to the cabin by way of the trail that edged the pond. "Sebastian?" She walked through the cabin and looked in the bedroom. He wasn't here. She walked back out to the den. His computer wasn't on the coffee table. She sat on the love seat and called him – of course the call went to voicemail. Of course...

She made a sandwich. If he had known she brought all this food for a week, he would not have approved. He told her maybe a few days. No – *she* suggested a few days. He said maybe. She took her sandwich and a cold beer and walked back down to the pond. Their folding armchairs still leaned against the stand of birch trees. She cleaned the leaves out of one, sat at the pond and ate her sandwich.

Her attention was drawn to the otter. It had poked its head out of the cool water and was watching her eat. The sow had a pup last year. Hopefully she'd have another baby this year. Kelly knew the sow lived alone – a solitary existence to be sure. She felt a certain kinship to the little otter – she had been living a solitary existence too. What the fuck happened?

The sun was setting – the sky had turned beautiful shades of honey-cream and crimson. It would be a remarkable day tomorrow. Kelly took her empty bottle and walked back up to the cabin. He wasn't anywhere around. Again she called him. Again her call went to voicemail. She cleaned up the kitchen and went to bed – alone.

Sebastian hadn't realized how comfortable the beds were in the little cabins. When he and his friends had driven up to assess and make improvements in the cottage, they stayed overnight in the guest cabins. He had shared a cabin with Michael. And sleeping in the same room with that man was torture. He snored. *God but he snored.* Now Sebastian had the room all to himself, his computer and his precious Wi-Fi. And when he laid on one of the twin beds to rest his eyes he hadn't planned on falling into a deep sleep.

The early morning sun peeked in through the windows. He woke and reached for her. Shit. He didn't sleep with her last night. He knew he was in trouble. Well, there was no sense in hurrying back to the cabin now. He opened his computer and checked on the DOW and the Nasdaq. And while he was at it, the S&P 500. Yes! His client would be very happy this morning. His wife not so much...

He called Kelly. She answered on the first ring.

"Where are you? You never came home last night."

"I'm sorry – I got caught up with this client and lost track of time."

"Sebastian, that's not the only thing you lost." She hung up.

Oh shit, she was mad. But he did get a lot of work done. Maybe he'd bring her breakfast. Kelly would like that, wouldn't she? Lately he wasn't sure what she liked any more. He had been keeping late hours at the office, and between her classes at the high school and her night class at the university they had seen very little of each other. And when he did get home, he couldn't shut down his mind. While she slept alone in their great bed, he worked alone in his office down the hall.

And he missed her birthday! But she knew the months leading up to April 15th were horrendous for him. He had tried reasoning with her. This was his business – his reputation! He was the sole owner, the CEO. Did she not hear him? Did she not understand? It was almost easier when he didn't have a wife. Before he married – before he met Kelly – he could focus all his attention, all his energies coddling his top clients. He could work at his office 24 hours a day if he had to. No one whined and begged him to come home. Home. Home to Kelly. God, what was he thinking? He called her again.

"Kelly, I'm done here. Can I bring you breakfast?"

"I don't know..."

"I bet they have bacon."

"Extra crispy?"

"I bet they do."

He heard her breathing into the phone. She should be breathing on his face.

"Okay. Bring me bacon. And scrambled eggs."

"Kelly..."

"I know... I love you too, Seb."

But just as he put his computer away, that call he had been waiting for came in. He knew this would only take a few minutes. Sebastian sat on the bed. This would only take a few minutes...

Kelly could tell the time just by looking at the sun. It was past noon and Sebastian still hadn't come back to the cabin. She hadn't had breakfast. He had promised her breakfast – scrambled eggs and bacon. Crisp bacon. But he still hadn't come back. She was hungry but didn't want to eat if he was going to bring her something.

She walked down the path and sat by the reeds at the edge of her pond. Her pond. This was her pond. It was quiet today. No wind, no ripples on the water. She kicked off her moccasins and put her feet in her pond. Her pond...

She heard his car door shut. Kelly grabbed her shoes and ran up the hill. The intoxicating perfume of the lilacs that grew outside the dooryard welcomed her as she neared the cabin. And she watched him climb the fieldstone steps, but he wasn't carrying her breakfast.

"Where's my breakfast?"

"There's been a change of plan." He opened the door and walked into their cabin. She dropped her shoes and followed in after him.

He turned and faced her. "We have to leave."

"Why do *we* have to leave?"

"Because I have to take a meeting – this is important."

"More important than us?" She walked through the den, into the bedroom and crawled up onto the great bed. She crossed her legs and pulled a pillow on her lap.

Sebastian followed her and stood in the doorway. She was sitting on their bed – alone. He should call his client and reschedule. He should...

"Kelly, this is important. It's important for us!"

"Not to *me* it's not!"

Sebastian turned away and picked up his jacket from the love seat. "Please. I have to leave." Again he stood in the doorway as he pulled on his jacket. "I still need to pick up materials from the office and..."

But she wasn't listening. Kelly rose from the bed and pushed past him. She strode into the den past the great hearth – past the shelving of reclaimed wood that held happier memories in cheap metal frames. Kelly stopped in the kitchen, turned and confronted him.

"I'm not leaving!"

"Don't be ridiculous." God, but she could be obstinate. "Do you want me to leave you here? Alone?"

"I'm already alone!" Kelly walked out the door, slamming it behind her.

He walked down the path and sat on the edge of the pond next to her. "Kelly..."

"We just got here and you haven't been with me." She looked at him. "And now you want us to leave!" Kelly turned back to the water.

"I'm sorry. This client..."

"Then go! Go to your client! If he's that important, go to him!"

"He's a she."

Kelly exhaled and again looked at him. "Fine. Go to her!"

"It's not like that."

"I know..."

They were silent for several minutes.

"Go... Go to your meeting."

"You want me to leave you here?"

"Yes. I'm done with my school – and I've got one college class left next week. I've got nothing to go home to."

"What about us?"

"Sebastian, you're never home! And when you are – you don't know I'm there!"

"I'm sorry..."

"That's all you are anymore."

"Kelly..."

"Go!" She looked sharply in his direction. "I'll be fine. I've got enough food for the whole week."

"Kelly..."

She turned to him. "I love you too, Seb."

"I'll call you."

She looked back out over her pond.

Sebastian stood. He touched her hair, caressing her auburn waves...

She waited until the sound of the engine faded, then walked up the hill to the cabin. She still hadn't had anything to eat, but she had lost her appetite. Kelly opened a bottle of wine and, taking a goblet from the cupboard, returned to her pond. She sat on the shore and put her bare feet in the shallows – and raising a toast to her pond, drank the burgundy liquid.

Sebastian had just enough time to stop at his office and grab his client's folder. As he was leaving, he received a call.

"Mr. Bonsignore, this is Laurie Berg. I'm sorry to be calling at the last minute, but we've had a family emergency. And I'm sure I don't have to tell you that your loved ones come first. Can we reschedule?"

By the time he returned to the cabin, it was pitch dark. And he didn't have a flashlight. Sebastian carefully made his way up the fieldstone path to the cabin. The door wasn't locked. He went into the cabin. She was nowhere to be found. Where was she? She couldn't have left – she had no means of transportation.

The weather had turned cold with a light mist in the air. He walked outside and looked down by the pond. Sebastian barely made out her body lying on the grass. The path was slippery – the mossy grass became like grease when wet. He knelt at her head.

"Kelly?" But she didn't move. He noticed the empty wine bottle. She was drunk.

Sebastian carried her up to the cabin. It was chilly in the rooms without a fire in the great hearth. He put her on the bed. Her clothes were damp. After using the bathroom he stripped her out of her clothes and pushed her into the middle of the bed. He joined her, pulling her shivering body to him, her back to his front. And they slept... sharing one pillow...

She woke – Oh she had a headache. Getting drunk on red wine always gave her a headache. And Sebastian was in their bed. She rolled on her front and, rising up on her elbows, looked at his handsome face.

"You're here..."

He kissed her forehead. "My client, the lady client had a family emergency and rescheduled. What do you think about that?"

"I think... I think I like you in bed with me." She lay back down and faced him. "I have to pee. Would you make a fire?"

"Yes, Love..."

She returned to bed. It was still cold in the bedroom. After making a fire Sebastian crawled in bed with her.

"I'm glad you're here..."

He kissed her. "Me too. But we're going to have to leave later today."

"But you're here now..."

"I'm here now..."

Kelly returned home from the teachers' dinner, an annual event when the instructors from both schools got together. Even Roger from the technical school joined them this year. The porch light wasn't on but his Porsche was in the garage. Good! He was home. Kelly ran up the porch steps and unlocked the deadbolt. She hurriedly opened the door and turned on the kitchen lights.

"Sebastian!" She pushed through the heavy swinging door into the dining room and turned up the dimmer for the chandelier. She turned on the hallway lights and walked upstairs – he wasn't anywhere around. Kelly checked her phone.

S. Bonsignore: Sorry. Taking a meeting. Will call. x

The 'x' was his way of sending her a kiss. But where was his meeting? In town? Out of town? For all she knew, his meeting might as well have been on the moon.

She was in no mood to cook. Kelly left the house and headed for the New London Grille for a subway. But the yellow crime-scene tape still blocked the door. The restaurant had been robbed the week prior, and as yet hadn't reopened. Change of plan. She pressed the number for Sammy's Pizza and ordered a medium pepperoni. She'd pick it up on the way home.

Kelly didn't go down into the basement very often. It was a finished basement – more of a man-cave actually and nicely decorated, too. She turned on the big screen

TV and sat on the large leather sectional couch. She ate the delicious greasy squares of pizza and watched the first season of *The West Wing* on Netflix.

It was getting late – very late. She texted her husband.

> *K. Bonsignore*: Where are you? Are you coming home tonight? Love K.

She really didn't expect him to respond. He usually turned off his ringer anyway. She went to bed.

Kelly woke in their great bed alone. He didn't come home... She took her phone off the charger stand and checked for messages. He had texted her.

> *S. Bonsignore:* Hi. Took taxi to airport. Will be in Chicago several days. I'll call. x

At least she knew where he was – and she knew where he wasn't. He wasn't in bed with her. She'd try to get ahold of him later.

The first week of summer was an empty time. During the school year she got to her classroom early and prepared for the day. She loved teaching – every day was an adventure.

She checked her phone. No texts, no missed calls.

Kelly was already on her second cup of coffee. She had several hours until it was time to leave for the university. This would be her final college class of the semester. She was one semester away from attaining her master's. Brie wasn't here to share her excitement – and Sebastian... Many nights he wasn't even home when she returned from her classes.

The drive to the university took 90 minutes – an hour and a half each way. That meant she didn't get home until almost midnight. When she began her studies just months after their wedding, he'd be waiting for her in their bed...

She loved crawling into bed when it was warm from his body...

She loved crawling into bed when he kissed her, feeling his warm breath on her face...

She loved crawling into that bed when he pulled her to him...

She loved crawling into bed and letting her husband – her Ulysses – the man who would love her always and forever make her body explode...

It was time to leave.

The drive back home after class seemed longer and lonelier... knowing there would be no one at home... knowing that Sebastian would not be there... knowing the great bed would be cold. She stopped and picked up a large pepperoni pizza.

She pulled the SUV into the garage, parking next to his Porsche. He'd be gone at least a week. Another lonely night. Another hot date with Sammy's Pizza. Another late night watching the second season of *The West Wing.*

She texted Gabriella and though it was early morning in Italy, they got caught up on their lives. Her own life seemed so mind numbing compared to the life Brie was living. And with Sebastian gone more and more, she was alone – more and more. Brie's life was certainly more glamorous and exciting – traveling through Europe with Raffaele. She was at his side in whichever city he played.

The last episode ended. It was time for bed. Kelly missed her friend...

Kelly was putting away the breakfast dishes when her phone alerted her to a call. She looked at the caller ID before answering. Finally! She quickly walked into the living room and sat in his chair.

"Hi!" She couldn't keep the excitement out of her voice, especially after not hearing from her husband for almost two weeks.

Sebastian yawned into the phone. "I'm going to be gone at least another week... I've got to wrap up some loose ends. I'll call you when I get back into town..."

Kelly exhaled into the phone, not holding back her frustration. No apology on his part... simply a statement of fact. Obviously his preoccupation with his business superseded all other thoughts – including her. She waited for him to say something. "Sebastian?"

But he had ended the call.

Upon his return he had called from the airport, asking her to pick him up. On the drive home she suggested they go directly to the cabin. He had seemed hesitant but said he couldn't take time – not right now. When they got home he went directly to his office in the spare room down the hall and there secluded himself for the remainder of the night. Again she felt excluded from his life.

Kelly woke and looked at his pillow. He hadn't come to bed. She heard him descending the stairs – she followed him into the kitchen. Sebastian was getting his first cup of coffee – and by the looks of him he hadn't gotten any sleep.

She silently approached him from behind intending to embrace him but he spun around, knocking his mug of hot coffee into her arm – splashing the contents on his hand. He mumbled an apology as he switched the hot cup to his other hand and shaking his burned hand.

Attempting to rectify the situation, she again suggested they take a few days off and drive out to the cabin. His response had been brusque.

"To hell with that damned cabin!"

She stood barefoot on the cold kitchen tile listening to his footsteps as he left the room through the heavy swinging door. Later that week, she let it be known that she no longer wanted the *'damn cabin'* either. The fact was she was only agreeing with what he wanted.

No, they wouldn't need it anymore – no more retreats, no more long weekends catching up with each other. It was a shame. That's all. A crying shame!

14

Memories

They were now only a few miles from the cabin. It would be over soon... She leaned her head back into the headrest and turning toward her window, closed her eyes...

She remembered the walks she and Sebastian took along the narrow winding road that led to the cabin. A thick growth of tall old sugar maples bordered the length of the road, the fingers of the uppermost branches intertwining, creating a natural arbor.

In the summer, flickering patches of sunlight penetrated the dense foliage creating kaleidoscopes of shadows upon their faces as they passed beneath the sheltering branches.

But autumn had been her favorite time to go on retreat. The leaves erupting in brilliant shades of rust, crimson and gold piled up knee deep along the roadside. She loved running ahead of Sebastian, kicking the leaves into the air as a child would. She came alive in the fall.

But her favorite season had to be winter because winter at the cabin was magical, especially when the moon was full. She remembered the weekend they celebrated their second anniversary. The water in the pond had barely frozen over – just a skin of ice. A full moon had shone white against the clear, cobalt sky – its ghostly image reflected upon the black water seduced its lunar trail straight to their bedroom window. Even Sebastian felt inspired by nature that weekend!

But spring most certainly was her favorite season. The little streams behind the cottage gradually opened, allowing the frigid spring-fed water to splash over stubborn ice shelves. Life was renewing itself in the spring. The lilac bushes around the cabin door were newly resplendent, intoxicating the air with their milky-violet glory. The crocus and tulips she had planted that first year sprouted, their green tips barely discernible as they protruded through the protective mulch.

She loved the little cottage and had so many wonderful memories here. It was her Never-Never Land. They could leave the reality of the city behind when they came here. But he had made up his mind about getting rid of their cabin. Kelly hadn't seen this side of him before. She was on the outside looking in. He had successfully pushed her away from his life and had not invited her back inside...

He drove down the private road that led to their cabin. The car's tires crawled over the roots that lay bare along the road, this narrow thoroughfare that had been carved through the woods. She rolled her window down and inhaled the country air. The overhanging branches extended through the open window, touching her creamy white cheek, the soft leaves brushing against her shoulder.

A front tire passed over a large knoll – the car lurched, jolting the book of poems from out of her lap. Kelly reached down between her feet and recovered it. Inspecting her book, she saw that some of the pages were bent. She never meant for Whitman to become a casualty.

Sebastian steered the car into an area that had been cleared of brush and lined with railroad ties, just large enough for one car. The ties were for aesthetic purposes only – there was no need for another parking place because no one else invaded their sanctuary.

He turned off the engine. Kelly withdrew from the car, leaving behind Whitman with its disfigured pages – the pages that no longer bore the texture of prophets. Walking alongside the steps of fieldstone, she took it all in one last time – the stand of birch trees, the little streams, the pungent smell of lilacs. Impulsively, she kicked off her moccasins and pushed her toes deep within the mossy turf – welcoming the sensation of pleasant agony.

Sebastian watched her get out of the car and noticed the book of poems lying askew on the bucket seat, its pages bent and soiled. Usually she brought Whitman into the cabin. *She really means to go through with it.* He was hoping she had changed her mind. Had he pushed her so far out of his life that she would not come back in if he asked?

Watching her walk barefoot across the lush lawn reminded him of their walks down the tree-lined road. She was so in tune with nature. He envied her appreciation of their personal haven. And though he wouldn't admit it, he truly was enraptured with her knowledge of the trees, the variant melodies of birds, the diversity of wildlife. And he did listen to her as she navigated around the marshes, streams and woodlands on their property.

She told him that summer was her favorite season. Then again she told him that winter and spring were her favorite seasons too. For him however, autumn was to become a bittersweet memory. The glorious blends of reds and browns reminded him of the color of her hair. He could not come out here again – especially in the autumn months! Seeing the color of her hair in the trees and on the ground would kill even a lesser man.

They had spent their second wedding anniversary – November 2nd – at the cabin. He would never forget how clear the night had been! Even *HE* noticed the crisp air, the full moon reflecting upon the thin ice. Truly he had been inspired – emotionally, spiritually, sensually.

During the winter, the bare branches of the trees lining the road hoarded pockets of snow. Only a breeze disturbed the serenity of the forest, releasing sparkling treasures from their wooden crevices. The wafting crystals gently assaulted those who walked beneath along the road. He loved watching her in the winter, her milky skin aglow, her emerald eyes sparkling, her cheeks rosy red from the crisp air! More than any other season, she seemed to thrive in the winter...

He remembered the morning after he returned from a three-week absence. He had had a series of successful face-to-face meetings culminating in signing on new high-end clients. The flight home had been delayed and he was pressed for time. Her voice had sounded like an angel's when he called from the airport. The suggestion that they go directly to the cabin was so tempting, but he had to complete the contract specifications for the new accounts before Monday and if he worked the rest of the weekend he could finish by late Sunday night. Then while working through the contract provisions he came across several inconsistencies and never made it to bed that night.

He felt lousy the next morning, not just from lack of sleep but from not being with Kelly. He missed her warmth, the scent of her body... It was these thoughts of her that had distracted him as he poured that first cup of coffee.

He heard her coming up behind him, and turning to greet her slammed his hot coffee cup against her arm – the scalding coffee burning his hand. She had backed off in astonishment. He was tired of being tired and couldn't contain his irritability. When she alluded to the cabin yet again he blew up.

Oh how he wished he could have taken back those words! If he hadn't been so exhausted, he would have told her she was the most important thing in his world, picked her up and personally carried her all the way to the cabin. But he didn't do anything – he simply left the room, leaving her standing on the cold kitchen floor – alone.

When they had talked later that week, she was so insistent they get rid of the cabin since it seemed they never used it anymore. Damn but she could be incorrigible...

Sebastian meandered by her little gardens as he followed the stone path to the cabin. He remembered how excited she got when the little buds busted out of the ground in the spring. He argued that he was not a nature lover, but his defense fell on deaf ears as she pulled him over to inspect each new growth. He enjoyed being a witness to her joy.

HE ENJOYED BEING A WITNESS TO HER JOY! Had his professional life smothered the life they once shared? He loved her. He had searched all his life for her, for Kelly – his Dulcinea. And now watching her climb the path to the cabin, he felt like he was watching his life end. Impulsively, he turned and walked back to the car.

As Kelly climbed the hill, she shoved her hands deep into her jeans pockets, feeling her hard thigh muscles – and remembered the weekends Sebastian and his three buddies had come up to clean the cabin. His excuse about attending two weekend conferences had been almost convincing, but it was just too much of a coincidence that his cronies were also absent those weekends. She was suspicious of his intentions until the clerk at the hardware store commented about Sebastian's unusual purchases: buckets, scrubbing brushes, drop cloths, mousetraps, rolls of pink insulation and electrical supplies – the list went on.

She didn't know what he was up to and he was probably up to no good – but she figured he couldn't get into too much trouble, considering the 'ammunition' he packed.

Upon his return that second Sunday evening, while he changed out of his clothes, she asked him about the meetings. She was already in bed, propped up on her pillows with her hands behind her head. She maintained a sober countenance as he bored her with a summary of the alleged conferences, trying very hard not to let on that she was NOT believing a word of his fabricated nonsense.

But Sebastian was a bad liar. And even if she hadn't already figured it out, her suspicions were put to rest the next weekend when they drove out to the property.

As he drove the car into the clearing, she remembered noticing the grounds were immaculate. Together they walked up the dirt trail leading to the cabin. He spoke of restoring the original fieldstone to the footpath. At the time she thought it was a funny comment considering this wasn't their property.

The little cottage, its doorway framed by lilac bushes of purple and white – just like out of a Whitman poem – was exquisitely clean and fresh smelling. It was all so lovely! Inside, the kitchen was complete with a two-burner propane stovetop, an apartment-size refrigerator, an apron front sink, shiny new granite countertops and new wooden cupboard doors.

Walking through the doorway, she entered a small sitting room which was dwarfed by a great stone fireplace and made cozy by a coffee table, a small loveseat and a thick rag rug. On one side of the hearth, tall bookshelves had been built using reclaimed lumber and would soon achieve a status of importance – holding treasures from weekends past: small bouquets of dried flowers tied with string, rocks of assorted shapes, colors and textures, and snapshots of special moments held for eternity in cheap metal frames.

The adjoining room was a tiny bedroom, filled with an enormous four-poster bed with several quilts and lots and lots of pillows – just how she liked it! *(Mmmm!)* She had a hunch that this was not due totally to happenstance, and certainly not a friend's cabin they were borrowing. Sebastian must have had a hand in the design somehow. But not until she happened upon the buckets and mops and mousetraps that had been crammed in a too-small closet did she finally put two and two together.

This was the cabin she had been asking for, but she couldn't let on that she knew. She had to feign ignorance – she was not about to spoil his anticipated surprise.

That Sunday morning after she had showered, he confessed his not-so-well-kept secret. She was more relieved than surprised now that she didn't have to keep her secret either. She had literally jumped on him, accidently spilling their drinks – which as she remembered made for an incredible morning of lovemaking. It seemed so fitting that Vivaldi's Concerto No. 1 in E Major had been playing on the iPod...

Now she stood before the door to the cottage, taking in for the last time the intoxicating smell of lilacs and silently cursing herself for not bringing the key. She lifted the padlock, knowing her actions were futile. Turning around, she noticed Sebastian walking back to the car. He must have forgotten the key too.

Kelly turned back to the door, squeezed her eyes shut and pressed her forehead against the rough exterior. This was *her* cabin – *their* retreat! No, she didn't want to let it go! She didn't want their marriage to end. She didn't want to let *HIM* go. Had her demands destroyed the life they once shared?

But she didn't know what to do. She didn't know how to make it right. All the pressures of this last year – all the visceral feelings of abandonment that she had experienced when she was just a twelve year-old girl – when her daddy, the first man she loved – died – crushed between train cars.

Now Kelly remembered those long-forgotten suffocating feelings... and she was like a tightly wound spring ready to explode.

Hearing the car door shut, she turned and looked back down the hill at Sebastian as he started his ascent. His worn leather jacket was open. In one hand he carried Whitman. In the other – he held the key.

15

The Beginning - Again

Kelly again was facing the door when he surmounted the hill and arrived at the cabin – her forehead leaning into the door, her hand still holding the padlock. He stood behind her. She spoke – but he barely heard her.

“Comfort me.”

He leaned close into her body, but did not dare touch her.

“Comfort me!” She said it louder and the tears came now in torrents.

“COMFORT ME!!!” She shouted the words.

Sebastian dropped the key and while holding Whitman, wrapped his arms around her.

Again she repeated her words, but they came out as a whisper. “*Comfort me...*”

He held her with every ounce of strength he had.

Now she wailed the words. *“Comfort me!!! Please! Comfort me!”*

He held her so tight he felt the rocking of her chest deep in his chest. But he still spoke no words. He dropped Whitman and felt he was holding onto his world. He *was* holding his world – his whole world. His arms were crossed on her chest, holding her shoulders. He didn’t think she’d ever stop crying, but he didn’t let go. He just held her for what seemed like hours. His arms were wet from her tears that spilled from her face.

She let her moccasins fall and lifting her hands, crossed her arms, placing her hands on his hands. He felt her breathing calm, but still he held her. He didn’t dare speak – he kissed the back of her head, then one ear, and finally craning his neck, her cheek – tasting her salty tears. And still he held her.

After several minutes, he spoke. “Kelly...” He said her name softly and with as much love as he could put into one name. “Kelly... what do you want?”

She took one last deep breath – still not looking at him – still he held her.

“I want my cabin,” she breathed the words. “I want our life. I want you.”

He let her go, quickly bent down and retrieved the key. He held the padlock with one hand while his other shaky hand managed to put the key in the lock and opened it. He unhooked the hasp, letting the padlock fall to the ground and pushed open the door.

Without words he lifted her in his strong arms, wet from her tears, and carried her into the cabin. Her head leaned heavy on his shoulder. He carried her into their bedroom and sat on the bed, still cradling her in his arms.

She put one hand on his chest, unbuttoned his shirt and pulled at his chest hair. He still hadn’t let her go – he still held her in his arms. Her hand roamed down, feeling his belly hair, then again up across his chest, feeling first one nipple then the other. Still he held her.

She looked at him with eyes so sad. "Comfort me..."

Sebastian laid her on the bed and kissed her, holding her head with both hands, letting his lips languish on hers. He pushed his tongue into her mouth, softly sucking on her tongue, making love to her with his tongue – all the while she held her hand on his chest.

He unbuttoned her shirt – she wore no bra – and opened it. He kissed one breast. Using both hands, he squeezed her breast into a soft mound, his tongue caressed her nipple. He loved her small breasts – his hands totally covered them. He felt her body respond.

His hand lovingly followed her shape down across her belly. He opened her jeans and unzipping them, forced his hand down under her panties. She opened her legs – he put his hand between her thighs.

With one hand she pushed her jeans down past her bottom and bending her knees, put her feet on the bed. He slid his hand behind her legs – and heard a groan from deep within her body.

"What do you want, Love?" He gazed into emeralds, wanting so bad to take away her pain.

"I want you... I want us." For the first time since he picked her up, her voice wasn't shaky – her tears had stopped. Sebastian quickly undid his trousers and pushed them down far enough to expose his growing erection. It had been so long since they made love. He lay on his side and pulled her to him, her back to his front. Kelly let out a long groan as he entered her. He kept one arm around her waist and the other hand on her hip, pulling her to him as he pushed deeper into her. She held on to his naked hip, pulling him closer. It took only minutes for them both to achieve a much needed orgasm.

And he held her, vowing never to let her go...

After working in his office all night – and after Sebastian had burned his hand on the hot coffee, he had retreated to the en suite bathroom and took his morning shower. He felt so bad about his knee jerk reaction to Kelly's suggestion about going to the cabin. But first he had to review the contracts before giving them to his lawyer.

Sebastian came out of the shower with a towel wrapped around his body and stood in their bedroom. Kelly was not there. He threw the towel on the bed and pulled his long hair back, securing it with a leather hair tie. Because he would be alone in his office, he dressed in jeans and a sweatshirt. Picking up his briefcase, he retraced his steps to the now empty kitchen. From the basement, he heard the sound of the clothes drier. He put his bare feet in tennis shoes and left the house without saying goodbye.

Kelly came back upstairs with a basket of clean laundry. Sebastian was nowhere in sight. She looked outside and didn't see his car. He had left without saying goodbye. She went upstairs to their bedroom – she saw his wet towel on the bed. She picked it up and pressed the thick, damp fabric to her face, smelling his body – and cried. This was not helping. She wiped her tears on his towel and quickly folded the clean laundry.

She walked into the en suite bathroom, turned on the water in the shower and waited until steam filled the room. She stripped and stepped into the large stall, letting the water flow across her body – and poured the fragrant jasmine shower gel into the palm of her hand.

She longed for the feel of his hands. She slowly caressed her neck *as his hands would...* touching her breasts *as his hands would...* hugging herself – *as he would.* Kelly leaned her head back and let the hot water from the rainforest showerhead cascade over her face. She longed for his touch – she missed his touch – she was starved for his touch... She remembered his touch those first few days she slept with him. Everything was so new – his voice, his body – his chest covered with soft black hair... Her fingers searching for his nipples... Listening to his breathing as it became deeper, more erratic, whispering her name, loving the sound of her name on his lips...

She touched her belly, her thighs, pressing her hands between her thighs... She felt her orgasm deep within her... She missed *him*... She wanted *him*...

Kelly left the shower and put on Sebastian's terrycloth robe. Then, wrapping her wet hair in a small turban towel, she returned downstairs to the kitchen. It was already the middle of the afternoon. She put together a turkey and cheese on rye and opened a beer. Picking up her tote bag, she walked into the living room where she sat in Sebastian's chair. She opened her laptop and began organizing her notes for the end-of-the-year meeting with her principal and the other teachers.

She felt a sense of calm in this room. Over the white marble fireplace mantel hung the colorful watercolor his grandmother had painted. In the corner, to the right of the fireplace was the chair in which she sat. It was Sebastian's La-Z-Boy recliner, the one he sat in while reading his papers. It was a large, overstuffed leather chair that didn't match anything. If his floor lamp was not on, the chair was not visible in that dark corner.

When she first toured the house, he had pointed out his chair and told her she could never sit in that chair. It was *HIS* chair. She remembered looking at him in response to his declaration – and laughing. She thought he was teasing her but there was no humor in his expression. Of course when he wasn't home she made it her favorite chair.

Kelly had worked for several hours transcribing her journal entries into her laptop. Before the meeting, she would use his printer to create her presentation – with talking points. She was one of three tenured teachers and had a reputation to uphold.

She looked at her watch and considered the time – it was late and Sebastian wasn't home. She put her files back into her tote bag. Before rising, Kelly looked at the framed wedding photo on the little side table. They were so happy then. What happened?

She returned to the kitchen – and couldn't stifle a yawn. She decided to turn in early. Before going upstairs, she put the bag on one of the stools. With his robe wrapped around her, she crawled into their bed, pulled his pillow to her face and cried.

Sebastian had spent most of Sunday at his office and got an enormous amount of work done. Around noon he went out and picked up a personal-size pizza and an iced tea. When he completed his work and updated his laptop, he felt good. Things were finally coming together. Now he needed to go home and be with Kelly.

The house was dark when he returned home. He touched the butcher-block countertop and thought back to when she first entered his kitchen. So many memories of that day – was it that long ago? He had only seen her in a dark bar, and then when she stood in his brightly lit kitchen her beauty had taken his breath away.

He couldn't get his fill of this woman, though she could be so bullheaded. Had their relationship faltered so badly that it couldn't be salvaged?

Her tote bag was on a stool. He softly touched the handles, knowing she had touched them last. Sebastian walked out of the kitchen through the heavy swinging door and into the dining room. He saw a light on in the living room – it came from the floor lamp next to his leather recliner. Evidently Kelly had been sitting in his chair.

When she first moved into his home, he had teased her that his chair was the only one never to sit in. It was *his chair*. Now he wished she was still in his chair. Sebastian sat in his chair for a few minutes. Their wedding photo was on the little side table. He turned the framed photo so he could see it easier. They were so happy then. What happened?

He yawned and stretched –

And woke!

It was morning. He had fallen asleep in his chair. He hadn't gone to their bed, hadn't slept with Kelly. It had been weeks since they made love. He quickly got up from his chair and raced upstairs to their bedroom. She was not in the bed. She must have already left for school. He sat on her side of the bed and touched his pillow. It was damp from her tears – he couldn't fix tears.

When she woke, he was not in bed – didn't he come home? Kelly showered, dressed and went downstairs – and saw Sebastian asleep in his recliner. He didn't want to sleep with her. She'd have her coffee with the other teachers at school. She picked up her tote bag and, taking her coffee creamer from the refrigerator, left the house.

During the long meeting she just couldn't concentrate. *He hadn't come to bed. He had slept in his chair.* She wanted to cry but held it together while she respectfully listened to her principal and other teachers. At noon she checked her phone – but there were no missed calls, no texts from him.

3:30. The meeting finally ended. It had been a long day and she hadn't heard from him. She really didn't want to go home to an empty house – surely he would be at his office. Kelly left school and drove around until she found herself in front of the restaurant that she and Sebastian were going to try – the new one at the mall.

She went in, found a stool at the bar and ordered a hamburger and a side of sweet potato waffle fries. She took a bite out of the hamburger, but really didn't have an appetite. As she left the restaurant, Cody and Tom were coming in. She spoke with them briefly and drove home.

The house was dark. His car was not in the driveway or in the garage. She parked and walked in through the front door. Kelly turned on the pendant lights over the breakfast bar. So many memories flooded her thoughts.

She remembered the first time she stood in this kitchen and how unnerved Sebastian had been. But that was also the first time they had sex. She never stayed overnight in her efficiency ever again. And they had made love every night, sometimes several times a night for weeks. She smiled at the memory, but then remembered there was nothing to smile about now...

Sebastian closed his office at 3:30 and headed home. Kelly should be back from her meeting. She hadn't texted him or called him all day. He tried reading his morning paper, but he had already seen all the news that came in on his *NYT* app. He went upstairs into their bedroom. Kelly had folded and put away their clean laundry and the towel he used for his shower had been hung to dry. He loved the way she took care of him. But they were in a tough time and he felt helpless, not knowing how to rectify the situation.

Sebastian didn't want to be in their home without Kelly and didn't want to prepare a meal without her – without Kelly. Before leaving he checked his phone one last time. He had a habit of forgetting to turn his ringer back on. No text, no missed calls.

He drove until he found a small restaurant, the hamburger place he and Kelly were going to try after she and Gabriella went shopping. He walked in and immediately found an empty stool at the bar. He ordered a hamburger, a side of sweet potato waffle fries and the house beer.

While he waited he noticed Cody and Tom a few stools down. Cody came over and good naturedly put his arm on Sebastian's shoulder. "What's with you two?"

Sebastian didn't understand the question. "What do you mean?"

"Kelly was here – you just missed her."

Sebastian lost his appetite. Without eating anything, he paid the tab and left the restaurant. He drove home. The lights were on – he walked in and saw her in the kitchen. She looked at him and asked if he had eaten yet.

"No." He sat on one of the stools. "Cody said you were at the restaurant. Did you eat?"

"No. I had no appetite."

Silence. And she started crying. He stood and approached her, but she put her hands up and turned and walked out through the heavy swinging door. Just as quickly she returned.

Through her tears she announced, "I don't want the damned cabin anymore."

He had never seen her so sad, so beaten. He wanted to pull her into his arms, but she would not want him to comfort her. She just stood there staring at him with her beautiful sad eyes.

"I can go out and close up the cabin tomorrow. I don't have anything pending in the office."

"I'm coming with you."

He wanted to spare her more pain. "You don't have to go."

"No." She seemed bent on making this as painful as possible. "I want to take one last look. I want to do that."

"Okay... Can we go to bed?"

"Yes Sebastian, we can go to bed." She left the room and walked upstairs to their bedroom, brushed her teeth, undressed and got into bed. Kelly waited for him but he never came up. She felt so alone. She pulled his pillow to her side of the bed and held onto it as she would his body...

He went to his office in the spare room down from their bedroom and quickly made arrangements to have Phil open the office in the morning. He finished some work, sent an email and then walked into their bedroom. He brushed his teeth, undressed and got into bed and lay on his side of the bed. Since she had his pillow, he bent his arm and rested his head on his elbow and watched her sleep...

Kelly opened her eyes. He was lying next to her – sleeping – but he never pulled her body to him last night. He didn't want her. Fine. She rose, padded out of their room to the guest powder room downstairs. She put coffee on. Soon he came into the kitchen. He asked her if she slept well.

"No. Did you?"

"Me neither." He pulled on his worn leather jacket. "Let's do this." He started out to the car.

"Just a minute." She ran back upstairs for her book. She never went to the cabin without Whitman, and even though they were closing up the cabin she wanted it for the drive back. Kelly met him at the car.

Sebastian waited until she buckled her seatbelt. "I have to get gas, first."

Kelly woke – and for a moment was unsure of where she was... Her shirt was open. Kelly reached behind her and touched his naked hip. Oh yes... they were at the cabin and he had comforted her... Thank God.

She pressed her body against his. Sebastian stirred and pulled her closer. He kissed her neck – she turned her head and looked at him. With his free hand he brushed her auburn hair behind one ear. She rolled over and touched his chest, drawing her fingers through the thick hair. He kissed her lips.

"Your eyes were so sad," he spoke softly. "Please, never let them be that sad ever again. It would kill me if I ever saw that awful sadness in your eyes – ever!"

"I missed you so much! All I wanted was you, but I felt like you were pushing me away and..."

"I am so sorry you felt that way. I promise I'll never let you feel that way ever!" He leaned in and kissed her again.

"I want you Seb..." She closed her eyes. "Hold me..."

He smiled. "You have me." They clung to each other – still with their shirts open, their pants down around their thighs.

She opened her eyes. "Kiss me..."

"Where?" He looked into her beautiful eyes and kissed another tear that had escaped down her cheek.

"Everywhere..."

And he did as he was told. He slowly removed her blouse and kissed her bare shoulders... and kissed and caressed her breasts, never wanting to stop kissing her breasts, his hands totally covering them. He sat up on the bed and slipped her pants and panties off.

She looked up at him and smiled. "Aren't you going to take off your pants?"

He pushed his pants down to his ankles, stood and stepping out of his shoes, kicked his pants away from him. Sebastian got back on the bed and lay on her body, her wonderful soft woman body and started kissing her breasts again. He stopped and looked in her eyes. "Where was I?"

"I'm not sure... But you're doing good now." She caressed his face. "If I were you, I wouldn't stop."

He kissed her mouth hard, kissed her face, her eyes and looked at her. "I almost lost my Dulcinea..."

"Never..."

"Do you need to use the bathroom?" It had already been a long day – it had already been a long couple days.

"Yes – I'd like to shower, too."

He smiled his crooked smile. She loved that smile. "I haven't turned on the water heater – it will be cold!"

"We'll get warm again." Kelly kissed his face, holding his head in her hands.

Sebastian grabbed her around her waist and pressed his face onto her belly. "Don't go anywhere!"

A look of panic crossed her face. "Where are you going?"

"I'm turning on the water heater. Don't go! Don't leave!" He ordered her as a man afraid he would lose his world again. He rose from the bed and as he walked to the kitchen, removed his jacket and shirt, throwing them on the loveseat. The cabin door was wide open – Whitman and her moccasins were on the ground. Quickly he retrieved them. After lighting the propane water heater, he dropped her shoes by the hearth and walked back into the bedroom.

The toilet flushed – he smiled as she returned to the bed. He got back into the bed with her, pulling the quilt up over her shoulders – she chilled easily – and handed her the book.

"Where was this?!" She held the book on her chest.

"Outside on the step."

"Thank you..." She tenderly kissed him... and kissed him again and again. He nestled between her legs, his body crushing her into the mattress.

She whispered, *"Sebastian, I want you – all of you!"*

"I love you, woman... I can never get enough of you..." He pushed his erection deep inside her. She gasped at the fullness – it had been too long. He pushed hard into her, just held himself rigid – not moving, just filling her. She wrapped her legs around his waist and asked him to love her.

With his elbows supporting his body, he closed his eyes and he rammed into her again and again – not wanting to stop. Feeling he was getting close, he opened his eyes – she was crying. She was crying so hard. He stopped moving.

"I want you so bad." Her chest was heaving, taking chaotic breaths between her sobbing. "I'm so sorry I doubted you. I'm so sorry." She put her hand across her eyes.

He kissed her lips, her face, and pushing her hand away, kissed her eyes – she kept whispering, "*I'm sorry...*"

"Kelly, we're back now... We're good now." With one hand he wiped her tears.

"Are we good?" The tone of her voice almost pleading...

He felt himself regroup. "You tell me if we're good!" And he resumed pounding into her. It took every bit of strength to keep thrusting into her. The bed quaked, the head board hitting the wall each time he slammed into her. She clung to his arms, squeezed her legs around his waist – and they came together as one...

He rolled over, taking her with him, making her lay on top of him.

"Please don't cry..." He caressed her face, loving her face, loving her...

Kelly inhaled deeply, stopping any new tears. She rested her head on his shoulder and kissed his chest hair. He grasped the edges of the quilt and pulled it up over them. They both slept the rest of the afternoon, the best sleep either of them have had in many days.

He woke first, reclaimed her body with his arms and dozed.

"We have no food." He was talking to the top of her head. "If we're going to stay here, we're going to have to make a run to Aggie's."

Kelly yawned into Sebastian's chest. She wanted to stay at least one more day at the cabin. Reality could wait.

"But I need to get up. You're pressing on my bladder." He kissed her forehead and helped her slide off him. He rose up off the bed. "I'm going to take a quick shower. Do you want to come in with me?"

He was standing in all his wonderful nakedness. She took her time, looking from his eyes to his legs. He noticed and struck a bodybuilder's pose.

"You are so bad!" she was laughing. "I think I'll wait until we have enough hot water for my shower... but thank you for asking."

"Your loss! I'll be right back." The minute he got in the shower, she heard him shout. *"Holy SHIT, this is COLD!"* She lay back on her pillow, closed her eyes and smiled. It was good to smile again.

He walked out with a towel wrapped around his body. Sebastian looked down at her. She was lying on the bed. He hadn't seen a sight that lovely in weeks. He dropped the towel and crawled back on the bed and kissed her mouth.

"Yes." She was grinning.

"Yes, what..?" He raised an eyebrow.

She turned her grin into a smile and answered, "Food!"

"Okay, let's go to Aggie's. By the time we return we'll have hot water." He leaned down over the side of the bed and pulled his phone from his discarded trousers. "Let me text Phil first and tell him he's got the office tomorrow – and maybe the next day, too."

Sebastian had hired Phil after he received his Honorable Discharge from the army. He was a local boy who married before he went into the military. Over the next eight years, he and his wife had three children – a pair of twin boys and most recently a baby girl.

Phil always had a knack with numbers and was completing a master's degree in accounting. He was smart, had a great work ethic and fit into Sebastian's business plan. He felt confident leaving Phil at the office while he was away.

Sebastian took out boxers from the tall wicker basket of clean clothes. He noticed Kelly watching him as he dressed.

"You keep looking at me that way and we're never getting out of here..."

The trip to Aggie's took about a half hour. While Sebastian drove he dictated a grocery list that included orange juice, and bacon and eggs for breakfast.

"I know we have beer – I should have put some in the fridge." Sebastian looked at her, but she was still writing. He squeezed her knee. Kelly looked over at him and grinned, so different from the sad expression she wore on the long drive up to the cabin.

Aggie's was bigger than a country store though not as impersonal as a supermarket. It offered the essentials and more that its clientele demanded, including a large deli department and a well-stocked liquor shop in the back. They had shopped at Aggie's often enough that the clerks knew them by name. The only drawback was that it was the only grocery for miles and closed early. It was already past five o'clock.

While Sebastian held the basket, Kelly chose items from their list, placing them into the basket which soon was overflowing. After packing their purchases in recyclable canvas bags, they left for the drive back to the cabin.

Kelly leaned against the headrest and looked at Sebastian through fresh eyes. Had she taken him for granted? She was very proud of him, but had she told him that? Every morning he dressed so sharply in one of his tailored suits and often wore the tie she bought for him, the one he wore at their wedding. And she knew he appreciated the feminine touches she had brought into his home – their home. She closed her eyes and slept...

Sebastian felt Kelly watching him as he drove. He usually knew what she was thinking, but now her thoughts could be all over the place. Was she still wondering if they were good? Did he not tell her that? Was she second guessing herself? Was she doubting him?

When she finally closed her eyes, he felt a sense of relief. She wouldn't feel secure enough to sleep if there were still questions in her mind. Shortly after they married, she had begun to transform his bachelor pad into a real home, bringing in her unique shabby chic style. Had he told her how much he appreciated the changes? Was he taking advantage of her love? He made a silent pact to open up to her, tell her how much he appreciated her. Tell her he loved her. Actually say the words. He returned to concentrating on his driving – he didn't want to miss that turn-off on the county road again.

By the time they arrived back at the cabin, the setting sun over the pond was low and shone like a fire across the sky. Sebastian retrieved the canvas shopping bags while Kelly started up the field stone steps.

While Kelly cut up the French bread and set out slices of meat and cheeses and other essentials of good sandwiches, Sebastian built the fire in the large stone hearth. The last time they were at the cabin he had chopped wood – now it was dry. And there were plenty of completed *New York Times* crossword puzzle pages for kindling. Soon he had a nice fire going. He looked over at Kelly who was preparing their food.

With the fire burning well, he went into the kitchen and standing behind her, wrapped his arms around his wife. She stopped arranging the food, laid her head back against his neck and put her hands on his arms.

"I love you, Sebastian." She was not expecting him to answer her with the same words – he rarely told her he loved her... Today however, she felt it was important for him to say the words – but she wasn't going to push.

He turned her around, held her to his chest and announced, "I love you, Kelly Isabella Cameron Bonsignore!" Sebastian kissed her hard. Kelly put her arms around his neck, not wanting to let go. She looked into hazel eyes shrouded beneath heavy brows – so focused on her right now.

He saw her tearing up. He kissed her lightly on the lips again. "Let's eat... now!" She laughed and wiped the single tear from her cheek. He carried the tray of food into the den, placing it on the coffee table. She brought in his Corona and her bottle of Zinfandel and a wine goblet.

They sat on the thick rag rug facing the slow burning logs in the stone hearth. He drank his beer out of the bottle – she poured her wine into the goblet. As they ate their sandwiches, they talked about Gabriella and Raffaele who were touring through Europe. Sebastian was grateful that his wife had urged him to watch his brother perform. If Kelly hadn't entered his life, he still would not have heard his brother sing. She even downloaded one of Raffaele's albums onto his iPod. Though he would never be a fan of opera, he would listen to his brother.

She poured more wine in her goblet – and stopped. He was looking at her so seriously. "What's wrong?" She thought things between them were good, but now she wasn't sure.

"Promise me..." He took her hand in his.

"Promise you what, Seb?"

"Promise me – if you ever feel I'm ignoring you or taking you for granted or I'm making you feel sad or if you feel lonely – tell me."

Her heart melted. "I promise!!" Kelly leaned into him and kissed him. She never wanted to not kiss him, kiss his lips... She pressed her face into his neck. Sebastian pulled his wife into his arms and holding her tight against his chest, pulled her down with him and lay on the rug. She rested her head on his chest – and listened to his beating heart...

"I love you, Sebastian."

"I love you, woman. God, Kelly, I love you." And they dozed in front of the fire until the embers were only a memory...

Sebastian woke and kissed the top of her head. He whispered, *"Are you awake?"*

Kelly raised her head and looked at him, her husband, her Ulysses. "I am now..." And she smiled.

He helped her roll off his body onto the rag rug and stood. He took the fireplace poker and cajoled and pushed at the dying logs until the flames reignited. He sat back down on the rug and took a sip from her glass of wine.

"You know, Phil is working for me now."

"I'm glad. He's taking some of the responsibilities from you, isn't he?"

"Yeah. He's smart..."

"I know, otherwise you wouldn't have trusted him with your business."

"Kelly, I'm going to be there for you more often now." He leaned in and kissed her face, her eyes, her mouth. "What would you think about making Wednesday nights our date night?"

"How do you mean?" She sat back and put her bare feet on his lap. While they talked he massaged her toes.

"I could drive you to school. And while I wait for you, I could set up my computer and get some work done."

Kelly exhaled loudly – his fingers working wonders on her feet. "There's a tavern about two blocks from the college. I think it's called Lanigan's. I heard some students go there after class."

"Do they serve food? If they do, we could eat dinner there, too."

"I think so. I love that idea." Bending her knees Kelly leaned forward, keeping her feet in his lap and kissed his face. "I love you... But now my sweet husband, I want to take a shower. Do you think we have hot water yet?"

"I'll check." Before he rose, Sebastian kissed her toes and moved her feet to the floor. He walked back into the kitchen and turned on the faucet.

He called from the kitchen. "Yes Love, you have your hot water." Before returning to the den, he stopped at the doorway and stood in awe at the sight. She was beautiful... His wife was beautiful. Her auburn waves were glowing, reflecting the tongues of the dying flames. He couldn't resist her – he entered the room and got down on the floor and kissed her hard.

She put her arms around his neck as he laid her on the rug and kissed her again. She touched his face, his soft beard and kissed his mouth. He put his hands on her chest, unbuttoned her shirt and kissed her breasts, sucking gently on her nipples. She didn't want to stop him, but she needed to get up. He began unzipping her pants – oh, she wanted his body, but not until she showered.

"Sebastian..." She was breathing heavier now. "Sebastian, give me two minutes..."

"Hurry!" He kissed her breasts... he kissed her belly...

"Holy crap, Sebastian! What the hell are you doing to me?"

"Loving you!"

She kissed him hard, then scooted out from under him and stood.

He put his head on his folded arms, then rolled over and looked up at her. "Hurry, woman!"

She laughed, drank the last sip of wine and walked to the bedroom. As promised she took a quick shower, but didn't wash her hair – the hot water wouldn't have sustained a full shower. When she came out of the bathroom he was waiting in bed.

She hung the towel on the bed post and crawled up on the great bed. Sebastian rose up and, collecting her in his arms, pulled her up onto his body. She stopped him. He looked at her with concern.

"I have to tell you something... um... something I did..." Kelly began but turned her head, avoiding his gaze.

"What did you do?" He looked at her, wondering what she was going to say.

"I was in the shower and, um... I masturbated."

"You did?" He smiled a crooked smile. "How long has it been since you did that?"

"Since before I met you..." She looked at him and quickly turned her head away.

Sebastian put his hand under her chin and made her look at him. "So what made you want to masturbate?" He was looking at her with that same crooked smile. Kelly loved that smile.

"I missed you and I wanted to feel your hands on me..." Though she was looking at him, she still appeared embarrassed. "I was taking a shower and I just started touching myself and, um, one thing led to another..."

Now he was intrigued. "How did you do it?"

"How? You mean, what did I do?"

"Yes, what did you do... actually, what did *I* do?" Now he was chuckling but not so much that she would stop talking.

"Well, like I said, I was in the shower and, um... I started touching..." Again she looked away.

"Are you embarrassed to tell me?" This could be such a turn on – could he tell her that?

"Kind of..." Now she was blushing.

He needed to find out what his wife did in the privacy of their shower. "Tell me... Where did you start...?" Sebastian's breath was on her face – she had wanted his breath on her face while she showered...

"Um... I touched my neck..." She put her hands on her neck and lightly massaged her skin down to her shoulders. Sebastian watched her – wanting to put his own hands on her skin...

"And...? What did you do next, Love?" He pressed his forehead onto her face, allowing her to talk without having to look at him – look into his eyes as she confessed her lovely dark secrets.

"I..." Kelly exhaled and closed her eyes... "You do it..."

Sebastian smiled his crooked smile as he touched her face and kissed her neck – his beard tickled her skin – but her only response was a soft groan that crept up from deep in her chest. His hand lightly roamed down to her shoulder – down her arm and back up to her shoulder. He loved touching her – he remembered the first nights they were together in his bed. He reveled in *her* touch, begging for *her* touch, loving *her* touch, dying for *her* touch...

Sebastian's hand found her breasts, her beautiful small breasts – his hand totally covering them. She could only respond with soft groans. He lowered himself on the bed – lowering himself next to her body – his wife, his Dulcinea. He licked her sweet nipples, taking his time, cupping her breasts into soft mounds, loving her breasts.

Kelly clutched handfuls of his long hair as he continued kissing and licking her breasts... Oh, she did love the softness of his tongue...

"I love you... I can never get enough of you, woman..." His hand explored her body, across her belly and down between her legs...

Her orgasm was instant, incredible, heart-stopping... "Love me... Love me please! *Now!*"

Sebastian rose up and carefully lay on her – and pressed into her while her body still pulsed from deep within. She wrapped her legs around his waist – crushing his waist – her hands holding tight onto his biceps. And the suddenness of his thrust heightened her already incredible orgasm – and she screamed his name as another orgasm overtook her mind, her body, her soul, her existence... And he thrust faster and harder than he ever remembered.

This whole masturbation scenario was so hot! After all these years with the same woman, who would have imagined that there could be new ways to blow his mind! And he came hard into the woman he loved – his wife... his Dulcinea.

It was still dark when she woke. Through the bedroom window, the full moon played hide and seek behind the stand of birch trees splashing its glow on them, filling the room with a bizarre disco-like quality. Kelly looked at the man who slept next to her – his arm and one leg lay across her body, his face next to hers on one pillow, his warm breath on her face.

She remembered their second anniversary – the moon had been full that night and inspired Sebastian to be more than attending to her sexual needs. Just the thought of his warm, extremely hairy body on her, under her, around her made her body yearn for him again. But he was right here. All she had to do was touch his face, his shoulder, his hip and she could have it all again – and again! It was all so peaceful and beautiful in their bedroom now.

She turned her head... Her hair tickled his face.

He woke, opening one eye. "Are you still here?" He pulled her even closer.

"I'm still here..." And she felt her body respond. The mere thought of him making love with her made her bottom muscles clench.

Sebastian pulled her on top of him. She bent her knees at his hips and lay on his chest – and he slid into her. He crushed her body to him. Her hips moved slightly, never disturbing the quiet of the bedroom. She kissed his handsome face, feeling his soft beard against her cheek. She put her head on his shoulder as he began pushing up his pelvis, meeting her body as she pushed down on him. He was so deep, he was so hard. Kelly so loved this man.

As they moved in unison his hands glided from her neck to her butt and back up again, all the while thrusting into her.

His touch enflamed her passion and Kelly increased her movements. She pressed her hips onto his body and growled his name as she came hard – he wrapped his arms around her and held on tight, sharing in her pleasure.

She stayed cocooned around this man, this man who she thought she had lost. This man who she had looked for and almost lost – because of her stupidity? Her pride? And the tears came. She couldn't stop – her tears dripping on his shoulder.

Sebastian knew what to do. He pulled the blanket up over her body and held her tight, not saying a word, not comforting her, not trying to fix tears. He just held her. Her breathing gradually calmed, her tears stopped. They slept with her still laying on him, his pillow wet from her tears – and they slept...

16

Make a Date

"I'm hungry..." She whispered in his ear, tickling his ear.

"No shit!" He turned toward her and laughed. He didn't need to ask how she was feeling this morning – if she was hungry she was feeling good. He kissed her quickly and crawled over her body. She stopped him and touching his beard, kissed him back.

"Up!" he ordered. She obeyed and they both raced to the bathroom.

The smell of bacon permeated the little cabin. Sebastian looked out the doorway, but couldn't see her. She must be down the hill by the pond. It was one of her favorite places. In the summer, she spent most of her time there. The shallow water boasted reeds where many kinds of birds and animals took refuge.

She knew so much about nature. The last time they were at the cabin, she gave him a tutorial on the wildlife near the pond. She had pointed out Kingfishers, Herons, Loons, turtles and otters. That same weekend while walking on their road, they had seen several mature Bald Eagles soaring overhead. And as they returned to the cabin, Kelly had pointed out a family of Pileated woodpeckers in the stand of birch trees.

He came to appreciate nature because she loved it – and if he was going to share her life, he had better know what made her happy.

Sebastian walked out the doorway and spied her down at the pond. He called to her – Kelly turned and waved her hand, acknowledging his call and walked up the hill to their cabin.

He filled two glasses with orange juice – one with a large green olive – and set them on the coffee table. He returned to his eggs just as Kelly came in the door.

"Bacon smells wonderful, baby!" She kissed her husband's cheek and hugged him around his waist. "Can I do anything? Or do you have it covered?" Kelly knew her way around a kitchen, but since she had been with Sebastian, she let him do most of the cooking.

"Pull off some paper towels and get two plates and forks please." She did as she was told. Soon they were sitting on the loveseat eating crispy bacon, sunny side-up eggs and drinking orange juice out of wine goblets.

"There was a full moon last night. Did you see it?" Kelly held a bacon strip to her lips.

"Full moon, eh?" He smiled that crooked smile. "Did we make love?"

"Yes, mister, we made love – I think twice." She leaned over and kissed him.

"Twice, huh?" He wiped his hands on a paper towel. "We'll have to do better than that next time." And he winked at her.

"We have to leave, don't we...?" She looked a little sad, but she also knew that they'd be coming out to the cabin again. It was always something to look forward to – coming out to the cabin.

"We have to be home by end of day unfortunately." Using his thumb, he wiped some egg yolk off her chin, then sucked his thumb – and gave her his best smile.

"I love you..." She didn't care if he said it back to her. She already knew the answer. These last two days proved it beyond her wildest dreams.

"I love you too, Kelly." He pressed her knee with his hand and looked at his watch. "And I'd like to take a walk down to our pond."

Kelly leaned into him – the man who loved her. "I'd like that too."

Sebastian stood and helped her rise. He put his hands on her shoulders and directed her through the kitchen and out the door. Together they walked down to her – their – pond. When they reached the bottom of the hill, he looked at her.

"I love you, woman. And I can never get enough of you..." Sebastian pressed her body against his chest, inhaling the scent of her auburn curls.

"Seb?" Kelly leaned into the man who promised to love her always and forever.

He enveloped her in his arms. "What, love?"

"I wish we didn't have to leave. I wish we didn't have to go home." She pressed her head against his beard, loving the feel of his soft beard on her face. "I wish we could stay here forever..."

Sebastian touched his wife's face, caressing her face with the back of his fingers, following her jaw line down to her neck. "Would you want to stay here forever?" He wondered if she was serious. "Quit your teaching position?"

"I don't know..." She wasn't sure – she loved her job, but she also loved this man. And she loved this man more than anything or anyone. "I don't know..." She closed her eyes, feeling her tears about to fall. "All I know is that I almost lost you – we almost lost us." And her tears came. No one could fix her tears.

"Love, I'm here." He put a finger under her chin, forcing her to look at him. "I'm not going anywhere. Okay?"

Kelly looked out over the pond. "I just don't want to live without you..."

Sebastian kissed the side of her face. "I'm not going anywhere. And if you wanted to quit your job and move to our cabin and live here forever – if that's what you wanted..."

But he didn't finish his thought. Kelly looked into his face – his beautiful face – and put her arms around his waist, hugging him tight and rested her head on his shoulder.

"No – I won't quit my job. But promise me we'll come out again... soon." She looked out over her pond again. "Promise me..."

Sebastian again pressed his mouth on her hair – breathing in her scent. "I promise. We'll come out here again."

Over the next few months they fell into a better routine, talking to each other and more importantly listening to each other. And as he promised, one night a week Sebastian drove Kelly to her night class at the state university.

She loved these date nights. The long drive to the university was spent talking about their week, sharing moments, bringing each other up to date on their individual lives. She had become a Boney James fan, the easy saxophone music serenading them during the ninety minute drive.

That first night, Sebastian had gotten into a conversation with the bartender. He recognized Kevin as the DJ who played at their wedding, and was impressed that the young man also moonlighted in a jazz quartet playing alto sax.

After her class, Kelly walked the two blocks to the small tavern. Her husband always sat in the same booth in the back. It was a secluded area, offering him a private work space – but also gave him and Kelly the opportunity for alone time.

"More coffee, Sir?" He looked up and saw his wife.

"You're out early." He stood and greeted her with a kiss. When they sat in the booth, they were both on the same side facing the wall.

"You two all set?" The waitress had been watching for Kelly.

"Hi, Millie! Can we get our usual? And put in an order of sweet potato fries, please."

"Sure can, Honey. Be right up."

Their usual was char-broiled bacon cheeseburgers and chocolate malteds. When the order arrived, they ate in silence, but they were with each other. Thighs touching thighs, elbows touching elbows, sharing the fries, laughing – but most of all, just sharing each other's company. Date night turned out to be the highlight of their busy weeks.

While they ate, Sebastian shared his news. "I'm going to talk to the folks at the Harbor Pub about getting a gig for Kevin and his group." He was always thinking, finding the best in people and advancing them to achieve greater successes. He had done that with Phil – now he was doing that with Kevin.

"I think we should make that a date night." Kelly finished her malted, slurping up the melted ice cream through her straw. "We could go dancing. What do you think of that, mister?"

Sebastian wiped the corner of her mouth and kissed her. "I think I should take my wife dancing."

"Right now, I want to make love to my husband. Let's go home." And she kissed him back.

17

Reality

He was lying on his back and he was snoring.

"Seb..." Kelly pushed on his body. Though it was morning and she had to get up early – still he was snoring. He had robbed her of those precious extra few minutes of sleep.

"What...?" He turned his head and looked at her beautiful face. "Was I snoring?"

She rose up on her elbow, kissed his face and lay back down again. It was almost time to be up anyway. He craned his neck to see the clock on the bedside table.

"What time is it?" But before she could answer, he rolled on his side and put his hand on her breasts, caressing first one, then the other. His hand stopped.

"Love, when is your period?"

She looked at him. "What a funny question. Why?"

He felt her breast again using just his fingertips. "I know you get fibroid lumps in your breasts before your period." He felt her left breast again, the one furthest from him, this time moving further under her armpit. "But this feels different."

She moved his hand away. "Let me feel..." and she felt the area he had examined. "I guess I don't feel anything."

He moved her hand and felt her breast again. "Don't forget, Love, I know your breasts better than you do." He lightly kissed her face and continued with the exam.

"Stop. You're scaring me."

Though his hand stopped, he did not remove it from her breast. "I'm sorry. It just feels... not the same."

"My period was a week ago. Remember?"

During the first couple days of her period, she refrained from having sex. He respected her wishes and cuddled with her all night, but she knew he was frustrated with her self-imposed monthly celibacy. When they resumed their lovemaking, he acted like he hadn't been with her for months. It definitely made for several passionate nights in a row, much to her delight.

"If it will make you feel better, I'll call my nurse practitioner. She'll probably do an ultrasound. It'll come back normal, like it always has before."

He resumed examining her breast. When he spoke, there was greater concern in his voice. "Why don't you get a mammogram? Isn't that what women usually do?"

"Yeah, women with *BOOBS!*" Kelly closed her eyes and turned her head away from him.

His fingers stopped moving. He pulled her chin, making her face him as he looked hard into her eyes. He kissed her lips. His hand traveled down her body and caressed her breasts. Then leaning over, he kissed both her breasts and licked and sucked on her sweet nipples.

"I love your boobs!" He continued caressing her breasts, his hand totally covering them. "I love you! Get them checked. This week. Please."

"Yes, mister." She kissed his face.

"Thank you, Love." He rolled on top of her and slipped into her like he had so many times before – and loved her.

Kelly showered first because she had to be at school early. Today was the first day of parent conferences. Most of her students – her kids – excelled in her classes. She expected a lot from them. A professional-looking sign posted in her classroom reminded them every day.

Expect the BEST!

Want the BEST!

Get the BEST!

Over the last twelve years of teaching, Kelly only had one student attempt to drop out of her class. She remembered this student. His name was Benjamin. During his years in grade school and junior high, he had somehow managed to pass all his classes with only a third grade reading ability. But when he became one of her kids, he quickly fell behind. When she received his request to drop her literature class, she met him after class. After a few simple questions, she realized he was smart but couldn't read the required material.

Kelly knew he and his younger siblings were in a single parent household and that Ben helped out a lot at home. She refused to accept the excuse that since he came from a non-traditional home, he couldn't keep up with the other students in her class. She had a cross section of America in her classroom of every ethnic background and social status – she was not about to let this young man slip between the cracks.

She set up time they could meet during the school day. Ben had a part-time job and couldn't jeopardize losing the extra income by staying after school. Kelly not only spent time tutoring him, but also created worksheets for him containing reading exercises he could complete over the weekends. Each week the reading material became more difficult, and each week he turned in beautifully filled-in worksheets. And although he understood the basic reading material, Kelly pushed him to increase his vocabulary.

But today would be different. She not only had to meet with parents, but she would be thinking about the lump Sebastian found. He was right when he said he knew her breasts better than she did. She always had small breasts – they just never grew.

The first time she met Gabriella, she couldn't stop staring at her large breasts. Gabriella offered to give her some of the overflow, a remark that not only broke the ice, but after much laughter, led them to become best of friends. And though Kelly may have envied the ogles Gabriella received from men, she was satisfied with what God – and her parents – gave her.

Her first husband, other than being a complete asshole, wanted her to get implants. He was obsessed with wanting her to be at least a B cup, or even better a C. After only a few months of marriage he refused to touch her breasts, telling her it would be a waste of his time. Their relationship didn't last another week – their split had turned nasty.

On the day their divorce became final, she and Gabriella had gone out to the Harbor Pub to celebrate. He walked into the bar and strode over to where the women sat at the horseshoe-shaped bar. He looked at her chest, then pointed to Gabriella's full bosom.

"Your friend here always had the goods, but you just wouldn't pump yourself up. You're not even a handful, *bitch!*"

A man who sat next to the women overheard the comment.

"Sir, I think you owe these lovely ladies an apology."

"Why the fuck should I apologize to *them*? That's *my* ex wife – the flat-chested one! And why the hell do you care? It's not your deal, man!"

The stranger rose from where he sat and stood to his full height. In a soft voice, he warned, "I'm a Marine, and I will not let a piece of shit talk such garbage to these two lovely women." He walked over to Kelly's ex and grabbing his collar, rudely escorted him out of the bar. Kelly noticed the stranger put a foot-plant on her ex's butt. The patrons around the bar, who were privy to the encounter, gave him an impromptu and raucous round of applause.

The big man returned to his empty stool next to the women and introduced himself. He was Roger McClennen, the carpentry and woodworking instructor at the technical school. From that time, Roger took it upon himself to watch over the two women – especially Kelly...

It was 7:00 a.m. Her first parents were scheduled at 7:15. This would be a long day for her. Kelly tried keeping each conference to twenty minutes. She and the parents would sit in comfortable chairs in her office – it felt more personal without a desk between them.

Seldom did Kelly have to give a less than spectacular report to the parents. She knew she inspired greatness in her kids – a fact not lost on the school district. She achieved tenured status early in her career and received yearly bonuses.

Sebastian had introduced the habit of putting smelly stickers on her high school-age students' papers. He remembered how proud he was as a young student when the teacher awarded his papers with a shiny gold star. Kelly wasn't sure about colorful stickers for teenagers, but after that first time when she handed graded essay papers back to her kids – each paper sporting a colorful sticker – the reception was eye opening. After that the students seemed to try harder to earn those stickers.

When Sebastian traveled, he often stopped at small, unique shops that sold fun stickers and brought Kelly back his latest finds. The parents also appreciated the colorful stickers and told Kelly they posted their older kids' essays and poetry on the 'brag board' along with their younger children's spelling and math papers.

One night when he was helping grade her students' homework, Sebastian found one of Ben's worksheets. He reviewed the student's answers to the questions and was impressed with the young man's insights into the material. Without asking Kelly, he placed a large, smelly dinosaur sticker on the paper. She noticed what Sebastian had done and was concerned it would give her student a sense that she was mocking him – but her concern was not warranted. When Ben saw the sticker, he was overjoyed and proudly showed his paper to the rest of his classmates. Kelly was so proud of her student and even more proud when he graduated the following year near the top of his class.

11:30. She could take a break. Closing her office door, she called her friend Lisa who was also her primary physician. Lisa's new assistant Rose took the call. Kelly impressed on her the importance of getting in this week to see her doctor. Rose offered to set up a mammogram before she saw Lisa, but Kelly knew it would not be possible. She started arguing with the woman – just make an appointment with Lisa. Please.

Rose put her on hold. Kelly hated to be put on hold. While she listened to the awful music, she pinched the bridge of her nose and started crying. Why was this so fucking difficult? Eventually Rose came back on the phone and said Lisa would see her whenever she wanted. Kelly asked for an appointment the first thing in the morning and hung up.

Looking at the clock, she needed to pull herself together – the next parents were coming in ten minutes. Kelly wiped her tears and took a drink of sparkling water. She looked in the mirror and whispered, *"It's showtime!"*

Sebastian was already preparing dinner when Kelly got home. She was grateful and told him so as she held him from behind – wrapping her arms tightly around his waist, pressing her face into his long hair, inhaling his scent. She so loved this man.

They sat at the butcher-block counter and together dined on grilled filet mignon wrapped in bacon, twice-baked potatoes and sautéed Brussels sprouts in butter sauce. Of course they drank her favorite Cline Ancient Vines Zinfandel. Kelly loved it when Sebastian cooked for her. The long day was forgotten as she enjoyed the small steaks and tender vegetables.

"Do you have any work to do tonight?" She finished her wine and wanted to be with him, hoping he had left his work at the office.

"I am all yours tonight." Sebastian kissed her hand.

Kelly pulled his head to her face and kissed his cheek, holding him close, feeling his soft beard against her face.

"Do you want to turn in early, Love?"

"Yes please..."

"Go upstairs and take a long, hot shower. You'll feel better." He kissed her eyes. "I'll clean up and be there shortly."

She kissed him again and left the kitchen.

Kelly stood directly under the rain forest shower head, the water cascading over her. She sensed when Sebastian joined her. He took her in his arms and held her, letting the water wash away the cares of their day.

"I want you Love, but not here." He shut off the shower. They didn't move – he just held her. She put her head on his shoulder.

"I love you..." Her tears coalesced with the water on her face – she pressed her face into his neck. He held her tight while she cried.

Sebastian put a finger under her chin. "Let's go to bed." He brought her face up to his and kissed her tenderly on her mouth.

He helped put his robe on over her wet skin. He wiped off with a towel as he followed her out of the bathroom. She crawled up on the large mattress and sat on the bed, still wearing his robe. He unceremoniously dropped his towel on the floor and joined her, sitting cross-legged facing her.

"I called Lisa. I'm seeing her first thing in the morning." Kelly looked down and then looked back at him, staring into hazel eyes shrouded beneath heavy brows.

"Do you want me to come with you?" If she wanted him with her, he would drop everything to be there with her.

"No..." She leaned into him and kissed his face. "I've seen Lisa before about my lumps and it's always turned out to be nothing." Her eyes glistened.

"You'll call me after the ultrasound?"

She nodded yes. But Sebastian knew Kelly well enough that she would agree only to mollify his concern. He pressed her. "I mean, really – promise me you'll call." His look was intense.

Avoiding his stare, she contemplated her clenched fingers and whispered, "I promise... I'll call you right away." She looked up at her Ulysses. "I love you..."

Feeling more confident, Sebastian laid her on the bed and opened her robe. He kissed her face, her eyes, her neck, her chest. He caressed her breasts, kissing each one, licking her nipples, cupping her breasts, his hands totally covering them. His hand roamed down her body. She opened her legs.

"Can I love you?" He was asking her. He had to know she still wanted him to love her.

"Sebastian... always and forever!"

He moved down her body and lay between her open legs. As he kissed her she reached down between her legs and fondled his head, grasping handfuls of his wet hair. He heard a groan coming from her chest. Sebastian could tell she was close – he knew her body so well.

Her back arched and she growled his name out loud. Oh, how he loved this woman!

Kelly pulled his body up onto her, wrapped her legs around him, kissed his mouth hard – and asked him to love her – *please, love her!* And he did as she asked, and thrust into her again and again and again, not stopping until she came again – her legs like a vise around his waist. And he came hard into the woman he loved more than life itself.

He woke early. The morning sunrise was only beginning to cast its grace upon their little part of the world. Kelly lay on her front facing him, her arms curled up around her head. He inhaled her breath, her sweet breath. On their first date night, he remembered how sweet her breath was on his face. He lifted the sheet off her body and softly caressed her back.

She stirred, opened her eyes and looked at him. "Hi..." She closed her eyes and turned over, her back to his front. She touched his feet with her own and exhaled.

Sebastian held her close. He kissed her neck, softly brushing his beard against her shoulder and spoke into her hair. "When is your appointment?"

"9:30. Lisa got me in right away." She turned her body into his and looked up at him. No more words were needed – her voice conveyed all the angst she felt. He pulled her closer. She felt his erection against her hip. "We can't this morning. I have to shower. And besides, my doctor is going to examine me." She turned her head away and closed her eyes.

"I thought as much." He leaned away from her. She heard the sound of his bedside drawer opening. Holding her close again he dropped something on her pillow.

She picked it up and looked at it. "A condom?" She was wide awake now.

"This way... you know... but only if you want..." Now he wasn't sure if his grand idea was such a grand idea after all.

"What if my doctor wants me to stop birth control? Are we going to use these?"

"We can talk about it then, but if it is your birth control I'll get a vasectomy. Or do you want kids?" They really had never talked about having children. Now that she was approaching 40, she felt like it was too late to consider it.

"No, we're too late – besides, I've got enough kids at school." She searched his face for a glimmer into his thoughts. "What about you? Do you want kids?"

"I thought of it, but after turning 30 I realized it wasn't for me. He kissed her face and continued. "Even if your lump isn't caused by birth control, I'm going to get one anyway. Those aren't good for you and I don't know why we didn't discuss the subject earlier."

"So... do you remember how to put on one of these things?" Kelly held up the small packet, flipping it over in her fingers. Then in her best spokeswoman voice, added, "It says it's textured and guaranteed to add to my pleasure."

Sebastian took the packet from her and opened it, ignoring her comment and giving her a sideways sneering lip. But she laughed anyway, then became perfectly still while he slowly rolled on the condom.

"Will it fit? I mean, it didn't say one-size-fits-all..."

"Quiet, woman. I'm trying to concentrate here." But the condom was too tight. He unrolled it and threw it on the floor. He looked at her – she was grinning.

"What are you smiling about?" He appeared so frustrated.

"We'll make up for it tonight."

He turned on his side and put his hand on her beautiful face. "Promise me you'll call me."

"I promise." And she cuddled with him until it was time to get up.

The drive to her doctor's office took only a few minutes. Kelly walked into the reception area, but there was no one at the registration desk. She sat and picked up a copy of *Car and Driver Magazine* and thumbed through the glossy pages from back to front, not really looking at the pictures. Christine the clinic's nurse manager came out.

"Sorry, Kelly!" She was holding files in her hands. "Come on back and we'll get you ready." They walked down the hallway and entered a private room.

"Have a seat and we'll get your vitals." She quickly and professionally took Kelly's blood pressure, pulse and temperature, and entered the results into her laptop.

"Did you want an ultrasound, Kelly?"

"Yes, Sebastian found a lump..."

"That's how it usually happens, you know. Partners are the first to find those things." Christine had known Kelly for many years. She put a comforting hand on Kelly's arm. "Are you worried?"

Kelly lied. "A little."

"You've had these fibroid lumps before, Kelly. Why now? What's different about his one?"

"Seb..." And she started crying. Christine waited for her to compose herself.

"Lisa will be right in. Take off your blouse and your skirt, too. She will want to do a pelvic I'm sure." She was about to leave, but thought better of it. "Kelly, do you want me to stay with you until she gets here?"

"No, I'm good. Thank you." After Christine left the room, Kelly disrobed and sat up on the table. She covered her lap with the paper sheet. A knock on the door – Dr. Lisa Goodwin came in.

"Hi, Kelly. I'm so glad you called." She sat at her desk and addressed Kelly. "Sorry about Rose. She means well, but she's new. Tracy got married, you know." Tracy was Lisa's former assistant. She knew everyone and their respective illnesses and complaints. Everyone loved Tracy.

"I had heard, I guess..." Kelly tried sounding interested.

"Okay, let's talk about you." Lisa pulled her chair closer to the table. "Tell me what's going on."

Kelly brought her doctor up to date on Sebastian's exam. Lisa was familiar with her fibroid lumps and had been through these exams several times before.

"Let's see what's going on." Lisa stood and listened to Kelly's heart and lungs. Next, she asked Kelly to put her right hand on her head. Lisa's fingers firmly pressed around one breast and under her armpit. "Now your left arm please." Kelly didn't say anything – this was the side Sebastian had found something not right. Lisa took her time, again pressing around the breast and again under the armpit.

She stood straight and told Kelly to put her arm down. "There's an abnormal mass on the side of your left breast. You're due for your PAP. I'd like to rule out any potential problems, okay?"

Lisa had her lie on the table and performed the exam quickly. She pulled the table leaf back out to its full length, allowing Kelly to straighten her legs, and covered her body with the paper sheet.

"I'm going to get you set up for an ultrasound. Christine will help. Try to relax..."

Christine entered the room, rolling the ultrasound machine on a small table. As she set up the machine, Lisa stood at Kelly's side and held her hands.

"Kelly, raise your arms above your head." Lisa smeared a little gel on her right breast, including her armpit. The gel felt cool. "I'm placing the transducer on your skin. This should not hurt. We've done this before." Lisa's voice was so reassuring, so soothing. The device glided around Kelly's breast and under her armpit. Then she smeared gel on the left breast and did the same procedure. But when she came to the area near the armpit, she stopped and moved the device around in one small area several times. Kelly noticed the look Lisa gave Christine.

"Okay, we're all done. Let's get you cleaned up." Lisa took a warm, damp cloth and wiped the gel from Kelly's breasts and armpits. She pulled the paper sheet up to her shoulders. "I'm going to look at the results. Why don't you get down and put your clothes on. You can sit in the chair." Before Lisa left the room with Christine, she added, "Try to relax, please."

Kelly put her hands on her face and cried – she cried harder than she ever remembered crying. She wanted her mom. She wanted Sebastian.

There was a knock on the door. It was Christine. "Sebastian is here. Can he come in?"

Kelly couldn't answer. She was crying too hard. Sebastian pushed through the door and saw his wife lying on the table. He gathered her in strong arms and held on tight. She held him around his neck and cried into his shoulder. The door closed silently behind him.

"Kelly... talk to me." Sebastian held her body, feeling her chest heaving with every breath. But she couldn't say anything. "Love, talk to me." He loosened his grip and with one finger under her chin, made her look at him. "Kelly..."

She closed her eyes and pressed her face against his chest. "Sebastian..."

"I'm right here, Love."

"They found a lump. A big lump." Her eyes were drowning with tears. "It's a big lump."

"Oh, baby..." He held her face between his hands and kissed her lips. Looking behind him, he found her clothes on the chair. Sebastian helped Kelly put her blouse back on, slowly buttoning every button with great care. He left her skirt and panties on the table next to her.

"Sebastian, it's bigger than it ever was. I'm so scared." Again she wept – again he gathered her in his strong arms, rocking her, loving her, comforting her...

After a few minutes, Lisa knocked on the door and came in the room. Kelly still sat on the table, her legs hanging over the side, the paper drape lying across her lap. Sebastian looking so handsome in his business suit leaned against the table with his arm around her – his other hand wiping the last of the tears from her face. Lisa sat at her desk and turned on her computer. She looked at the two people who weren't looking at her.

"I have the preliminary results." Lisa turned the monitor so Sebastian and Kelly could see the image. It appeared as a condensed group of small greyish, oval-shaped blobs, mostly looking uniform. One larger blob, the tumor, was darker and irregular in shape.

"One of the fibroid tumors may be malignant, but we won't know until we get in there."

Kelly leaned her head into Sebastian's. He kissed her hair.

Lisa continued. "I would usually do a needle biopsy first, but I can already see this as abnormal." She waited until her patient understood what she was saying, then continued. "I'd like to do a lumpectomy as soon as possible. How long would you need to request time off from teaching, Kelly?"

"How much time off would I need?"

"If all goes well, maybe a week. You'll be sore."

Kelly looked at Sebastian, then back at the doctor. "But you don't know for sure if it's malignant?"

"I'll be straight with you. I think it is."

Sebastian squeezed Kelly's shoulder and asked the next question. "Who will do the surgery, the lumpectomy?"

"I'll have Scott Elliot do the surgery. He's an excellent surgeon, Sebastian. He'll take good care of Kelly."

"Where do we go?"

"Dr. Elliot operates at the Boardwalk Surgical Plaza. This will be an outpatient procedure." Lisa turned her attention to Kelly. "As soon as you get your affairs in order, you call me and I'll schedule it."

"If it's cancerous, what do we do?" Kelly looked at her husband, who held her tighter.

"Kelly, there are options of course. You don't have a history of breast cancer in your family, so I would not expect this to reappear if that's any comfort."

"What about a mastectomy?"

"Taking the whole breast isn't warranted unless Dr. Elliot finds positive lymph nodes."

Kelly looked at Sebastian – he kissed her forehead and again asked the next question.

"Doctor, what about chemotherapy?"

"Sebastian, because you caught the fibroid tumor early, I don't think you should be concerned. Having said that," she turned her attention to Kelly. "Our oncologist will get in touch with you. She'll review your chart and talk to you."

"Lisa, it won't be a problem getting time off. I'll talk to my principal today and request a medical leave. You can schedule me any time tomorrow."

"And I'm in town," Sebastian assured Lisa. "I'm not going anywhere." He smiled at Kelly and kissed the side of her face.

Lisa stood. "Okay, you two. I'll get in contact with Scott and we'll get this scheduled right away." She looked at Kelly. "I know this is a lot to take in, but do your body a favor and try to relax."

Lisa approached Sebastian and put her hand on his arm. "Stay in the room as long as you need." She pressed Kelly's knee and left the room.

"I have to go back to school."

"Kelly, you've just had a shitty morning. Are you sure you don't want to go home?"

"I'll drive myself crazy thinking about everything if I go home, even if you're there." She smiled at him. She didn't think she could ever cry again. "I won't stay after fourth period. And it'll give me time to talk with my principal."

"When will you be home?" He pressed her for an answer. He really didn't want to let her out of his sight.

"I can be home by 1:30."

"Okay..." Suddenly he swore under his breath.

"What?" Kelly frowned – Sebastian never used foul language.

He stood, turned around and jammed his hands deep into his pants pockets. "I have a late afternoon dinner meeting. I've been trying to get this guy signed on for months." He stared at the floor, trying to figure out how to juggle everything today.

She knew she was complicating his usually well-scheduled life. Kelly reached for him, grasped his lapel and pulled him back to where she sat, making him stand between her legs. "Keep your meeting." She kissed his mouth, which was now scowling.

"And don't scowl! I hate it when you make that face." She put her hands on his tie, the one he wore at their wedding. "Besides, I want to call my mom. And if you're there too, I'll never stop crying." She smoothed the tie, pressing her hands onto his chest.

He cupped her face in his hands and kissed her lips. “I’ll make the meeting short. Promise!”

“I know...”

Sebastian helped his wife get down from the table. Kelly dressed and slipped on her shoes. He walked her out to her car and waited until she got in and started the engine. She rolled down the window. Sebastian leaned down, resting his forearms on her door.

“I’ll see you at home later.” He kissed her through the open window. She smiled up at him, her husband – her Ulysses. She rolled up her window and drove off to her school.

18

Revelations

Third period classes had ended and Kelly found herself in a sea of teenagers, many of them her students. Choruses of *'Hi! Mrs. B!'* followed her down the hall. She went directly to her classroom and walked through the open doorway.

Terese was filing paperwork in the cabinet. She had been Kelly's assistant for many years. The woman was Jamaican by birth and loved wearing colorful tunics and mama-muumuus, as she called them. She had grown up in Atlanta and hadn't lost her charming Southern accent. When she noticed Kelly, she went up to her and hugged her tight. "What's up, sista?"

Kelly brought Terese up to date on her impending surgery. Before she could say another word, Terese wrapped her in her large arms and hummed softly while she swayed back and forth. Kelly gratefully let her friend comfort her and hugged her back.

The fourth period bell rang. Terese told her not to worry about anything. Kelly was grateful for her support. Now she had to see her principal. As she opened the classroom door, her kids came rushing in. She knew each student by name and greeted each one as they entered the classroom. She turned to Terese and made the hand sign for talking on the phone, mouthing *I'll call you.*

She walked down the empty hall to the main office. Mr. Jorgenson had been the principal for most of her tenure at the high school. His assistant Claudia was on the phone when she walked in. Claudia smiled at her, pointed to his door and motioned for her to walk in. Kelly silently thanked her and walked into the office.

"Kelly, please come in." Mr. Jorgenson stood, walked around his desk and greeted her. "Please have a seat."

He walked back to his chair and sat. Putting his forearms on the desk and folding his hands, he leaned forward. "What can I do for you today? Claudia said you had a doctor's appointment?"

"Yes, I did... um, I had one. I need to take a medical leave." Oh shit, there go the tears. Kelly bowed her head and squeezed her eyes shut, her tears falling onto her lap.

Mr. Jorgenson picked up his phone and asked his assistant to come in. Immediately the door opened.

"Oh, sweetie..." Claudia came in. She sat in a chair next to Kelly and put an arm around her shoulder.

"Claudia, Kelly needs a medical leave. Would you help her fill out the request?" Mr. Jorgenson addressed Kelly. "You take as long as you need. Do you hear me?"

She sniffed back her tears and smiled at him. "Thank you, sir."

Claudia stood with Kelly and escorted her out of the office.

After Kelly left the clinic parking lot, Sebastian drove to his office. Phil was completing a phone call when he walked in. From the one-sided conversation he surmised Phil was speaking with a prospective client. He was typing on his keyboard as he spoke and confirmed the contract would be emailed immediately. Phil hit send and graciously thanked the new client.

He pulled off his Bluetooth headset and looked up at Sebastian. "Kelly...?"

"Breast cancer – that is, we're pretty sure." Sebastian sat in an upholstered leather chair across from Phil's desk, leaned forward and put his elbows on the armrests. He closed his eyes and covered his bearded jaw with his hands.

"Sorry." Phil's grandmother died from breast cancer when he was a teenager. Now that he was a husband and father, he was more than sensitive to family illnesses and the tragedies they could inflict, not only on the nuclear family but the extended family as well. "What can we do?" *We* meant his wife Emily and all Sebastian's friends, who would no doubt rally around Kelly and give whatever support was needed.

Sebastian sat back in the chair and looked out the bank of windows behind Phil. "They're going to do a lumpectomy tomorrow."

"The doctors don't know for sure it's cancer?" He felt comfortable talking with Sebastian. They had known each other for years.

His eyes focused on Phil. "No. She – the doctor – is sure. You know, I found the lump." Sebastian looked past his friend to the cloudless sky. "There's one thing you can help me with – if you have the time."

Phil didn't hesitate. "I have time."

"I have a dinner meeting later this afternoon with a prospective client. Sam Jeffries. You know I've been courting him for weeks. I think we can bring him on board. He'd be a good high-end account."

"What do you want me to do?" Phil was already looking at his calendar.

"Come with me. Sit in on the meeting."

"Sure, I can do that." This would be the first time Phil was included in this type of meeting. He was ready – and eager to prove himself.

"Good. If all goes as planned, I'll excuse myself and you and Sam can go over, you know, the more mundane points of the contract." Sebastian felt he had insulted his friend and continued quickly. "I'm sorry..."

"Seb, today mundane, tomorrow Power Lunch!"

Sebastian laughed. It was good to laugh. He enjoyed Phil. On the credenza behind his desk he had arranged framed pictures of his growing family. Sebastian regretted not taking any pictures of Kelly this last time they were at the cabin. Again he was lost in thought...

> *He remembered how sad Kelly was on their last drive to the cabin. She had cried and he couldn't comfort her. That drive was so long, so frustrating. But as he drove, all the memories of their life together*

had flooded back – their first date, their wedding, their honeymoon. So bittersweet. And then Kelly's meltdown at the cabin door. He was grateful that she wanted to save their relationship, save their marriage, save their love. That afternoon was so intense and she was so sad. But she let him comfort her.

Now Kelly was dealing with something he couldn't fix but at least he could comfort her. And he would as long as she needed him. Isn't that what the wedding vows instructed? To the end of time? Until death do us part? Death...

Phil's phone rang. Sebastian excused himself and went into his office. Their suite was on the second floor of an old refurbished library building located away from the downtown business district. With its front pillars and domed roof, it had so much character. The tall windows in each of their offices overlooked the lake, the same lake in which Kelly had accepted his ice cream marriage proposal.

Wednesday nights during the summer, sail boaters put on an exhibition, their watercraft making lazy circles out on the cold lake. Families set up their portable armchairs along the boardwalk and watched what they called the sailboat races. From their vantage point in their offices, Sebastian and Phil had a perfect bird's eye view of the armada. When they worked late on those days, the sight of the early evening sun glistening off the white sails was spectacular.

Their offices were also the perfect spot from which to view fireworks. The last Fourth of July, Phil brought his twins Brody and Jase to the office. Sebastian and Kelly enjoyed watching the young boys as they reacted to the colorful explosions with wide-eyed wonder.

Though they had decided not to have kids, Sebastian wondered if that had been a mistake. Phil seemed so happy with his family. And he doted on his new baby girl, all dressed in pink with a teeny rubber band holding her teeny blonde top knot. But he and Kelly had entered into their relationship later in life – too late to consider starting a family.

His phone vibrated in his pocket – he had forgotten to turn on his ringer again. Without looking at the caller ID, he answered it.

"Hey, mister..." It was Kelly. She spoke so softly. But even whispering, her voice sounded like an angel's.

"Hi, Love." He listened to her breathing.

"I received an open-ended medical leave." Her voice was shaky. "Mr. Jorgenson was so good. All he said was to keep him in touch with... with me."

Sebastian had met Mr. Jorgenson at several school functions. He was also a family man – no doubt he understood life's detours.

"I'm leaving school early, Seb. I'll be home by noon."

"I'm sorry I can't be there with you. Are you going to call your mom?"

"Yup, and Brie."

Sebastian laughed. "You had better call Gabriella. If she finds out you didn't let her know about your surgery, she'll kick your ass."

Kelly laughed, but not her usual happy laugh – more like a mournful laugh. "She could do it, too."

"Tell your mom I'll cover her plane ticket. Understand?" He could hear his wife breathing into the phone. He wished her sweet breath could be on his face right now.

"Yes, sir..."

"That's better. Phil is joining me for my dinner meeting. He'll wrap things up so I won't have to stay. I'm hoping to be home by 7:00 at the latest."

"Bring me a sub sandwich?"

If she was talking about food, she was feeling better. "Tuna. With Provolone. And chips?"

"You know me so well, Seb."

"I love you, Kelly." Except for her soft breathing into the phone he heard only silence.

Then she spoke. "Seb?"

"Yes Love?"

"I hope you get this guy."

He sensed her smile – he knew her so well. "Thanks, Love."

He checked the time. "Phil, let's get our shit together for this meeting! Sam won't know what hit him!"

Before she called her mom, Kelly took a Corona out of the refrigerator and walked out onto the deck. She sat on the bench swing – she loved this swing. She and Sebastian were at the Home Depot when she saw it and asked him if he'd buy it for her. He said he didn't know if it would fit in with everything else on the deck and didn't seem interested in discussing it. They left without buying it, but the next morning when she walked out on the deck, she saw the swing – the same swing with the green and white striped awning. Without her knowledge, Sebastian had called Roger and Cody and asked them to pick up the swing from the store and deliver it to his home. They set it up after Kelly had gone to bed.

She loved Sebastian so much and knew he wouldn't deny her anything. This swing would always remind her of his kind heart. She took a couple long drinks of the cold brew, then called her mom. It only rang once.

"Hi, Kelly! What's up with my girl?"

She blurted out her news. "Mama, I think I have breast cancer." Oh, the silence on the phone could have swallowed a truck. When her mother finally spoke, her voice was so calm, so soothing, so her mom.

"Honey, you've been to the doctor?" She wanted information. Kelly hated playing twenty questions and she wasn't about to let her mom do that now.

"I saw my nurse practitioner. They did an ultrasound and found a tumor."

"Are they going to do a lumpectomy, honey?" Shit, that should have been her next sentence. Her mom was good.

"Yes. Tomorrow. In the morning, I think." Kelly knew her mom was not going to be happy. She'd have no time to get here in time for the surgery.

"I'm coming. I can book a flight this evening."

"You don't have to come here, Mama. Seb will be with me. It's an outpatient procedure and we won't even have the results right away and..."

"Are you kidding me? I'm coming. Done!" Whenever her mom said *done*, she knew not to argue.

"Mama, Sebastian said he'd cover your ticket."

"You tell that man of yours not to worry about me." Kelly heard her mom clicking the keys on her laptop. "Let's see... I can get a flight out of Grand Junction within an hour, leave Denver later this evening and be in town early tomorrow morning. Do me a favor – make a reservation at that hotel I stayed at for your wedding. That was nice."

"Mama, you can stay here."

"Oh, bull, Kelly. Sebastian does not need his mother-in-law underfoot while he's taking care of his wife." Her mom never swore, and 'bull' was as close to the F-bomb as her mom would ever say.

"Now you text me with the information where the surgery will be. Do you know the time yet?"

"No, my doctor is calling me this afternoon. I'll know then and I'll text you right away. Promise."

"I love you, Kelly! You tell that man to wrap you in his strong arms and take care of my girl."

"Thanks, Mama. Love you, too." And she hung up.

And no tears. She took another long swig of her beer. Now Gabriella. But instead of calling, Kelly texted her.

> *K. Bonsignore*: Brie. I may have breast cancer. They're doing a lumpectomy tomorrow. Seb and my mom will be here. Just wanted you to know. Love, Kelly.

That's done. She looked at the time. Sebastian should be preparing for his dinner meeting about now. This had been a long day. She decided to take a long, hot shower and go to bed.

She listened to Neil Young on her iPod while reading *Song of Myself*, one of her favorite Whitman poems. She must have dozed because the sounds of creaking stairs woke her. Kelly smiled, knowing he'd be with her momentarily.

He entered the room and took off his suit coat and tie. She looked up at him.

"Come here, please... I want you..."

Sebastian stood at her side of the bed, leaned over and kissed her mouth, his hand supporting his body on the headboard. Kelly pulled at the leather tie-back, letting his long hair fall across his face. She held his head in her hands, pushing her tongue deep into his mouth.

He quickly stripped and crawled onto the bed, holding his muscular body over her. Sebastian kissed her, his tongue following the outline of her lips. He caressed her breasts, his tongue softly licking her nipples. He looked at her – his wife, his Dulcinea. How he loved this woman, how he would do anything for her, to take these next few days from her. To take away the pain she was about to endure, the loss she would feel.

He slipped into her and just held still. Her knees were locked at his sides, her hands on his biceps. He kissed her, making love with his tongue as he made love with his body.

"What do you want, Love?" Sebastian searched her emerald eyes brimming with tears.

"Just love me... Please love me." And she began crying, crying so hard. And he did as she wanted and thrust into her, pushing into her, deeper, more of him, more of his love. He came hard into her, but she didn't achieve orgasm.

Sebastian rolled over, pulling her with him and lay on his back. Her head rested on his shoulder. Her tears had stopped but her heart still pounded in her chest. He held her tight, his strong arms enveloping her – not letting her go.

He felt her smile on his neck. Kelly raised her head and looked into his face, the face of the man she loved more than life itself. She kissed him.

"Did you bring my sub?"

Sebastian laughed. If she was hungry, she was okay. "Yes, it's downstairs."

Neil Young sang about a death down by the river...

19

Family

Ruth's flight from Denver had arrived earlier that morning. After resting only a few hours, she went to the Boardwalk Surgical Plaza.

She entered her daughter's room and witnessed the love between husband and wife. Sebastian sat on his wife's bed, holding her hands, stroking her arms, talking in whispers. Kelly wore a hair net covering her auburn curls. He brushed a tear from his wife's eye – she pushed her head against her husband's hand. Ruth softly knocked on the door. Sebastian looked up.

"Come in, Ruth." He leaned down and kissed Kelly's lips. "I'll let you and your mom have some time." Sebastian kissed his wife again, then got up and pulled a chair close to the bed for Ruth.

"Thank you, Sebastian." She kissed his cheek, feeling his tears. Ruth sat near her daughter's bed.

"Mama, they might take my breast. I'm scared." And Kelly's tears started anew. Ruth put her hand on her daughter's face and tucked a stray curl back under the hair net.

"What's your greatest fear, my girl? What are you afraid of?" She kept lightly rubbing her only daughter's arm.

"I don't know. I guess it's the thought of having cancer and a piece of me getting cut off... you know?"

"Would it be different if it was your eyes?"

"What?" Kelly looked hard at her mom. "I don't understand."

"Honey, you still have the most important things that God gave you – your ability to see, hear, taste, listen and smell." Ruth paused, making sure Kelly was listening closely. "You can still see the glories of God, the colors of His world. You can still hear the songs of the birds, the sounds of the waves crashing on the rocks. You can still smell the morning air after a cleansing night rain and the scent of your favorite stargazer lilies. And you can still taste a fine wine – and chocolate!"

"Chocolate?" Kelly smiled at her mom, who knew better than anyone how to put things into perspective. "Guess my boob is kind of inconsequential?"

"Oh it's definitely a part of you, my girl. But your breast does not define you. Your soul, your heart – the people you love and whom you have chosen to share in your life, those are the important things, those are what define you – not your breast."

"Thank you, Mama."

Ruth rose from her chair and kissed her daughter's face. "I'll get Sebastian. I'm sure he's anxious to see you before you go in for your surgery." When she turned, he was standing at the door. She walked over to her son-in-law and hugged him. "She's ready."

He returned to his wife's bedside and softly caressed her face – the face of the woman whom he loved more than life itself. Dr. Elliot came into the room and addressed the couple.

"I've looked at the films again. This tumor is quite large. I'm going to check the lymph nodes, Kelly. If the lymph is involved, a mastectomy unfortunately will be needed. I just want you to be prepared."

"I want my wife."

"With all due respect Sebastian, I want to hear it from both of you that you've thought about the consequences of a mastectomy."

Kelly whispered, *"I have... I know."*

"If however there are no lymph nodes involved, I will only perform a lumpectomy. If that's the case, I'll still be taking quite a bit of muscle from that side of your breast." Now he looked at both Kelly and her husband. "There will be a definite disturbance to the shape of the breast."

Dr. Elliot brought up the subject of reconstructive surgery. Kelly shook her head no.

Sebastian agreed with Kelly. "If it's all the same to you, I'd prefer you save my wife's life."

Kelly squeezed his hand and looked at the doctor. "I think I'd like my life saved, too. My breast can't smell roses."

Sebastian gave her a crooked smiled, leaned over and kissed her lips.

"I'm going to have my nurse give you something to relax, Kelly." Turning to Sebastian, Dr. Elliot added, "I'll let you know as soon as I get in there."

Without taking his eyes off his wife Sebastian thanked the doctor.

The nurse came in and injected a drug into Kelly's IV. "This should take effect immediately, Mrs. Bonsignore." The nurse capped the syringe and left the room.

"Thank you, Seb." The relaxing drug had already taken effect – she was fighting it.

"Thank you for what?" Sebastian held her hand. He leaned in to hear her fading words.

"Agreeing with me... about the recon... you know..."

"I love you more than just your breasts." He kissed her mouth. She attempted a pucker, but that didn't happen either.

"So glad..." Her eyes closed, but she kept her hand clasped in his, not wanting to let go – and he not wanting to leave his wife. How could one woman upset his neatly organized life so much? What if he had decided not to go to the pub when Roger called? What if he had never seen her eyes, her beautiful emerald eyes? What if...

Dr. Elliot and two orderlies came into the room. "Mr. Bonsignore, we're going to take Kelly now." Dr. Elliot put his hand on Sebastian's shoulder. "We'll take good care of her."

He leaned down one more time and kissed her lips, wishing he could wave a magic wand and be transported back to their cabin...

> *Walking down the dirt road... The thick growth of tall old sugar maples bordered the length of the road, the fingers of the uppermost branches intertwining, creating a natural arbor. In autumn, the leaves which erupted in brilliant shades of rust, crimson and gold, piled up knee deep along the roadside. He loved watching her run ahead, kicking the leaves into the air as a child would. She came alive in the fall...*

"Sebastian?"

He stood and watched as the orderlies wheeled Kelly's bed out of the room. He turned to Dr. Elliot. "She's my life..."

The surgeon put his hand on Sebastian's shoulder. "I'll let you know within the hour."

"Thank you." Sebastian stood alone in the room, not knowing what to do. He paced from the door to the window that overlooked a parking lot. Nothing. He felt so lost. He was a man with an agenda, a well-planned agenda, and this beautiful redhead upset his life to the point that he literally felt lost without her.

A nurse came into the room. "Mr. Bonsignore, we've set up a private reception room for you. I think there're some folks waiting to see you."

He figured it would be Phil and probably Roger too. But when he walked in the room he saw Raffaele and Gabriella.

"Oh My God! You're here! Why are you here?!" He reached for Raffaele and clung tightly to his big brother. Sebastian never cried, but now the tensions of the past 24 hours caught up with him and his tears streamed into his beard. Brie stood next to them and held Sebastian's hand. He loosened his hold and looked at his brother and again asked, "Why are you here?"

"Because you're my little brother and I love you."

Sebastian still couldn't believe his brother was here with him, supporting him. He turned his attention to Gabriella, who was extremely pregnant.

"And what's this?" He opened his arms to his sister-in-law, enfolding her in a hug and kissed her cheeks. "You really do look wonderful!"

"Thank you, Seb. I feel wonderful." Raffaele put his arm around his wife's shoulder.

"Does Kelly know?" Sebastian hadn't taken his eyes from her large belly.

"No, it was supposed to be a surprise." Brie looked at Raffaele. "We were planning on coming to see you both in a few days and..."

Raffaele finished his wife's sentence. "... and I think I'll be house hunting. We'd love to move here, close to you and Kelly. Raise our family here."

As awful as this day was, he was so happy to see his brother.

Ruth walked into the room. "Sebastian, were you surprised to see these two?" Then turning to Gabriella she asked how she was feeling.

Sebastian wished he could feel happier about their reunion, but he was so worried about Kelly. His thoughts were on the woman, that beautiful redhead, his wife who promised she would love him always and forever...

And he knew Raffe understood – how could he not understand? His first wife and their unborn child dying so tragically so many years ago – and now Gabriella, the woman who healed his heart was pregnant with their child. Of course his brother understood.

A soft knock on the door brought him out of his thoughts. Dr. Elliot came into the room. He approached Sebastian and asked if they could talk privately.

"This," Sebastian pointed to the people in the room. "This is my family and they are all here for Kelly. Say what you need to say." He sat in one of the upholstered chairs.

"Mr. Bonsignore, Kelly had positive lymph nodes." He sat in an adjoining chair. "I've already sent samples to the lab. But," he paused, looking down at his folded hands and then back at his patient's husband. "Her tumor was aggressive. I had to perform a mastectomy."

"How is my wife?"

"Actually, she's doing very well considering. She's strong, Sebastian. Her vitals are stable. She's in recovery. You can go in and see her in a few minutes. My nurse will let you know." Dr. Elliot stood and before leaving the room looked at the small gathering and smiled. "Kelly is obviously in good hands."

Ruth moved to the now empty chair. She sat and held her son-in-law's hands in her own. "I'm so sorry."

"Thank you." He looked kindly at his mother-in-law. "I'm so glad you decided to come." He looked at Raffaele. "And I'm so grateful that you and Brie are here."

"We wouldn't be anywhere else, little brother."

Dr. Elliot's nurse came into the room. "Excuse me... Mr. Bonsignore, you can see your wife now."

"You go ahead," urged Ruth. "We'll have plenty of time to see Kelly later."

Sebastian thanked his mother-in-law and kissed her on the cheek. He rose from the chair and followed the nurse. They walked down a short hallway and entered the recovery room.

"Dr. Elliot gave her some strong pain meds – your wife will be out until at least tomorrow morning. But sit here for as long as you'd like."

Sebastian pulled up a chair and sat by his wife's bedside. She had a large white bandage on her chest. She looked so peaceful. He slowly pulled the hair net off her head. He touched her leg and put his head on her hip – he felt her stir.

Sebastian raised his head and looked at her face. "Hi, baby..."

Her eyes barely opened – she must have heard him. Kelly mouthed *I love you.* He put his head back on her hip and stayed that way until the nurse came in.

"Mr. Bonsignore, go home, now." She urged him, her voice soothing. "Go home and rest. Get a good night's sleep and come back in the morning. She'll need you then."

Sebastian hesitated.

"Go on, now." She gave him a reassuring nurse smile.

He walked out of his wife's room, retraced his steps down the hallway and entered the private family room. Ruth saw him first and put her hand on Raffaele's arm. Now everyone looked at Sebastian.

"She's... ah... Kelly's going to sleep until morning." His eyes glistened. Ruth walked up to him and put her arms around him. He leaned over and enveloped his mother-in-law in his strong arms.

"Thank you for being here, Ruth. Thank you." While he hugged her, he looked at Raffaele.

Communication between siblings is powerful. And the look the brothers gave each other spoke volumes. Gabriella felt the energy and knew in her heart she would never share that bond. But then Raffaele looked at her and clasped her hands tighter, silently confirming his commitment to her, his wife, the mother of his child. She leaned forward and kissed her husband. Brie looked at Sebastian.

"Go and be with your brother. Ruth and I will be okay."

Ruth nodded, then turned back to Sebastian. "Go with your brother for the rest of the day. Gabriella and I will be fine."

Sebastian looked at Brie, not knowing what to say.

"Ruth and I can do some house hunting. The faster we move here the sooner I can be here to help Kelly."

Raffaele stood and helped Gabriella get to her feet. He lovingly kissed his wife and watched as she and Ruth walked out of the room together.

"Come on little brother. We're going to have a drink."

Sebastian stopped at the nurses' station, making sure the nurse had his cell number and would call him when Kelly came out of the anesthesia. After Sebastian turned to leave, Raffaele whispered to the nurse he was going to get his brother drunk.

The brothers walked out of the surgical plaza building into the late afternoon sun.

"Let's get a bite," Raffaele suggested to his brother. "Are you hungry?"

"I haven't had anything to eat at all today."

"Good. Harbor Pub it is. They have food, right?" They got into Raffaele's rental and drove down to the lake. After quickly finding a parking space, the brothers walked into the bar. Raffaele chose a table in the corner and they sat.

"Stay here." Raffaele got up and walked to the bar. As if in a clandestine operation, he spoke to the bartender in hushed tones. The bartender looked over at the table where Sebastian sat and nodded.

While waiting for his order, Raffaele looked back at his brother. Sebastian's elbows were on the table, his head in his hands. Raffaele had missed out on so much of his brother's life, traveling the world, barely keeping in touch. He had a lot of making up to do – but today he would help his little brother through this next critical part in his life. Sebastian would be at Kelly's side for the near future, no doubt putting his business affairs on hold. The least he could do was be there for his brother, for Kelly and hopefully he and Gabriella would find a house move-in ready.

The bartender returned with his order on a little round tray – four glasses of whiskey on the rocks, two of them doubles. Raffe had to keep his wits about him while he temporarily unburdened Sebastian of his pain. He carried the tray back to the table.

"Here we go little brother. Drink up." He put the doubles in front of Sebastian, then sat down and sipped from his glass. Sebastian took a long gulp and almost choked.

"What's this?"

"Jameson Irish Whiskey. Drink." Sebastian studied his brother and frowned, then took another drink. Raffaele sat silently. If his little brother wanted to talk, he would listen.

As Sebastian was nearing the bottom of his second glass, Raffaele flagged the bartender. He had asked that they not be bothered, but if he gave him a sign the bartender would personally serve them another round. And now four more drinks were put before the brothers. Raffaele had also requested that after the first round, all of his drinks be just water – only Sebastian would receive the whiskey. Tonight he would take care of his brother.

And Sebastian began talking. The table was far enough away from the speakers that the music wouldn't drown out their conversation. He talked about Kelly, how they met in this very bar. And her eyes – her emerald eyes...

"Man, she had eyes that could see right through me..." He looked at Raffaele, trying to focus on his brother. He shook his head and looked down at the table – but kept talking. "You know she wanted to have sex on our first date?" He took a long drink of his whiskey and looked hard in his brother's eyes. "Holy crap, Raffe... she was so... sexy, so... responsive... you know... she had an orgasm the first time I went down on her..."

Raffaele wasn't sure he should be listening to his brother's very intimate albeit drunken talk, but it certainly wasn't anything that different from his first night with Gabriella...

> *After the groom's dinner at Sebastian's house, Raffaele had followed Gabriella to her condo in his rental car. As she unlocked the front door, he reached under her car coat and touched her hips, caressing her*

figure from her waist to her thighs, sensually touching her body lightly with his fingertips. When she opened the door, he turned her around and holding her close, kissed her hard, pressing her body against his, her full breasts crushing into his chest.

"My God, Gabriella, you are going to be the death of me." Raffaele was breathing as if he had run a marathon.

"Raffaele, if you die right now I will kill you!" They laughed, cutting the intense sexual tension. She took off her coat and turned to him.

"Do you play?" She pointed to the white baby grand in the corner of her living room. Casually throwing his jacket over the arm of a chair, he walked over to her piano.

Brie went into the kitchen and opened her liquor cabinet. "Raffaele, would you join me in a brandy?"

As he sat at the piano bench, Raffe answered, "Yes please Gabriella... if you have one."

He pushed the bench further back from the piano, giving his long legs more room and lightly touched the highly polished ivory keys. He began playing a Rachmaninoff adagio, a piece he knew well.

Brie walked over to the piano carrying the large brandy snifters. She placed one in front of the open top board near the music rack and sat on the bench at his side. He stopped playing and picked up his brandy. They toasted each other, sipping the amber liquid.

"You are so beautiful, mia Gabriella."

"Thank you, Raffaele, but you can call me Brie."

"Non! I would never abbreviate such a beautiful name!" Holding his brandy in his left hand, he wrapped his right arm around her waist, pulling her close. He kissed her mouth, caressing her lips with his tongue. She moaned and lifted her head, exposing her neck to his lips. He kissed her neck, lightly licking her skin as he kissed her. His kisses traveled down to her breasts and, supporting her body leaned her back and put his face onto her heaving cleavage, kissing and licking her breasts.

"Gabriella, if you only knew how much I admire you... Your sensitivity, your beauty, and yes my darling, your breasts." Again he kissed her lips. "Bella Gabriella, we should practice the duet for the wedding – but before we do, I need to drown in your beauty..."

He took a deep breath, and looking into her eyes, confessed he wanted to put his mouth on her, to taste again her face, her breasts, her body... "Ti prego di dire di sì..."

Whispering, she answered him, "Si Dominicci, per favore!" He stood and, walking behind the piano bench, took her hand in his. He bowed low, kissed the back of her hand and turning it over kissed her palm, tenderly flicking his tongue across it.

"Where is your bedroom, mia bellissima Gabriella?"

She escorted him across the vast living room to her bedroom. "Let me freshen up. Sarò ma un minuto... Attendere per me!"

"Per sempre, bella Gabriella!"

While she was in the bathroom, he walked into her bedroom, closing the door behind him. He noticed her iPod on the tall dresser. Picking it up from the docking station, he scanned through her music and chose a Brahms' selection for piano. He put it on repeat and replaced the iPod back on the stand.

Brie could hear the music coming from her bedroom. Brahms, Opus 118. Oh, this man had good taste in romantic music – and he was definitely setting the mood.

She removed her blouse and bra and looked at her reflection in the mirror. Never had a man had such an effect on her. And when he kissed her... oh, when he kissed her he licked her skin. Shivers went through her body as she remembered the touch of his soft tongue on her mouth, her neck, her breasts...

Brie smoothed back her long hair, pulling it up in a temporary bun high on her head and securing it with two pins. Her hands followed her neck, down across her chest, fondling her own breasts. Soon he would lick and suck on her large areolas. Brie gently pressed her full breasts together, feeling her nipples harden as she touched them, exhaling at the mere thought of his tongue...

She removed her trousers and thong panties. As she slowly stood, she drew her hands up her legs and between her thighs – would he taste her? Bring her to orgasm with his mouth? It had been so many years since a man had bothered to give her pleasure. Pressing her fingers between her thighs she felt her body responding – craving the feel of his tongue on her.

She turned on the faucet and stepped into the shower, letting the steaming hot water cascade over her skin. Squeezing jasmine shower gel into the palms of her hands, she washed her body, feeling her skin as she hoped he would. Her fingers explored her body... pressing one finger into her... tasting herself on her finger. She wanted him to taste her...

Gabriella opened her bedroom door. Raffaele turned and put his hand on his chest and gasped. She was wrapped in a large lavender bath towel – just a towel. He walked to her, took her hand and led her to the bed. He leaned in and chastely kissed her mouth.

"Gabriella, this has been my dream. E il mio sogno si è avverato stasera."

He reached behind her and pulled out the pins that held her long brunette hair, allowing her thick tresses to flow down her back. Slowly he pulled the towel from her body, letting it fall at her feet. He took her hand and kissed it, kissed her arm, her shoulder, her neck and *again her lips. When he kissed her, he also licked her, tasting her freshly bathed skin.*

She put one hand over her breasts – he pulled her hand away, then backed up and considered the woman now standing before him in all her naked glory. Her cheeks were flushed, her large brown eyes glistened, her nipples hard – he knew she was sexually excited. A smile played on her full lips.

His eyes traveled down to her breasts, her very large round breasts. He had noticed her dark areolas through her flimsy blouse while at his brother's house and now he looked at them – naked and beautiful. His breath caught in his throat... remembering another woman...

With trembling hands, he touched her full breasts, following their shape from under her arms to her nipples, caressing them, adoring them.

Looking into her large brown eyes he leaned into her and kissed her lips again. "Gabriella," he spoke in low sensuous tones as he would an aria... "You have answered my every prayer."

Taking her face in his hands, he kissed her eyes, her lips... "My heart has been empty for so long. Until you my beautiful Gabriella, I was a man alone. My heart and my soul were so damaged..." He kissed her face again, combing his fingers through her hair, touching her shoulders, her arms – and again her full breasts. "Gabriella, if you only knew how you have healed my heart tonight."

"Raffaele," she looked up into his eyes, trying to fathom the sadness he felt. "I don't understand."

Tears welled in his eyes. "Just these past few hours with you have shown me there is hope for my tortured soul."

"You have endured a terrible loss?" She pressed her hands to his chest.

"Yes, a terrible loss... a tragic loss." He lowered his head. Gabriella placed her hands on his face, forcing him to look at her. And he spoke...

"Her name was Annalisa... Annalisa Katarina."

"Tell me about her. Please..."

"I had only known her for a brief time when I asked her to be my wife..."

"What happened? You don't have to tell me..."

"No. I want to. I need to so you will understand my grief."

"Tell me... I will listen..."

"I was touring. My beautiful Annalisa was at home. She was killed..."

"Oh my God, Raffaele..."

"A truck... struck her car..."

Brie touched the face of the man who was confessing his sorrow. "I am so sorry."

"My Annalisa... she was pregnant..."

"Oh my God... And the baby?"

"... died with her... my wife and my child..."

Gabriella held him close... Speaking softly into his ear, she made a promise. "Let me bring comfort to you tonight, let me... let my heart and my body bring you comfort tonight..."

With trembling hands, Gabriella again pressed her palms against his chest, feeling the beating of his heart. "Love me tonight, Dominicci... Let me love you..."

"Yes..." Raffaele exhaled loudly and closed his eyes. With trembling fingers Brie unbuttoned his shirt. When she came to the last button, she smoothed the shirt away from his chest and explored the thick black hair that covered his body, caressing his nipples...

He, too, began the gentle assault on her body. Raffe was enamored with her European naturalness and drew his fingers through her thick pubic growth. Reaching down between her legs, he pressed his fingertips on her – and heard a catch in her breathing. Again he kissed her mouth, licking her lips as he kissed them, sucking on her tongue...

On one knee, he knelt before her and kissed her inner thighs. Seizing her hips, he pushed his face deeper into the top of her thighs, licking her... lingering for minutes... inhaling her dark musk...

"Oh God, Dominicci, your tongue is so soft..." She closed her eyes, feeling light-headed and supported herself by holding his shoulders.

He stood and held her in his arms. "Bella Gabriella, my dreams have all come true tonight... You have brought solace to my soul... my heart... to my very existence.... May I make love with you?" And he kissed her deeply. Taking a step back, he guided her to the edge of her bed... "Please bella Gabriella, lay on your bed."

She never took her eyes from him as she eased her body up on the bed – lying across the mattress, putting her head on the large pillow.

He put one knee on the bed and, supporting himself with his arms, balanced his body over her without touching her. His face was above hers, so close he felt her breath on him. "Please Gabriella. Vorrei fare l'amore con lei."

"Si Dominicci. Voglio fare l'amore per me."

He stood and slowly pulled his shirt out of his trousers and off his shoulders. He unbuckled his belt and unzipped his pants, letting them fall to his feet.

Gabriella raised herself on one elbow. She was the silent observer to her own private strip show. The thick, soft, curly black hair that covered his chest and six-pack belly also covered his legs and forearms.

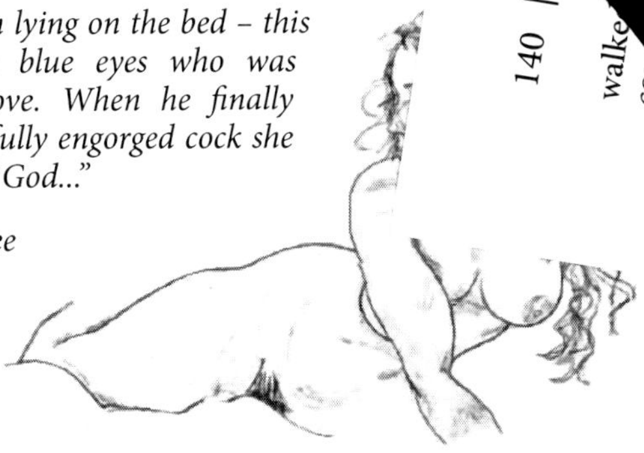

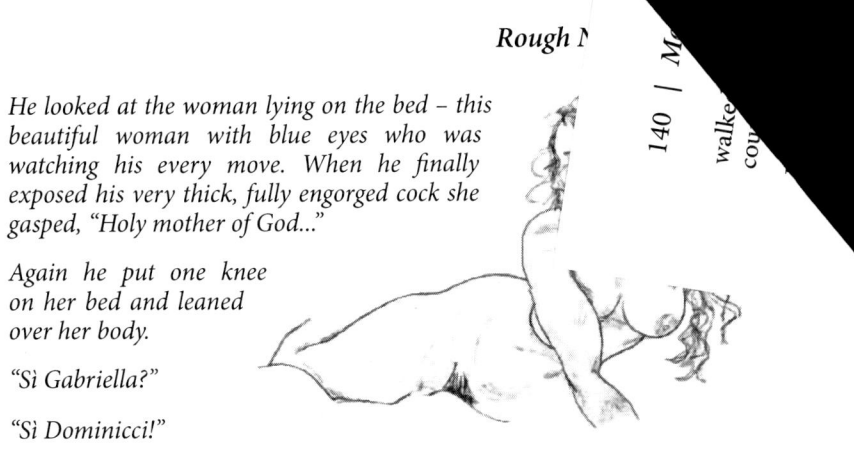

He looked at the woman lying on the bed – this beautiful woman with blue eyes who was watching his every move. When he finally exposed his very thick, fully engorged cock she gasped, "Holy mother of God..."

Again he put one knee on her bed and leaned over her body.

"Sì Gabriella?"

"Sì Dominicci!"

While the bartender delivered one more round of drinks, Raffaele asked for a large order of sweet potato waffle fries, enough to put something in his brother's stomach. He didn't want Sebastian to have to deal with a hangover in the morning, too.

Their order came quickly – Raffaele shook extra sea salt on the fries. Sebastian leaned with one arm on the table. After eating a few fries, he put his forehead on his arm. He repeated the movements – sit up, eat a few of the salty fries and rest his head on his arm. He asked Raffaele if the nurse had called.

"No Seb. Kelly is still resting. Let her rest. Tomorrow will be a big day for everyone."

"You're right." He slurred his words. "Cuz you're my big brother."

"I know." Raffaele put his hand on his brother's shoulder. He glanced at his watch. It was time to go. He left folded money as a tip and helped his brother to his feet. He was taller than Sebastian and let his brother lean on him. They exited the bar. As the cool fresh air hit Sebastian in the face he temporarily became aware of his surroundings and tried walking on his own, but in the opposite direction from where the car was parked. Raffaele commandeered his brother's body and guided him to his rental. Opening the rear passenger door, he poured Sebastian's frame into the back seat.

While he drove back to the house, he called his wife. "I'm staying with Seb tonight. Will you be okay?" Gabriella was only seven months pregnant. He was sure nothing would happen in the next twelve hours.

"I'm here with Ruth. She's staying with me in our room tonight." He could hear Ruth in the background. "Raffaele, I'm fine. Be with Sebastian... be with your brother."

Her voice was soothing to his ears. He loved his wife, and he loved that she wanted him to stay with his brother. "Gabriella, I love you. Thank you!"

"I know, Raffaele. I love you, too."

He walked down the long staircase with halting feet, his hand carefully holding the railing. The house was dark as he crossed the expanse of the dining room and pushed through the heavy swinging door. Sebastian stood in the kitchen – the room where Kelly had propositioned him so many years ago. He was unsteady as he d through his kitchen – his fingertips followed the edge of the black soapstone ntertop. It was too quiet...

Returning through the heavy swinging door he again entered the dining room, this time turning on the light. The antique chandelier lit up – too bright. It hurt his eyes. He fumbled for the dimmer switch...

Off in the corner of the living room, he noticed his floor lamp was on. He didn't remember turning it on – Kelly must have been sitting in his chair. He walked over to his chair. All his *New York Times* newspapers had been neatly folded. He turned off the light.

Sebastian found his way back upstairs to their bedroom. *Their bedroom*. For years, it had been his bedroom – he had shared it with no one. No other woman ever came into his bedroom. Only Kelly.

The bed wasn't made. When Raffaele had brought him to the bedroom, he had laid on his side of the bed. Now he walked around the bed and collapsed on her side. He put his head on her pillow – it smelled of her... her body, her scent...

"Seb?" Raffaele had heard him walking around the house. "Are you okay?" But he realized his brother was already sleeping. He waited in the bedroom for a few minutes, listening to his brother's shallow breathing before he returned to the futon bed down the hall.

20

Smelling the Coffee

Sebastian smelled coffee. He opened his eyes – where was Kelly?

Oh yes, surgery...

Oh yes, Raffe had taken him out last night...

Oh yes, he drank whiskey...

Oh yes, he got drunk...

Oh yes... coffee!

Raising his head off Kelly's pillow he saw his brother sitting on the edge of the bed holding a large stoneware mug.

"You got me drunk." He put his head back on her pillow.

"You needed it." Raffaele's voice was soft – soft like a lion tamer's soothing voice. Sebastian looked at his brother with wary eyes. He sat up and took the mug.

"Just coffee... right?" He sipped the black liquid. "Oh, this is strong." But still he drank.

Sebastian put the mug down and walked unsteadily to the en suite bathroom. When he came back into the bedroom he stood by the bed and touched Kelly's pillow – appearing as a helpless little boy who had lost his best friend.

"Seb – Ruth and Gabriella are with Kelly. Let's get breakfast. *Then* we'll go see your wife."

The brothers drove to the same restaurant where they ate the morning of the wedding. Upon entering the restaurant, they were quickly escorted to a booth. Raffaele asked for coffee immediately. The young waitress lingered at their table, obviously enchanted by the two handsome men who weren't looking back at her. She left and within a few moments brought their coffee and two menus.

Raffaele had already decided. "Pancakes and crisp bacon. And bring two tall bloody marys. Right away. Please."

Sebastian hadn't taken his eyes off his brother since they sat. "Are you retiring?"

"Yes. I'm just recording now. I'll play an occasional concert, but I won't be touring anymore." Raffaele sipped his coffee. "I guess I just needed a reason to settle down and when Gabriella told me she was pregnant I realized she – my family – was my reason."

"Was it a planned pregnancy?" Sebastian was going to get a vasectomy as soon as possible. And Raffaele's words concerned him.

"Yes... well, yes and no. I knew it wasn't good for Gabriella to be on birth control pills, so I got a vasectomy. But we didn't wait long enough after, you know, waiting until all the little swimmers were gone." He looked around, wondering where their bloody marys were.

"Were you happy? *Are* you happy?"

"Never happier." Raffaele smiled. "I think Gabriella was apprehensive about telling me, you know... But I couldn't have been happier." He took another drink of coffee, again looking over the high back of the booth for their drinks. He turned back to his brother. "She's my life Seb, you know? She's my second chance..."

Their drinks and food arrived simultaneously. Raffaele frowned at the waitress, but thanked her.

While Sebastian pushed at his bacon with his fingers, Raffaele took a large drink of the vodka-laced drink.

"Come on, Seb. Eat." Raffaele poured syrup on his pancakes. "You're going to need your strength today. And Gabriella and I are going house shopping." He ate the last of his bacon. "That reminds me – give me the name of your realtor."

Sebastian still hadn't touched his pancakes, but at least he ate his bacon. He pulled his cell phone out of his back pocket and scrolled through his contacts. "I'm forwarding her number. She's good. She'll find what you want." He put his phone down on the table and drank more of his bloody mary.

"Seb, you can't go see Kelly if you're hopped up on vodka."

He knew his big brother was right. Wasn't he always right? Sebastian smiled and cut into his pancakes, pouring copious amounts of syrup on the stack. He glanced at Raffaele, who was giving him his *that's a good boy* smile. Picking up his fork, he ate. Yes he was hungry.

Raffaele had cleaned his plate. While he watched his little brother eat, he called Gabriella.

"How's your friend?"

"She's good. Not a lot of pain right now. You know they had to cut through nerves."

"We're coming in a few minutes. We're having breakfast. *Grazie, Gabriella. Ti amo.*"

"*Lo ti amo troppo, Dominicci.*" He loved when she called him that name. He loved *her*.

Raffaele winked at his brother. "Come on. Let's go see Kelly." Sebastian pulled the celery stalk out of his brother's glass and ate it as they walked out of the restaurant.

While his brother drove to the surgery center, Raffaele relaxed against the headrest and remembered the night Gabriella told him she was pregnant.

Lately, Gabriella had been sleeping so much more. Even when his concerts were over early, Raffaele found her in their bed sound asleep.

On this night after his shower, he had crawled into bed with Gabriella. She always wore a silken nightgown. She was lying on her side. He lightly kissed her shoulder

– she rolled onto her back. He kissed her mouth, licking her lips as he kissed, then slowly pulled down her nightgown, exposing her beautiful breasts. But before he could drown in her full bosom she stopped him. He looked at her face. She had been crying.

"*Oh, mia cara Gabriella!* What is wrong? Why the tears?" Her face betrayed a story he did not yet know – and her eyes were so sad. "Please, *mia bellissima Gabriella*. Tell me so I can take away your pain."

"Raffaele..." She turned away from him and shed fresh tears. But he stopped her, pulling her back until she was again looking up at him.

"Raffaele... I'm pregnant..."

With those two little words, 'I'm pregnant' he was magically transported back almost twenty years to Bologna in Italy.

> *He had finished a successful run at the Teatro Comunale di Bologna, one of the finest and oldest opera theaters in the world. He and his wife Annalisa were returning home from dinner. They spoke of traveling to America.*
>
> *They had just settled into their bed. He pulled Annalisa close and began kissing her face, her lips, licking and kissing her neck, her full breasts. Holding her close he pressed his body against her breasts, but she pushed him away. With tears in her eyes she whispered that her breasts were tender – because she was almost two months pregnant.*
>
> *'I'm pregnant.' Those two little words changed his world and altered his place in the universe. Suddenly something in his life was greater than he and she – suddenly their life would include their child.*
>
> *That night they had made slow passionate love. He couldn't get his fill of his Annalisa. In the afterglow of their passion, he lay with his head on her belly, holding her close, kissing her belly.*
>
> *Before they could plan their trip to America, and while he was away touring in La Bohème, Annalisa had gone shopping with her girlfriends. On the way back from the shopping center a truck had crossed the center line and crashed head long into the women's car, splitting it in half – killing only his wife and their unborn child...*

It took him only seconds to process Gabriella's words – and time stood still. Was this a terrible nightmare that would repeat itself throughout his life? Or were the words *'I'm pregnant'* on some cosmic plane be a chance for redemption – redemption for his heart, his soul, his world.

She was his second chance at love – Gabriella had opened his wounded heart and healed the jagged scar. Silently he prayed to Annalisa and their unborn child – forgiveness for finally putting their memory to rest and strength to welcome his future.

And her tears flowed. Making fists, Gabriella covered her eyes. He kissed her lips and drew back the sheet. Pulling up her satin nightgown, he placed his hand on her naked belly.

"*Bella Gabriella* – you have made me so happy!" Raffaele leaned down and kissed her belly, then pulled her body close to him.

"You aren't mad..." Her voice was steadier now.

He looked into her brown eyes glistening with tears. "*Ti amo, mia bellissima Gabriella!* How could I ever be mad at you? I love you!" He kissed her face. "You please me every day."

She returned his kiss and looked lovingly into his eyes. "We are going to have a baby..."

"*Si, bella Gabriella!* We are going to have a baby!" He caressed her belly again and kissed her beautiful face – kissed the mother of his child.

Kelly woke to her favorite smell in the morning. Coffee! She smiled but felt as if a ton of bricks pressed on her chest. Her right hand wouldn't move – it had an IV in it. Ouch. She moved her left hand. It worked. Good. Her chest was wrapped tight, but she felt no pain – just an awful pressure. She closed her eyes and enjoyed the smell of freshly brewed coffee.

"Good morning, my girl."

Oh, her mom's voice! Her mom's sweet voice! Kelly turned her head and looked at the woman sitting at her bedside – the person holding the coffee! Coffee!

Kelly tried sitting up. That hurt. She felt the head of her bed slowly rise. What a relief. Now she could see everything. The nurse who made the bed move talked to her. She held a chart with faces – smiling faces, angry faces, crying faces.

"Mrs. Bonsignore, how's the pain?" The nurse pointed to the chart.

"No pain... Just, um, pressure."

"Good. Dr. Elliot will be in here shortly." The nurse put the chart down and walked out of the room.

Feeling frustrated, Kelly again looked at her mom. "Mama?"

"Honey, the breast is gone." Ruth waited for her daughter's reaction before she went on.

Kelly pulled at her hospital gown, but the ties at the back held tight. She rubbed her chest with her left hand, feeling the thick bandages under the thin cloth. She closed her eyes as she spoke to her mom. "Um... I can still see God's glorious colors... and smell the lilies... That's something, right?"

"That's something." And Ruth smiled.

Kelly sat quietly for a few minutes, collecting her thoughts. "Where's Sebastian?"

"He's having breakfast with Raffaele."

"With who?" Kelly was confused – until she looked up and saw Gabriella in the doorway.

"He's having breakfast with my husband." Brie walked in and stood at her bedside. "Hi, Kell."

Ruth kissed her daughter's forehead and let Gabriella take her chair.

"You're here! You're really here! Why are you here?"

Gabriella laughed. "That's the same thing Sebastian said when he saw his brother yesterday."

"Yesterday? You've been here since yesterday? You and Raffe?" Kelly's thoughts were all over the place. She tried getting her head around the fact that her best friend wasn't in Europe but was sitting right here by her side.

"You've been out of it, girl." Brie stood. "Your mom brought you coffee." From behind her, Ruth moved the rolling tray over to the bed.

"Can you reach your cup, honey?" Ruth turned the cup so the handle faced Kelly.

"Yeah, that's better. Thank you." But as she tried picking up the heavy mug with her left hand, she winced in pain. "Shit! Fuck!" Remembering her mom was in the room and, in spite of her newfound pain, she laughed. Brie picked up the mug and held it to her friend's lips. The coffee was hot – Kelly took a breathing sip. Satisfied, she put her head back on her pillow.

"Raffe took your husband out for breakfast. They'll be back shortly."

Now Kelly really looked at her friend. "Brie, are you pregnant?"

Brie backed up a step and showed off her super-sized belly. "Surprise!"

"Oh, wow! You're really pregnant!"

"Seven months."

"When were you going to tell me?"

"Actually, we had planned coming here in a few weeks anyway." She held the cup again for her friend. Kelly took another large sip.

"You know I'm going to start crying..." And her tears began. Brie joined in with her own tears – Kelly crying out of happiness for her best friend and Brie out of sadness for her best friend.

Kelly looked up and saw Sebastian – her Ulysses – standing in the doorway. Now her tears came in sheets.

In a heartbeat he was by her side. He gingerly put his hand behind her neck, leaned in and kissed her lips – her lips wet and salty from her tears. He whispered, *"My Love..."*

She tried lifting her left hand but failed. Her chest muscles ached whenever she moved that arm. So she just leaned her head into his and let him comfort her.

Raffaele appeared and seeing Gabriella, walked directly to her. He looked passionately into his wife's eyes and stroked her full baby bump. Brie asked if he and his brother had breakfast.

"We did. I got him to eat all his pancakes."

Gabriella looked hopefully at her husband. "I could eat some pancakes."

Raffaele hugged his wife around her shoulders. "Didn't you and Ruth already have breakfast?" He looked quizzically over at Ruth who nodded yes.

"Always hungry," and kissed his wife's lips. "Let's go eat and leave these folks alone." But before they left the room, Raffe walked over to his brother and touching his shoulder, signified he wanted to speak to his sister-in-law.

"Be well, my dear Kelly. You have so many people supporting you." He looked back at Brie, and again turning to his sister-in-law, added, "You introduced me to my wife and for that I am eternally grateful." Tears filled his eyes as he kissed her cheek.

"Kell," Brie stood behind Raffaele. "We'll be back – after you've seen the doctor." They left the room together.

"Seb, would you give me more coffee?" He moved back to his wife's bedside and held the mug for her. She took bigger sips of the cooler coffee. He kissed her forehead.

She gave him a look. "You slept in your clothes!" Kelly carefully lifted her left arm and tugged at his wrinkled shirt sleeve. "As I recall, I met you like this."

"Lucky me." He kissed her again. A knock on the door drew his attention.

Dr. Elliot entered the room. "How are you, Mr. Bonsignore?"

"I've been better, thank you."

The doctor addressed Kelly. "Alex my nurse tells me you don't have pain, just pressure. Is that still the case?"

"Yes, I think. And I can't raise my left arm." She tried raising it, but just as quickly put it down.

"That will come in a few days. Don't worry." He put his clipboard on the tray table. "You know we performed a mastectomy on your left breast."

"Yes, my mom told me." Kelly looked at her husband, who hadn't taken his eyes off her.

Dr. Elliot continued. "You had a positive lymph node in your armpit. I took what is called a sentinel node plus a few of the surrounding nodes. The one node was cancerous, but the others were clean I'm happy to say."

"What about chemotherapy?"

"I'm having our oncologist Dr. Janice Kusch talk with you, Kelly. She'll go over all the results regarding your positive lymph node findings and discuss if chemo is warranted. She should be here early this afternoon."

"When can I bring my wife home?" Sebastian moved closer to the bed. "When can she be discharged?"

Dr. Elliot picked up his clipboard. "Kelly, if there are no complications, you can go home tomorrow morning." He turned to Sebastian. "Will there be someone at home with your wife?"

From behind, Ruth spoke up. "Sebastian, I can be there for her. While you're at work, I'll stay with my daughter."

"I don't have to work." He was again trying to figure out how he was going to juggle all these new responsibilities in his life.

"You have to work!" Kelly made her words light. "You have to support me in the manner to which I have become accustomed!"

Sebastian winked at Kelly. "I guess I have my orders."

"Mr. Bonsignore, unless you have more questions I'll leave you alone." Looking at Kelly, Dr. Elliot added, "I'll have your pain meds and breakfast brought in shortly." He excused himself and left the room.

While holding his wife's hand, Sebastian spoke to his mother-in-law. "Ruth, I'll get the guest room prepared for you. We'll help you move out of the hotel this evening..." He paused, gathering his thoughts. "Would you stay for a few minutes? I'll be right back."

He left the room, peered down the hallway and spotted Dr. Elliot at the nurses' station. Sebastian quickly walked up to him.

"Excuse me. Dr. Elliot, may I have a word?"

"Yes of course..."

"I don't know if Kelly's cancer was caused by her birth control pills but I want her off them immediately."

"That's a good observation, Sebastian. She should refrain from taking her birth control tablets while she's on chemo." He paused and consulted his clipboard. "How can I help you?"

"I want to get a vasectomy. Can you recommend a urologist? This might be a good time to get the surgery done, you know... while we're... you know."

"Yes. There's a fine urologist on staff here. I'll contact him and have him get ahold of you today. Can he call you on your cell phone?"

"Yes. Thank you!"

"Mr. Bonsignore, are you sure? Why now? It can't just be because you want your wife to quit her birth control."

"We've talked about it. We're both almost in our 40's and we're not having kids."

"If you're sure..."

"We're sure. Thank you."

When Ruth saw her son-in-law enter the room, she picked up her purse. "I helped Kelly take her meds. I'll let you two have some alone time." She leaned close to her daughter and kissed her cheek. "See you in a few hours, my girl."

After Ruth left the room, Sebastian asked Kelly if she needed anything.

"Help me eat my breakfast. All I want is the poached egg, some toast and juice."

And he did as she asked. He cut into the egg, dipped a corner of toast into the gooey yolk and carefully – and lovingly – fed his wife. When she had eaten all she wanted, he held the glass of orange juice to her mouth.

A nurse's aide entered the room. Sebastian asked the young man to lower the head of Kelly's bed and take away her breakfast tray.

"Did you have enough to eat?" Sebastian took a napkin and wiped his wife's mouth. "Can I do anything else for you?" He pushed the tray table toward the foot of her bed and rearranged her sheet and blanket, making her as comfortable as possible.

"One thing... Tell me about your dinner meeting."

Sebastian sat next to his wife's bed, uncharacteristically eager to share the confidential proceedings of the meeting. "... and it turned out that Phil and Sam Jeffries were in the same unit in the army. Phil just didn't recognize the name. The funny thing, Phil was supposed to ride shotgun, but as soon as he and Sam realized they served together, I sat back and let Phil run the meeting. He was fantastic! And we have a new account!"

He looked over at Kelly who was obviously enchanted with his story – she was sound asleep. Sebastian sat more comfortably in the large chair and dozed.

21

Dr. English

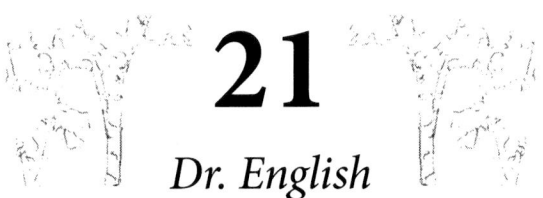

His cell phone vibrated. Sebastian looked at the caller ID, but didn't recognize the number. Phil was taking all his calls today. He almost declined the call but his curiosity got the best of him. "Hello?"

"Mr. Bonsignore, this is Matt English. Dr. Elliot gave me your number."

"You're the urologist!" Not wanting to disturb his wife, he rose from the chair and walked out in the hallway.

"Yes. Dr. Elliot said you wanted a vasectomy?"

"Yes, as soon as possible. My wife..."

"I'm aware of the situation, Mr Bonsignore. If you want, I can get you in at the end of the day today."

"Thank you. What do I need to do before I come in?"

"I suggest you shower and bring a jock strap with you. Do you have someone who can drive you home? And who is your regular physician?"

"Um, I don't have one."

"In that case, I'll have you come in early. My office is on the third floor in the south wing. Mr. Bonsignore, are you currently taking aspirin or ibuprofen?"

"No, no I'm not. How long will the appointment take?"

"Including getting your medical history, the prep and the actual surgery – probably less than two hours. Could you come in around three this afternoon?"

"I think so. Can I make a call and get right back to you?"

"Certainly. When you call back you'll get Carolyn, my assistant. I'll let her know you'll be calling and she'll take care of everything. Good luck to you, Mr. Bonsignore."

Before calling his brother, he checked the time and thought of all that had to be accomplished in only a few short hours – including transferring Ruth's things from the hotel to his home. But the guest room hadn't been prepared... Sebastian quickly punched a number in his cell phone.

"Roger here."

"Roger – Seb."

"How's our girl?"

"She's good." He knew Roger felt a sincere devotion to Kelly. "She's coming home tomorrow."

"No kidding! That soon?"

"Yes, and I need you and Cody and hopefully Tom, too."

"Name it."

Anything he needed, Roger would come through big time. Sebastian reviewed what had to be done – get rid of the futon bed and desk from his office and make it into a nice guest room for Kelly's mom. And schlep over Ruth's belongings from the hotel.

"That's it?"

Sebastian had to smile. Ever since their first adventure cleaning up and renovating the cabin, he knew he could count on his friends.

"Can you come to the surgery center and pick up my duplicate house key? I'll have you make copies."

"Yup. I'll get Cody and Tom together – probably Michael, too – and get that room fixed up. And we'll move your mother-in-law's things. Don't worry, Seb."

"Roger..."

"Hey, take care of our girl."

Sebastian punched the call-back number for Dr. English. The phone rang only once before Carolyn answered. She had a lovely voice. Maybe he could steal her away from the good doctor and hire her as their office receptionist.

"This is Sebastian Bonsignore."

"Yes, Mr. Bonsignore. I've been expecting your call. Are you able to come at three?"

"I can. I had to get some things in order. My wife had surgery yesterday and..."

"No worries. Dr. English said there were extenuating circumstances. And Mr. Bonsignore," Carolyn added in her very professional manner. "After the procedure, I'm giving you the names of several GPs. You need to get established with a doctor."

Sebastian silently snickered. *They're ganging up on me.* "Thank you... I'll be there at three."

He put his phone in his pocket as he walked back into his wife's room. Kelly was awake.

"Who was that?"

"My doctor."

"You don't have a doctor." She yawned. Oh, how she wished she could stretch.

"My urologist. I'm getting a vasectomy this afternoon."

"Really? Are you sure?" She tried sitting up in bed, but thought better of it.

"I thought we talked about this." He sat on the edge of her bed.

"But," now she really tried sitting up. "What if I'm not here... something happens to me... and you meet someone and..."

"You did *NOT* just say that!" He stood. He was angry, a feeling he had never felt toward Kelly.

"I'm sorry..." She had never seen him look that way at her – except of course that awful morning in their kitchen.

Leaning over her, he put his finger under her chin and brought her face up to look at him. Though still frowning, he softly kissed her lips. "Without you woman, I will die a miserable, lonely death."

She looked up into his hazel eyes and whispered, *"Promise?"*

He kissed her again – thankfully his eyes had lost their anger. Sebastian glanced at his watch. "As soon as Raffe and Brie get back, I'll have to leave. I have to shower and get my jock strap."

"You don't own a jock strap." She knew him so well.

"I also have to buy bags of ice." He made a mental list of what he needed.

"Frozen peas."

He lost his concentration. "What?"

"Frozen peas. They stay frozen longer than ice in a bag."

"Really?"

"Really. Now kiss me!" And he did as he was told.

Kelly had finished eating her lunch and was napping. While he waited for Ruth, Sebastian called Raffe, asking for a ride home after his surgery. Hopefully he and Brie wouldn't lose too much time in their quest for the perfect house.

As he finished the conversation with his brother, Ruth came into the room. He brought her up-to-date on his impending procedure. "And Roger is coming to pick up this key." He took the spare key off the fob. "Could you give it to him?"

"Of course." Ruth put the key in her sweater pocket. "But... are you sure about the surgery?" She put her hand on his arm, much as she would with a parishioner she might give counsel to in her church. Sebastian understood her concern.

"Kelly and I had discussed having kids and we're both in agreement. I want her off birth control pills. I don't know if that's what caused her cancer, but I'm not taking any more chances with her health."

Ruth put her hand on his bearded face. "So, you're saving my daughter's life – again."

Sebastian enfolded his mother-in-law in his strong arms. Then bidding her goodbye, left his wife's room.

Raffaele arrived at the doctor's office at 4:30. Sebastian was waiting in the recovery room – an ice pack on his crotch.

"You okay, little brother?"

"No... Yes. At least it's done."

Raffaele sat on a chair next to his brother. "What made you decide to get snipped?"

"I wanted her off birth control. Kelly and I figured we were too old to begin a family." He then remembered that his older brother was about to be a father. "Raffe, I'm sorry..."

"Look, this baby wasn't planned," Raffaele offered. "But I love Gabriella. After my beautiful Annalisa and our child died..."

Sebastian hadn't heard him speak of his late wife since her untimely death. He remained silent while his brother composed his emotions.

"I have met some stunning women in my line of work, many of whom would have gladly opened their legs to me and bore me many children." Raffe played with his expensive watch. "But when I met Gabriella, I knew my life would never be the same. She was and is everything I have ever wanted in a woman, in a wife since my Annalisa died – and now as the mother of my child."

"You fell in love with her at my house..." Sebastian picked at his melting ice bag, rearranging it to gain more ice over his bruised balls.

"When we made love," Raffaele looked up from his watch. "When we made love I knew we would never be apart. And we haven't. Like you and Kelly, when she's not in my line of sight, I don't feel complete."

Dr. English entered the room where the brothers sat. "How are you feeling, Mr. Bonsignore?"

"Sore..."

"You'll be sore for at least a day. No physical activity of any kind. Sit and rest. Let yourself heal."

He assured the doctor that he would not be doing anything or going anywhere for that matter. "Dr. English, please excuse my manners. May I introduce my brother Raffaele?"

Raffe stood and shook the doctor's hand. Dr. English scrutinized his face.

"Oh, my goodness! Dominicci! It is an honor to meet you! My wife and I have attended many of your performances."

"Thank you, Dr. But I've retired to the recording studio. My wife and I are moving here to be closer to my family, my brother."

"I do hope you'll be happy here." Now the doctor turned back to his patient. "Carolyn has given you several names of physicians?"

"Yes, thank you."

"Take my advice. Establish yourself with a doctor." And then addressing Raffaele too, he continued. "These are good physicians. Both of you need to make sure you are fit, for yourselves and for your wives. I've seen my share of men who never see a doctor – or see one too late."

Dr. English shook Sebastian's hand, then again Raffaele's hand and exited the room. Raffaele helped his brother stand.

Carolyn came into the room. "Mr. Bonsignore, here's a prescription if you need it. I've already called it in. It should be ready when you get to the pharmacy."

Raffaele took the paper and thanked her. As she walked out, Raffaele commented on what a nice voice she had.

"Yeah, I agree," Sebastian breathed, trying to stand straight. "I'm thinking of hiring her as our receptionist."

After picking up the prescription, the brothers returned to the surgical center. Together they slowly walked down the hall to Kelly's room.

When she saw him walking slightly bent over, she couldn't help razzing him. "Oh, my poor man!"

Sebastian gave her a sardonic scowl and quickly sat by her bedside.

"You want one of your meds?" Sebastian nodded. Raffaele opened the prescription bottle, shook out a pill and poured water into a cup.

"Thanks..." He swallowed the pill.

Raffe stepped closer to her bed. "Kelly, where's Gabriella?"

"She'll be right back. She went to talk to the nurses about finding an obstetrician."

Raffaele left the room in search of his wife.

Sebastian caressed his wife's hand. "I'm going home, but I needed to see your pretty face first."

"I love you, Seb."

With tears in his eyes, he looked lovingly at his wife. "I love you, too."

"Go home. I need to rest and you need to be there for me!"

Raffaele and Brie returned to the room. "Okay little brother. Let's get you home. We're stopping at the grocery store?" He helped his brother stand.

Sebastian leaned over his wife's bed and kissed her lips. "I'll see you in the morning, Love." He and Raffaele slowly left the room.

Kelly waited until her husband was out of earshot before she started crying. Brie sat in the chair next to her and held her best friend's hand.

Upon arriving home, they saw Roger's pickup truck and a small moving van parked in the driveway. Raffaele pulled up and raised a questioning eyebrow.

"I asked my friends to fix up the guest bedroom for Ruth. I've been using it as an office, but with Kelly and her recovery I figured Ruth would be more comfortable in a room down the hall from our bedroom." Sebastian opened his car door.

"Wait." Raffaele walked around the car and holding out his arm helped his brother stand. They slowly walked up the front steps.

Tom exited the house as Raffaele opened the door. "Hey Seb! How's Kelly?"

"She's good. She's coming home tomorrow."

"That's what Roger said. Excuse me." And he hurried down the steps to the van.

"Are you hungry, Seb?"

"Yeah, I thought I'd order a pizza. What about you and Brie?"

"I'll have some pizza with you. Gabriella and Ruth will eat dinner with Kelly. I'll pick them up later and bring Ruth back to your house."

Raffaele unpacked the grocery bag. "Frozen peas? You on a health kick little brother?"

"No. Kelly said they stay frozen longer than ice." Raffaele dutifully stashed the small bags into the freezer.

Sebastian's friends had transformed the guestroom from his home office to a beautiful, comfortable bedroom suite. He looked in the room, but couldn't believe what he saw.

"It's beautiful! But how did you do it? And when did you have time to paint the walls?"

Roger affectionately draped his arm around Sebastian's shoulder. "Connections, my friend."

He was so pleasantly in awe at what his friends did for him – again. He looked over at Raffaele. "I should probably lie down now."

Raffe escorted his brother into his bedroom. Sebastian stopped him. "I want to be on Kelly's side – please."

Raffe did as he requested, slowly helping his little brother sit. He picked up his brother's feet and swung his legs effortlessly onto the bed. "Good?"

"Yeah, I'm good. Thank you."

"I'll get you a fresh bag of peas." Raffe left the bedroom and returned downstairs.

Roger came into the room and took one look at his friend. "Vasectomy?"

"Yeah. How did you know?"

"Had one. Not that I needed to, you know." Sebastian knew Roger rarely dated. But in the event that he should get lucky, he didn't want to take any chances with a pregnancy.

"Rog, I'm going to order a pizza. What does everyone want?" Roger called out to his friends and asked their preferences. A cacophony of ingredients rang out: pepperoni, green olives, extra cheese, bacon, peppadew peppers, sun-dried tomatoes... and the list went on. Sebastian gave his phone to Roger and had him order what they wanted.

Raffaele brought up a new bag of frozen peas and handed it to Sebastian, who put it on his crotch.

"Raffe, before you leave tonight, help me take off my trousers. If Kelly finds out I slept in my clothes again I'll never hear the end of it." Raffaele winked at his little brother and ruffled his long hair.

Roger still had Sebastian's phone when Kelly called. He came into the bedroom. "Your wife wants to say good night."

"Hi baby. Did Raffe get you home? Are you comfortable?"

"I'm fine. I'm sore. But I bought the frozen peas like you said." He missed his wife. He loved the sound of her angel voice. Sebastian listened to her breathing. He knew she was crying. Even though he couldn't fix tears, he wanted to be there with her – he wanted her with him in their bed.

Through her tears, she whispered, *"I love you, Seb."*

"I love you, Kelly. I miss you. I miss you in our bed. I miss you in my arms." Now he could really hear her crying. He wished he hadn't said those words to her, but he couldn't help himself. He missed his wife. "See you tomorrow, Kelly. I love you..."

"See you tomorrow, mister. I love you, too..."

Dr. Janice Kusch the oncologist came in while Sebastian had his surgery. She explained to Kelly and Ruth that chemo was warranted, suggesting it begin within two weeks and continue for six months. Also, the regimen would be two weeks on the chemo drugs and two weeks off. Kelly would have to come in for an intravenous injection on the first day and then take meds orally for the remaining 13 days.

Ruth asked about the side effects. Dr. Kusch explained that some women experience hair loss and nausea. It all depends on the person.

"My nurse will contact you in two weeks to set up the appointments. And Kelly, you're not on birth control anymore. Because of the chemical makeup of these drugs I highly discourage you from getting pregnant."

The next morning, Dr. Elliot came into Kelly's room. His nurse Alex made the head of the bed rise. She closed the privacy curtain and, after carefully removing the IV, untied her hospital gown.

"Kelly, I'm going to take off the dressing and inspect the incision." As Dr. Elliot began cutting the thick bandage, Alex tried taking Kelly's mind off the doctor's actions by engaging her in idle conversation.

"I was named Alexandra, but since I was the only girl with four brothers..."

Though she tried concentrating on their conversation, Kelly was more interested in how her non boob would look. Dr. Elliot gently touched the incision that ran laterally from about an inch to the left of her breast bone to an area under her armpit. A thin, flexible tube came out of the incision under her armpit. On the other end was a little pump. Alex explained that the pump would extract fluid that would continue building up for the next week.

Kelly looked down but only got a brief glimpse of her non boob while Dr. Elliot checked the drain tube. Since her other breast was so small she really didn't see much of a difference, except of course the nipple was gone. In fact, because of the build up of fluid they actually appeared similar.

The privacy curtain moved – Ruth's head appeared and asked if she and Sebastian could come in. Before Kelly could say anything, Dr. Elliot told them to please step in so he could explain how to drain the pump. Ruth and Sebastian stood at the foot of her bed.

Kelly looked up and noticed her husband staring at her chest. She couldn't read the look on his face. Was it fascination? Fear? Curiosity? Dread? Maybe he thought she looked hideous. She willed him to look at her. Finally their eyes met – and he mouthed *I love you*. Oh, thank God. Dr. Elliot interrupted her thoughts.

"Alex, please give the written instructions to Rev. Cameron. This pamphlet explains how to maintain the sutures and also how to drain the pump. I'd like to make sure you all understand." As Dr. Elliot showed Kelly how to drain the pump, Ruth watched closely, following along with the written instructions in the trifold pamphlet.

Sebastian hadn't taken his eyes off of Kelly. Now he looked down at the instructions and scanned the pages.

Ruth spoke to the doctor. "Yes Dr. Elliot, we can do this." Then looking at Sebastian she asked, "We can do this, right?"

"Whatever my wife needs, yes."

"What do you think, my girl?"

Kelly smiled up at her mom – then her tears started. Ruth knew her daughter's tears and moved to her side, ready with tissues.

Dr. Elliot waited while she composed herself. He put a hand on her shoulder and continued in his stern, cautionary voice. "Rest your body, Kelly."

He looked at Sebastian. "Are there stairs in your home?"

"Yes, but we have an en suite bathroom and a powder room on the main floor."

Dr. Elliot again turned his attention back to his patient. "Limit yourself, Kelly. Limit your physical activity. Spend an entire day either upstairs or downstairs. You should be able to move your left arm within a few days, but keep it as immobile as possible. I don't want those sutures opening. And do not shower above the waist until the sutures come out."

Sebastian had been listening to the doctor's cautionary directions, though he hadn't taken his eyes off his wife.

Ruth spoke up. "I'll be living with my daughter and son-in-law for a week or so." She turned to Kelly. "I'll be there for you, too."

"I'm going to wrap a surgical dressing on your incision." Alex helped Kelly sit up while Dr. Elliot wrapped the gauzy bandages around Kelly's upper torso. She winced.

"Sorry Kelly, but I'm wrapping it tight to keep the fluid build-up to a minimum." He finished and taped it securely. "Do not remove the bandages until our follow-up in one week. My office will call you to set up the appointment."

Dr. Elliot took off his sterile gloves. "I understand Dr. Kusch has recommended chemotherapy. I'd like that drain removed before you have the first injection."

As Alex disposed of the used dressing he continued, his voice softer. "I'm sure you'll have questions. Our nursing staff answers questions 24 hours a day." Dr. Elliot put on his fatherly face and smiled. "You did well, young lady. You'll be just fine."

He patted Sebastian's shoulder. "And I don't have to tell you to take care of your wife."

"Reverend Cameron," Dr. Elliot shook hands with Ruth. "It was a sincere pleasure meeting you."

Kelly looked at Sebastian. "Are you driving me home?"

"No. Raffe is waiting for my call and he'll pick us up."

While he was waiting for his brother's call, Raffe and Brie had gone to the supermarket. They knew Ruth would prepare many of the meals. He dropped his wife off at the house so she could put away the groceries. Raffe had also called the maid service and arranged for the ladies to come in and change out Sebastian and Kelly's bedding, clean the bathroom and do a once over on the house in general.

After Dr. Elliot and Alex left the room, Ruth asked Kelly if she was ready to go home.

"So ready!"

Sebastian texted his brother. "Raffe. We're ready."

Before coming to the surgical center, Kelly had packed a bag containing sweats, including a pull-over hoodie. She held it up with her right hand, not knowing what to do.

"Here..." Sebastian grasped the hoodie and asked her to put her right arm in the sleeve. He carefully pulled the soft garment over her head, across her left shoulder and down to her waist.

Kelly looked at her mom. "I feel so helpless."

Ruth put her arms akimbo. "There are many adjectives I would use to describe you, but helpless is not one of them!" She leaned in and kissed her daughter's tear-stained cheek. Kelly looked up at Sebastian and smiled.

"That's my girl." He wanted to pull her into his arms and hug her tight. Instead, he held her sweatpants at her feet and pulled them up as she slid off the mattress.

A nurse's aide came in the room with a wheelchair. With Sebastian's help she walked a few steps to the wheelchair. They all headed down the hallway to the elevators.

"Mama, how do you like your room?"

"Oh my goodness! Sebastian and his friends transformed that office into the Taj Mahal! You won't believe it when you see it!" Ruth looked up at her son-in-law. "I may never leave." And she winked at him. Sebastian winked back and smiled down at her.

22

Home

Entering the front door of their home, the smell of bacon pleasantly assaulted their senses. Tom stood at the stove with a flour sack dish towel wrapped around his waist. Cody stepped out from the open refrigerator door holding a large roast wrapped in butcher paper.

"What's going on here?" Sebastian marveled that someone other than himself was cooking in his kitchen.

Cody placed the roast on the countertop next to a bowl of Idaho Gold potatoes. "I thought I'd prepare you and your family a pot roast for an early dinner." He had also purchased a bunch of carrots from the local farmer's market. A large Dutch oven was on the stove.

"Tom, that all smells so good. And I'm done with hospital food!"

"When you're settled, I'll bring you up a plate of French toast and bacon."

"Yes, thank you. Really!" Kelly turned to Sebastian and grinned. "Bacon!"

"If you're hungry, I know you're feeling better." And he kissed her mouth. He had missed kissing his wife and he wanted to do it again – and again. But for many reasons he controlled himself, a reaction that was foreign to him around her.

"Let's get you upstairs." Raffaele opened the heavy swinging door leading to the dining room. As they entered, an incredible sight greeted them. Bouquets of beautiful flowers were spread out on the dining room table. Tall vases, short vases, round and square vases with blooms of every shape and size and color.

Sebastian was visibly stunned. "What's this? Who are they from?"

Tom came in the room, wiping his hands on the dish towel. "I had kept them at my florist shop until this morning. It would have been too much bringing them from the hospital."

Walking to one of the arrangements, Sebastian pulled an envelope from its plastic holder and opened a card. His lips moved as he silently read the message enclosed. "Oh my goodness... It's from one of my clients." He opened another card. "This is from Phil and his wife..." And another card. "And this one too is from another client... I'm amazed."

Ruth spoke up. "Sebastian, you are a kind, generous man. Your clients know that about you. And when your wife's world got knocked off its axis, your friends rallied around you both."

Kelly came up to her husband and leaned into him. "They're beautiful!" She walked among the bouquets and stopped at one with stargazer lilies. She inhaled the intoxicating perfume of the white blossoms – remembering the prophetic words her mother spoke while in the pre-surgery room.

"Mama, these are stargazers!" Kelly pulled the little envelope from its plastic holder and opened the card. As she read it, Sebastian walked over to her.

"Seb, this is from Mr. Jorgenson and the teachers." An additional card was tucked in with the small envelope. Kelly pulled out the note and read it out loud. 'When you're feeling better, I'll bring you my jerk chicken. Love, Terese.' Seb, you have to try Terese's jerk chicken. Seriously, it's the best!"

"Mrs. B.," Brie steered her friend toward the staircase. "It's time we get you upstairs..."

"Honey, I'm going back into the kitchen." Ruth looked at the loving family that surrounded her daughter. "I think you're in good hands. I'll check on you in a few minutes."

"Thank you, Mama..."

Brie held Kelly's arm and helped her up on the first stair. Raffaele quickly intervened.

"My beautiful Gabriella. Please, let me." He turned to Kelly. "Do you mind?"

"No, Raffe. Thank you."

He stood on Kelly's right and put his arm around her waist. "Okay, slowly..." And they began climbing the stairs, one step at a time. Gabriella and Sebastian followed close behind as they surmounted the staircase and continued walking down the hallway to her bedroom.

Kelly wanted to be on her side of the bed. Raffaele helped her sit and removed her moccasins. And as he did with his brother after his surgery, lifted Kelly's legs and swung them carefully onto the bed.

Sebastian stood at their bedroom doorway until she was settled. He walked into the room and sat on his side of the bed. He leaned over and kissed his wife.

Kelly closed her eyes and smiled. "This is what I've missed."

That evening they all enjoyed the pot roast that Cody and Ruth prepared. Sebastian had called Roger and Michael to join them. Tom and Raffaele carried dinner trays upstairs for Brie so she could eat with Kelly in her bedroom.

Ruth raved about how Sebastian's office had been transformed into such a lovely guest room. And from Raffaele she got caught up on his search for the perfect house. Sebastian enjoyed the normalcy of the evening, and hoped he and his friends could all get together again soon.

But it was getting late – and he wanted to be with his wife. Brie and Raffaele said their goodbyes with Roger and Michael leaving soon after. Tom and Cody cleaned up and put the leftovers in the refrigerator.

Before going to bed, Kelly's mom drained the fluid from the little pump. Sebastian quietly watched from the doorway...

The room was dark, their shadows as one. Sebastian lay on his side facing his sleeping wife... thinking... Breast cancer was an incredibly disfiguring illness. Personally he didn't care. He didn't marry Kelly's body. He married her spirit, her heart, her soul – and those emerald eyes. He didn't care if she had one breast or no breasts. But how did she feel? How did she feel about losing a breast?

He was the outsider looking in. They hadn't talked about that. Was she worried he wouldn't want her anymore? Be repelled by the sight of a healed scar? He already had seen her non boob as she called it when the doctor inspected the incision. He had looked more out of curiosity than anything else. But because it was part of her – part of the woman he loved – it didn't make a difference to him. He loved her – breast *and* non boob.

He needed to reassure her that he wanted her – breast or no breast, scar or no scar. When he could, he would make love to her in the most sensual way he could, loving her, loving every part of her – kissing her, kissing every part of her.

She had doubted him once – and if she hadn't opened up to him at the cabin door, they might not have ever gotten back together. Would she doubt him again? Would she doubt his love for her? But now in the darkness of their bedroom he dozed...

She was too warm – she still wore her hoodie and sweatpants. And she felt like crying, but would her crying wake her mom just down the hall? Her mom wanted to drain her pump this evening. She knew Sebastian wanted to, but she had let her mom do it. Would he see that as usurping his right as a husband to care for his wife?

Kelly lay on her back, her right hand resting on his hip... thinking... She wanted him – a natural response lying so close to him... But would the sight of her scar repel him? Would he still love her with only one breast? She needed to let him know she loved him – that no matter how he felt about her, she would always love him.

She whispered, "This was quite the day..." When he didn't answer, she assumed he was sleeping. She squeezed his hip – he put his hand on hers. His hand traced her arm up to her shoulder, her face. He caressed her face. She kissed the palm of his hand.

"I love you, Seb..." And the tears came. He inched himself closer to her. He slid one arm under her pillow and put his other arm around her waist, his hand on her hip. His forehead met her face on her pillow. He kissed her cheek and lay his head on her pillow again – and held her.

"I love you, woman. Please don't cry." Of course her dam burst and she couldn't help herself. But she cried quietly, taking long, deep breaths. And the more she cried, the closer he held her. He was so gentle, so loving, so... Sebastian. And in the darkness of their bedroom they slept.

He had held her throughout the night. He never left her side, and woke with his arm around her waist, his hand holding her hip. When Kelly woke, she turned her head and looked at the man who was looking at her. His hazel eyes shrouded beneath heavy brows penetrated her very soul. No, he wasn't going anywhere. Her fears as she slipped into her dreams last night were foolish. Only death...

She tested her voice. "I have to pee..."

He sarcastically repeated her words. "I have to pee?" He raised his head and kissed her face. "Not 'Oh Sebastian, love of my life.' No! 'I have to pee!'"

"Stop!" Kelly backhanded his arm. "I'm going to laugh and I won't be able to hold it!"

He arose from the bed, pulled on his trousers and walked around to her side. He pushed his arm under her shoulders and raised her body – slowly – and pulled her legs over to the side of the bed. "How's that?"

"Good." She put her hands on her chest. "I feel a lot of pressure."

With his help, Kelly stood. "Oh... pressure..." Sebastian helped his wife to the bathroom and closed the door. While he waited, he laid out the large disposable cup and sterile wipes on the mattress.

Michael was coming today to hook up a wide screen 4K TV in their bedroom. The only TV in the house was in the basement rec room. Sebastian wanted Kelly to pass time without going stir crazy. From inside the bathroom, he heard the flush.

"I'm done. Bring me unders?" Sebastian retrieved a pair of panties out of her drawer. He helped her put them on, then together they walked the short journey back to their bed.

"Should we drain the pump now before you get comfortable?"

"Yeah – I want to take my hoodie off, too."

Sebastian took hold of the bottom of the garment and in one movement, carefully pulled the hoodie over her head. He heard his mother-in-law's footsteps outside their door.

"Ruth, would you come in to our room please?"

Ruth opened their bedroom door. She still wore her nightgown and robe. "Good morning, you two. How was your night?"

"Good, thank you Mama. Sebastian held me all night." And she kissed her husband again.

"That's how it should be, my girl. So what's on the agenda?" She stood at the foot of the king sized bed. Sebastian turned to her.

"I'm going to drain Kelly's pump. Would you make sure I do it correctly?"

"It looks like you have everything ready. Go ahead, Sebastian."

And just as Dr. Elliot had illustrated, Sebastian adeptly opened the little pump, releasing the suction and drained the brown fluid into the disposable cup. With a sterile wipe he cleaned the pump and tubing, then collapsed the pump, engaging its suction and closed the cover.

Ruth winked at her daughter. "Perfect. Okay, I'll leave you two. I'm going down to fix coffee."

"Mama, Seb programmed the coffee maker last night. There's coffee now."

"Thank you, young man. That was very nice of you." Before leaving the room, Ruth lingered a few moments longer, taking in the love that surrounded her daughter and son-in-law...

After flushing the drained liquid, he returned to his place next to his wife on their bed. "Are you ready for your morning meds?" Kelly leaned into Sebastian and kissed his face. He put both hands on her bare thighs and leaning in, kissed her mouth – a real kiss. She groaned. Oh, she wanted to feel his weight on her.

"Yeah, I want my meds, please. Can I have them with my coffee?"

"Yes," kissing her lips again. "I'll bring them both right back." He hurried downstairs to the kitchen.

Ruth poured her first cup of coffee. When Sebastian came into the kitchen she offered him a proposition. "I thought you and your brother would like to spend the day together. Brie and your wife and I have some girl talk to catch up on. Do you mind?"

He began pouring coffee in his cup and in Kelly's mug. "Kelly would love that. I could show Raffe around to some neighborhoods he might like." He stuffed the prescription bottle in his pocket. From the refrigerator, Sebastian retrieved Kelly's French Vanilla creamer, pouring quite a bit in her mug.

"Want some creamer, Ruth?"

"Yes... Thank you, honey." As he left the kitchen with the two full cups, Sebastian realized this was the first time Ruth had called him that endearing term.

He backed through the heavy swinging door into the dining room and paused – and looked over the field of colorful blooms that filled the large table. The smell was incredible. He set the mugs down, then putting the handles together, lifted them as one, and picked up the vase of stargazer lilies.

As he carefully made his way up the stairs, he made a mental note to bring several more of the vases up to their room before he left.

He stopped at the doorway to their bedroom and took in the sight. Kelly lay on her back – her eyes closed. She wore nothing except her underwear and the gauze dressing that covered her chest. He missed being with his wife. But he still couldn't do anything about it. *I can't make love to my wife... I have to take care of her until she feels better. I can do that. I love her. I love all of her – especially those emerald eyes!*

23

Girl Talk

The king size bed was perfect for a day with just the girls. Kelly and Brie sat up against the headboard while Ruth sat in the middle of the grand bed. Between them were trays filled with snack crackers, mascarpone cheese, grapes, watermelon slices, green olives, radishes and more of their favorite munchies. Ruth drank wine while Kelly and Brie drank sparkling water on ice.

"So, um..." Kelly looked at her mom and almost second-guessed the question she wanted to ask Brie, but asked it anyway. "Gabriella, how was your honeymoon night? You've been having sex with Raffe since the night of the groom's dinner."

Ruth took a drink of her wine. "You know, I thought so... But I'm too much of a lady to say anything." Kelly's and Gabriella's eyes widened with surprise. Ruth laughed, feeling proud of herself that she was able to shock her grown daughter.

"Mom!" Kelly almost choked on her water. Ruth popped a grape in her mouth and shook her head. She looked at her daughter and winked. But Brie knew Ruth's limits.

"Raffaele is so hairy! I love it. What about Sebastian?"

"This is where I'll excuse myself, you two. Besides I need a refill. Finish your hairy-man talk before I return, okay?" They all laughed as Ruth moved to the edge of the bed and walked out of the room. As soon as they heard her descend the stairs, Kelly answered her friend.

"Way hairy. I love his chest and his belly. I play with his chest hair all the time." She spread mascarpone on a cracker. "You know, his ex wanted him to wax his chest?"

"No way! So, what about... you know..." Brie looked sideways at Kelly. She knew the brothers shared more than body hair.

Kelly spoke in a stage whisper. *"Sebastian is bigger than any man I've ever been with... Thick, too."*

"Oh God, so is Raffe! Long and thick." The girls laughed. Brie scooped some of the creamy mascarpone on a cracker and put some watermelon slices on her plate.

"So, what does Raffe think about you not shaving?" Several years ago, Kelly invited Brie to come with her for her Brazilian wax appointment. Brie said she'd come along but wouldn't get one. She liked being natural.

"He's so European." She closed her eyes and sighed. "Oh God Kelly, he is just so fucking hot!"

Ruth softly knocked on the door, announcing her return to the bedroom.

"Are you girls done with the hairy descriptions?"

Kelly and Brie looked at each other and giggled. "Yes, Mom! Come on in!"

"Good, because Michael is here to hook up the TV."

Kelly liked Michael. He had a unique look about him and it just wasn't his crooked nose. He wore his shoulder-length jet black hair tied in a Samurai ponytail – a look he began in college. It had served him well on the rugby field.

When he entered Kelly's bedroom and saw he had an all female audience, he felt a bit self-conscious. But he worked quickly as he hooked up the new, really too big television. And though he was getting silly suggestions from the three women sitting on the large bed – calling them his personal peanut gallery – he soon enjoyed the cheap abuse.

After completing the relatively simple operation, he checked to make sure all their favorite cable channels were working, even installing a few of his personal favorite apps. Meanwhile, Kelly and Gabriella were already deciding what they'd watch during the rest of the afternoon.

"Is there anything else I can do for you ladies?"

Gabriella realized Kelly was in pain. This episode took more out of her than either one of them had anticipated. "Thank you... You did great."

Ruth also noticed Kelly's discomfort and knew it was time for her daughter to rest. "Michael, would you like to bring home some roast beef leftovers?"

"Yes ma'am, that would be nice. Thank you."

"I thought as much. Come on." Ruth excused herself and escorted him downstairs.

Brie looked at Kelly. "You look tired."

"I think I am tired." And she yawned. "My stitches come out this week – and I get rid of my friend the pump." Another yawn took over her face as she asked Brie to help her to the bathroom.

After sending Michael off with a full dinner of leftovers, Ruth came back into the room. "Kelly, you look tired. How about you take your meds and lay down for a nap." She put her hand on her daughter's forehead.

"Let's get these dishes out of here." Brie and Ruth picked up the empty trays and set them out in the hallway.

Ruth walked into the bathroom and brought back a glass of water with Kelly's meds. She took the little pills out of her mother's hand and sipped the water.

"Thank you, Mama." Kelly was grateful for her mom's presence. She knew her mom would be returning home to Grand Junction after her chemo regimen began, but that wasn't for another week.

Brie yawned. "Kelly, I'm taking a nap with you."

"I think that's a good idea. You need your rest too, Brie." Ruth turned on the TV for the girls and put the remote between them on the bed. She put several large quilts on the bed.

"I'll be downstairs. I'm going to fix something good for dinner." And she threw the girls kisses.

Kelly had a hard time getting comfortable, but soon her pain meds kicked in and she closed her eyes. Brie came out of the bathroom and crawled into the great bed next to her best friend. After scrolling through the movie options, she chose *Love Actually*. She pulled a quilt over her large belly and settled down for a nap.

It was good being with Ruth and Kelly again. The last time they were all together was in Colorado for her quick wedding ceremony to Raffaele. She felt blessed that her favorite people in the world were with her for the most important event in her life – that is, up to this time. The most important event would be happening in just two more months. Never in her wildest dreams did she think she'd meet and marry such a wonderful man. He really was everything and more than she had ever wanted.

She had met men before who got off on her breasts – it got old quick. *My eyes are up here, asshole!* But Raffaele adored her breasts as much as he cherished her. He didn't see them as an entity of their own – instead he treasured them as he would her heart...

> *Their wedding night was one of the most wonderful nights of her life. She had chosen an ivory fairy-lace bridal pajama for her wedding night – a two-piece lingerie set, very see-through.*
>
> *After a brief reception with their friends, they returned to their honeymoon suite at the Two Rivers Winery and Chateau. Raffaele had lifted her easily in his strong arms and carried her into the two-room suite. She thought he would never let her go. He just held her with tears in his eyes. Her wonderful, sensitive man!*
>
> *Excusing herself, she went into the adjoining room and quickly stripped and slipped into her naughty, erotic pajamas. Not that he needed anything to inspire his libido, because he was already a titan in the bedroom. Since that first night together, they had made love every night without fail. He always made sure she had at least two orgasms – the first using his sweet tongue and another while making ferocious love, using his whole body, pushing her, making her experience the pleasures up to that time she could only have imagined...*
>
> *Brie cracked open the door, finding where her beloved husband waited. He had already undressed, carefully folding his clothes and placing them on a chair. He was a perfectionist and it showed in his concerts – and in their bed. She watched him move unseen. He had the silkiest, most beautiful thick black hair covering his body. She loved his body, his very Italian body. She opened the door and walked into his arms.*
>
> *Raffaele put his hands on her bare waist and spoke in a whisper. "Mia moglie... Io sono veramente beati." He raised one of her arms and asked her to turn around.*
>
> *"Mia bellissima Gabriella – you are even more beautiful tonight. You thrill me."*
>
> *She pulled him close and whispered in his ear, "There is no crotch in my bottoms..."*

The look on his face was remarkable. He took a step back and with one hand inspected the area, pressing his fingers on her exposed skin.

"You have pleased me tonight."

"Raffaele, I have done nothing."

"Mia bellissima Gabriella, you have breathed life into my soul." His statement of love brought tears to her eyes and she couldn't hold back her emotions.

"Why the tears, mia bellissima Gabriella?"

"Because I feel the same way. Because since you have come into my life, I feel like I have been reborn." They held each other tight. On their honeymoon night, when their passions should have taken priority they held each other close, professing their love for each other, honoring each other with their words – and their tears.

He led her to their bed – the bed they had made love in as man and woman the night before – now the bed they would make love in as husband and wife. He slowly untied the silk ribbons that held her chemise, letting it fall from her breasts. Raffaele kissed her lips hard, pushing his tongue deep into her mouth. While he was making love to her with his tongue, he caressed her full breasts, his thumbs rubbing gently on her nipples.

Raffaele lifted his wife with ease, placing her in the middle of the grand mattress. He gracefully mounted the bed and knelt at her feet. He leaned down and opening the delicate lace material, tasted her silky skin, his tongue exploring her body – loving every part of her. She bent her knees, spreading her legs wider and groaned out loud as she felt her orgasm pulse through her body.

With trembling fingers, Raffaele slowly untied the silk ribbon on her pajama bottoms. He leaned back on his ankles and pulled the pajamas off, exposing her bare legs. He looked at his wife, lying naked on their bed with her legs spread wide – for him.

Gabriella caressed his face as he kissed and licked her breasts, sucking on her large areolas, feeling her hard nipples in his mouth. She softly called his name, pressing up her hips, feeling his erection between her legs.

"Mia bellissima Gabriella, may I make love to you?" From the first time they were together he asked permission to make love to her. That was just how he was and she hoped he would never change.

"Yes, Dominicci," she exhaled her words... "Yes, please!"

Brie could never get her fill of this man – this man who loved her, who honored her with his words, his tongue, his body. While his arms supported his body, he began thrusting into her, pushing deeper, thrusting harder, his hips gyrating round and round. With every thrust, her large breasts quavered, which only increased his fervor. Through rasping breaths, he asked her if she was ready to come with him.

She looked up at his face, the face of the man she loved, and put her hands on his arms. Gabriella softly cried as she answered him... "Yes, oh my God... Yes..."

And he pushed deeper, thrusting deeper, pressing his body onto her harder while he came hard into her – and as she achieved her second orgasm, she breathed his name, "Dominicci! Dominicci! Dominicci!"

Supporting his body on his elbows so as not to crush her breasts, he kissed her mouth, her face, her eyes – whispering his love for her...

Even now, so many years later, Gabriella still remembered the feeling of his wonderful body bringing her body to such hard orgasms. He was so loving, so attentive – always and every time assuring her that she was loved and loved well by him.

24

Carolyn

"We found Brie and Raffe a house."

They had settled into their bed and were relaxing after a long day. That afternoon, Kelly had her sutures removed along with that awful little pump. She showered before coming to bed. Now she lay on her back cuddling with Sebastian. He lay on his side, sharing her pillow, holding her close, one leg draped across her legs. She felt safe – she felt loved.

"Where's the house?" She played with the dark hair on his arm.

"It's only a few miles from here. It's an old estate property."

"What's special about this place? I know Brie liked that two-story brick not far from your office building."

"You know Raffe isn't touring anymore and this estate also has a carriage house he'll convert into a recording studio." He nuzzled her face, wishing he could do more. He wore his boxer briefs, his confined erection pressed against her hip.

"Is it a large property?" She felt his erection – and tried ignoring the heavenly feeling by playing with his thick chest hair.

"Yeah. I think so. And it's also move-in ready, something they required on their wish list." The touch of her fingers on his chest made him uncomfortable.

"Furniture too?" God, his erection was so hard, so long... digging into her hip. She took a deep breath and let it out slowly. He held her hip tighter, pulling her body even closer to him.

"No, but Raffe thought you and Brie could go furniture shopping." He kissed her mouth – he couldn't help himself. And he knew she responded – not that they could do anything about it.

"I'd like that..." She paused, giving him a last kiss – and looked into his eyes. "I start chemo next week."

Sebastian loudly exhaled, relieving the sexual tension, and pressed his forehead on hers. He kissed her cheek. "How do you feel?"

"I feel good." She snuggled her face into his neck. "How are you?"

"I miss you..." He kissed her auburn curls.

Her hand stopped in the middle of his chest. "I miss you too..."

"Can I pull up your shirt?"

"No – not yet! Please!" In a reflex action, her hand immediately covered her chest.

"Okay... Okay... It's okay..." He eased her hand from her chest. Sebastian caressed her breast through the T-shirt, rubbing the palm of his hand over her nipple, feeling it harden. "Baby, I've already seen everything... right after your surgery. Remember?"

Kelly looked at him – tears welling in her eyes. She turned her head – her tears escaped and ran down the side of her face. He put a finger under her chin and made her turn back to him. Sebastian kissed her tears...

"I won't if you don't want me to... I promise..." He moved down her body and kissed her T-shirt covered breast.

"Seb...?"

"Yes, Love... I'm right here... I'm not going to do anything you don't want me to do." And he kissed her mouth chastely...

Again she looked at him, her husband, her Ulysses. She whispered, *"Okay..."*

"Okay, what Love?"

"Okay, you can..." And she cried harder.

"Baby, I love you. I didn't marry your breast. I married you. I love you. I won't if you don't want me to..."

"No... I want you to..."

Sebastian again professed his love to her. Slowly he lifted the edge of her T-shirt, exposing only her breast. He kissed her nipple... his tongue licked her sweet nipple.

She whispered, *"... all of me..."*

She arched her back. He pushed her T-shirt up to her shoulders, exposing her scar. He looked one more time into her eyes. Her tears came in torrents. She was bawling, crying out loud, not even trying to stifle her tears. And she turned her head away from him.

Sebastian ignored her tears and gently – very gently – kissed her scar, kissing her scar from her breastbone to her armpit. And he held her, enfolding his wife in his strong arms, just holding her close, waiting until her crying subsided – not fixing her tears. And as long as it took he held her.

After what seemed minutes her breathing became more regular, her chest quit heaving, her tears stopped. With one finger under her chin, he pulled her face back to look at him. And she looked at her husband, her Ulysses.

"My Lord woman, I love you!" Sebastian tugged the quilt up over their bodies and pulled her closer. And they slept well into the morning, sharing one pillow...

His meeting lasted longer than he had planned. Phil wasn't with him – his little daughter had the flu and his family needed him at home. Of course Sebastian understood.

The week earlier Ruth had returned home to Colorado. He pulled up to the garage. The only light was the motion detector flood. Many times Kelly forgot to turn on the porch light when she left the house.

Sebastian entered his home and pushed through the heavy swinging door into the dining room and listened. The house was quiet, except for the muffled sounds of the TV from the second floor. He ascended the stairs and looked into the bedroom – the only light came from the TV. Kelly was nowhere to be found and the bed was unmade.

He knew she had her injection a few days ago and surmised she must be with Gabriella. Removing his suit coat and tie – tossing them on the bed – he walked into the en suite bathroom and turned on the light. Kelly lay on the floor next to the toilet.

"Oh Kelly..." He knelt on the floor at her side and felt her face – it was cool. She must have been sick, but for how long? He had meant to be home much earlier – how long had she been on the tile floor?

"Hi..." Her eyes barely opened. "I feel like shit."

"Can I take you to bed?" He wasn't going to move her if she felt like throwing up again. She was in charge.

"Yeah. I think I'm done."

He gathered her in his arms and brought her to the bed – and sat on the mattress holding her. He felt guilty not being here for her, even though she usually refused his help when the effects of the chemo hit her. Sometimes she just had dry heaves as she knelt on the floor until the nausea subsided.

"How was your meeting?" She talked into his stiff shirt collar.

"Long." He pressed his face against the top of her head and kissed her hair. He knew she wasn't up for any lengthy explanations. He stood and laid her body on the mattress.

"Cold..."

He pulled the sheet and one quilt up over her shoulders. She wouldn't wake now until the morning. He used the bathroom, stripped to his boxer shorts and crawled into bed.

"Seb..."

"Yes, Love?" He moved closer to his wife's body, listening to her whispers.

"Seb..."

"I'm right here, Kelly." He put an arm around her waist and pulled her closer to him – back to front, legs against legs, sharing one pillow.

"That's what I wanted..."

Sebastian had an appointment with Dr. English to check his swimmers. He considered calling Gabriella, asking her to come over, but she was due in a few weeks and he didn't want to take chances with her health. He had let Kelly sleep in. He poured the extra coffee in an air pot so she could have a cup later.

The heavy swinging door opened – she looked a mess.

"Good morning, Beautiful!"

"Fuck off, Sebastian."

He met her at the doorway and pulled her into his arms. He had already showered and dressed and was ready for work. "Do you want me to help you shower?" To him she was always beautiful – but he wasn't going to push it this morning.

"No – you're ready for work. Don't be silly. Phil is still home with his baby, right?" She looked into his eyes, challenging him to argue.

"Yes, just me today. But I'm hiring an office manager." He told her about Carolyn. After his last appointment with the good doctor, he learned she had been working at the clinic less than a year. She was a single mom who could use more income and better health benefits, including dental. He was going to make her an offer she couldn't refuse and had already made an initial offer by phone. Now he would see her in person and get her answer.

"Is she pretty?" Kelly poured creamer into her coffee mug.

"Oh, yes, she's gorgeous..." Sebastian purposely emphasized his words, hoping to get a smile out of his wife. "She's tall with long blonde hair, blue eyes and a great figure."

"You're an ass." She turned and kissed her husband's cheek, then turned back to the butcher-block counter.

"I know. Do you want breakfast?" He stood behind her and putting his arms around her, pulled her against him, holding her close, wishing she didn't feel like shit.

"No, Raffe and Brie are coming over." With one hand, she held his arms while breathing in her first sip of coffee. She put her cup down and turned around.

He kissed her chastely. "I love you."

"I know...." She lay her head on his shoulder. "Thank God."

Sebastian entered the doctor's office hopefully for the last time. Although the staff was professional, he knew *they knew* why he was here and what he'd be doing in the privacy of that small room. X-rated magazines and videos were available for the men who needed that extra incentive. He never needed any outside encouragement. He just pictured Kelly half naked in a hot tub – that's all the motivation he had needed.

Carolyn was busy filing and entering information into her computer.

"Good morning, Carolyn." When he greeted her, she looked up and opened the privacy window.

"Good morning, Mr. Bonsignore. We're running a little late this morning. Please have a seat and we'll be with you shortly."

"Carolyn, I don't mean to interrupt you, but have you thought about coming to work for me?"

As she entered more information, Carolyn spoke quietly. "Actually, I have. I've already talked to another person who wants to transfer to this office." She looked around, not wanting anyone else in the office to overhear the conversation. "But I would still have to give Dr. English a two-week notice and train in my replacement."

"That's just fine. We really need you at our office."

Carolyn's phone rang. She listened and acknowledged the caller. "Okay, I'll send him back." She looked up at Sebastian. "They're ready for you, Mr. Bonsignore. Go on back."

"Thank you. I'll send you some paperwork you can complete in your spare time."

Carolyn mouthed *thank you* and closed the window.

A young female tech escorted him to the little room. *Embarrassing!* Gene had escorted him last time. Where was he? Sebastian knew that this young lady knew what he was about to do. She was blushing. Shit. If ever his dick was going to shrink, this was the moment. She closed the door behind him. He expected her to say a cheery 'Good luck.' Thank God she had the sense to not say anything.

He remembered this room. On the left, a monitor and DVD player for the X-rated movies was next to a stack of girlie magazines. He needed none of these. All he needed were the memories of his wife making love with him. A narrow bed with a clean paper sheet was on his right. On the bed lay a little cup wrapped in plastic. He tore off the plastic, uncapped the cup and placed it back on the bed.

He leaned against the bed and unzipped his pants. With eyes closed, he remembered the hot tub – and Kelly. God, he loved that woman. She was so beautiful – especially with those pieces of cloth she called a swimsuit barely covering her body.

That night after he had talked with his brother, he didn't think they'd have time to make love before the pizza arrived. But if he had to choose between cold pizza and hot Kelly, she would win every time...

> *The tub was large enough that she could float on her front, her naked ass at the water level – and standing behind her – fucking her hard – ramming into her – thrusting into her, again feeling her orgasm...*

... grab the cup.

Securing the cover, he placed the cup on the lazy susan in the wall. He washed his hands and hoped the hallway would be empty when he emerged from the room. *Shit*. This was not his lucky day. There she was. Little miss tech – blushing. He avoided looking at her.

"Come with me, please." She escorted him to another room and placing his file in the plastic holder, let him go into the room alone.

He sat in the chair beside the doctor's desk and waited. He hated waiting. He was not a patient man. He wanted to make love to his wife – really make love to his wife. The two weeks she was taking chemo drugs were the times he would just hold her – but the two weeks when she wasn't on her chemo regimen they could enjoy each other, love each other...

A knock on the door brought him back to the present. Dr. English came in, shook his hand and sat at the desk. He opened the file folder.

"Mr. Bonsignore, you've been doing your homework." He smiled. "What I'm looking for is what we call a state of azoospermia, meaning no sperm in the ejaculate. And I'm genuinely surprised that your count is very low, almost nil. I would still use some kind of birth control for the next month at least."

"Um..." Sebastian wanted to ask a question. He felt embarrassed – that this situation was so different from other men. "I have a question."

"Anything, Sebastian. I've heard it all. Trust me."

"Okay, well, I tried putting on condoms, but, um, they're uncomfortable... Too tight." He looked at the ceiling.

"I wouldn't worry. There's a trick to using those things – but having said that, I'll give you some samples that might work better for you." He stood, opened a cupboard door and took a box from the shelf. "These larger condoms might be better for you. I understand your hesitancy talking about this." Dr. English sat and looked again at his files. "When is your wife off her two-week chemo regimen?"

"She just had her injection a few days ago and she's on meds for another week at least."

"So you'll have a few more days to masturbate." As he spoke, Dr. English entered the information into his computer. He stopped and turned to his patient. "Sebastian, keep up your good work. I know it's hard to go through this. But trust me – it'll be better for both you and your wife in the long run." He closed the laptop. "How is your wife tolerating the chemo?"

"I found her asleep on the bathroom floor last night." Sebastian remembered how cold she felt when he had put her to bed. "She vomits sometimes, but mostly it's dry heaves."

"I know. My wife had breast cancer several years ago and we went through the same thing."

"I didn't know... I'm sorry."

"We do what we can for our wives, the ones we love more than life itself." He and Sebastian looked at each other, both understanding the true meaning of those words.

Dr. English closed the file. "Let me know if those work out for you. I really expect you to be clean in another month."

Sebastian stood, but asked one more question. "Is there a take-home test? I felt pretty stupid when the young miss tech out there escorted me to the room."

"I am so sorry, Mr. Bonsignore. I didn't know. Gene usually escorts the men, but he's out with sick children today."

"Sounds like that's going around. My business partner is out with a sick baby today too."

"Wait here. I'll get the home test." He exited his office and returned within minutes holding a small box. "This contains two tests. Use one in about two weeks and another in a month. Let me know the results. Good luck to you."

He shook Sebastian's hand and escorted him out of the room.

Before introducing Carolyn to Phil, Sebastian shared some of her background with him. She had been married, but divorced shortly after the birth of her second child. She had graduated college, but because of the divorce never attained her dream of becoming a lawyer. Sebastian showed Phil a copy of her college transcript.

He waited while Phil digested the magnitude of her qualifications. "She's got a degree in criminology with a minor in sociology. This woman is smart."

Phil reviewed her transcript. "She's taken so many pre-law classes... abnormal psychology, critical reasoning, law and economics..." He looked up at Sebastian. "That course in abnormal psychology makes her the perfect fit to take care of us!"

"Yeah, she's smart. After she graduated all she could get was as an assistant in a doctor's office? I don't get it."

"Seb," Phil interjected. "I would probably be in a similar situation if you hadn't hired me. It's a bitch out there in the real world. I mean, I had attained the rank of Master Sergeant, and all I could look forward to was working at some tedious job, much like Carolyn had."

Sebastian didn't know what to say. He saw the potential in Phil. He saw the potential in people, even if they didn't see it in themselves. Just as he saw the potential in Kevin, whose jazz quartet now had a steady gig at the Harbor Pub.

The following Monday, Sebastian came in late. He and Kelly made love that morning – twice. She was off her chemo for two weeks and was feeling good. Carolyn would be joining the business soon. Sebastian told her to take an additional week off and enjoy her family before coming to work for him.

"Phil, how's your little girl?"

"Gracie is just fine, thanks! How are you doing?" Phil winked at Sebastian. "Kelly must be off her chemo?" He was putting the latest tax preparation publications into the file cabinet.

"Why do you ask?"

"Because you're smiling, boss." And Phil returned to his desk, shaking his head and grinning. "So what's up for this week?"

"Carolyn starts in a few days."

Phil was a hard worker and Sebastian knew he could achieve great things, but he also took calls during the day which cut into his work. The addition of Carolyn as office manager would minimize Phil's receptionist duties so he could concentrate more on his work. And he was within months of graduating, and had already found the perfect place on the wall behind his desk for his diploma.

"Phil, how old are your twin boys?"

"They're turning ten next month. They're growing so fast..."

"Carolyn's two boys are three and six I think."

"She mentioned her kids when we met, but I didn't know their ages."

Sebastian again thought about him and Kelly not having kids. Was that the right thing to do, having his vasectomy? And what would his wife think when she discovers what else he did... But there was something more important he needed to do... He had been thinking about it for weeks and would write a first draft later that day.

"Seb? Would you want me to show her the ropes? How we work? Files and such?"

"What? Oh... Yes, please. I'm back full time now – for at least two weeks. When Kelly goes back on her chemo, I'll be home more with her. But for now I'll share in training Carolyn."

"I'm looking forward to having someone keep us better organized."

"So," Sebastian sat at Phil's desk. "What's been going on? Bring me up to speed."

25

A New Life

While Sebastian met with Phil, Kelly spent the day with Gabriella. Because his wife was a week overdue, Raffaele refused to leave her side. Having Kelly visiting allowed him to supervise the renovation of the carriage house into his recording studio.

Gabriella and Kelly had gone furniture shopping, purchasing some pieces locally but gained the majority of pieces online. Soon the UPS trucks were rolling up. New carpeting had been installed, hardwood floors cleaned and polished, and some of the rooms painted. A guest room became a nursery for their little boy, whenever he decided to meet the world. Raffaele and Gabriella had already chosen a name – Tommaso Finnean, in honor of their paternal grandfathers.

"Raffaele wants to feel my belly every time Finn kicks." Gabriella was sitting on one of the new couches and Kelly had her hand on her friend's belly. "He's almost frantic about it. It's like he's afraid everything will go away, like Annalisa... you know?" During one of their girl talks, Gabriella had shared the story of Raffaele's first wife Annalisa and their unborn child.

"It's getting to be so uncomfortable. After we make love, all I want is a little breathing room between me and my very hot and hairy husband." She gave Kelly an ironic smile. "He asked my obstetrician if it was okay for me to have an orgasm. I was so embarrassed."

"What did your doctor say? I mean, I've never been pregnant – is it safe?"

"Sure. That is, Dr. Lockart assured us that it was quite safe for me to experience an orgasm. But she told Raffaele that during my final weeks of pregnancy, he should be more attentive to me. Holy crap, Kell – I don't know if I can stand him being more attentive!"

Though Brie laughed, she loved how her husband cared for her and their child. She had never felt so loved in her entire life.

"The doctor said we could have sex only if I felt up to it. Shit Kelly, I love having sex with Raffaele. His lovemaking is... well, I just love his style." Brie sighed and Kelly laughed, though she could only imagine. If the brothers were anything like each other in the bedroom, she knew Brie was having the best sex of her life.

"He always makes sure I have my orgasm before he has his. Seriously? Who does that?"

Kelly gave Brie one of her knowing smiles. "Sebastian..."

"I should have known." Brie changed position, moving so she could lean into the overstuffed cushions. Kelly pushed a small pillow behind her friend's lower back.

"So... how are you making love with Raffe with – you know..."

"Very carefully!" And the women laughed.

"But seriously, we've been doing it doggie style." Brie looked shyly at Kelly. "It's just easier on me. And holy shit Kell, he loves it." The friends had known each other forever – and now that Brie wasn't teaching at the high school Kelly missed these long chats. She sat back into the couch cushion and cuddled up next to Brie.

"I can appreciate his anxiety." Kelly leaned over and put her head on Brie's large tummy – and felt something push against her face.

"Oh! That was a big one!" She looked up at her friend who had a shocked look on her face. "Brie... what's wrong?"

"I think it's time. I think my water just broke!"

"Not on the new couch!!" Kelly stood and quickly helped Brie stand.

"Call Raffaele! This is it!" Brie started walking, dripping water down her bare legs. Kelly picked up her cell phone and pressed the speed dial key, but the call went to voicemail.

"Kelly, let's go... *NOW!*"

She helped Brie out the door and to Sebastian's SUV.

"Kelly, get a garbage bag."

"Brie, it's okay..."

"KELLY-GRAB-A-GARBAGE-BAG!"

Shit. Kelly left Brie standing at the passenger door as she scurried into the garage and ran back out with the box of lawn and leaf bags, pulling one out as she ran back to the car. Kelly put a bag on the passenger seat. She helped Brie in and buckled her seatbelt.

Kelly began the short drive to Mercy Hospital. Brie's obstetrician knew she was overdue and would be expecting a call any day. She called her doctor.

"This is Gabriella Bonsignore. I'm coming in! My water broke!"

"Mrs. Bonsignore, drive up to the emergency door and we'll bring you in."

"Drive up to the emergency driveway. They're waiting for me. Shit! Where's Raffaele?"

"I'll try calling him again." Kelly pressed redial... Raffe answered on the first ring.

"Raffaele, I'm driving Gabriella to Mercy Hospital! Meet us there! You're about to have a baby!"

Brie screamed! ***"Raffaele! I'm having our baby!"***

"I'm leaving now. Tell Gabriella I'm leaving now. *Gabriella, sto lasciando ora!* Oh, my God, Kelly, we're having a baby!"

Kelly looked at Brie, who by now was breathing heavy, taking in light gasps and blowing out with a *whoosh* sound.

"Hang in there, Mama... we're almost there!" A car cut them off – Kelly expertly avoided the potential fender-bender. "Asshole!"

Brie put her hands on the dash. "Kelly, Annalisa was killed in an automobile accident." She took in several small breaths. "We've got to get to the hospital in one piece."

"Yeah, well as long as those fuckers stay out of my way." She looked at Brie, who was concentrating on her whoosh whoosh whoosh breathing.

Brie let out another piercing scream. "I don't know if we're going to make it!"

"Holy shit, Brie. Hang in there, girlfriend!" Kelly put her foot on the gas and passed cars as if driving the Porsche. Within minutes, she arrived at the emergency driveway. Several nurses in colorful hospital scrubs filed out and met the SUV.

Brie opened her door and screamed again. "I can feel the baby coming... ***NOW!***"

Two sets of hands pulled her out of the seat and placed her on a gurney. One of the nurses knocked on Kelly's window. "Park over in the lot across the street and come to the neonatal ward on the 4th floor."

Kelly parked in the hospital's lot. After depositing the plastic bag in a nearby dumpster, she ran across the street, almost getting hit herself by an oncoming car. *Holy crap!*

Upon entering the hospital lobby, she ran to the bank of elevators. *Come on... come on... Finally!* When she arrived on the fourth floor, she saw the sign directing her to the neonatal ward. She skipped down the hallway and stopped at the nurses' desk.

"I'm Kelly Bonsignore – Gabriella Bonsignore's sister-in-law."

"Ma'am, they're getting Mrs. Bonsignore ready. You can go back if you want."

"Her husband will be coming up."

"Have him check with us and we'll escort him back to be with his wife."

Kelly waited until Raffaele came down the hall.

"Where's Gabriella? Where's my wife?"

A nurse called to him. "Mr. Bonsignore? Raffaele?"

"Yes... my wife..." And before he could say another word, the nurse pulled him by the arm and escorted him down the hallway into the birthing room.

Under her breath, Kelly whispered, "*Good luck, Raffe...*" She returned to the elevators.

Gabriella had been stripped and prepped for the birth of her baby, but there was no time for an epidural. A strap around her large belly monitored her baby's heartbeat. Two nurses assisted Brie at her side.

"*Mia bellissima Gabriella...*" Raffe kissed her forehead, tasting her perspiration. Brie looked up at her husband and smiled – and let out a yell.

"Ohhhhh! I want to push! I have to push! Can I push? I have to push!"

Dr. Bernice Lockart stood at the end of the narrow bed between Brie's legs. "Gabriella, I can feel the baby's head. He's in a good position. Whenever you're ready, let us know."

Raffaele stood at her head, holding her hands. Brie took several deep breaths and looked up at her husband.

"Stay with me, my love... we're going to have a baby..." She took a deep breath, closed her eyes and with everything she had in her pushed – and ***screamed!*** And crushed his hands.

"Good work, Gabriella... Okay, rest... Wait... Okay, and can you give me another good push?"

Brie took a deep breath and bore down, again she held Raffaele's hands and growling his name *pushed!*

"Wait now... Okay, he's coming. I can see his shoulder. Wait. Can you give me one more push?"

Brie mustered everything she had in her and *pushed*. She pushed until the doctor told her to stop. She heard her baby's cries. Brie looked at Raffaele. He was crying, his tears falling from his cheeks onto his wife's face. She pulled his face down to hers – and kissed him.

"Mr. and Mrs. Bonsignore, here's your baby boy!" Dr. Lockart placed the partially swaddled baby on Brie's chest.

Raffaele cupped the baby's head in the palm of his hand. He leaned down and kissed his son. He looked at his wife – his beautiful wife who healed his broken heart and gave him back his life – and chastely kissed her. *"Ti amo, mia bellissima Gabriella..."*

"Mr. Bonsignore," Dr. Lockart spoke to Raffaele, but he didn't hear – he was concentrating on his beautiful wife and their new baby. She repeated her words.

"Mr. Bonsignore. Raffaele. Would you like to cut your baby's umbilical cord?"

"Yes... oh yes..." A nurse handed him a surgical scissors and pointed to the area he should cut. Carefully, slowly, he positioned the scissors and cut...

"Good job, Mr. Bonsignore."

One of the nurses picked the new-born up from Brie's chest. "We're going to check out your baby now."

"Just relax, Gabriella. I'm going to examine you." Dr. Lockart sat on a stool and brought a lamp closer to Brie's body.

"You have a small second-degree tear. I'm going to put a few stitches in so you'll heal faster. I'm going to numb you – you'll feel a little prick." Brie winced when she felt the small needle injecting anesthetic into her perineum. The doctor waited a few minutes.

"Gabriella, let me know if you feel this."

"Feel what...?" Brie and Raffe were concentrating on their baby. Tommaso Finnean Bonsignore was getting weighed and measured, finger and foot printed, and having a tiny bit of his blood drawn. He was not happy and let everyone in the room know how he felt.

"Okay, I'll be quick. I'm going to put in a running stitch. It will heal quicker and you'll never know it was there."

"Gabriella, il mio amore... La ringrazio." And Raffaele wept...

26

The Best Medicine

"No swimmers."

"Huh? What?" Kelly turned her head, brushing her auburn curls against Sebastian's face.

"I said," while pushing strands of her hair behind one ear. "I'm clean – no swimmers."

"Yeah? So... does that mean no more condoms?" It wasn't that she minded the condoms – at least they could make love, but they couldn't be spontaneous and the spontaneity of their sex was just one of the many things she loved about her husband.

"I've already scheduled an appointment for this afternoon. If I'm clean I'd like to take my wife to our cabin."

Their faces were inches apart, her emerald eyes looking directly into hazel eyes shrouded beneath heavy brows. They hadn't been to the cabin for over six months. During her chemo, Kelly didn't feel up to the long drive. And she had some hair loss – the new growth was silver.

Three weeks prior, she had her last injection and her oral meds were officially done this last week too. She felt good. Kelly felt like her old self. And unfortunately with the addition of the silver, she looked like her old self.

"I think – Yes! I want to go to our cabin with my husband!" She kissed him hard and whispered, *"Please be clean!"*

Sebastian kissed her back, letting his tongue taste her lips, making love to her with his tongue. Turning onto his back, he opened a packet and rolled on the super-sized condom. He had ordered a box of assorted colors. Today the color was green.

Cuddling close, she laughed. "I'm going to make love with the Green Hornet!"

He looked at her and, grinning his crooked smile, made a buzzing sound in her ear. She squealed with laughter. He grabbed her and pulled her onto his body, making her sit on his large erection.

"Take me, woman!"

And she did...

Kelly called Mr. Jorgenson and let him know she would be in the following Monday to resume teaching. Granted it was close to the end of the school year, but she wanted to finish the year with her senior class.

During her recuperation, her kids had sent her cards and bouquets. Even her former student Benjamin had heard of her cancer. He had written her a heartfelt note, wishing her a speedy recovery. He was in nursing school, and her cancer diagnosis had inspired him to concentrate on becoming an oncology nurse. Kelly cried when she read his letter and kept it safe, tucking it in her bedside drawer.

She loved coming to their cabin in the spring. All the bulbs she had planted that first summer were blooming. Yellow and pink crocuses edged the fieldstone on the hill leading to the cabin. And yellow-and-white daffodils and deep-blue early spring iris bordered the perimeter of the little cabin. When they left last fall, Sebastian helped Kelly cover the dormant bulbs with hay mulch. Every spring she was eager to pull the hay away and expose the resplendent new blooms.

When he purchased the cabin and surrounding grounds, it was just that – a cabin, a blank slate. Over the years, Kelly had transformed it into a magical place – an Eden, lush with colorful gardens. And now from early spring to late fall, something always bloomed. Even Sebastian came to appreciate all the lovely colors.

Kelly met her husband at the door. He came home with a clean test. She had been hoping for a good result and had already packed and was ready to go.

Sebastian had alerted Carolyn and Phil the week prior that he hoped to be out of the office the entire week. With all the preparations made, they decided not to wait until morning – instead leaving for the cabin that night. While driving, he promised himself he would make sure Kelly knew how much he loved her...

He remembered the weekend at the cabin on their second anniversary. They slept, ate and made love in their grand bed. Kelly had renamed the cabin their Love Shack. That was also the first time they had made love in front of the great stone hearth. Just the thought of being with his wife for almost an entire week already gave him an aching hard-on. She noticed how uncomfortable he was in his leather bucket seat.

"Um, should we stop by the side of the road? I mean, really Sebastian. Are you that lusty after my skinny old bod?"

"Woman, I am *always* lusting after your beautiful bod! Haven't you figured that out by now?" She only laughed and returned to reading out of her book of poems. And soon she slept.

But he couldn't stop thinking of his wife and the hell she had gone through. She had conquered cancer and come out the other side stronger than ever. And this was the week he would express his love for her any and every way he could.

Before leaving town, they stopped at the New London Grille and bought sub sandwiches. That evening, they ate the sandwiches by the great hearth. The fire was burning well, the crackling of the logs only adding to the serene atmosphere.

Sebastian removed his shirt. Kelly leaned forward and touched the thick hair that covered his chest and belly, combing through the soft hair with her fingers.

"I can't get over your first wife wanting you to wax your chest. She was so stupid."

Sebastian took her hand and kissed the palm, pressing her hand to his face. "I want to make love with you tonight – here, in front of the fire." He poured more wine in her goblet.

"Thank you, baby." She sipped the burgundy liquid.

"Kelly, you know a little about my ex. What about your first husband? What was he like?"

Sebastian had never asked about him, and she never offered any information. Up to this minute, it had been ancient history – a part of Kelly's past he didn't need to know. Now while sitting next to the slow burning fire, he asked her.

Kelly's first marriage was just a blip in her life – she never really thought about her ex. Of all the bad decisions she had made in her life, this one was the worst. After taking a long drink of her wine, she began...

"I had just moved here and begun my teaching career – and between lesson planning and getting the feel of my classrooms, I felt swamped. I had stopped at the post office. Stevie – his name was Stevie – worked at the front desk. We started talking..." She paused and drank more wine. All this talk about her ex was making her thirsty, and surprisingly a little unnerved.

"Anyway, while we were talking I found I liked his off-the-cuff humor. I thought he was funny, albeit in a crude sort of way."

Sebastian hadn't taken his eyes off her, even as he drank his beer.

"So," she continued, looking into Sebastian's hazel eyes. "We agreed to meet for a drink later. And one thing led to another as they say and about a month later he moved in with me."

"You both lived in your efficiency?"

"Yeah, talk about cramped quarters. But I thought I was in love. Go figure." She leaned into Sebastian and kissed his cheek. "But our living arrangement would have caused problems at my school, so I decided to get married."

"Just like that?" Sebastian brushed her hair behind one ear, touching her cheek with his thumb.

"Yeah, just like that. He was fun at first – always cracking jokes, sometimes they were hurtful jokes. But I just owned it up to his sarcastic humor." She took another sip of her wine.

"Brie knew him from high school, and when she found out we were dating she clued me in on him. She said he made his classmates laugh but made the teachers so mad. He was written up a lot and sent to the principal's office at least once a week. I guess from what she said he wasn't that popular. Anyway, he finally dropped out of high school, and until I started dating him she hadn't thought of him again."

Kelly looked at Sebastian – he hadn't taken his eyes off her. "After a while our relationship went south and I threw him out of my apartment. I guess I got tired of his bullshit and told him to pack his shit and move out. And while I was at school he moved out."

Sebastian frowned. "Weren't you worried about him trying to get back at you?"

"Oh Sebastian, you're getting ahead of yourself." She smiled, but it wasn't her happy smile. "When I got home that evening, I asked my super to change the locks on my door. But before he could do that little chore, Stevie slipped into my apartment that night and assaulted me."

Kelly knew saying this would enrage Sebastian. But she had already said more than she originally planned on sharing.

"He woke me. He overpowered me..." She took a big drink of her wine and swallowed hard. "And he tried to rape me."

Sebastian closed his eyes. She hurriedly continued.

"I kicked him in the groin – hard."

Sebastian's eyes opened – wide.

"I knew it would only temporarily stop his assault, so I kicked at his sternum. I sent him flying off my bed and he hit his head on my dresser." She watched Sebastian's reaction. "I called him a low-life piece of shit and yelled at him to get the fuck out of my house." She smiled now as she remembered the end of that encounter. "When he ran out of my apartment, his pants were still hanging off his ass."

Her eyes glistened. The memory of her final encounter with her ex-husband still affected her. Sebastian felt her body tense – again he touched her face. "Remind me not to get on your bad side."

She looked into his hazel eyes and exhaled through pursed lips. The fire in the hearth was dying – only glowing logs remained.

He brushed the bangs out of her eyes. "You never called the police?" He was concerned for his wife and the memories she still held deep in her heart.

"No..." She looked at the sparking embers while she spoke. "I had no proof – my word against his. And frankly I didn't want the publicity." She pondered her next words, as if reconsidering her options. "Looking back, I should have said something, but I already had made so many bad decisions."

Sebastian again touched her face. "When Roger was making over the guest room for your mom, he told me he threw your ex out of the Harbor Pub. He said it was the best feeling he had in a long time."

A smile crossed her face at the memory of Roger manhandling her ex.

"Why did your ex even bother you?"

"He was angry because he had received divorce papers the same week I threw him out – the same week he assaulted me." Kelly drank more of her wine, tipping the goblet to get the last drops. Sebastian poured the last of the bottle into her glass.

"Oh, he was pissed. Since I had already been talking with a lawyer about ending the marriage, it took only my signature to finalize the document. Stevie was served before the end of the week."

"What happened?" He caressed her face with the back of his fingers. "I mean, how did you know the relationship had ended?"

"Stevie was just being a dick, excuse the expression." She looked at Sebastian, wondering how much she should share about Stevie's behavior. But she trusted him. "He wanted me to get breast implants."

Sebastian shut his eyes tight. When he opened them they glistened with anger. She continued, knowing anything she said would be kept in his heart – deep in his heart.

"After I refused to get implants, the only way he wanted to have sex with me was from behind..."

"What do you mean, *behind*?" Sebastian's face betrayed renewed anger.

Again, she wondered if she really wanted to share this with him. But it was a part of her past, and her past was part of her. "He made me lay on my front and he screwed me from behind. Or he made me kneel and he'd screw me like that."

"Did he ever...?"

"No! Never!" Kelly knew what he was asking. "Stevie was never that crude – he was just rude."

"I know we've had sex like that," Sebastian spoke softly. "But you never said anything – you never said you didn't like it."

"When Stevie did it that way he was trying to hurt me. That's the only way he got off – screwing me from behind. And when he came he just laid on me, telling me how good it was. God Sebastian, he was such an ass!"

"Did you have a... when he did that to you?" Sebastian swallowed more of his beer.

"No. Never. He just pumped a couple times, got his rocks off and he was done." She looked hard at Sebastian. Oh what was he thinking? "He wasn't you." She touched his face, caressing his beard. With one hand, she undid the leather tie and combed her fingers through his long hair, pulling his hair forward in her fists. "He wasn't you..." She pulled his face to hers and kissed him. "Thank God he's not you!"

Sebastian kissed her lips, tasting her lips, making love to her with his tongue.

Again she whispered. "*He wasn't you...*"

Sebastian lay her down on the rag rug, opened her shirt and licked her nipple, caressing her breast, loving her breast. He also kissed her scar, following the red line from her breastbone to her armpit – she let him kiss her full chest.

"You take my breath away! I want to make love with you Seb..."

"Yes..." But he had an edge to his voice. "You know I would never hurt you..." Kneeling between her legs, he pulled her shorts and panties off her legs. He stood and removed his jeans and boxers. As he nestled between her open legs, she sat up and pressed her hands on his chest.

Kelly looked carefully into his eyes. "I want you from behind."

"Why?" Sebastian couldn't believe she said she wanted him like that. "But you said he did that to you..."

"I know, Sebastian, but he's not *YOU* – and you need to know that. Really know that!" She pulled his face to hers and kissed his mouth hard. "He's not you!"

Kelly turned around and got on her hands and knees. Sebastian knelt behind her and touched her beautiful round ass. He sidled up on his knees until his hard cock barely touched her – and stopped. Kelly sat up on her ankles and turned to him.

"Sebastian, please... I want this. I want you..." She kissed his lips and lovingly combed her fingers through his thick chest hair.

"I love you, Kelly."

"I know you do... Love me now. Please."

He eased her body back onto the rag and slowly – oh, so slowly – pushed his engorged cock into her and held still. She whispered his name. He pulled out and pressed slightly into her again.

"Please, Sebastian..." She begged him to love her, love her the way he used to love her before she had told him about Stevie – the way he loved her the night he asked her to marry him.

Sebastian thrust into her, thrusting so hard her face rubbed on the rag rug. He held her hips and continued mashing into her. Kelly yelled out his name, trying to cope with the force of his thrusts – faster, harder, deeper.

She grasped at the rug as she came hard, harder than she ever had before with Sebastian. He gripped her hips, thrusting even after he had climaxed, thrusting again and again – and she felt the electricity running down her legs – another orgasm mounting within her.

He finally ceased his thrusts and pulled her with him as he collapsed on his side.

"Holy shit, Sebastian... That was incredible!" He held her close to him. She felt the sweat from his chest and belly against her back.

He exhaled into her hair. *"I can never get enough of you, woman..."*

Kelly smiled and whispered, *"I know..."*

And they slept on the rag rug in front of the large stone hearth...

Kelly woke before Sebastian. She picked up her clothes and stealthily left the cabin, closing the door silently behind her, and walked down the path to the pond. Sitting behind the reeds so she wouldn't disturb the tranquil setting, she observed the wildlife. A great blue heron ignored her presence – it had found a small perch. As the bird tipped its head high, the small fish slid down the bird's gullet.

Further out in the water, Kelly spied an otter sow swimming on its back with her pup. It had captured a crayfish and was happily munching on the small crustacean. The first year they were at the cabin Kelly had discovered the otter's couch under a small knoll at the shoreline. At that time Sebastian wasn't too impressed with her find.

She heard him coming up behind her. "Shhhh... come here... there's a mallard hen with her brood."

Sebastian carried two coffee mugs with him. As he crouched down next to his wife, he handed one to her. He followed her gaze and watched as the duck swam near them followed by about ten ducklings.

"Brood?" He assumed brood meant ducklings, but he wanted to know more.

"The babies, silly. When the ducklings are following the hen, their mom, they're called a brood." Kelly and Sebastian sat on the edge of the pond near the reeds.

"You made good coffee. This is exactly how I like it." Kelly leaned in and kissed her husband. "Oh, see that smaller duck over there?" She pointed out a duck further along the shore. "That's a northern pintail hen."

"I can't tell the difference between a mallard and a pintail."

"Okay, watch when the mallard hen displays her wings..."

"Displays?"

"Flaps her wings... When the mallard hen displays, you'll see blue speculum feathers..."

"You lost me."

Kelly put down her mug and rose up, kneeling on the soft grass. She pointed to a bird farther out in the water. "Look! There's a loon with her hatchlings!"

"Hatchlings? I thought they were a brood."

"Listen... Baby ducks are ducklings and when they're following their mama, the hen, they're called a brood." She looked at Sebastian, who was frowning. She ignored the look and continued. "Loon babies are hatchlings when they hatch. See? And when they're a little older, they're called chicks."

Kelly pointed to another loon farther out in the water. "Look how she's carrying the chicks on her back!" She sat on her feet and took a long sip of her coffee.

Sebastian was always amazed at the amount of knowledge Kelly possessed about nature and the surrounding woodlands and waterfowl. He remembered back when he first met her at the Harbor Pub. She wanted to introduce him to nature, but he resisted. What a fool he was. But after several years of prodding, he finally appreciated her world. And now he loved learning about the outdoors, especially since she was his teacher.

"We're coming down to the pond tonight, Sebastian. I want you to listen to the loon calls."

"Whatever you want, Love. I'll build a fire pit. Would you like that?" He finished his coffee and placed the empty mug on the ground.

She kissed his mouth. "I'd love that!" Kelly lay back on the soft mossy grass. "Make love with me. Right here..." She wiggled out of her shorts.

Sebastian stood and removed his jeans and boxers. She looked up at him and laughed. "You are always ready!"

He lay down next to her. "That's because you're in my life, silly." He echoed the name she called him when they watched the ducks.

"Oh, that's so sweet!" Kelly crawled up on her husband's body, sitting astride his extremely hard erection. She leaned down and kissed Sebastian's lips, first softly, then crushing her mouth against his, consuming his tongue, making love to him with her tongue.

He held her close to his chest, pinning her to him, letting her tongue taste his mouth, his face, his eyes. So many things he loved about her, but her sweet kisses were still his favorite.

"Love me, woman..." Sebastian pushed her hips up and let her slowly come down on him – slowly – until his length filled her...

Kelly whispered, *"I love you so much... always and forever..."* She kissed her husband, loving her husband, drowning in her husband's love. He put his arms around her and held her close, knowing if she moved he would come too soon. He wanted this moment to last – his wife atop him, loving him, letting her beautiful woman body cover him.

He would always treasure this moment – making love with his wife down by the shoreline, the great blue heron strutting nearby among the reeds, the loons carrying their chicks out in the middle of their pond, the mallard hen leading her brood by the shore, the early morning sun still low in the cloudless sky, a soft breeze rustling the leaves in the stand of birch trees – and his wife's warm breath on his face. Oh, yes, this was a moment he would keep deep in his heart. Always and forever...

That afternoon as promised, Sebastian made a small fire pit. There was enough fieldstone around the property to create the perimeter and walls. He hauled sand from down the shoreline for the base, and created a teepee of logs from the pile he had chopped the previous year. And he sharpened the ends of sapling branches for the bratwurst and marshmallows. Everything was ready for their date night.

With the fire pit completed, he walked up to the cabin. In his fist he carried a bunch of blue cornflowers. Sebastian closed the door quietly behind him. He tied the green stalks together with string.

It was warm in the bedroom. Kelly was taking a nap lying on her front in the nude. She had opened the window, letting in a cool spring breeze. He placed the delicate blooms on his pillow and crept up on the bed. She stirred when she felt his body press into the mattress. Sebastian put his hand on her legs. Kelly turned over and smiled at her husband, her Ulysses. He couldn't remember a lovelier sight than this – his wife, lying on their bed, looking at him with those beautiful emerald eyes.

"Did you build my fire pit?" She pulled his body, making him lay on her.

"Yes Love, your fire pit is ready. I even sharpened sticks for the brats and marshmallows."

"Wow, you really do love me!" And she kissed him. "And you're sweaty. I took a shower earlier. I bet there's enough hot water for you."

Sebastian laughed and kissed his wife. "Yes, ma'am." He got up and removed his pants and boxers. She loved watching him strip. His body was beautiful – his chest and belly as well as his forearms and legs covered with thick soft black hair. Such a sight – and it was all hers.

"Don't move!" And he escaped into the bathroom. While he was in the shower Kelly discovered the small bouquet of blue cornflowers. Oh, she loved that man. She sat up and clutched the impromptu bouquet to her chest – and cried.

Sebastian came out of the shower and saw his wife crying. "What's wrong?"

"You gave me flowers!" And the tears started anew.

"These are happy tears?" Leaving his towel on the floor, he got up on the bed and kissed her face, wiping the tears with his fingers.

"These are happy tears..." And she kissed him back. Sebastian kissed her shoulder, caressing her breast. Kelly held his head close to her heart and pulled on his long wet hair until his face touched hers. "Seb, what would I do without you?"

"Love, you'll never have to worry about that." He kissed her eyes, loving his wife... "Tell me what you want..." Sebastian kissed her tears.

"I want you to hold me and never let me go..." She closed her eyes – loving the feel of his soft beard against her face.

He kissed her lips. "I almost lost us because of my carelessness." He kissed her again, chastely, lovingly. He nestled between her legs. "I will never be so stupid again – I will never *not* tell you how I feel, never *not* tell you I love you... Never let you feel abandoned or alone or unloved."

She stroked his smooth back, moving her hands across his shoulders, following down his spine... "I know... Thank you..."

And they made love on that bed – slowly... She wrapped her arms around his neck, kissing his neck, his shoulders, her legs locked around his waist. She never wanted him to stop loving her, never wanted him to stop...

Sebastian slightly turned and bending one knee brought his leg up, giving him more traction as he pressed into her. Physically making love with her was the only way he had to show her his love. She was the wordsmith – he was the caveman. He was never a poet, never a writer, never someone who could lace words together in such a way that she would know how he felt – truly felt about her. This was the only way...

And she shed tears. He watched her cry but didn't stop. He knew her tears and these weren't tears of sadness. He knew these tears. These were tears of love – full, complete love. Tears of adoration for the man she married, for the man to whom she gave her life, her love, her body, her soul. And he would cherish these tears as he cherished the woman who shed them.

And as the first night they were with each other, they came together in mutual orgasm, loving each other, vowing to treasure their love, caring for each other, honoring each other – until the inevitable death...

27

Starry Starry Night

That evening, Sebastian filled a box with all the essentials of a good date night: a bucket for the Corona beers, bratwurst and buns, mustard, marshmallows, matches and kindling, and beach towels if they decided to go for a midnight skinny dip. Kelly carried the folding armchairs.

The dusk of night was upon them. The sun was low – horizontal streaks of red, lavender and hazy shades of peach blessed the early evening sky. Kelly set the chairs close together by the fire pit.

"Sebastian, I love it! When did you become so talented?"

He put his arm around his wife, pulled her to him and whispered into her hair, *"I thought you knew how talented I was..."*

She pressed her hands on his chest, feeling his heart beating. "I do know how talented you are!" Kelly closed her eyes and kissed her husband's lips – loving the feel of his beard against her face. She opened her eyes and looked into hazel eyes shrouded beneath heavy brows. This image would forever stay in her heart. This man, her husband, her Ulysses – Sebastian would forever be a part of her life, her heart, her soul. Always and forever...

The fire he built was perfect. They propped their feet up on the raised perimeter of fieldstone while roasting their dinner. When the beer-infused brats were properly blackened, they were pulled off the sticks and placed in buns. Kelly spread her favorite brown mustard on her brat – Sebastian preferred his plain. She ate one while he ate two and they both enjoyed the ice-cold beer.

A log fell into the crackling fire resulting in a cluster of glowing embers swirling up to the heavens. As she watched the glowing sparks dance in the cool air, Kelly noticed the stars dotting the heavens. She pointed up to the constellations so bright in the night sky.

"There's the Big Dipper!"

Sebastian's eyes followed where she pointed. "I know the Big Dipper. I was a boy scout!" He said the words with great pride.

"Is that how you learned to make a fire pit? And a fire?" She looked at his face – his beautiful face.

"I know where to build a fire and how to start a fire. I also learned how to make a fire pit in scouting, but it wasn't this nice."

"You really did a nice job. I told you I was impressed."

"You said, dear wife, that you were surprised."

"Well, I was surprisingly impressed!" And she leaned into him and kissed his lips. "I love my surprisingly impressive husband!"

"Nice recovery..." and he kissed her back. "And I know the Big Dipper, although it's been a while since I've enjoyed looking at it so much." The fire cast flickers of light on Kelly's face – he couldn't remember when she looked so beautiful. "So tell me about the stars, Love." He meant it, too.

"Okay, so if you know the Big Dipper... Do you see the pointers?"

"No... Where am I looking?" He looked up at the Big Dipper, but wasn't sure where else to look.

"Okay, look at the bowl of the Big Dipper... The two front stars of the bowl are the pointers."

"Yeah, okay... I see them now. Why do you call them 'pointers'?"

"Because they point to the North Star. So, when you face the North Star – Polaris – you are facing north."

"Yeah, I think I knew that..."

"Did you also know you can never get lost on a starry night? Just look in the sky and see the Big Dipper..." She pointed up and made an outline of the formation with her finger. "If you know where the pointers are, you'll find the North Star."

She was looking up at the sky when she felt his beard brush her cheek. She looked at Sebastian in time to get kissed right on her lips.

"I love you, woman." He pulled her head forward and kissed her harder, pushing his tongue into her mouth.

She responded with a groan that came from deep within her body. "I love you too, mister." She fondled his beard, her fingers tracing up to his ears.

"So before this gets out of hand, tell me more about the stars." His lips were lightly pressed against her mouth. As he spoke, she inhaled his warm, sweet breath.

God, she loved this man. He smiled his best smile, the one that he showed her so many years ago in the bar – the smile she could never resist. Even now she would have gladly drowned in her husband's love. But he wanted to learn more and for a man who was so resistant to nature she wasn't going to lose this moment.

"So Polaris is the tip of the tail of Ursa Minor – the Little Dipper." Sebastian again looked up into the sky. "Now..." she instructed him with her finger in the air. "Follow your pointer in the other direction. See that bright white star?" Again he followed her finger to where she pointed.

"Yes... The real bright one?"

"Yes, that's right. That's Regulus in the Leo the Lion constellation." She looked at Sebastian, making sure he really wanted to know this because she really wanted to tell him about the stars. "Now see what looks like a reverse question mark?"

"Wait..." Sebastian couldn't immediately see that damned question mark... then he saw it. "Yes, okay, I see it!"

"That's the tail of the Lion. Neat, huh?"

"That really is neat. I never knew that."

"So, okay, see kind of that darkness where there's only a few bright stars in the foreground? That's the plane of the Milky Way Galaxy, the area between galaxies..."

While she looked up, Kelly drank from her bottle of beer. She turned to Sebastian, but he wasn't focused on the night sky– he was staring intently at her. "Thank you."

"Seb, thank you for what?"

"Thank you for finding me."

The peace of the night was broken with a mournful call.

"That's the loon... Listen..." And the loon call echoed across the pond, followed by an answering call from farther away. "Loons don't mate for life, which is sad."

"You and me, Kelly... We mate for life."

"I dearly hope so." And she leaned in her chair and kissed her husband's lips. She took his hand and held it, lovingly caressed his knuckles with her thumb. And they sat silently, listening to the loons and an occasional splash from a fish jumping for an insect dinner.

"Would you like to roast some marshmallows, Love?"

"Yes..."

He reached down beside him, retrieved the bag of marshmallows and handed her two new sticks.

"Good, you bought the jumbo marshmallows. Next time, let's remember to get graham crackers and Hershey bars."

"S'mores?"

"S'mores!"

"If you want, we can make a run to Aggie's tomorrow. We'll be here all week." Sebastian looked at the heavens. "We're supposed to have good weather."

"I'd like that." Kelly leaned in and kissed him.

They pushed the large white puffs onto the sticks and held them over the logs. But Sebastian held his too near the fire and it burst into a flaming torch. He brought it close to his face, and blew out the fire from the nearly incinerated marshmallow.

"Let's try this again..." He ate his mistake and successfully roasted another marshmallow. They took turns eating them off each other's sticks. But as Kelly fed one of the toasted treats to Sebastian, she got some in his beard and mustache.

"Seb, there's marshmallow all over your beard!" Kelly touched the sticky, melted goo that had already started to harden. "I can clean that off..."

"I've got a much better idea!"

She played coy. "Pray tell!"

He rose from his chair and began pulling her up. But Kelly complained that she only got to eat a few roasted marshmallows. He ignored her protests.

"Let's get into the water."

She looked out over the pond, the water appearing black. "Are you sure about this?"

"Yes Love, I'm sure." He kissed her, promising to keep her warm if the water was cold.

"I'm game if you are." They stripped. Sebastian stepped into the water first.

"It's a little cool, but it's not bad..." He held her hand as she followed him into the water. They walked out into the sandy shallows. With each step the water rose higher on their legs. He let go of her hand and fell back into the water, splashing her as he partially submerged. Kelly did a shallow dive into the water, propelling her body out into deeper water. Sebastian waded out to where she stood.

"Come with me." They walked out a little deeper. He turned and holding her close, lay on his back in the cool water. He pushed off with both feet, swimming a backstroke. Kelly put her head on his chest, feeling his muscles as he moved through the black water. Soon she looked back and noticed their fire pit slowly fading behind them.

"We need to go back, Sebastian." He made a lazy turn and continued his backstroke, Kelly still lying on his muscular body, still listening to the beating of his heart...

They wrapped their wet bodies in large beach towels and held hands while sitting by the dying fire. They shared the last bottle of Corona.

"This has been a good day." She gazed into the fire, watching the sparking remnants of embers.

Sebastian lifted her hand and kissed her knuckles. "You're feeling good, Love?"

"I'm tired, but I guess that's to be expected."

"I want you to rest as much as you want this week. We won't leave until Saturday."

He knew Phil and Carolyn were more than capable of running his business. Carolyn had quickly learned the ways of the office, which meant Phil didn't have to screen incoming calls. His workload increased, which made for a more productive business. Sebastian even gave Phil a bonus for bringing in new clients. And with her background in criminology, Carolyn had shown the men how to perform more extensive research on prospective clients.

Sebastian could also conduct more out-of-town business meetings with prospective clients, though he hadn't shared that information with Kelly yet.

She stifled a yawn. "Can we turn in?"

"Yes – let me carry you to the cabin. We'll leave the chairs here." He wrapped the towel around his waist and, pulling her towel around her shoulders, lifted her in his arms. Kelly rested her head against his chest as he climbed the steep hill to the cabin. He kissed her forehead, but she had already fallen asleep. He carried her through the rooms and lay her on their bed, covering her body with the quilts.

He leaned over her and whispered, *"I can never get enough of you, woman."*

28

Foreshadowing

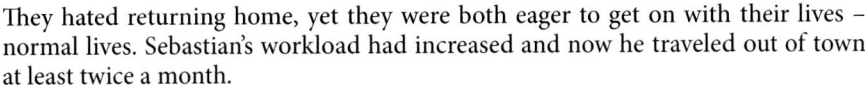

They hated returning home, yet they were both eager to get on with their lives – normal lives. Sebastian's workload had increased and now he traveled out of town at least twice a month.

Kelly felt better than she ever had, and was busy with her summer school students. Her high school graduates could take the class and possibly test out of college level English Comp in the fall. When she first approached her principal about beginning this course, she was met with apprehension. Mr. Jorgenson didn't know if any graduating students would be interested in taking a summer-school class. But his fears were put to rest when these classes became so popular Kelly had to add another five-week class toward the end of the summer.

Because of her health, she couldn't teach the first summer course. But she was definitely up to teaching the second one. She felt stimulated being back in the classroom setting. And she was ready to begin teaching her regular high school classes in the fall. Soon her days were once again filled with her students. And of course Sebastian was with her most nights helping her grade papers. And like before, many nights she went to bed covered in shiny stars and smelly dinosaur stickers...

Wednesday nights became date nights. Usually they went down to the Harbor Pub and enjoyed Kevin's jazz quartet. They enjoyed dancing to the soothing tones of the music which brought out Sebastian's romantic side – even more than usual if that was possible. They would dance close together or enjoy a low-key swing – Sebastian gently pushing her away, spinning her around and pulling her back, again holding her close.

As he escorted his wife back to their table, Sebastian tried taking in everything special about this evening. Kelly was healthy – she shined out on the dance floor. And he felt more in love with her than he ever had. He blessed the day he met her, and was grateful that she saw more than his scruffy beard and wrinkled shirt. Sebastian knew his life was blessed because of her – because of this beautiful redhead...

"Let's go home." Sebastian looked into her eyes. "I have to leave town tomorrow."

"Are you flying out?"

"No, it's just a four-hour drive and I'm taking my new BMW x6. I want to stretch her legs and see what she can do."

"When do you leave?"

"Tomorrow evening, right from the office. I want to get to the hotel early and be fresh for my meeting."

Kelly never asked about his clients. It wasn't that she wasn't interested in his business, because she was. But he only discussed the confidential details with Phil and Carolyn.

"When will you be home?"

"Friday, mid day. It's an early breakfast meeting. I'll leave right from the meeting." He took her hand and kissed her knuckles.

"Good. I hate it when you're gone."

"I could have Phil take the meeting."

"No. He's got kids who like to see their dad home for dinner. You go, and I'll plan something special for us to do Friday night."

Sebastian leaned across the little table and kissed his wife. Her eyes were always so beautiful in the Harbor Pub. He didn't know if it was because of the lighting in the pub, or the fact that when he first saw those emeralds, he knew his life would change forever...

"Let's go home. I want to make love with my wife." They said their goodbyes to Kevin. Sebastian took Kelly's hand and together they left the bar.

He stopped outside of the pub door. "Our life is perfect. Lots of memories here..."

Kelly pulled him close. "All my memories of you start right here."

"I love our life..." Kelly rested her head on Sebastian's chest, listening to his beating heart.

He was trying to catch his breath. They had started their lovemaking on the bed, and finished next to the bed on the white Berber carpeting. "I love our life, too... If you don't kill me first!"

Kelly rolled off her husband's body and lay beside him. She propped herself up on one elbow and played with his chest and belly hair.

"I mean it – we're both doing so well. And it's not that I don't love my high school students, because I do. But now that I've got my master's, I want to teach college level literature."

"Where?" Sebastian kissed his wife's forehead. "At the community college in town or where you got your degree?"

"I like the professors there, but I don't like the drive. Here would be good."

"Then do it."

Kelly looked deeply into her husband's eyes. "Just like that?"

"Just like that." Sebastian checked his watch. "Let's shower and hit the hay. I want to get to the office first thing in the morning."

"Just let me have a few more minutes of *you* – okay?"

He couldn't turn down such a request. Sebastian put his arm under her head and pulled her close. "I love you, Kelly."

"I know you do." She kissed his face. "I love you, Seb – always and forever."

They eventually got up and showered. By the time they returned to bed, Sebastian was ready to make love to his wife again. As he lowered himself into her arms, Kelly pressed her face into his neck. She loved the feel of his beard tickling her face, his long hair becoming tangled in her fists as he pushed her body into incredible orgasms.

"I never want this to end... I love you so much." She kissed his lips, his neck, his shoulder...

"It will never end, Kelly. It will never end." Sebastian kissed her face and held her tight. "I promise. It will never end."

Carolyn took good care of her boys, as she referred to Phil and Sebastian – keeping them organized, fielding calls and generally keeping the two men in line. They were grateful for her help. Since graduating from college, she had wanted to pursue a law degree. But within months of joining Sebastian's business, he convinced her that her strengths were in numbers and statistics. Carolyn had a great math aptitude, and enjoyed the challenge of examining the financial statements of prospective clients.

Through Sebastian's encouragement, Carolyn applied for and was accepted into a master's program in forensic accounting. She could take many of the courses online, and the rest were taken at the same university where Kelly received her master's degree.

Carolyn's classes met Tuesday nights, so she left work early those days and came to work late the following day. She never dreamed her life could get any more exciting than it was now. And because of Sebastian and his faith in her, she was realizing greater things for herself and her children.

Their morning had been busy. The week before, Carolyn had vetted a prospective client. Now Phil and Sebastian met with the woman at a luncheon meeting, and they rocked it, signing papers on the spot. But it wasn't until they had left the restaurant that Sebastian gave Phil an unexpected high five.

"That was big!" Phil hadn't seen this side of Sebastian very often. He felt proud that he had brought the client to Sebastian's attention.

After returning to the office, Phil opened his laptop. "Seb, we haven't done any research on this guy." There was concern in his voice over the out-of-town meeting Sebastian had personally arranged for the following morning. Phil was trying to find some information on the client.

"I'm good with it. Besides, I want to see what my BMW x6 can do. I'm leaving town right after work. Don't worry about it."

Phil looked up from his monitor. "I wish Carolyn had researched him."

"She's busy with her kids now." Carolyn had taken the week off to care for her children who were both battling colds. "Besides, we haven't had any issues up to now."

"If you say so." Phil didn't want to belabor the discussion, but he couldn't keep the concern out of his voice. He still wasn't comfortable about this prospective client.

"Phil, weren't you leaving early today?"

"Yeah, this is parents' night at St. Anne's middle school. Some pre-Thanksgiving gathering."

"Why don't you head out? I'm leaving around six thirty – I'll close up."

Earlier that day, Kelly had gone to the salon where they styled her hair for her wedding. The hairdresser matched her original hair color, and after an hour of anticipation showed her the finished product.

"No more silver! I love it." Kelly held the mirror as the stylist turned the salon chair in a circle, giving Kelly a 360° look at her new-old color.

After leaving the salon, Kelly spent the afternoon with Gabriella and Finn. She loved being an aunt to Brie's baby, who was already eight months old. Raffaele was accepting some out-of-town dates, but mostly he was in the recording studio.

He and his manager had started a record label highlighting young talent. Musicians and singers of all backgrounds often filled their recording studio. Many times he would have his son strapped to his chest as he sang at the mic. Finn enjoyed listening to his father's strong voice. Raffaele's record producer even suggested the next album cover be a photo of his baby sound asleep on his daddy's chest.

"Kelly, would you and Sebastian be Finn's godparents?"

"Oh, Brie. Yes! We'd be honored!" She reached over and brought the baby over to her lap, letting him sit on her bouncing legs.

"That's what I thought. Do you think your mom would do the honors and baptize Finn?"

"She wouldn't miss it for the world. My mom loves you and Raffe – and this would give her a chance to meet Finn." Kelly brought the baby to her face and inhaled his baby smell. "Why don't you call her?"

"I will." Brie watched as Kelly held the baby close to her face.

"I'm going to be your godmommy!"

Brie laughed, but then she got serious. "Kelly, do you and Sebastian regret not having kids?"

"Um..." She kissed Finn's exposed tummy. "I don't think so. Sebastian really never showed an interest in having kids and, well you know me. By the time I get home from school I've had my fill of kids – except this little one!" Kelly blew raspberries on his bare tummy. Finn's high-pitched squeal filled the house, his little arms beating against his sides. "Brie, he's perfect."

"I know..."

"Raffe's a good daddy?" Kelly's full attention was on Finn as he drooled on her jeans.

"Kelly, I'm surprised that I get to have my baby at all!" Brie picked up her phone and scanned through pictures until she found the shot of Raffaele at the professional studio condenser microphone – with the infant strapped on his chest, sleeping soundly just below his daddy's chin.

"Look at this! It's just the craziest thing you've ever seen! Finn loves his daddy!"

Kelly took the phone and perused through more pictures, laughing at some, cooing at others. While she held him close, Finn reached for her necklace and pulled.

"Oh no you don't, little one." Kelly carefully opened his fingers and pulled the rock pendant out of his hands. "You can't have this."

"That necklace is so neat, Kelly."

"Sebastian had it made for our anniversary. I swear Brie, that man is the most thoughtful human on the planet!"

"Where is that man anyway?"

"He's out of town this afternoon. He's got a new client – *yes he does*!" She couldn't get her fill of the little boy who was entranced with his Auntie Kelly talking baby-talk to him.

"Did he fly out?"

"No – he's got to test out his new BMW. Holy crap, Brie – boys and their toys!"

The front door opened and Raffaele came into the room. Finn saw his daddy and screamed with exuberant joy, holding up his chubby hands and grabbing air. Raffe took his son's small compact body and swept him up in an arc, holding the baby high above his head. *"Ciao, il mio ragazzo!"*

Kelly winked at Brie and stood. "I'm going to leave, girlfriend. Let's do breakfast tomorrow morning. Sebastian won't return from his meeting until almost noon."

"I like that idea. Call me."

This had been a long day. She'd be alone in their bed tonight, but then tomorrow she would plan a special homecoming for Sebastian. She was tired, and after eating some of his leftover herb pasta and chicken piccata she went upstairs.

Kelly brushed her teeth and changed out of her clothes into one of Sebastian's T-shirts. Usually she would have taken off her necklace before bed. Tonight she kept it on – wanting to feel closer to *him*. She put her cell phone in its charger stand on the bedside table and pulled his pillow over to her side of the bed.

The really too big television was still in their bedroom. Sebastian had wanted to move it out of the room, but Kelly liked it – the TV stayed. Scrolling through the favorites menu, she chose an old black and white movie. As she fondled the rock pendant between her fingers, her last thoughts were of him – her husband, her Ulysses.

29

Revenge

He couldn't keep a job. They said it was his attitude.

His dad – was he his dad? His mom said this one really was, but who knew – anyway, his dad began using his head as a punching bag when he turned 12. Happy birthday, Stevie. Fuck me!

In his junior year he almost flunked out of high school, but not because he wasn't smart enough – he was. He just couldn't put up with the bullshit in his classes. His teachers didn't understand him, writing him up as a disruptive influence. He wasn't disruptive – he was funny! His classmates laughed when he said shit to his teachers.

He dropped out of high school in his senior year but made up for it with a high-scoring GED. With that bullshit behind him he could get on with his life.

He stayed in a basement room in his mom's house. His dad, like all the other men in his life, had left years ago. He had some dead-end part time jobs and then got a good job at the post office mailroom sorting outgoing mail. He was earning good money but he told his mom it was only a part time job so he could stay at her house.

Stevie was becoming Stephen and was finally coming up in the world. After five years at the post office he had a savings account and spending money. And he got married – to a teacher no less. Definitely upped his respectability quotient. She was nice to him and laughed at his jokes – guess she could see through his bullshit. She had really cool green eyes and curly red hair. No figure, but that could be fixed eventually. They lived in her efficiency apartment.

Before he got married, he hadn't seen a lot of action – but his wife liked to fuck and they did! She gave pretty good head, too, but also wanted him to go down on her. Not his cup of tea, though if that's what it took to get fucked then so be it. He went down on her occasionally, but more often than not he just wanted her to spread her legs and let him have his way with her.

He didn't care if she had an orgasm or not – that's not what women wanted anyway. They just wanted a dick in their cunt and a man on top – or behind. That became his favorite way to fuck – her lying on her face and fucking her from behind. That way he didn't have to see her little titties. No difference between looking at her chest or her back – definitely not much there to get excited about anyway.

He had good insurance from the post office and he had savings. He tried convincing her to have her titties fixed. Jesus, at least a B cup would be an improvement – a C would let him really enjoy himself. He figured he was sliding the slippery slope when all he wanted was to fuck her on her knees, doggie style. She had a great ass – what more did she want?

Apparently, she didn't *want* any more. She threw him out of her apartment. He left, packing his shit in a box and leaving before she got home from work. Good riddance! Thank goodness he could still move back with his mom.

But he wasn't done. That bitch couldn't tell him what to do. His whole life he had put up with people telling him what to do. He was an adult now and she had no business kicking him out. He still had his key. That night, he took his mom's car and drove over to the apartment building. He waited outside her apartment – their apartment! Stevie waited until her bedroom light went out and then waited another hour. He was going to surprise her with a good fuck.

The key slipped into the lock, the door opened, the apartment dark. Her bedroom – their bedroom! – was off to the left. He made sure he didn't crash his shins into her stupid coffee table. Why she had that piece-of-shit in this small apartment was anyone's guess – she never had any taste. Her bedroom door was closed. What the fuck? That door was never closed. She had better not have a new roommate!

He turned the knob and pushed. There she was. Sleeping – alone. His baggy jeans were already unzipped. Easy peasy. He walked quietly to the bed... With one swift movement, Stevie pulled down the covers and forced her T-shirt up over her head. As Kelly struggled with her T-shirt, he yanked her underwear down - then while pushing down on her chest, he pulled out his dick.

Oof! He hadn't counted on legs! She kicked him right in the nuts! That bitch! But he still had the upper hand. He grabbed one of her legs – but she kicked him with the other leg and sent him flying off the bed. He hit the floor hard, banging his head against her piece-of-shit dresser.

Kelly stood over him as she pulled up her pants. "Get the fuck out of my house, you low life piece of shit." She screamed so loud! Christ, he never knew she had it in her. Stevie scrambled to his feet with his tighty whities down at his knees, and ran out of the apartment. As he gimped to his car, he swore he would get his revenge! Now more determined than ever he'd get his revenge...

He was served divorce papers within a week! When did she have time to see a lawyer? She must have been planning this all along! She had used him for what she wanted out of him and then threw him away. That bitch! Well, she'll get hers. He knew where she hung out – her and that bitch friend of hers Miss Boobs-A-Plenty. Why the hell didn't she want to look like that? He threw the documents in the garbage.

Stevie drove his mom's car down to the Harbor Pub. He knew exactly where she'd be. Her and that big-breasted bitch always sat in the same place. How predictable. There really wasn't an original bone in her body – except when he was giving her his bone! Ha! He still had it! This was the kind of humor people never appreciated.

He walked into the dark pub and made a beeline over to where Kelly and her bitch friend sat at the horseshoe-shaped bar. Hell, she didn't even know he was standing behind her. Stevie brusquely bumped her shoulder with his open hand, jostling her body forward into the bar. She turned and looked at him with that stupid *what the fuck* look on her face. What a bitch!

He pointed to her friend's rack. "Your friend here always had the goods, but you just wouldn't pump yourself up. You're not even a handful, bitch!"

A man who sat next to the women chimed in. "Sir, I think you owe these lovely ladies an apology."

"Why the fuck should I apologize to them?" Stevie was pissed! He was talking to *his* ex wife. This old dude had nothing to do with his business and he told him so. "That's *my* ex wife – the flat-chested one! And why the hell do you care? It's not your deal, man!"

The man rose from where he sat and stood to his full height. Oh shit – this guy was big. And in a voice Stevie swore rumbled from deep in the man's balls warned, "I'm a Marine and I will not let a piece of shit talk such garbage to these two lovely women."

The Marine walked toward him – maybe this wasn't the brightest idea he ever had. But before he could get out of the way, the big dude grabbed his collar and rudely forced him to walk to the exit. And adding insult to injury, the son-of-a-bitch planted a foot on his tailbone, propelling him out into the late afternoon shadows. Before the door closed, Stevie heard the people around the bar applauding.

He wasn't sure when it would happen, but he would get his revenge not only on his fucking ex but now on that fucking Marine, too. That son of a bitch better watch his step. He had friends. Sometime, somewhere when they least expected it – Bam! He'd get his revenge. No one pushes around Stephen!

He forgot about that day. Life went on and he had a pretty good life. His job was secure. He had moved out of his mom's basement and into an apartment with a woman who was stacked. It felt so good squeezing her big globes when they fucked. If his ex had just wanted to get pumped up they might still be together. But as long as his girlfriend put out he was satisfied.

The days at the post office were becoming monotonous, sorting the outgoing mail was getting old. But a few years later in late September, something happened that would eventually change his life. Stevie came across a whole bunch of those larger wedding invitation envelopes. He hated handling them – that odd size always fucked up the system.

He noticed a familiar name on the return address sticker. ***Kelly Isabella Cameron***. What the fuck? That's his ex's name. She was getting married? But that wasn't her address. He knew that area of town – it was the east end of the city where the wealthy people lived. He looked around at his coworkers – no one was paying any attention to him. No one ever did, which was fine by him. He slipped one of the large envelopes under his shirt – he'd check it out later.

That night, before his girlfriend got home from work his curiosity got the best of him. Stevie needed to know the contents of the envelope. He carefully tore open the flap and pulled out the printed card. He held the card under his bedside lamp and read...

Kelly Isabella Cameron
Daughter of the Reverend Ruth Cameron
and the late Frederick Cameron
and
Sebastian Giordano Bonsignore
Son of his treasured parents
Rosabella and Vicenzo Bonsignore
Request your presence to
Witness their wedding vows.

November 2nd
St. Catherine's Chapel

4 pm with reception
Immediately following at the Harbor Pub

Well fuck me. So the bitch is getting married. And this time to a rich guy. Fucking bitch! She found herself a sugar daddy. Stevie sat on his bed and opened his laptop. He Googled the name – Sebastian Giordano Bonsignore. Christ! He's a financial advisor with his own business! She'll probably quit her nowhere teaching job and get fat. Shit! This Bonsignore guy could afford to give her big titties – maybe as big as her friend Miss Boobs-A-Plenty.

Fuck her and her rich boyfriend. Fuck them all. He slammed the cover shut. But instead of tossing the invitation and envelope, he stashed them in his dresser drawer. He never knew when something like this might prove very valuable.

After several years, inflation hit and some workers at the post office were let go. Stevie was one of the lucky ones – his job was reduced to part time. His girlfriend had quit him a while back and he was again living in his mom's basement. He needed another part-time job.

He got a call. One of his buddies who worked at a hardware store got arrested and put in county lock-up. His cousin contacted Stevie and asked if he could cover Ronnie's hours for a few months – part time, three days a week. Sure. He could do that. The manager of the hardware store taught him how to make keys from blanks. Easy peasy. No brainer. And that was his job for the time his friend was in the county lock-up.

Over the years, Stevie had grown a beard and let his hair get long, stuffing it under a navy blue Milwaukee Brewers baseball cap. He had to look half-way respectable. This was a good gig as long as he kept his temper in check.

It was a slow day. Stevie had just returned from his break when he observed two men resembling Laurel and Hardy walk into the store. As they approached his kiosk, he recognized the skinny dude as the queer who owned a plumbing supply store. The other guy, the big dude was telling the queer what to write.

"Kelly's mom will love that color. Sebastian said to make it nice and he'll be blown away that we had time to paint."

Stevie recognized that unmistakable deep voice. That was the asshole who threw him out of the Harbor Pub. Son-of-a-bitch!

"Hi." The queer was doing all the talking. "We need two copies please."

Then the big dude – the fucking Marine – held out the house key.

Stevie took the key. He knew the Marine didn't recognize him – he looked so different with a beard and his baseball cap pulled low over his eyes.

While he cut the blank, it dawned on him – Sebastian and Kelly. Sebastian was the rich guy that Kelly married! This must be their house key, but he'd better make sure. He'd make small talk...

"Are you doing renovations on your home?"

"No, we're fixing up a room in our friend's home. This is his house key."

Stevie sized up the Marine. His friend Ronnie was about his size – and he knew he needed some extra cash, especially after being out of work for a few months. He also knew Ronnie would do anything for money. He had a mean streak, and if he asked him to fuck over someone, he could do it. Now he had to make sure he could put his plan into action.

Stevie handed one copy to the Marine who took it, putting a nice thumbprint on the bow of the key. Perfect.

"Oh, shoot," Stevie said, sounding confounded. "Give that key back. I think I messed up."

Roger handed the copy back to Stevie who pretended to throw it out. Because the kiosk walls were high, Stevie pocketed the key and threw away a blank. He made two more copies, put them into a small paper envelope and wrote out a charge slip.

When the men left his kiosk, he took the house key from his pocket and, fastening it to the brace, quickly made another copy. He then dropped the original key into a small envelope. If he could get Ronnie on board with this plan it could be epic – and he would finally get his revenge.

But his friend had really fucked up – he had to spend another year at the work farm. Jeeze Ronald, you certainly know how to fuck up a good plan! But Stevie could wait. He had waited this long – another year won't matter.

He managed to keep his temper in check and was given more hours at the hardware store. Between working at the post office and here, he was bringing home a tidy sum. The money he was going to pay Ronnie would be money well spent.

After almost a year, Ronnie was released for time served. Stevie picked him up from the work farm. While they drove back to his mom's house, Stevie explained his plan and hoped Ronnie wouldn't fuck it up too much.

He had already called Sebastian's business office, pretending to own a start-up company – not even on the radar yet. Stevie had done his research and knew the correct buzz words to say that would get Sebastian interested. He said his company was out of town and wanted to meet in an early breakfast meeting. This way, he figured, Sebastian would leave later in the day, stay overnight and be ready for the fabricated breakfast meeting the next morning. He'd be too far away to interrupt Ronnie while he was fucking over his wife – *his* ex wife!

When the awaited evening finally came, Stevie convinced Ronnie to wear a ski mask and latex painters' gloves. But when he put the gloves on, Ronald complained they were too tight. Stevie pressured him, emphasizing that it was important to keep them on his hands at all times.

"Now, you know what you have to do." Stevie reviewed the plan with his friend. "You're gonna find her in bed and fuck her over, right Ronald?"

"I'm going to fuck her over."

"She likes it hard, Ron. Fuck her hard. She'll scream, but that's how she likes it. Do it hard."

He was already smiling. "She likes it hard, that's what you said."

"You got it!" He slapped Ronnie on his back.

"And don't forget to wear this condom, Ronnie!" Stevie gave him the Trojan condom, already out of the foil wrapper. "That's important! Wear a condom. And leave this house key on the kitchen counter." He held up the little brown envelope. "You have to leave *this* key on the kitchen counter, Ron. Got it? They have to find *this* key with that asshole Marine's thumbprint on it. Got it?"

But Ronnie's mind wandered... Stevie had promised him a thousand dollars. The things he could buy for a thousand dollars... After spending over a year in county, he would do just about anything for that kind of money.

Stevie slapped him aside the head. "Ronnie... Focus! I'll be parked outside the house so you can make a quick getaway! Got it?"

He turned back to his friend. "Got it! Thanks Stevie!"

Shortly after midnight, Stevie and his accomplice drove up to Sebastian's house and parked across the street. The porch light was on. Clutching the little envelope in his gloved hand, Ronald stepped out of the car and walked up the driveway.

Stevie watched Ronald carefully avoid the motion detector flood.

He watched Ronald walk up the front steps.

He watched Ronald put the duplicate key in the deadbolt lock... The door opened.

Stevie watched Ronald enter the house and push the door closed behind him.

Now Stevie waited...

Ronnie opened the little envelope and let the key slide out – it dropped on the butcher-block counter. He was going to earn his money, the money Stevie promised him. He unlaced his boots and took them off, moving them with his bare feet into the corner.

He slowly pushed through a heavy swinging door and entered a large dining room. He'd never seen such a large dining room. Ronnie touched the wall and finding a light switch, pressed it. The light had been dimmed before it was turned off and the antique chandelier glowed with a soft light. "Pretty..."

Ronnie walked around the main floor but couldn't find a bedroom – it must be up the stairs. He quietly made his ascent to the second floor. A light came from a room down the hall. He heard voices. He crept closer to that room and looked in. The sounds were coming from a TV. Gilligan was running from the Captain. Ronnie watched the black and white episode for a few minutes – then turned his attention to the bed. The TV cast enough light that he could see the sleeping woman.

Oh, she was pretty. He would like this.

He took off his pants and underwear. He hadn't fucked anyone in a very long time and he was ready! But when he tried putting on the condom, the latex gloves he wore stuck to it. Ronnie removed the gloves and with his bare hands rolled the condom on his thick, stubby dick.

He crept closer to the bed and walked around to the side where she slept. This would be fun. He put on the ski mask and pulled it down across his face, adjusting the eye holes.

The woman woke. She sat up and ***SCREAMED!*** Oh No! Don't scream! He hated that noise! Ronald backhanded her. The woman collapsed on the bed. Now he would have fun. He pulled the quilt away from her body, grabbed her underwear by the crotch and tore them off her legs. Ronald lumbered up on the bed and spreading her legs, knelt between them and pushed into her tight cunt. His mask twisted on his face – he pulled it off so he could see her. She was pretty.

The woman opened her eyes and kicked him, pushing her legs between their bodies – he punched her on the side of her head. He continued fucking her but he couldn't really feel anything. He pulled out and ripped off the condom, discarding it on the floor. He pushed back into her hard until he climaxed.

But he wasn't done – he hadn't fucked anything in over a year and he was just getting started. Ronald rolled her over. He knelt between her legs and fucked her. The woman came to and fought him. He hit her again. She fell back on the bed.

He pulled her hips up, again pushing his dick into her cunt. While Ronnie fucked her he pushed a fat finger deep into her rectum, pushing his finger in and out, in and out. He pulled out and pushed his fat cock into her butt and fucked her hard. Oh she was tight. He pumped hard and fast, holding her hips, digging his dirty fingernails into her soft flesh – warm liquid spread down his thighs.

Shit! The woman woke again – she screamed and clawed at her sheets. Supporting his weight with one hand on the headboard, he hit her hard in the back of her head. Before her body slumped onto the mattress, he climaxed into her ass. Oh this was fun!

Ronald rolled the woman on her back. Her mouth was open. He knelt at her pillow and grabbing her hair, lifted her head. There was so much blood on his dick and on her face – the white light of the TV making her blood appear black. He pushed his cock deep in her mouth and began jacking off in her throat.

The woman made gurgling sounds. He thought she was waking – but before he could hit her again, she bit down on his dick.

"YOU FUCKING BITCH!" He slammed his fist against her head. He grabbed onto the top of the headboard with a bloodied hand and got off the bed. While holding his bruised cock, the woman's gold necklace caught his eye. He growled, *"This is mine!"* and grabbed the stone, yanking the slender necklace from her neck.

Ronnie retrieved his pants and fled out of the bedroom and down the stairs. He ran across the dining room and pushed with bloody hands against the heavy swinging door, making it bang with a thud against the kitchen wall. Forgetting his boots, he ran out through the front door naked from the waist down, still holding his pants and the woman's necklace in his bloody hands.

Where's Stevie?

Where's Stevie's car?

Where was Stevie?

Kelly fumbled for her cell phone and grasped it tightly in her hand. Opening one eye, she carefully pressed 9-1-1.

"911 operator. What's your emergency?"

Kelly could only whisper her words... *"I'... b... help...help..."*

"What's your address, ma'am?"

Kelly knew her jaw was dislocated – she spoke slowly, forming her words carefully. She told the operator to please hurry...

"Stay on the phone with me, ma'am. Is the person who did this still in your house?"

"No..."

"Stay with me, ma'am."

Kelly found her voice... *"Seb..."*

"Stay with me, ma'am. The police are on their way. Stay with me..."

Kelly heard sirens – a lot of shouting – many footsteps coming up the stairs.

Kelly knew help was here.

Kelly slipped into a coma.

Kelly's last thoughts were of Sebastian, her Ulysses – always and forever...

30

Lt. Joseph Rafferty

Sebastian was settled in the hotel room and had been sleeping for a few hours. His cell phone rang. Before answering, he looked at the time and the caller ID. He didn't recognize the number.

"Hello?"

"Mr. Bonsignore? Mr. Sebastian Bonsignore?"

"Yes, this is he..." He rose up on one elbow.

"Mr. Bonsignore, this is Lieutenant Rafferty. Your wife has been assaulted."

"What?" Sebastian sat up. "Is this a joke? Who are you?" Again he looked at the name on the caller ID.

"Mr. Bonsignore, I'm sorry, but this is not a joke. Your wife was assaulted in your home."

"What the hell!" He pushed back the covers and sat with his feet on the carpet.

"Sir, your wife is in the hospital. How long will it take you to get here?"

"I'm fucking out of town!" He stood and turned on the bedside light. "It'll take me at least four hours."

"Sir, what airport are you near?"

"Um... I don't know." He put the palm of his hand on his forehead. "I'm down near Burnsville at the Sheraton."

"Sir, there's a regional air field just south of you. We'll send an air ambulance for you."

"Why? Why are you sending a helicopter?" He pulled his pants on with one hand. Kelly might not survive the assault? God in heaven, what the hell happened! "I'm leaving now."

Sebastian quickly pulled on his shirt and slipped barefoot into his Tommy Bahama loafers. Without checking out, he raced into the parking lot and got into his BMW. After entering the name of the airport into the GPS he drove like a madman until he found the small airfield.

A security guard met him and let Sebastian know he received a call from the police. The air ambulance would be here in about 90 minutes.

"Thank you." He called Raffaele.

"Hey Seb, what's up?"

"Kelly's been assaulted. I don't know any details, except she's in the hospital."

"Which hospital?"

"God, I'm not sure. Find her. Please. The police are sending a copter to pick me up."

"You got it. I'll call you when I find her."

"One more thing. Call Phil. Please. Call him and tell him what happened."

Sebastian paced behind the security fence. What the hell happened to her? *Who* did this to her?

The security officer stopped him. "Sir, what about your car?"

He looked at his new BMW – and back at the officer. "I don't care..."

He was in the helicopter. His cell phone rang. It was Raffaele calling. Sebastian declined the call and texted him...

> *S. Bonsignore:* Can't hear. Text me.
>
> *R. Bonsignore:* Kelly's really fucked up. Whoever did this was brutal. You're not going home for a few days.
>
> *S. Bonsignore:* What do you mean I'm not going home?
>
> *R. Bonsignore:* Scene is a mess. Please get here.

The copter landed on the hospital's helipad. Sebastian was escorted to the elevator and down to the waiting area. He found his brother.

"What the hell happened?"

"Someone really fucked her up. She's in surgery."

"Why? Where's a doctor? What the hell is going on?"

A woman dressed in a business suit entered the room. "Sebastian Bonsignore?"

"Yes – yes, that's me. Please tell me about my wife. What did they do to her?" He looked like a man possessed. Strands of his long hair had come out of the neat leather tieback and hung across his face.

"I'm Rene Andresen – your wife's patient advocate. Your wife was assaulted. She has a dislocated jaw and a concussion." The woman waited until Sebastian digested what she was telling him. "Sir, your wife was raped."

"Oh, God!" He backed into a chair and sat down hard. Sebastian didn't know if he should cry or yell, so he did both – emitting a mournful wail heard throughout the ward.

Raffaele immediately sat beside his brother and held him tight. Now he addressed the woman. "Do they know who did this to my sister-in-law?"

"Sir, the CSU is at your brother's house right now. As soon as they know anything, they'll be in touch." Her pager buzzed. "Excuse me..." She left the room.

"But who...?" Sebastian watched as the woman left without answering his questions. He couldn't wrap his head around the whole scenario. His cell phone rang. He looked at the caller ID. It was Carolyn.

"Yes Carolyn..."

"Phil just contacted me. I'm so sorry. Have you seen her?"

"Thank you… I haven't yet." Sebastian leaned forward, pressing his elbow on his leg and resting his forehead on his clenched fist.

"I've done some research from home. Your business meeting was a ruse. I'm thinking whoever contacted you wanted you out of the house and preferably out of town." When Sebastian gave her no answer, she continued. "The number was from a cell phone registered to a Stephen Ward. Do you know that name?"

"No... Stephen... Oh God! Carolyn, do some checking for me. Find the name of Kelly's first husband. His name was Stephen. Court records would have that."

"I'll get right on it." She ended the call.

He looked at his brother. "Kelly may have been raped by her ex husband."

Raffaele didn't know how to comment – he didn't know anything about that chapter in Kelly's life. But he knew her mom needed to know.

"Seb, shall I call Ruth?"

Sebastian hung his head and closed his eyes. "Oh, God... Ruth. Yes, please..."

Rene returned to the room. "Mr. Bonsignore, you can see your wife, but she's heavily sedated. And one more thing... She must have bit her rapist. The CSU found DNA in her teeth."

For some perverted reason, Sebastian felt very proud of his wife. She must have put up one hell of a fight.

While his brother followed Renee into the ICU, Raffaele made the call. He knew he would wake her – it was early morning in Colorado. The phone rang only once.

"Hello?"

"Ruth? This is Raffaele Bonsignore, Sebastian's brother."

"Yes. Hi, Raffaele. Is everything okay?"

"Ruth, I need you to listen to me..."

"Just a minute." He heard her moving around. "Okay, I'm listening Raffe. Go on."

"Kelly has been assaulted. She was raped."

"Oh, my dear God in heaven!"

"She's in pretty bad shape. She's had surgery... she's in a coma."

"Surgery? What surgery? What were her injuries?"

"Whoever did this dislocated her jaw and gave her a concussion."

"Oh, my dear God..."

"I'm chartering a private jet. Can you get to the Grand Junction airport?"

"Yes. Oh, dear God... If you're doing all that, does that mean she might not make it?"

"I'm not sure. All I know is that Sebastian was out of town and they flew him back in an air ambulance."

"Okay, you tell me what to do, Raffaele."

"I'll text you. Just get to the airport. And Ruth... She could really use your prayers."

"Thank you, Raffe... Thank you."

Sebastian tentatively followed Renee into the ICU. A man's voice softly called to him.

"Mr. Bonsignore? My name is Andrew. I'm your wife's nurse."

He stopped and looked at the man dressed in bright blue scrubs. "Can I see my wife?"

"Yes, sir. Please follow me." Andrew escorted him to Kelly's bedside.

If he hadn't known the body lying in the bed was his wife, he would not have recognized her. The head was stabilized with a cervical collar – the face purple, the eyes black and swollen shut. One side of her skull had been shaved – a track of staples closed an arc-shaped incision.

"Sir, the trachea tube introduced in her neck is attached to a ventilator. Because her jaw was dislocated, the surgeon conducted a procedure called a tracheostomy that provides an alternative breathing route. We're monitoring her heart with an external pacemaker. And this..." he pointed to a screen with many graph lines and pulsing numbers, "is monitoring all her bodily functions."

Andrew waited until he was sure Sebastian comprehended all he told him, then continued. "Mr. Bonsignore, your wife is in a medically induced coma to help her body heal."

Sebastian looked at the nurse. "They said she was *in* a coma."

"Sir, yes she is, but we don't want her waking on her own. She'll be like this for at least several weeks depending on how she heals."

"What do you mean?" He took a step forward and carefully touched his wife's hand – his Dulcinea...

"Mr. Bonsignore... There were extensive injuries to her rectum and perineum, and your wife will need further reconstructive surgery. I'm sorry to be so graphic sir, but you need to know what she's going through." Again Andrew waited, watching Sebastian as he digested all the information given him.

"Sir... Mr. Bonsignore... The police are here."

"What?" Sebastian wasn't listening. He was concentrating on the numbers flashing on the monitor, hoping one of them would tell him that his wife would come out of this terrible situation.

"Sir, the police are here. Lt. Rafferty wants to talk with you. I told him I'd contact him when I saw you."

Sebastian spoke in a daze. "Yes. Yes... that's fine..."

"Sir, if you'd come with me now."

"Sure..." Reluctantly, he left his wife's side knowing he couldn't do anything for her. He looked at the nurse. "Andrew... Will my wife live? Will she come out of this?"

"Mr. Bonsignore, I'll do my best to see that she does. But her injuries were so severe. Whoever did this was big and strong – very strong."

Andrew picked up his desk phone and asked for an escort. He thanked Andrew and followed the orderly down the hall to a private room. When Sebastian opened the door, he was met by a tall distinguished-looking African-American police officer in full uniform.

"Mr. Bonsignore? I'm Lieutenant Joe Rafferty. I spoke to you on the phone."

Sebastian walked into the room – a long wooden table and several chairs took up much of the space.

"Yes... Um, good to meet you... Thank you..." He took a chair. A plainclothes detective approached the table.

"Sir," Lt. Rafferty spoke, though Sebastian wasn't registering anything he was saying. "This is Detective Rhodes."

"Thank you for meeting with us, Mr. Bonsignore." Sebastian saw his lips moving but didn't hear the words. He put his arms on the table, palms up and directed his question to the police officer.

"Who did this to my wife? Do you know who did this?"

Det. Rhodes took a chair across from Sebastian. He appeared so young and wore a business suit without a tie. "Sir, we arrested the man who raped and assaulted your wife."

"Who?" He looked hard at the detective. "Who?"

"Mr. Bonsignore, do you know the name Ronald Wolff?"

"Ronald?" Sebastian looked from the detective to the officer and back to the kid sitting across from him. "No, no I don't. Did he do this to my wife? Did they tell you he ripped her apart?"

"Yes sir." Lt. Rafferty interjected, stepping forward. "We're aware of her injuries. I'm so sorry."

"But why did he do this? I don't understand..." Sebastian was so close to tears, but he needed to keep it together.

"Sir," Det. Rhodes again took on an objective air. "Here's where we're confused. Do you know a Roger McClennen?"

"Roger? Yes, he's our friend. He walked Kelly down the aisle at our wedding."

"Sir, we found his finger print on a house key in your home."

"Well, yes... About a year ago, he did some renovation work for me and I told him to make copies of my house key."

"Sir," Det. Rhodes spoke carefully. "We don't believe Mr. McClennen had anything to do with the assault – we're just trying to connect the dots here."

Sebastian looked at the detective. "Roger is our friend, but I think I can help you to connect your dots."

"I'm listening..." The detective took notes in a small notepad.

"Many years ago, Kelly... my wife... Her first husband tried raping her. She never reported it because she overpowered him and threw him out of her apartment."

Det. Rhodes looked up from his writing. "How does Mr. McClennen fit into this scenario, sir?"

"Her ex husband's name was Stephen – I think Stephen Ward. After their divorce, he verbally assaulted Kelly in the Harbor Pub." He looked directly into the young detective's eyes. "There were many witnesses." Sebastian remembered the conversation he and Roger had at his house. "Roger manhandled her ex – Stephen – out the door. I bet somehow Stephen and this Ronald guy were in cahoots together."

"Do you think Mr. McClennen could shed some light on this?"

"Yes!" Sebastian pulled the cell phone out of his back pocket and pressed Roger's number. Even though it was well before daybreak, the phone rang once.

"Seb! What's up, buddy?"

"Roger, can you get down to Mercy Hospital right away?" He was watching the detective when he spoke to Roger.

"Why? What's up?"

"I'll explain. Ask for Lt. Rafferty when you get to the front desk. They'll bring you up to this room."

"Be right there."

Sebastian was grateful for so many reasons that Roger was his friend. He would always consider him not only a dear friend, but as close as a brother could be.

Det. Rhodes stopped writing. "Sir, did this Roger give any indication that he knew what happened to your wife?"

Now Sebastian was pissed. "*No!* He had nothing to do with it. *Christ!* Listen to me. My wife might die. Roger didn't do this! *Christ!*" And finally he put his face in his hands and broke down.

At Lt. Rafferty's suggestion, the detective left the room. After a few minutes he returned and handed Sebastian a bottle of water.

"Thank you..." He drank from the bottle and leaned back in his chair.

"Sir, I'm sure Roger is not involved. We just had to make sure."

"Well I'm sure." He looked at the detective askance. "And that's all you need to know."

Twenty minutes later, the door opened. Roger's large frame filled the doorway. He looked at the men gathered in the small room. Lt. Rafferty spoke first.

"Mr. McClennen? Please have a seat." Roger took the chair next to his friend.

"Roger... Kelly was attacked this evening in our home."

"What the hell?" Roger looked at the other two men in the room, then back to Sebastian. "What happened to our girl?"

"Rog... Kelly was raped. They messed her up real bad. They don't know if she'll make it."

Roger hung his head – pressing his fingers on his eyes. He quickly composed himself and wiped his face with both hands.

Sebastian took a deep breath and continued. "The police found a copy of my house key with your finger print on it."

"What the hell?" Roger looked again at the two men in the room.

"Sir," Det. Rhodes interrupted. "We know you don't have any involvement in this matter."

Though still puzzled, Roger visibly exhaled.

"Rog, where did you and Cody have the spare keys made?"

He thought for a moment. "We went to Mitchell's Hardware in the city. I remember because our next stop was at Gorman's Paint and Wall Covering next door."

"Do you remember who made the copies?" Sebastian wished he could be with his wife right now instead of in this pseudo interrogation room.

"Yeah..." Roger gathered his thoughts and closed his eyes... "Caucasian male, scraggly beard and a blue Milwaukee Brewers baseball cap." He looked up at the officer. "You don't see many Brewers caps in Minnesota."

Sebastian turned his attention to the detective. "You talk to that guy. I'm willing to bet you'll find a connection between him, Stephen Ward and Ronald."

"Ronald?" Roger spoke to Sebastian. "Ronald who?"

"Rog, the man who raped Kelly was Ronald Wolff."

"Shit, Seb. Ronnie just got out of county lock-up. He spent over a year at the work farm."

Det. Rhodes looked sharply at Roger. "And you know this because...?"

Roger became defiant that this ass with a badge was questioning him. "I know this because that piece of shit was brought up on B&E charges for vandalizing the New London Grille. While I served in the Marines as a Gunnery Sergeant, I was an MP. Now I do ride-a-longs with the police. We arrested him outside of the restaurant." He looked pointedly at the detective – and in his deep voice demanded, "Check it out!"

Det. Rhodes appeared frustrated. He pushed his fingers through his short curly brown hair and rose from his chair.

Sebastian's brain was fried. "Do you remember the date you had the spare keys made?"

"Yeah Seb," his voice softened. "It was the day after Kelly's surgery..."

Det. Rhodes stepped forward. "What surgery was that, if I may ask?"

The detective was finally out of bounds. Abruptly Sebastian stood – knocking the heavy table forward.

"Breast cancer! Any more questions?"

The young detective slunk back into a corner of the room and whispered, "*Sorry, sir...*"

Roger put a hand on his friend's arm and pulled him back down into his chair. Sebastian addressed Lt. Rafferty. "I'll find the date. I'm willing to bet that the guy who made the copy of the house key is somehow involved."

Lt. Rafferty's phone buzzed. He listened for several minutes, thanked the caller and put his phone way. "That was Det. O'Reilly. She questioned Ronald Wolff. Seems Ronnie gave up Stevie..."

"Stephen Ward?"

"Yup. Apparently Stevie wanted some revenge against your wife, Mr. Bonsignore. From what I gather – and I'll get more information soon – Stevie chose Ron Wolff because he was built like you, Mr. McClennen. Stevie wanted to pin the rape on you."

Roger slammed his large fist on the table. Sebastian reacted quickly, putting his hand on his friend's clenched fist. He turned his attention back to the young detective.

"So what about Stevie? Are you going to arrest him, too?"

Det. Rhodes walked forward, flexing his shoulders and adjusting his suit coat. "Mr. Bonsignore, it will be my pleasure to arrest this piece of shit." He looked at Lt. Rafferty. "If it's okay with you Joe, I'll get going on the warrant."

"Go!" Det. Rhodes left the room.

As he was leaving, another officer entered the room. "Excuse me... We found this with Ron Wolff." She handed a clear, plastic evidence bag to Lt. Rafferty.

"Thank you." Lt. Rafferty gave the bag to Sebastian. "Sir, does this belong to your wife?"

Roger watched as his friend opened the bag and poured into his hand a stone hanging from a gold chain – caked in blood.

"This was the necklace I gave Kelly for our fifth anniversary – two weeks ago.... The stone was from our pond. She found it the first year we were at our cabin..." As he handled it, blood transferred onto his fingers. He slowly wiped the blood from the stone, exposing a single diamond. "Kelly... Um... She always took her necklace off before going to bed. She must have kept it on last night. And he took it from her."

Sebastian looked at Roger and whispered, *"He took so much from her... from me..."*

"Keep the necklace, Mr. Bonsignore. We have enough evidence to book Ronald. We wouldn't need her necklace.

"Thank you... Now I want to go home... Please..."

"Sir, you can't go home – your home is a crime scene."

"That crime scene is my *home!*" Again Sebastian sat back in the chair, clutching the necklace in his closed fist, desperately trying to halt his tears.

A knock on the door interrupted the tension. Roger stood and opened the door to Raffaele. He nodded at Roger and took a step into the room and addressed the police officer.

"May I come in?"

"Lieutenant," Sebastian's voice betrayed his exhaustion. "This is my brother Raffaele."

Roger tried reasoning with his friend. "May I suggest you go home with Raffe?"

Raffaele sat across from his brother in the chair once occupied by the young detective. After Sebastian had made that first call, Raffaele had driven to his brother's home. The EMTs had already taken Kelly to Mercy Hospital and the CSU team was on site. Though he was not allowed to go upstairs, he still got a glimpse of the carnage.

"Seb, you're going home with me. Besides Ruth should be arriving in the next couple hours. You two will need each other."

Sebastian's eyes were raw, his long hair a mess. He didn't know what to do, which way to turn – he was lost without Kelly... Kelly – his wife, his heart, his soul, his Dulcinea, his reason for living.

Suddenly his words came back to haunt him – *Without you woman, I will die a miserable, lonely death.* He lay his head down on his folded arms and openly wept, not trying to be strong anymore. Roger and Raffaele put their hands on the man whose life was in such chaos.

"Come on, buddy..." Roger stood and helped his friend get to his feet. Sebastian looked at Lt. Rafferty.

"You got Ron Wolff. You get Stevie, you hear me?" Raffaele and Roger supported Sebastian's frame as they escorted him out of the room.

"I want to see Kelly before we go... I want to see my wife!" Both men looked at each other and nodded – they half carried him back into the ICU.

Andrew was standing at Kelly's bedside when he saw the men approaching. He quickly spread a light blanket on her body covering her modestly from the waist down.

"How's my wife?" Sebastian wasn't looking at Andrew – instead he looked at his wife and her exposed breast. Several sticky electrodes were on her chest and shoulders.

"Mr. Bonsignore, there's no change, which is good. I was just checking her vitals." Andrew looked at the trio of men. He acknowledged them and quietly cautioned, "You can stay for a few minutes." Andrew removed the electrodes from her skin and pulled the blanket up over her shoulders.

Roger cried. The Marine who had seen battle, who was as big as a mountain, who was as tough as they come – Roger cried when he saw what that son-of-a-bitch had done to the woman he loved in silence. He couldn't take his eyes off the damaged body lying on the bed... Her bruised and swollen face, her dislocated jaw – the trachea tube inserted into her neck and hooked up to the ventilator was literally her lifeline – wires attached to her shaved scalp monitored the electrical activity of her brain.

Sebastian whispered, *"They took her hair... God..."*

"I know Seb..." Raffaele was devastated himself and couldn't find the words that would give his little brother comfort.

"Sirs... Go home. There's nothing you can do for her. I'm sorry."

"You call me when she..." Sebastian was desperate for any sign of life. "You call me... when she wakes... you call me..."

The men collected their friend and practically dragged him out of the ICU, walking as one to Raffe's car.

"Roger, help me bring him to my house?"

"Yeah. I'll help get him home." Roger steered his friend into the back seat, but before he could buckle him in Sebastian lay down. "He's good. I'll follow you."

While he drove, Raffaele called Gabriella. She only knew her husband received a call from his brother, but didn't know the reason why.

"How's Sebastian?"

"I'm bringing him home with me." He paused, considering his next words. "Gabriella, Kelly's been assaulted. She was raped."

"Oh God!"

"*Caro mio...* She's in the ICU. Seb is staying with us for a few days."

"Of course, of course."

"And Ruth is coming in. She should be arriving at the airport within a few hours."

"Raffaele, I'll have everything ready. What else do you need me to do?"

"*Caro mio,* Roger might be staying with us, too."

"We have more than enough room. And Raffe..."

"Yes, my baby..."

"I love you."

"I know you do... *Grazie a Dio.*"

31

Coping Skills

Ruth arrived early the next morning and drove directly to the hospital. Gabriella met her outside the ICU.

"I was just with Kelly and I need to prepare you... She has so many injuries, Ruth. Her face is bruised and swollen. They had to perform surgery to relieve the swelling of her brain." Gabriella didn't want to overwhelm the woman with details, but didn't want her to be unprepared when she saw her daughter.

Ruth looked up at Brie. "Let's go see my daughter." They walked arm and arm into the ward.

A woman in pink scrubs met them. "Reverend Cameron, my name is Mari. I'm your daughter's nurse this morning."

Ruth put her hand on Mari's arm. "Take me to my daughter, please."

Mari nodded at Brie and together they escorted Ruth down the aisle. They stopped at a bed – Ruth didn't know why they were stopping.

Gabriella whispered in her ear. "This is Kelly..."

She looked at the body in the bed. *"No!"* Ruth crumpled to the floor. Mari and Gabriella caught her small frame and walked her to a chair at Kelly's bedside.

"Stay with her – I'll get some water." Brie held Ruth's hands while Mari returned with a glass of water.

"Here, drink this..."

Ruth looked up at Mari and whispered, *"Sorry..."* She sipped the cool water.

"My God. What did he do to her? I don't even recognize my own daughter!" She put a hand on Kelly's bed, caressing the white blanket. "I don't know what to do..."

Brie's hands rested on her shoulders. "Just be here for her."

"I'll leave you two. Let me know if you need anything." Mari excused herself and returned to her desk.

"Brie... What happened? Who did this? Why did he do this?" Her questions were many but Brie had few answers. Raffaele hadn't explained everything to her, just what she needed to know at the moment.

Brie walked across the aisle and brought another chair. The women sat by Kelly's bedside listening to the ventilator breathe for her. There were so many machines, all monitoring her many bodily functions.

"I don't know who this is..." Ruth broke down, sobbing into her hands. Brie rubbed her back, comforting her – not knowing how to rationalize this awful situation. She stayed by Ruth's side, listening to her quiet sobbing.

"Do I pray for her quick recovery?" Ruth looked into Brie's eyes, hoping for answers. "Or do I pray for the Lord to show mercy on my daughter's soul and bring her home..." Again she cried, unable to hold back her emotions...

Brie suggested they go back to her home and rest. As they walked out of the ward, Ruth thanked Mari for her kindness – and for caring for her beautiful daughter.

After Ruth was settled in the guest room, Brie silently entered the nursery. She picked up her sleepy baby and sat in the rocking chair. Finn suckled for a few minutes before Brie broke the suction and moved him to her other breast. After a few minutes she stood and laid him back down in the crib on his side – placing his favorite green giraffe next to him.

Brie walked down the hall and into her empty bedroom. She lay atop the comforter in their grand bed for a brief nap. And she cried...

After making coffee, Raffe came upstairs and stood in the doorway to their bedroom, listening to his wife. He closed the door behind him and crawled on the bed. He pulled her body to him, hoping her tears would stop – but when she felt his arm around her, she cried harder.

In the dim light of their room, she looked at her husband and caressed his face. "Raffaele, Ruth didn't recognize her own daughter – *I* didn't recognize her. Her face was so bruised. Her eyes..."

"I know." He kissed his wife. "I changed Finn while you were gone."

"Thank you... Honey, when Ruth saw..." Brie swallowed hard. "She asked me if she should ask God to show mercy and take Kelly home."

He knew the extent of her injuries, but was shocked that Ruth would ask God to let her daughter die.

"Raffe, you know more than I do about what happened to Kelly. What are her injuries? What did that guy do to her?"

He turned on his back, held his wife closer and spoke to the ceiling. "*Caro mio*, Kelly was raped and sodomized." Brie gasped. Raffe pressed his head against hers and wondered if he should continue. He softly exhaled and again addressed the ceiling. "He must have tried raping her mouth too. The doctors, they found fecal tissue in her mouth."

"I don't want to hear any more. No wonder Seb was devastated. Does he know all this?"

"I don't know."

"They shaved her head... Kelly just had her hair colored before she came over to see me yesterday afternoon." Brie rose up on one elbow and put her hand on her husband's chest. "Kelly was going to plan something special for him tonight."

"I know..." Raffaele rose from the bed and kissed her forehead. "Rest my baby... I'm going downstairs and check on my brother."

When Sebastian woke, he reached for Kelly – and realizing she was not in his bed, rolled over and put his arm across his eyes... and wept.

Someone knocked on the closed door. He took a deep breath and growled. "Go away!"

Raffe opened the door but didn't enter the room. Sebastian rose from the bed and walked into his brother's arms. All Raffe could do was to hold him, feeling his brother's wracking sobs and knowing there was nothing in the world he could do to ease his little brother's heart-breaking pain.

"Come upstairs, Seb." This was a critical time for his brother, but Raffe couldn't force him to join him upstairs.

Sebastian exhaled loudly. "Okay... Let me wash my face. I'll be up." He turned and walked into the bathroom, not bothering to close the door behind him. Raffaele returned to the kitchen alone.

Roger had gone out earlier and picked up a box of sticky buns. While he waited for Raffe, he ate one with his coffee. After a few minutes, he heard footsteps coming up the stairs.

"I think he'll be up." Raffe took a mug from the cupboard and poured a cup. "How does this happen, Rog?"

"I wish I knew. I guess Kelly's ex was a real piece of work. And for him to manipulate Ronnie that way..."

Raffe took one of the breakfast treats out of the box, and with his coffee sat at the table across from Roger. "From what I've heard, Ronnie wasn't really all there – kind of slow I guess, ya know? And it seems like no one ever got him help." He looked up. "There's my little man!"

Brie entered the kitchen from the back stairs holding Finn. When he saw his daddy he leaned out from his mommy's arms. Raffe took his son, cradling him in one arm.

"He's grown, hasn't he?" Finn looked at Roger and smiled.

"He likes you, Rog." Brie poured her first cup of coffee. "How did you sleep?"

"Fine, Brie. Thank you for opening your home to me."

"Of course. It's our pleasure." Brie opened the square white box that sat on the counter. She leaned in and inhaled the aroma of the freshly baked pastries. "Oooh! Sticky buns... With pecans!"

Taking a table knife she cut one of the indulgent glazed pastries in half. "Who bought these bad things... Roger?"

"Yup. I wanted this morning to be less hectic."

"That was very sweet of you. Thank you." She walked over and putting her arm around his shoulders, kissed his cheek, then moved a chair next to her husband and sat.

"I nursed Finn again before we came down. He's good for a few hours." She caressed her son's head. "Raffe, yesterday I asked Kelly if she and Sebastian would be godparents to Finn."

Raffe heard noises behind him and took his attention from his baby, but Finn grabbed his daddy's nose – Raffaele turned back to his squirming son and kissed his face.

Brie put her hand on her husband's arm and whispered, "... *Sebastian...*" Brie stood and put her arms around her brother-in-law.

Sebastian put his head down on her shoulder. "Kelly loved you so much, Brie."

"Oh, Seb, she still does – and she still loves you, too!" Brie took his hand and brought him to the table. Roger pulled out a chair next to him.

"Thanks, Rog."

Brie poured a cup of coffee. "Seb, would you like coffee?"

"Yeah, thanks." He took the mug from her and held it between his hands, warming them. His tears started again. "These were Kelly's favorite stoneware mugs..."

Roger put his hand on his friend's shoulder. "I love Kelly, too. You know that."

"I wish you had done more than kicked her ex in his ass. I wish you had kicked that SOB to the fucking moon... sorry... the moon." Sebastian looked apologetically at Finn, who thankfully wasn't paying attention to him – he was touching his daddy's eyes.

"Don't worry..." Brie assured him.

Sebastian drank more coffee and leaned back in his chair. Through bloodshot eyes, he glanced at Roger. "I want to go home. I want to see... I don't know what I want to see."

Roger looked hard at his friend. "For one, you're not going alone. And for two, I don't think it's a good idea."

"... Please..." Sebastian could barely keep his eyes open – he was exhausted, tired, sad, grieving, angry...

Roger knew if his friend had his mind set on something, no one could talk him out of it. "Like I said, you're not going alone." He pulled off another piece of his sticky bun and slowly ate it. "I'm coming with you."

Before they left, Roger poured another cup of coffee and ate a third sticky bun – attempting to delay the inevitable.

They pulled up to the garage. The crime scene tape hung across the front door. While they sat in the idling vehicle, Roger called Lt. Rafferty.

"Joe, Roger McClennen here. Sebastian wants to inspect his home. Are we okay to go in?"

There was a long pause before Lt. Rafferty responded. "CSU is done – but I have to tell you. It's a mess."

"Got it. Thanks." He looked at his friend. "Seb, are you sure?"

"Rog... I need to see..."

He got out of the truck and followed Sebastian as he walked up the front porch steps. Roger put his hand on his friend's arm and asked him one last time. "You're sure?"

"Whatever he did to my wife, he did it in our home. Yes. I'm sure."

Roger pulled down the crime scene tape. He put the key into the deadbolt lock and opened the door, allowing Sebastian to enter his home first.

The kitchen was mostly undisturbed, except for the bloody handprints on the inside of the door... and bloody footprints on the floor. Sebastian walked toward the heavy swinging door that separated the kitchen from the dining room. Roger again met him at the door and pushed it open. Sebastian stepped through the doorway into his dining room. He waited until Roger followed him in, letting the door swing shut.

"Oh God!" Roger followed Sebastian's startled gaze. The inside of the heavy door was smeared with dried blood – Kelly's blood.

"Come on, Seb... let's get out of here..." But Roger's words again fell on deaf ears.

Sebastian proceeded across the dining room to the stairs. He stopped. Each stair held evidence of blood – Kelly's blood. As he began his ascent, Roger again tried stopping his friend, but his actions were in vain – he followed him up the stairs.

Sebastian walked down the hallway – Roger moved in front of him and stopped him.

"Seb, let me look first. Please." He put his hands on his friend's chest, impeding his movement, feeling Sebastian's pounding heart. "Please!"

Sebastian exhaled and closed his eyes, finally whispering, *"Okay."*

Roger put his hands on his friend's shoulders, squeezing them as a sign of great affection. He turned and walked the few steps until he stood on the threshold of the bedroom – and saw the wreckage left behind.

He put his hands on the door jambs. This could have been a scene out of his memory – a war-torn Afghan village. There was blood on the white Berber carpeting – large splotches of blood. Roger entered the room and followed the trail around the far side of the bed. The sheets were saturated with blood and tissue, as was the pillow. The tall headboard was smeared with blood as well as the wall showing evidence of blood spatter.

As part of his ride-a-longs, Roger followed many CSU teams as they investigated crime scenes – he knew that every piece of evidence told a story. And this bed told a very violent story. He knew her injuries. Ronnie had held nothing back...

He closed his eyes, halting the tears before they fell onto his face. He knew Sebastian would be shocked if he saw this scene and right now the former Marine had to be stronger than his friend.

"*Oh God...*" Sebastian stood at the doorway to the bedroom.

"Seb – buddy. You don't want to come in." Roger quickly walked back around the bed and met him before he could come any further into the room. "You don't want to see this." Roger held his friend and pushed him back into the hallway. But he was overpowered – Sebastian broke free of his hold.

He watched helplessly as Sebastian walked through the bedroom, carefully avoiding the trail of blood. He stopped at Kelly's side of their bed and grasped the headboard. Realizing he had touched her partially dried blood, he quickly backed off and wiped his hand on his shirt, making a dark red mark over his heart.

"Let's go. You've seen enough." He approached Sebastian, who still held his hand over the bloody smear across his chest. "It's time to go." Roger led his friend out of the bedroom.

While driving back to Raffe's home, his cell phone rang. He pulled the phone from his shirt pocket. "Roger here."

"Roger, Joe Rafferty. I just spoke to ADA Susan Ryan. Ward is being charged with accessory to a crime. Susan said it's a Class B Felony. There's no wiggle room in this one."

"Good."

"But... If his wife dies, Ron Wolff will be charged with murder – and Stephen Ward's charges will be upgraded to accessory to murder. Either way, those two will never see the light of day again."

Roger took a deep breath, trying to mask his emotions. He looked over at Sebastian who was leaning against the door.

"I hear you. Thank you, Joe."

Sebastian glanced over at Roger. "Who was that?"

"Lt. Rafferty."

"Oh?" He slowly sat up straight in the seat. "Did they get Stevie?"

"Yup. He's not going anywhere, Seb. The courts will see to that."

Sebastian again leaned into his door, his forehead pressed against the window, his hazel eyes looking at nothing. "I want to see Kelly."

"Did you say something Seb?"

Without looking up, he softly repeated his words. "Yeah... I want to see my wife."

"Sure buddy." Roger engaged the turn signal and drove in the direction of the hospital. "Do you want me to come in with you?"

"Yeah... if you want."

Roger parked, and together he and Sebastian walked in. Upon entering the ICU, Andrew greeted them.

"Sebastian, there's no change in your wife's condition." Andrew pulled up her chart on his laptop and quickly scanned for any new information. "She's stable, which is good."

He thanked Andrew and began walking down the aisle to his wife's bedside. Roger's heart would break if he saw her again like that. How many times had he wanted to tell Kelly how he felt about her – and now he might never get the chance. He sat down heavily on a chair near the nurse's desk, hung his head and quietly wept.

Sebastian approached his wife's bed. He stood for a few minutes watching the numbers and pulsing graph lines on the machines. The whole scene was surreal. Kelly was supposed to be waiting for him at home. She was going to plan something special for them. He never thought this would be his reality.

He stood on what would be her side of their bed – and leaning over her body, kissed her bruised face and whispered, *"I'm here, Love."* He sat on the chair at her bedside. With every ingestion of air from the ventilator, he silently watched her chest rise and fall – and he remembered their last time out at the cabin. She had been teaching him about the ducks...

> *It was a moment he would keep deep in his heart forever – making love with his wife down by the shoreline, the great blue heron strutting nearby among the reeds, the loons carrying their chicks out in the middle of their pond, the mallard hen leading her brood by the shore, the early morning sun still low in the cloudless sky, a soft breeze rustling the leaves in the stand of birch trees – and his wife's warm breath on his face... Always and forever...*

Sebastian put his head on her bed and wept. He felt a hand on his shoulder. Looking up, he saw Roger.

"Come on, Seb. Let's go home." Sebastian put a hand on his friend's arm and nodded. Roger briefly looked at his girl, then helped her husband slowly rise from the chair and escorted him out of the ICU.

32

Imitation of Life

She woke him.

"Kelly..." He looked up at the woman. "Kelly? You're here?"

"Yes, silly. I'm here. I never left."

"But you did."

"I'm here now..."

He loved the feel of her hands on his body... feeling her hands reaching for him. He moved closer to the woman who occupied the warm spot on the mattress. He felt her fingers in his beard, her fingers combing through his chest hair. He felt her fingers... her fingers... just the lightest touch of her fingers against his skin gave him permission to accept her comforting presence. Her face was close to his – he inhaled her sweet breath...

"Love me, Sebastian..."

He held her face in his hands. Her eyes were so green – so much brighter than he remembered. He took off her shirt.

"Your breasts... They're both there!"

"I had the surgery. I'm whole again. See?" She pulled his hands up to her breasts. "Feel them, Sebastian."

He loved the feel of her small breasts – his hands totally covered them.

"Love me, Sebastian..."

And she was under his body. He pressed his now fully erect cock into her and kissed her lips.

"Love me, Sebastian..."

He thrust hard into her, pushing into her, holding her head between his hands.

"Love me, Sebastian..."

"I'm trying... Kelly, I'm trying!" He was shouting the words. "I love you Kelly... I can never get enough of you... I love you..."

"Love me, Sebastian..."

He was exhausted – he was exhausted yet he still tried loving her... his wife... his Dulcinea... He was exhausted... and collapsed on her body.

"Sebastian, love me..."

He looked into her face. It was purple and bruised – her eyes black and swollen shut.

He screamed! Sebastian scrambled off the bed – his pants at his knees. He turned on the ceiling light. There was no one in the bed. He had ejaculated on a pillow. She was not here. It was a nightmare. He heard a loud knocking on the door. It was Raffaele.

"Are you okay? Sebastian!"

He pulled his pants up to his waist and opened the door.

"Seb, are you okay? I heard you yelling."

"I had a nightmare. Kelly was here." He pointed to the wet pillow in the middle of the bed. "I was making love to her..." He was embarrassed. Raffaele picked up the pillow and pulled off the pillowcase.

"Raffe, I'm sorry."

"I've got coffee on." Raffe walked the few steps back to the laundry room and tossed the pillowcase in the open washing machine. "Come upstairs. It's just you and me."

"She was there. I swear she was..."

"I know." Raffaele pushed the coffee mug into his hands. "Drink."

"Last time you told me to drink you fed me whiskey."

"You needed it. You need coffee now."

Sebastian picked up the mug and sipped the hot coffee.

"Ruth will want to go see Kelly today. Did you want to go with her?"

"Yeah, we should go together. Where is she?"

"Brie and Ruth are taking Finn for a walk. They won't be gone long."

"When did they leave?"

Raffaele looked at his watch. "About an hour ago. They're at the park just a block from here."

Sebastian looked down at his coffee cup – his eyes glistened with fresh tears. "Roger didn't think I overheard his conversation with the police officer." He lost his voice as he related what he heard the officer tell Roger. "If Kelly – if my wife dies – Ron will be charged with murder... *and Stevie with accessory to murder.*" His last words fading to a whisper.

"Shit. I'm sorry you heard that... I should tell you. Phil called."

Wiping his eyes with a napkin, Sebastian asked, "Oh? What did he want?"

"He thinks this thing that happened to Kelly..." Raffaele took another long drink of his coffee. "He thinks it was his fault."

"I'm the one who insisted on going." He kept the napkin pressed to his eyes with both hands. "He even tried talking me out of going on this business trip."

Raffaele put his cup back on the table. "You need to tell him that."

Sebastian folded the napkin and wiped up a drop of coffee from the table. "I will, first thing tomorrow. I'm going into the office."

"That's probably a good idea. Kelly needs to heal and you need to try to regain your footing."

He looked hard at his brother. "Raffe, how did you do it?"

"Do what, Seb?"

"Get over Annalisa."

Raffaele took another long drink of his coffee. "I never have forgotten Annalisa if that's what you mean."

"But you went back on the concert tour just a week after her death. It was in the trade magazines."

"I didn't know you were checking up on me." He smiled. "I had to. If I didn't go back on the stage I think I would have died." He returned his brother's gaze. "You have Kelly, Seb. She's still there. You have hope, little brother."

Sebastian's eyes again filled with tears. He shut his eyes tight in the hope of holding them back, but in spite of his efforts the tears ran down his face.

"Seb, I hear Brie and Ruth..."

He quickly wiped his face with his sleeve – and realized he had slept in his clothes for a second night. Kelly would not be happy.

"I'm going to shower and change." After Roger had brought Sebastian back to Raffaele's, he had returned to his friend's home and packed a suitcase for him.

"Brie put fresh towels and washcloths in your bathroom."

"Thank you." Sebastian stood and left the kitchen, returning to the basement guest bedroom.

As he watched his brother leave, Raffaele knew what he had to do for him – and hoped Brie would agree.

When they came back from their walk, Brie left the stroller at the bottom of the porch stairs. She lifted Finn out of the stroller and carried him up to the house. Ruth sat in one of the rocking chairs on the massive front porch.

"Brie honey, you go on in. It's such a nice morning... I'm going to sit out here for a few minutes."

Gabriella took a warm afghan from another chair and draped it across Ruth's legs. "I'll see you in a few minutes." Brie kissed her cheek and went into the house. She saw her husband sitting at the kitchen table and handed their sleepy son to his daddy.

"*Ciao, mia bellissima Gabriella.* How did Ruth do?"

Brie caressed her husband's shoulder. "I think the walk was good for her."

"Seb wants to go to the hospital with Ruth."

"That's a good idea." She sat in the chair next to Raffaele.

He kissed his son's forehead. "Do you want me to put this little one down?"

"I have to nurse. On our way back, I could feel my milk letting down. I'm so sore..." Brie put her arm around her husband and kissed his cheek. "Roger's truck is gone. Where did he go?"

"He left. He said he needed to get back into his classroom." Raffe stood. "I'll carry our boy up to the nursery."

They walked into the living room, and while leaning against each other, ascended the grand staircase to the second floor.

Ruth walked into the kitchen just as Sebastian returned from his shower.

"You look a little better honey." She patted his side.

"Have you had lunch, Ruth?"

"I tell you, I'm not hungry. But you go ahead."

Raffe entered the kitchen from the back stairs. "Hey, Ruth. Are you hungry?" He walked to the refrigerator.

"No, but I think Sebastian is."

Raffaele opened the large refrigerator and pulled out a bowl of pasta salad, sliced rare roast beef, mayo and mustard. From the cupboard he took out a bag of Kaiser Rolls.

"Seb, help me make some sandwiches." The brothers stood at the counter and together made several sandwiches, arranging them on a large platter. Sebastian carried the platter and bowl of pasta salad to the table. Raffaele put out a stack of paper plates and cups, napkins and forks. He poured lemonade into a large pitcher and also placed it on the table.

"Ruth, are you sure you don't want some?"

She looked at the food. "It does look good. Maybe I'll have half a sandwich."

"There's enough for all, Ruth. Please take whatever you want." They all sat at the kitchen table and began eating. No one spoke. Brie finally returned.

"Was that boy of yours hungry, Brie?"

"Oh, Ruth – always! I don't even have to pump. He's so greedy for my milk." Brie sat at the table and put some salad and a sandwich on her plate. Again they ate in silence.

Sebastian took a large drink of his lemonade. "Ruth, do you want to come with me to see Kelly this afternoon?"

"Yes Seb, thank you. I'd like that."

Ruth was quiet as Sebastian drove to the hospital. He escorted her to the ICU ward. Kelly's nurse greeted them.

"Good afternoon, Sebastian, Reverend Cameron."

"Mari, please call me Ruth."

"Thank you, Ruth. Kelly will be ready in a few minutes. Dr. Schmitt's assistant is changing Kelly's dressings."

Sebastian looked toward her bed and saw the privacy curtain had been partially pulled across her bed – a man he didn't recognize was touching his wife's body...

Mari noticed the concern on Sebastian's face. "Mr. Bonsignore, Van is very caring – he's also giving your wife a sponge bath."

"Why the sponge bath?"

"It accomplishes two things." Mari spoke kindly to him and Ruth. "First, it keeps infection down and the act of rubbing her skin helps her circulation. We do this every day, especially to her arms and legs. We also change her bedding. And we've been turning her three times a day so she won't get bed sores. This also encourages healing to her injuries."

Sebastian and Ruth waited by Mari's desk until Van pulled the curtain open, securing it at the front of the bed – and watched as he passed out of the ward, pushing a rolling tray that held bloody dressings.

"You can go down now. There are two chairs for you at the bedside."

"Thank you, Mari."

"Of course, Ruth."

Sebastian held Ruth's arm as they slowly walked down the aisle to his wife's bed. Kelly lay on her side, her body stabilized with pillows. It had been three days since the attack and the bruising on her face was beginning to heal. Her eyes weren't as swollen, and if it wasn't for the faint discoloration of green and yellow on her face, Kelly appeared as if she was asleep in her own bed.

They sat in the chairs – Ruth keeping her small purse on her lap.

"Ruth, I dreamt Kelly was with me last night."

"Oh dear, honey. Did you have a nightmare?"

"Yes..."

"After my husband – Kelly's father – died, I swear he visited me many times."

"How long ago was that? Kelly never talked about her dad."

"That was about twenty-six, twenty-seven years ago. Kelly's father was a brakeman on the Denver and Rio Grande Western Railroad. Of course, that was also when it was an active working railroad. Now, you know, it's mostly a tourist train." Ruth began taking off her sweater – Sebastian reached behind her and helped.

"Thank you, honey." Ruth touched her daughter's bed, feeling the soft blanket between her fingers. She continued her story – conjuring up both sweet memories and terrible sadness. "It was just a hundred and fifty mile run – about ten thousand feet above sea level. But my Fred was very proud of his old Tunnel Motor..."

Ruth noticed Sebastian's questioning stare. She smiled as she remembered her husband's explanation. "That old locomotive was called a Tunnel Motor because the rear air intakes were relocated down to the walkway level of the car body. That modification, he told me, drew in cooler air and solved the problem of overheating inside the long tunnels. Safer, you know, for the crew..."

"You knew a lot about his job? His train?"

"When you're with someone as long as I was with Fred – you know, we talked when he was home. And I did learn about his job." She smiled... remembering... "My Frederick was proud of his work. He was responsible for all communication between the engineer and the crew. You know, throwing track switches, moving cars, signaling... and coupling and uncoupling of the cars."

Sebastian wanted to know more. He encouraged Ruth to continue talking about Kelly's father. "Sounds like an important job."

"Oh honey, without my Fred, that train didn't move!" She listened to Kelly's ventilator for a few minutes. Ruth looked down at her lap and opened her purse.

"I have a picture..." From a secret pocket, she retrieved a laminated Polaroid photo. She held the photo with reverence, tracing the sealed edge with one finger. Ruth handed it to the man sitting next to her – the man who shared her grief.

"During the summer, Kelly's dad took her on the train with him on day trips. I tell you, they were like two peas in a pod back then. I remember when I took this picture..."

> *"Well, you're up early!" Ruth kissed the top of her eight-year old daughter's head.*
>
> *"Hi, Mommy! Daddy's taking me to work on his train today!" As Ruth poured her first cup of coffee, she asked her daughter when they'd be leaving.*
>
> *"As soon as Daddy gets ready..." Kelly quickly finished scooping up her Cheerios, slopping milk back in the bowl. Ruth brought her coffee to the kitchen table and sat across from her daughter. As she sipped the freshly brewed liquid, she smiled at the young girl with emerald eyes and a head full of curly red hair.*
>
> *"Do you know where you're going today?" Ruth knew that her husband's train kept scheduled routes but distances changed day by day. She hoped today's train would be a shorter route so her daughter wouldn't get bored – if that could ever happen. Any amount of time Kelly spent with her dad, no matter the distance traveled, was special.*
>
> *"Nope..." Kelly was eating the last of her cereal. "But Daddy said we're hauling a load of lime rock."*
>
> *"Where's your cap, Kelly?"*
>
> *Ruth looked up and saw her husband stealthily tip-toeing into the kitchen. He put his finger on his lips as he raised the small blue-and-white striped engineer's cap over his daughter's head. As he was about to place the cap on her head, Kelly looked up. The cap landed on her upturned face.*

"Daddy!" She dropped her spoon in her cereal bowl, squirmed out of her chair and hugged her father around his waist. She looked up at him with wide-eyed adoration.

"You all set, Kelly-Belly?" He held her small shoulders in his large hands.

"Yup!" And she hugged her dad again. Then straightening up, she put her engineer's cap tighter on her head. Ruth watched as her husband and daughter interacted. What a pair – father and daughter, sharing the same auburn colored hair, although his was now peppered with silver.

Ruth stood and picked up her Polaroid camera off the counter. "I want a picture, Fred. Hold Kelly?"

Her husband bent down and, grabbing his 50-pound daughter by her waist, hoisted her up – and with one large arm, held her to his chest. Kelly hugged her dad tight around his neck, leaning her head against her father's bearded face.

"Ready... Smile!" Ruth pressed the red button. A thin plastic card ejected from the camera.

"Okay, Kelly-Belly, let's go!" Fred set his daughter back on the black-and-white checkered linoleum floor.

Ruth cautioned her husband. "Don't let her climb those cars when you're setting the brakes, Fred."

"No, that's not a job for my Kelly-Belly." He looked down and winked at his daughter, whose unkempt curls were bursting out from under the small cap.

"Little girl," her mom reminded her daughter. "Don't forget your lunch!" Kelly picked up her kid-sized silver lunch bucket from the counter.

"Okay, we're off." Fred approached his wife, bent his tall frame and kissed her tenderly on the lips. "I love you, Ruthie."

"I love you too, Fred. Be careful out there."

Fred picked up his heavy grip and hoisted it on his broad shoulder. Taking his young daughter's hand, he led her out through the kitchen door into the early morning sun.

Ruth sat back in her chair and drank more of her coffee, waiting the appropriate amount of time before she could peel open the Polaroid picture. Carefully, she pulled back the flimsy plastic exposing a perfect photo. Her husband and her daughter – both red heads, two peas in a pod and inseparable...

Sebastian had never seen pictures of Kelly as a little girl. But even in this old Polaroid, her emerald eyes sparkled. He chuckled at the mass of red hair poking out from under her blue-and-white striped cap. He handed the photo back to Ruth.

"Like I said, that train ran through La Veta pass through the Mule Shoe loop. There was very little radio service in the mountains. Not like now where everything is satellite. These were the old radios. There were two engineers that day. Max and Nick... such fine men. And Gordon... Gordy was the conductor who, you know, monitored the freight." Again Ruth paused – again feeling the heartache of her memories...

"Where was I? Oh yes... They had to change channels on their radios at least three times going through that mountain pass. The engineer would radio Fred about the channel change, and he'd acknowledge the order and change the channel on his radio."

"You said this happened several times on each mountain pass?"

"Every time they went through the mountains. You had to be on your toes working those trains."

"So what happened...? If you don't mind me asking, Ruth."

"No... No, I don't mind." She closed her eyes as her words brought her back to that terrible day – that terrible day that changed their lives forever. "That train was climbing the east slope of the Tennessee Pass – a steep grade up a ten thousand foot mountain pass." Ruth softly exhaled. "Like I said, that old locomotive was pulling too many cars. This was an older engine – not like the modern diesels you have today."

She looked up at her son-in-law. "You know, those engines weren't nearly as powerful and couldn't pull as many cars up that steep grade." Ruth again closed her eyes and bowed her head...

"Fred's orders were to uncouple the last twelve or so cars while they were stopped on the siding before, you know, they began the climb up that pass. He uncoupled the cars and engaged the hand brake on the front car. But from what I was told, after he the set out the flares in the knuckle prior to departing, the hand brake didn't hold, and while he was closing the angle cock on the main train, the set out cars managed to roll into him..."

"Oh Ruth! I'm so sorry..."

She opened her eyes, staring at nothing, and slid her hand across the soft white blanket. "Thank you..." Again she put her head down – a low hum rose from deep in her chest as she remembered... "Like I said the radio transmission was crap. And from what Nick said, my Fred didn't hear the call to change channels." Ruth's attention turned back to Sebastian. "Gordy assumed Fred heard the call, too. And they didn't discover what happened for almost ten minutes."

Ruth put a tissue to her eyes. "The toughest part of the story was that my Fred wasn't killed instantly. He died alone on those tracks... And that's what still haunts me to this day."

Sebastian could see Ruth was still affected by those horrific events that had transpired so many years ago – the day her beloved husband died. And now they were sitting at the bedside of the woman who might also die. He put a comforting arm around his mother-in-law. "Is that why you wanted to be part of the church, Ruth?"

"Oh, partly I suppose." Ruth again looked up at the man who sat next to her – who sat with her at her daughter's bedside. She exhaled... "At that time Kelly was going through the terrible tweens, and we argued all the time. She hated me. And when her dad died, she hated us both – me for not understanding her, and her dad for abandoning her." Ruth again placed her hand on the white blanket that covered her daughter. She continued, her words spoken as if in a dream. "We had such shouting matches..."

"But you got back together. You married us."

"Yes, but it wasn't until her senior year in high school. And then she left for college. She attended Arapahoe Community College. It was only four hours away." Ruth gazed at her daughter's shape under the blanket. "Like they say – distance heals relationships."

Ruth looked up at Sebastian. "Honey, I'm not surprised she never talked about her dad. Her father's death broke her heart, and to this day it's still a painful memory."

Sebastian took his mother-in-law's hand in his – her hand was ice-cold.

"Anyway, where was I? Oh yes... I know my Fred visited me those first nights, almost as if he were saying goodbye. I was afraid at first, but then I looked forward to his visits. After a while, maybe three or four weeks he quit coming." Ruth affectionately placed her other hand on his. "I do believe my daughter was with you. Can you find comfort in that?"

"I think so... But I don't want her to visit me just to say goodbye."

"Oh, honey, my Frederick was dead when he visited me. There was no wishing about him coming back. You, however... I believe Kelly's spirit visited you, maybe to comfort you."

"Thank you, Ruth." He put his arm around her shoulder and together they listened to Kelly's breathing...

After a week, Ruth returned home to Colorado. She was reluctant to tell Sebastian – she suggested they take a walk in the nearby park.

"Honey, I know your heart is breaking." She held onto his arm as they walked. They were pushing Finn in his stroller. "If you were one of my parishioners, I'd know what to say. But this is too close, too personal."

Ruth cried – Sebastian put his arm around her shoulders. They continued walking along the paved path near the frozen pond.

He stared off into the distance. "I'll call you if there's any change..."

Ruth looked up at his kind face. "Yes, please. I would like that." She used her free hand to wipe her tears. And they walked on for another twenty minutes until Finn began fussing. It was time to go back.

The following week, Gabriella and Sebastian took Finn for a walk in the park – Sebastian pushed the stroller.

"I got a call from the hospital this morning. They're removing Kelly's trachea tube and bringing her out of the induced coma."

"This is good news, isn't it?"

"I asked Dr. Schmitt if this was the right decision... But she said they didn't want to keep the trachea tube in her any longer than necessary." Sebastian stopped walking and looked across the frozen pond. "The doctor was concerned that a bacterial infection could cause pneumonia." He turned back to his sister-in-law. "Like it could get any worse, you know?"

They continued walking. "I wish Ruth could have stayed longer, but she needed to get home to her church."

"You'll tell her about this development?"

"I don't know, Brie. I don't want her to get her hopes up. I don't want to get *my* hopes up, you know?"

"When are they bringing her out of the coma?"

"This afternoon. I'm going down there in a few hours."

"She's healing well?"

"She... Kelly's been in that induced coma for over three weeks. And the doctors were able to complete the final reconstructive surgeries on her. Brie, they've been so good to her."

"I was down there earlier this morning. Her color is good. She looks like she's sleeping."

"I know. It's frustrating. When I'm visiting I tell her to open those beautiful eyes, but I don't know if she can hear me."

"You don't know she can't hear you. There's so much about a person in that state that even the doctors don't understand."

"I've been talking to her Brie – telling her I love her, telling her to come back to me."

"I can't imagine..."

"Did Raffaele ever talk to you about Annalisa? And how he went on without her?"

"He's told me what I needed to know. Even though he's said I've given him his life back – and this little sweetheart. I know her memory is still with him. But he's comforted by her memory, I think. You can't turn off a memory."

They walked along the paved walkway for a while longer.

"We should get home. I need to nurse this little guy."

"You and Raffe have it all..."

"You and Kelly will have it all again, Sebastian. Don't sell my friend short! She's tough. You know how tough she is." Brie lightly put a hand on his back.

"Yes, I do." They walked back to the house.

33

Follow Your North Star

Sebastian visited Kelly every day, sometimes twice a day... sitting by her bedside listening to her shallow breathing – so quiet compared to that awful machine. And each evening when he returned to the bedroom in the basement, he cried.

He hardly slept. And when he did sleep, he dreamed of his wife – and he cried. He was tired when he woke – and he was tired of being tired when he went to bed at night. He didn't know how he could keep up with this pace. If it weren't for Phil and Carolyn his business would have suffered.

Before she was brought out of her induced coma, the surgeon removed the appliance that held her jaw in place and a nasal feeding tube had been introduced. She was transferred to a room on the rehabilitation floor. Sebastian had chosen a private room with tall windows that let in the last rays of the day. When they were at the cabin, many evenings she would sit at the edge her pond and watch the sun as it slipped beyond the horizon, behind the tall tamarack larch on the distant shore...

She loved her cabin. But they almost lost everything back then – back when their communication had failed so badly. He thought... and she thought... If only they had talked to each other. The drive out to their cabin had been so frustrating for him, so sad for her. He remembered watching her get out of the car...

> *She had left her book of poems on the seat. Usually she brought Whitman into the cabin. He feared she wouldn't change her mind – and their love would be a thing of the past.*
>
> *Watching her walk barefoot across the lush lawn reminded him of their walks down the tree-lined road. She was so in tune with nature, the sounds of the birds, the smells of the colorful blooms. He envied her appreciation of their personal sanctuary. If he let her go, he would have lost his life, his world, his love.*
>
> *He finally stood behind her at the cabin door. She spoke, though he barely heard her.*
>
> *"Comfort me." He remembered leaning so close into her body, but feared touching her – would she push him away?*
>
> *"Comfort me!" She said it louder and the tears came in torrents.*
>
> *"COMFORT ME!!!" She shouted the words. That was his cue. He wrapped his arms around her. And she had repeated those words but in a whisper. He held her with every ounce of strength he had. She began wailing the words. "Comfort me!!! Please! Comfort me!"*
>
> *And he held her like he was holding onto his world. And he didn't think she'd ever stop crying, but he didn't let go – he just held her for what*

> *seemed like hours. His arms were wet from her tears that spilled from her face. And he comforted her – he comforted her...*

If only he could comfort her now – if she'd only look at him, he would comfort her. If she'd open those beautiful emerald eyes, he would comfort her. But she didn't – and he couldn't.

But he could be there for her – be there for her when she decided to wake up. He set up a portable desktop at her bedside. Phil and Carolyn communicated through emails and texting. And he would take meetings but he wouldn't leave town. Phil was now responsible for any out-of-town business.

The holidays were upon them. Wreaths and potted poinsettias decorated the nurses' station. Many of his friends were joining Phil and his family for Christmas dinner, including Michael and Roger. Carolyn and her two boys would also be there. Phil invited Sebastian, but he felt no holiday spirit. He preferred staying with his wife.

Dr. Laura Schmitt had visited Sebastian in the private room, instructing him to watch for any movements in his wife's fingers or toes, and any eye movements. And she encouraged him to speak to Kelly. And he did. From the time he arrived in her room until he left her side at the end of the day, he shared all his confidential client information with her.

> *[You said you couldn't share that information with me, silly... Now I know all your secrets...]*

The daytime staff had left for their holiday festivities. The rehab floor was quiet. From his pants pocket, he pulled out a small velvet bag tied with a satin ribbon. He opened the bag and tipped the contents into the palm of his hand. The diamond in the arch of the stone sparkled, reflecting the late afternoon sun that shone through the tall windows. He had taken her necklace back to the jewelry store where it had been created. The jeweler cleaned up the stone and put it on a new gold chain.

He lifted the delicate chain. The simple grey stone with black bands – the banded chert in the shape of a heart – twirled back and forth like a pendulum. As he watched the pendant's movement, the crisp bands ran into the grey as tears welled in his eyes. He closed his eyes, remembering when she found the stone. It was on their first trip to the cabin. At that time, he wasn't that interested in learning about nature...

> *"Look!" Kelly was wading near the water's edge picking up pretty rocks. She picked up what looked like a plain flat grey stone and showed it to him. Looking at it he wasn't too impressed, although the shape did resemble a heart.*
>
> *"It's a banded chert! Isn't it beautiful?"*
>
> *To him it resembled an agate, but where an agate was red and brown with distinctive bands this was more of a two-toned flat rock with bands of grey and black.*
>
> *"It's not an agate." Sebastian dismissed it – he was looking for real agates and skipping stones.*

"No silly, but it's the cousin of an agate." She held it up so he could get a better look at it. "It's got banding and a chochoidal fracturing pattern, see?"

When he still didn't seem impressed, she continued. "The bands form similar crystal granules like an agate but they're so tight that the rock is opaque rather than translucent." Sebastian continued looking for his flat stones.

"Well, I love it." Kelly slipped it into her shorts pocket and continued helping her husband look for his skipping stones...

The last time they were at the cabin – when she was feeling so much better after her chemo regimen was completed – he remembered that heart-shaped rock. He looked for it on the bookshelves made of reclaimed wood, hoping she had added it to the accumulated rocks she discovered every year. There! He found it. The heart-shaped... what did she call it? Oh yeah, banded chert. Before they left the end of that wonderful week, he pocketed it. He wanted to make her something special for their fifth anniversary.

After they returned home, while she was teaching her summer school classes, Sebastian took the stone to the jewelers. He told the head jeweler what he wanted – a single diamond set in the polished stone that would signify her North Star. This would be remarkable if he could pull it off.

Sebastian got the call a month later that the necklace was ready. While his hopes were high, he couldn't get over how beautiful the necklace actually turned out. The highly polished stone was brilliant, the black bands on the grey stone more pronounced – and the diamond placed high in one of the heart's arches symbolically pointing north. Now he had to surprise her. Kelly knew he was a bad liar, so somehow he had to hide this splendid gift.

For their anniversary Sebastian suggested they go to their cabin. Everything was ready. But she must have known something was up as he impatiently pushed her out the door.

Kelly buckled up and looked at him. "What?"

He looked at her. "What what?"

"What are you up to? That's what what!"

"Nothing..." Sebastian winked and pulled out of the driveway. Kelly looked at him one more time before exhaling in loving exasperation. She opened her Whitman and began reading. This would be such a good weekend if he didn't blow it.

It was late when they arrived at the cabin. The necklace was in his jacket pocket. They both walked up the fieldstone steps to their cabin. Kelly unlocked the padlock.

"Do you want to build a fire tonight? It's cool and it would be nice to lie in front of a warm fire." Sebastian agreed and brought in an armful of wood. Together they built the fire. Soon the dry logs ignited into a roaring inferno, warming the little room. Kelly took off her jacket.

"I'm going to light the water heater..." Sebastian got up and while he was in the kitchen pulled the necklace out of his jacket pocket and stuffed it in his front pants pocket. He lit the water heater. Returning to the room where Kelly waited, Sebastian made a point of throwing his jacket on the loveseat, implying he had no surprises there.

He sat on the rag rug next to his wife. Kelly didn't like the silver in her hair.

"You know, I don't care if you cover the silver or not. I like it." He kissed her lips – chastely, lovingly... Making love to her with his tongue. He held her shoulders and pushed her to the floor.

"Are you going to make love to me first or show me what you've been hiding?"

"I'm not hiding anything!" She was too smart for her own good. He could never keep anything from her – except when he hid her wedding ring. Now that was big! Sebastian kissed her again and lay at her side, propping his head on his raised arm. "Why do you think I'm hiding something from you?"

"Because I know you, Sebastian. I love you and I know you... and this is our anniversary weekend!"

He closed his eyes. Kelly kissed his eyes and caressed his face, feeling his soft beard. "Give it up, mister." She pushed him onto his back and straddled his hips. The inside of her thigh pressed on the small rock in his front pocket.

"What's that?"

She scooted down from his hips and put her hand into his jeans' pocket. He let her find it. The necklace was wrapped in a small velvet bag. Kelly held up the bag. "You're holding out on me, Seb!"

"Open it..."

Still sitting on his legs, she pulled at the satin ribbon. "Oh my goodness...!" Kelly moved off his legs and sat on the rug. She pulled the gold chain from the bag until the little stone appeared.

"It's my banded chert... with a diamond!" She held the polished stone in the palm of her hand, admiring the simplicity and beauty of it. "It's

wonderful... It's the best you've ever done!" Kelly leaned down and kissed her husband's lips. "It really is the best."

He sat up. "You know what the diamond means?"

She looked at the diamond in one of the heart's arches. "No. Tell me."

"It signifies your North Star." Oh boy, he should have known this would have brought on a torrent of tears. She was crying – oh boy, was she crying! He pulled her into his arms. While she cried, he assured her that she could never get lost as long as she followed her North Star.

"That's right," she sniffled through her tears. "You are my North Star... always and forever."

"Can I put it on?" Sebastian took the delicate gold chain and carefully opening the clasp attached it around her slender neck. She touched the stone, fondling it.

"I love it... I love you."

"Kelly, I'm putting your necklace on..." As he carefully clasped the hook, he felt her pulse against his wrist.

[I love the feel of your hands on my body... I can never get enough of you...]

He positioned the stone at the base of her throat, covering the scar from her tracheostomy. "Follow your North Star, Kelly... Come home to me."

[Yes, that's right! Follow my North Star... You remembered...]

He leaned down and kissed his wife's lips.

[I love you, Sebastian... Kiss me again... kiss me again...]

It was late. The hallway was empty. He enjoyed this quiet time with his wife. Before he left, he read another Whitman poem to her. She had always found so much comfort in the poet's words. And he knew she loved *Song of Myself*, so once again he opened her book to the well-worn pages and read the poem, starting from the beginning...

"I celebrate myself, and sing myself,
And what I assume you shall assume,
For every atom belonging to me as good belongs to you..."

His cell phone vibrated. He checked the caller ID before answering. Carolyn was taking all his calls. It was Roger.

"Everything is done."

"What do you mean, Rog? What is done?"

"Your home. Your home is ready for you to move back in, buddy." Roger waited for his friend to speak. He knew not to push Sebastian. He had known his friend long enough – he knew him well.

Sebastian knew this day would come, but it was almost comforting to be holed up in his brother's basement. He felt safe there. It was dark in that room – he could lose himself in that room. He had dreams of Kelly in that room. Would she know where to find him if he moved back to his – their – bedroom?

Again, Roger waited for a response. When he heard only breathing, he continued. "Yeah Seb, the CTS team did a great job. And I took the liberty of getting you a new mattress, sheets, pillows – and new carpeting."

"I don't know what to say..." Sebastian loved Roger, and knew his friend was only doing what was best for him. After all, who would know him better than Roger – the man who introduced him to his wife. *His wife...*

"It's okay, Seb. You'll get the bill."

"Thank you." Sebastian chuckled, "Really... Thank you."

"You know I did it as much for you as I did for Kelly."

"I know..." He put his phone away – and casually spoke to his wife as if she was merely dozing on a lazy Sunday morning. "I have to go. I'll be back in the morning. I love you."

He leaned over and kissed his wife's lips. "Come back to me, Kelly." He left the room, closing the door quietly behind him.

[I'm here... Don't go... Sebastian... I'm here...]

Sebastian drove home for the first time since the attack. The neighborhood homes he passed were lit with brilliant hanging icicles, glowing Santa sleighs and reindeer with bobbing heads. He pulled up in his freshly plowed driveway. The flood lights came on but his home was dark – not even the porch light was on. He used to caution Kelly to always keep the porch light on. Safety reasons, he said.

Slowly he walked up the dark porch steps and put his key in the lock. Roger had installed a new deadbolt lock in the door and dropped the keys off with Phil at the office. Only Sebastian had the keys – no copies were made.

Pushing the door open, he entered his kitchen. The last time he was in his kitchen – the morning of the assault – he ate breakfast with Kelly. He only had time to eat a bran muffin and coffee. She had an omelet. He ate standing at the butcher-block counter while she sat on one of the stools. But he remembered to kiss her goodbye. He never left her without a kiss – he would give up everything to get one of her sweet kisses...

He stood at the doorway to his – their – bedroom. There was a new quilt and spread on the bed. The carpet was also new. He and Kelly had made love on the carpet the night before – the night before...

Everything he did now would begin *the night before*... His life was made up of three chapters... Before Kelly. With Kelly. Without Kelly.

He walked into the en suite bathroom. Her makeup and perfumes were where she left them on the Carrara marble countertop. Her towel and his stolen hotel robe that she always wore – that he would never wear again – still hung on the back of the door. Walking back out into the bedroom he saw the TV. He had wanted it taken out – Kelly wanted it to stay. It would stay.

It was late. He walked out of the bedroom and down the hall to the guest room. He vowed not to sleep in their bed until she was home with him.

> *Sebastian reached over and pulled his wife to him. He felt her body, her soft woman body. He caressed her face, his fingers gliding across her lips. She kissed his fingers. He pulled her face to his, kissing her lips, his tongue pushing into her mouth, making love to her with his tongue...*

And she vanished. She was never there. She hadn't been there for over a month. Yet he dreamed of her every night. He was almost eager to leave her bedside each evening so he could see her in his dreams.

Then he was angry. Why the hell did she have to come into his life? Why couldn't she have stayed home that afternoon? Why didn't *he* stay home that afternoon? His life was fine without *her*. Why *her*? What was so special about that redhead? And why shouldn't he be angry? He had every right to be angry! She needed to open her eyes! Those beautiful goddamned emerald eyes!

"Good morning, beautiful." Sebastian looked down at his wife. The night staff had already drained her urine collection bag and repositioned her so she lay on her side. She looked so peaceful, as if she were sleeping in their bed. He leaned down and kissed her forehead.

> *[I missed you... Thank God it's you, Sebastian...]*

He carefully turned his wife onto her back and pulled the blanket up over her chest. He centered the necklace on her throat. Kelly still had no movements in her fingers or toes – he checked several times a day.

He brushed his wife's hair, her beautiful auburn waves, helping the new growth cover that awful half-moon scar. And he gave her sponge baths. She was his wife – he would bathe her. There was no argument. The physical therapist instructed Sebastian how to massage her legs and her arms.

Many times, he brought food in for the staff that took care of his wife. They appreciated the home cooking, especially when he made fettuccine. And he called Ruth, even when there was nothing to report. Sometimes he would prop up his phone at Kelly's ear so she could hear her mom's voice...

> *[Mama, I can hear you... Mama, I'm here... I love you, Mama...]*

It was late. He had a breakfast meeting early in the morning. But before he left, he tried one more time to get a response out of Kelly. He massaged her arms and legs, he kissed her lips, her eyes, caressed her head.

> *[I can feel your beard against my face... I love you, Sebastian... I can smell your sweet breath, Sebastian... kiss me again Sebastian...]*

"Kelly – you've got to wake up!"

> *[I'm here... Sebastian, I'm here...]*

He was tired... tired of coming here every day and not having her respond to anything he did or said... tired of all the one-sided conversations. He missed talking to her in their bed at night, in the dark of their bedroom, their shadows as one, their whispers the only signs of life. He had gotten used to her body lying next to his – she was so warm, so soft. She was his safe haven, the one constant in his life...

"Talk to me!"

[I'm trying... I love you, Sebastian... I'm here, Sebastian...]

The staff down the hall heard him, but he didn't care. He needed her to wake up.

"Wake up! Wake up! ***Wake up!***"

One of the nurses approached the room. He gave her a look that made her quickly return to her desk. This was his wife. *His wife.* And he needed her to come back to him.

"Kelly... I love you."

[I love you too, Sebastian... You're my Ulysses... I love you... always and forever...]

Before he left for the night, he again sat at her bedside. Again he centered the banded chert pendant over her scar.

[I love my necklace... I'm following my North Star, Sebastian... I love you...]

He looked at her fingers, willing her fingers to move – just one little movement. Tell me you're in there! But there was no movement. Nothing. And there hadn't been in over three weeks. Nothing.

Sebastian pushed his chair into his makeshift desk, picked up his briefcase and took one last look at Kelly, his wife, his Dulcinea. Again he leaned down – his face touching her face – and kissed her lips.

[Kiss me again Sebastian...]

He breathed in her ear..."I love you, always and forever..."

[Sebastian... always and forever... always and forever...]

He walked out of her private room. The door closed silently behind him.

[Don't go... I'm here, Sebastian... I'm here... I'm here... Please Sebastian...]

In the late afternoon shadows of her room, the final rays of the setting sun shone through the tall windows – and glistened off a single tear...

34

Dreams

Let's go home. I have to leave town tomorrow.

Are you flying out?

No, it's just a four-hour drive and I'm driving my BMW x6. I want to stretch her legs and see what she can do.

When do you leave?

Tomorrow evening, right from the office. I want to get to the hotel early and be fresh for my breakfast meeting.

When will you be home?

Friday, mid day. It's an early breakfast meeting. I'll leave right from the meeting.

Good. I hate it when you're gone.

I could have Phil take the meeting.

Would he mind? I mean, you're scheduled, but it is only an overnight, right?

Yes. In fact if I ask Phil, he'll probably fly out early in the morning. Let's go home. I want to make love with my wife.

Our life is perfect. Lots of memories here.

All my memories of you start right here.

He had been sleeping, holding his wife close as he had done ever since their first night together. The television cast its ghostly light on their bodies. And though the volume was turned down, he swore he heard something on the stairs. He raised his head and looked at the doorway. Maybe he was hearing things. Putting his head back on her pillow he pulled his wife closer and dozed.

He woke, aware of a presence in their bedroom – a dangerous presence. He sat up and saw a large man naked from the waist down standing at Kelly's side of the bed.

Sebastian yelled out loud. He got out of bed and stood, looking at the stranger in his room. Again he yelled at the man. Get out!

Sebastian watched Kelly sit up and scream.

Yes Kelly! Scream!

> But the stranger in the room backhanded Kelly and she fell onto the bed. The stranger pulled off the covers.
>
> Kelly! Wake up!
>
> He watched the stranger lumber onto the bed and rape his wife.
>
> Kelly! Wake up!
>
> Kelly pushed at the stranger's body with her legs.
>
> Yes Kelly! Fight!
>
> The stranger hit Kelly in the head. She fell onto the mattress.
>
> He watched the stranger turn her over and rape her while she laid face-down on the bed.
>
> Kelly! Wake up!
>
> He watched the stranger rape his wife. He watched the stranger pull her up by her hips. He watched the stranger sodomize her – fucking her so hard, tearing her body apart.

"KELLY!" Sebastian woke. He was in the guestroom bed. He'd had a nightmare! Oh dear God, Kelly...

He arose and stood in the doorway, leaning against the jamb, trying to catch his breath – and gradually became aware of sounds coming from his bedroom. He tentatively walked the few short steps down the hall and looked into his bedroom. The TV was on, but he didn't remember turning it on. He walked to his bedside table and picking up the remote, turned it off.

He showered, dressed and made his way downstairs. Thank goodness he programmed the coffee maker before going to bed. He poured a cup and added French Vanilla creamer. Because it was Kelly's he somehow felt closer to her – tasting the sweet coffee as she would. He looked at his watch. It was time to go see his wife.

He stopped at the office first. Phil was already out at a breakfast meeting. Carolyn was taking a call. When she saw Sebastian, she put up one finger and quickly finished the call.

"Good morning, Sebastian." Her voice was soothing. He was glad he had hired her. She was good for him and Phil. She was smart and pretty – a deadly combination.

"Anything new this morning, Carolyn?" He started going through the stack of mail on her desk. Any 'get well' cards had ceased coming weeks ago.

"Phil is out with that client you and he met with last week. He's finalizing the contract this morning." The phone rang and Carolyn answered it – her voice was so mellow. What was the line from that Lionel Richie song? Oh yeah... She had a voice that was *'easy like Sunday morning.'* Sebastian grinned at the association.

He walked into his office. Carolyn kept it in order – there were no urgent matters on his desk. He was grateful that she and Phil were running his business. He gathered together a stack of paperwork, put it into his briefcase and left the office.

Christmas had been a non-holiday this year. New Year's Day was a non-event. Kelly's birthday would be a non-event, too. He had no reason to celebrate – and he wasn't going to celebrate anything until she was back with him. He promised himself they would celebrate all the holidays and her birthday in one week – when she came back.

The head nurse on the rehab ward met him when he arrived. "Good morning, Mr. Bonsignore. How are you this morning?" Karin was always so upbeat, always smiling. But she could also be so strong, especially when he needed a shoulder, an ear, a hug.

"Good morning, Karin. How's Kelly?"

"She's good. We turned her onto her right side. Danny moved your desk and chair." Danny was Kelly's night nurse. He had cared for his mom when she was dying from ALS. Sebastian knew Danny had a soft spot for Kelly, caring for her as if she were his own daughter.

He thanked Karin and began the short walk down the hall and entered her private room.

[Sebastian... I missed you Sebastian...]

"Hi, baby." He walked around the bed. Kelly appeared as if she were sleeping. Her blanket had slipped off her shoulder. He knew she got chilled easily – he pulled the blanket up to her ear and kissed her forehead.

[I was cold... thank you, Sebastian...]

He put his briefcase on the desk and sat on the chair. He exhaled softly and looked out the tall windows... Soon his attention turned to his wife... appearing so peaceful... as if she was in their bed... sleeping. He put his hand on her face – and noticed the telltale trail of tears.

"Kelly... Kelly!" He stood and pressed on her shoulders, causing her head to move on the pillow. He put his hands on her face, softly wiping his thumbs across her closed eyelids. "Kelly! Are you in there? Please! Kelly!" He put his hands on her face and aimed her closed eyes at him. "Kelly!"

And it happened. Tears escaped from her eyes. "Kelly! You're back! Kelly!" Her eyes opened as more tears escaped – her beautiful emerald eyes.

Sebastian pressed the call button. Karin came to the door. "Yes, Mr. Bonsignore?"

"She's back! My wife is back!" Sebastian looked up at Karin. "She's back!" While he was talking, Kelly blinked her eyes and more tears escaped.

[I'm trying to come back to you, Sebastian... have faith... I'm here...]

"Look! She's back! My wife is back!" Sebastian continued to press his hands on his wife's face. Karin sadly nodded and left the room.

"You're back..." He kissed her lips, lingering on her lips...

[I love you, Sebastian...]

He again pressed the call button.

Karin returned to the room. "Yes, Sebastian?"

"I want to make arrangements to move my wife home! I want her home with me!"

[Yes, Sebastian... I want to go home... to our bed...]

"Mr. Bonsignore, just because her eyes are open..."

Kelly eye's focused on the nurse – and frowned.

Sebastian's anger spiked. "Why in hell can't I bring her home?"

Karin walked over and stood beside him. "Sir – Mr. Bonsignore, she is going to need 24-hour care. Can you do that?"

He looked at Karin as if she had grown an extra nose and couldn't mask his irritation. "Yes, of course I can!"

Ignoring his tone, she replied, "Well, if that's the case then... I'll prepare your wife's discharge paperwork."

He watched her leave the room, silently regretting speaking to her that way. But he also was impatient to bring Kelly home. He leaned over his wife and kissed her lips. "We're going home. You and me, we're going home!"

[Yes... I want to go home... our home...]

Karin returned to the room followed by Dr. Schmitt.

"Mr. Bonsignore," her voice was soft but stern. "I'll have to do a final check on your wife's injuries."

"Yes... I unde :stand." As he spoke to the doctor, Sebastian refused to take his eyes off his wife. "When can you do the exam? She's in there... Kelly, my wife, she's in there. I want to bring her home so she can come back to me..." He didn't mean to cry, but his emotions – frustration? – took over and he couldn't hold back his tears.

"Mr. Bonsignore, I can schedule it for later this morning." Dr. Schmitt then asked Karin to page her assistant.

Sebastian didn't want to leave his wife's side.

[Sebastian... Bring me home... I want to go home... please...]

"I'll be back. I love you, Kelly."

[I love you too, Sebastian...]

Dr. Schmitt performed an exam on Kelly's injuries. Before Kelly was weaned off her induced coma, the surgeon had completed the last of the reconstructive surgeries. After this final the exam, she spoke with Sebastian.

"Mr. Bonsignore, I see no reason why your wife couldn't go home with you. The incision on her skull has healed well, as have her other injuries." She took Sebastian's arm and walked out of Kelly's room. "Karin tells me that you're hiring a full-time nurse to care for your wife?"

"Yes. I can't care for her alone."

"May I suggest you contact Danny? He's been your wife's nurse since she arrived. He knows Kelly, and he cares for her. I think that would be a good match."

"Thank you, Dr. Schmitt. I agree." He remembered Danny read Whitman to Kelly at night. Yes, he was comfortable with Danny caring for his wife.

"As soon as you prepare your home, I'll discharge your wife."

"Thank you, Dr. Schmitt." With both hands he shook the surgeon's hand. "Thank you."

He returned to his wife's bedside. Her eyes were closed and she was frowning. "That's not a good face, young lady." Sebastian leaned in and kissed her. "If I didn't know better, I'd say that's a scowl on your face. You didn't like it when I made that face..."

Kelly opened her eyes and managed a small grin.

[I hate it when you scowl...]

"That's my girl." He sat on the edge of her bed, his hip resting against her leg. "I'm bringing you home in a few days." Sebastian leaned over and kissed her – his chest lightly touching her body. A soft moan rose from her chest.

[I miss your weight on me... I miss you Sebastian...]

"I know you're in there... and you're coming home." He kissed her again... and she closed her eyes...

Sebastian hired Danny as Kelly's full-time nurse. Since she needed him around the clock, he would stay in the guest room. And she slept in her bed – their bed, though it took a few nights to figure out the logistics of sharing his bed with her. Eventually he became comfortable sleeping next to his wife – and he was happy.

With Danny's help, Kelly was weaned off her feeding tube and she began eating many small meals throughout the day. She still had no voice, but Sebastian knew his wife. He knew when she was hungry, he knew when she was tired, he knew when she needed him to simply hold her and let her cry. He knew her so well...

"Seb..." His name came out as a raspy mumble.

"Kelly? Did you say something?"

"Yeah..."

He made a movement to turn on his bedside light.

"No... me..."

"I'm here, Kelly. I'm right here." He kissed his wife's cheek and pressed his body against hers. "I'm right here."

"...Good... thanks..."

"Thank you for what, Love?"

"Home..."

Sebastian felt her head turn on their pillow. "How are you feeling, Love?" He rubbed her chest, feeling her breast under the soft T-shirt material.

"Think good... better... feels good..."

"You're back, Kelly." He kissed his wife's face.

"Back..? Happened... to me?"

"You don't remember?" As far as he was concerned, if she never remembered anything of the assault, it would be fine with him. She didn't need to relive those terrifying minutes.

"No... Um, not sure..."

"What aren't you sure about, Love?" He touched her chest, her shoulders and again centering her necklace over her trachea scar.

"...Nightmares... not sure what is real... I think... want to cry..."

Yes. Nightmares – nightmares he hoped would soon fade from her memory.

"It's okay... I'm right here. I'm not going anywhere." He tried assuring her so she felt safe – safe to cry while lying in his arms – safe to forget those awful dreams, that awful night.

"Hold me... Seb..."

He moved closer to his wife, putting one leg across her thin legs, holding her hip and pulling her against him.

"Good..." And she cried.

The early morning sunrise shone through the tall windows of their bedroom. Sebastian had slept with his head on her pillow – like they had every night since that first night they spent together. He felt her head turn toward him.

"Hi..." Her voice was so soft, but it was her voice.

He looked into her eyes and whispered, *"Kelly... you're back."* He leaned in and kissed his wife on her lips.

"I think I have to pee..." Sebastian remembered when she said those words after her cancer surgery – and he had made fun of her. He wouldn't make fun of her today.

"Okay, let me help you." He helped Kelly stand and, while supporting her body, walked as one into the en suite bathroom. He removed her adult diaper and gave her privacy by looking away.

"That feels so good... hate those things..."

"I promise, you won't have to use them very much longer."

"Good... I think I'm done." He helped his wife rise and walked her back to the bed. She looked up at him, her beautiful eyes glistening. "Sebastian... I'm hungry."

And he laughed. He hadn't laughed in so long, but her words brought about a full belly laugh from him. Kelly looked up at him and smiled.

"Let's get you some food!" Sebastian picked up his phone and made a call. "Danny, we're ready to go downstairs! We're having breakfast!"

35

Giving Comfort

Over the next six weeks, Kelly's strength and stamina greatly improved. Through the physical therapy she received from Danny, and her husband's constant devotion, she was walking without assistance – even conquering the stairs.

At their last breakfast together, Danny was happily relieved of his caretaking duties. He wished his patient well as they celebrated with orange juice poured into crystal wine goblets. Sebastian gave him a personal check, over and above his fee – and included a healthy donation to ALS research, which he tearfully accepted.

The early morning rays of the sun woke Sebastian. He looked at the time – and couldn't remember sleeping so late, except when they were at the cabin. Their night time sexual appetites always caused them to sleep well into the morning. His arm was wrapped around his wife's thin waist. He nuzzled her face, breathing in his wife's scent.

Kelly woke and looked into hazel eyes shrouded beneath heavy brows. It felt so natural waking up next to her husband. She was lazy this morning and would have liked to lie in bed a bit longer – cuddling into her husband's warm body. Unfortunately nature's call overruled her wishes. After kissing his lips, she rose and walked into their en suite bathroom, not bothering to close the door behind her.

"Sebastian!"

Alarmed, he rose and hurriedly went to her – but he was hit in the head by an empty toilet paper roll which she had thrown with deadly precision. *Really?*

After she had eaten a breakfast of French toast and bacon, Kelly lay down for a late morning nap. She slept for several hours at a time when she napped, and Sebastian would usually stay in their bedroom catching up on work. But today, since her appetite had returned, he went down to the kitchen and made pasta.

Sebastian measured three cups of unbleached flour on a large bread board, mixed in kosher salt and made a well with the flour. He cracked three eggs into the well – and breaking another egg, carefully separated the yolk, adding it to the well. He poured several glugs of extra virgin first cold press olive oil into the eggs, and finally about one quarter cup of water.

With a fork, he whisked the eggs and olive oil, gradually adding the flour as he did. When the dough was still rough, he added flour to his hands and proceeded to knead the dough, pressing his full weight into the soft mound. After ten minutes, a round bald head of dough had been created.

Sebastian wrapped the dough in plastic wrap and let it rest. As he washed his hands, he heard a knock on the door. Wiping his hands on a dish towel, he opened the door to Gabriella.

"Hi, Brie." He leaned in and kissed her cheek. "Come in." She thanked him and entered his large kitchen.

"Kelly's okay?" She sat on one of the stools at the butcher-block counter.

"She's doing fine." He put the towel down. "Why didn't you bring the baby? You know she loves when Finn visits."

"We need to talk."

Sebastian knew what was coming. He and Brie hadn't really talked about that night. It was their secret – his and Brie's. But still, she was right. They needed to talk.

"Does Raffe know?" He pulled a wrapped package out of the freezer and put it on the counter.

"Yes he does. He's the one who suggested I go to you."

"I don't understand." Sebastian opened the package and put several large chicken breasts on a plate. He stopped and frowned at her. "My brother asked you to come to me – to have sex with me..." He rewrapped the remaining chicken, returning them to the freezer.

"Your brother loves you..."

"Gabriella, excuse me, but that's one hell of a way for my brother to show his love." He stood at the butcher-block counter looking at her, supporting his body with both hands on the counter.

"When Annalisa died, Raffaele was inconsolable..."

"Christ, Brie! You didn't know him then. What are you talking about?" Sebastian looked at the heavy swinging door that separated the kitchen from the dining room, hoping Kelly wouldn't come in while he and Brie were having this conversation.

"He told me." She put her hand on one of his, but he pulled away. "Seb, please..."

"What? Did you come here to have sex with me again? Round two?" Picking up the hand towel, he walked away from her and leaned against the black soapstone counter across from the stove. Still clutching the towel, he folded his arms across his chest.

"No, that's not why I'm here." Brie knew this would be a hard conversation, but she didn't expect him to be that angry.

"So tell me what my brother told you, Brie. Enlighten me, please."

"When Annalisa died... Raffaele said he wanted to die."

Sebastian's countenance softened as she spoke. He could identify with the feeling of hopelessness that his brother felt.

"After the funeral, Raffe holed himself up in his apartment – the apartment he shared with Annalisa." Brie paused, hoping she was getting through to Sebastian. When he finally uncrossed his arms, she continued.

"He knew you were hurting. He said you were having nightmares – he had nightmares about Annalisa, too."

"So what? Someone came to him and fucked him so he'd feel better?" He turned and threw the terrycloth towel on the counter.

"That's not fair!" Brie rose from the stool. She walked around the butcher-block counter and faced Sebastian. "And that's not what I did – and that's not what happened to Raffe. A very good friend knew he was hurting, just like you were hurting."

Sebastian looked at the floor, then back again at Brie. "Who was this friend?"

"It doesn't matter who it was. But she was a dear friend..."

"Is this dear friend still in your husband's life? Is she still around to give your husband comfort?"

"Really!? Are you listening to yourself?" Brie wondered if this was such a good idea after all. Maybe she just should have let it be. She turned to leave, but he stopped her with his question.

"Tell me about this friend, Brie."

"She's an opera singer. From what Raffe told me, they were both in *La Bohème* and had toured together. She's quite famous actually, although I know you've never heard of her." She smiled. "You don't listen to opera."

Sebastian looked down at the floor. "No I don't – but I love my brother."

"Look. I came over to make sure there wasn't any awkwardness between us, but I guess I was wrong. This was a bad idea."

"Brie, I love my wife. What we did – it was impulsive, and I guess you thought I needed it. Maybe I did." He looked hard at his sister-in-law. "But you are my brother's wife. Can you comprehend how crazy this all sounds?"

"Yes, I can actually." She turned and walked toward the door. "Yes I can. But Raffe was the one who suggested I come to you. Can you deal with that?"

He again closed his eyes. "No Brie, I guess I can't."

She left his house, leaving Sebastian still leaning against the counter.

Brie walked to her car. She started the engine and clung to the steering wheel, resting her forehead on her hands. That conversation with Sebastian was not her finest moment. What did she think would be accomplished by confronting him? What she did – what her husband wanted her to do – was unforgivable. If she could do it over again, she would have told her husband to go fuck himself. But she didn't.

Oh God, what if Kelly found out what she did – what she and Sebastian did? Her best friend would never forgive her. But it wasn't Sebastian's idea, yet he didn't tell her no either. Fuck. This was so fucked up...

> *"Gabriella, are you awake?" Raffaele's pressed his face against his wife's long hair, inhaling its perfume. He loved her hair – the way it cascaded down her back almost to her waist.*
>
> *He pulled her closer to his body, her back to his front. Brie felt his hand reach between her legs. He pressed his fingers into her and felt her arousal.*

"My baby. You are always ready for me." Gabriella leaned her head back, allowing her husband to kiss her neck. "But tonight, my baby, I want you to do something for me... For Sebastian."

She turned on the bed and faced her husband. His hand caressed her hip. She reached up and felt his face.

"Raffaele, what do you mean?"

"Mia bellissima moglie, do you remember when I told you about my Annalisa?"

"Raffaele, why are you bringing her up now? I don't understand. But, yes, I remember." She kissed his lips, tasting his tears. "You told me you wanted to die..."

"Gabriella, mia bellissima moglie... Yes, I wanted to die. Do you remember I told you someone saved my life? Do you remember that story, my baby?" His breath was warm on her face.

"Raffe, you told me the story of the woman who came to you. She knew you wanted to die." He had told her a good friend came to him in his apartment and spent the night. Not only spending the night with him, but making love to him – passionately. Not holding back anything or any part of her body.

"My Gabriella, she comforted me when I wanted to die. Do you know that?" He kissed her lips... "Do you know that, my baby?" Again he kissed her face, then moving lower, kissed her breasts, loving her breasts, drowning in the cleavage between her beautiful breasts...

"Don't you know what the feel of your body – your breasts – can do for a man? Mia bellissima moglie, just touching your beautiful body can bring a man back from the brink of death..."

"What are you saying, Raffaele? What are you asking?" She guessed what he wanted, but she needed him to say the words.

"Mia bellissima moglie, if I asked you to go to my brother, to comfort Sebastian during this terrible time in his life – if I asked you to comfort my brother, would you... if I asked?" Again he caressed her breasts, loving her large areolas, causing her nipples to harden under his touch.

She was silent. Her husband was asking her to break their marriage vows, to lay with her brother-in-law, her best friend's husband. Brie raised her body on one elbow. "Is this what you want? You want me to lay with your brother?" She could barely make out his face in the dark of their bedroom.

"Sì, mia bellissima moglie..." He pulled his wife's face down to his own and chastely kissed her lips. "That was how I was saved from death. You saw Sebastian today. He cried so much. And I know he does not sleep. His grief is too great."

"I know. I saw his tears, too. Just the thought of Kelly..." Brie returned her husband's kiss. "If you want me to go to Sebastian, I will. Yes, Raffaele, I will."

"Gabriella, go now. Please. Go now."

She arose from their bed and turned on her bedside lamp. By the glow of the small lamp, he watched as she removed her silken nightgown and sleeping bra.

"My God, Gabriella, you are a beautiful woman."

She opened her closet door and took out a full-length floral caftan. She stepped into it and zipped it up. "Raffe, you are sure?"

Though he didn't answer her immediately, she surmised he was not sure. She knew he loved her, but now he was asking her to be with another man – his brother. This could be such a huge mistake on both their parts – and knew she would be the one to suffer the repercussions.

Without looking at his wife, he whispered," Sì, mia bellissima moglie..."

Brie leaned over the bed and kissed her husband. After turning out the light, she left the room, silently shutting the door behind her. Taking a deep breath, she walked down the back stairs to the kitchen and continued into the basement to the bedroom where Sebastian slept...

Before Brie came back to their bedroom, she went into the bathroom down from their room and showered, even douching while in the shower. After having sex with Sebastian, she wanted no part of him entering into their bed.

She opened their bedroom door – Raffaele lay on his side.

"Raffe..." She touched his shoulder. He turned over, feeling her bare breasts against his arm. He pulled his wife closer, her head resting on his shoulder. He said nothing to her. But his emotions wouldn't allow him to rest – he couldn't control himself.

"Gabriella, il mio amore. Vorrei fare l'amore con voi?" His breath was warm against her throat.

"Dominicci, sempre. Per favore." Of course, Brie would always love her husband – she would always make love with him.

He kissed his wife passionately, feeling her breasts press against his chest. Moving lower, he licked and kissed her breasts, sucking on her large areolas.

It had been only minutes before that Brie had made love with another man – her husband's brother. Sebastian had easily brought her to orgasm several times. She loved the feel of his beard on her skin, his beard touching her face, his beard touching her breasts, his beard touching her thighs – his beard touching her sensitive clit. She reveled in the feel of another man's hands on her body. Sebastian had been so ready to make love to her in so many ways. He enflamed in her a yearning she didn't realize she was missing.

But now she was with her husband. And she knew Raffaele would cherish and adore her until the ends of their lives.

He knelt behind her and turned her onto her belly, helping her rise to her knees, caressing her beautiful round ass. His hips gyrated as he made love to his wife, her soft groans inspiring him to thrust harder, pushing into her, pressing his fingers into her soft flesh. She braced herself by clutching onto the sheets as he brutally thrust harder into her again and again.

Brie whimpered, softly crying. "Raffaele, not so much... please, Raffe." But he only thrust harder, pushing harder, mashing against her body, his fingers causing bruise marks on her skin.

She called out. "Raffaele, you're hurting me!" But he ignored her pleas. He grunted as he pushed into her, audibly growling as he shoved into her. Brie collapsed under the pressure, lying on her front – but he wouldn't stop. Raffe grabbed her long hair and pulled hard while he pummeled into her. She cried out loud, shouting, begging him to stop. But he would not stop – his blind rage made him thrust harder.

"Stop! Raffaele! You're hurting me!" But she couldn't get away. His heavy body, plus the strangulating hold he had on her hair hindered her movements.

"Dominicci! Stop!" Brie was crying, sobbing, her face pressed into her arms. She couldn't move – she was in shock.

Raffaele came back to reality and gasped, "I'm sorry, mia bellissima Gabriella... I am so sorry." He slipped off her body and lay at her side. He tried reaching out to her, but she pushed him away.

"What the hell, Raffe?" She choked on her tears.

"I'm sorry, mia bellissima Gabriella. I'm so sorry. Please forgive me."

"Christ, Raffe!" She spoke into her arms, trying to stifle the onslaught of new tears. "If you didn't want me to go to your brother, why the hell did you ask me? I thought that's what you wanted? But your response just now was full of hate!"

She eased her body into a sitting position and pulled the sheet across her breasts. Every muscle in her body ached. "You weren't making love to me! You were fucking me!" Her tears stopped and her anger took over.

In the dim light of their bedroom, Raffaele looked at his beautiful wife, but he offered no response.

"Raffaele, are you jealous that I was with your brother? You asked me to go to him! Christ, Raffe! Get your shit together." But he remained silent.

Brie arose from their bed in disgust and threw on her bathrobe.

"And while you're thinking about it, I'll be in the other guest room." She walked out, closing the door hard behind her...

Brie put her car in reverse and backed out of Sebastian's driveway. This was a mistake – so many things had been mistakes. Her marriage was falling apart. Raffaele was so distant, and they hadn't made love in weeks. She put the car in gear and drove home.

Sebastian walked through the heavy swinging door into the dining room. He listened for any noise coming from upstairs. The TV wasn't on in the bedroom, so if there were any noises he would hear them. He walked into the living room and sat in his leather chair. He pulled up the arm and reclined the chair.

That conversation with Brie was so uncomfortable. Was it really necessary that she come into his home and confront him like that? What happened between them should have stayed between them – and forever a secret. But what about Raffe telling Brie to go downstairs to his bedroom – in their home – and comfort him? That's nonsense. That's crazy. He'd like to forget about the whole thing.

Again he listened for any noises coming from their bedroom upstairs. Good. Kelly still slept. He would take a nap in his chair. He picked up the afghan and covered his legs. Crossing his arms on his chest, he sighed... and dozed...

> *He had been crying... When he was upstairs in his brother's kitchen, he could barely control his emotions. But he completely lost it when he went back downstairs into the spare bedroom. And because Kelly didn't like it when he slept in his clothes, he removed them before getting into the full-size bed.*
>
> *He hadn't been sleeping that long, if at all. And if he did sleep, it was always a restless sleep. He would doze... wake and cry... doze and cry. His world was in an uproar and he didn't know how to resolve it. He was tired, but he couldn't sleep. He was sad and all he could do was cry. He was exhausted.*
>
> *Sebastian had barely dozed again when he sensed the bedroom door opening. Was this another bad dream? Was he dreaming that Kelly – or another terrible nightmare – was haunting him? He raised himself up on one arm.*
>
> *"Who's there?" He turned on the bedside lamp.*
>
> *"It's me, Sebastian. It's Gabriella."*
>
> *He looked at her. She was wearing a floor-length caftan. He sat up. "Brie, what do you want? Is everything okay?"*
>
> *She slowly unzipped her caftan, letting it fall from her shoulders. Gabriella stood before him in all her naked glory.*
>
> *"Brie, what are you doing here?" God in heaven, she was a beautiful woman.*
>
> *She turned off the bedside lamp. He felt the bed groan under her weight as she sat near him. She put a hand on his chest.*
>
> *"But..."*
>
> *"Sebastian, hush. I'm here to help you get through the night..." And before he knew it, Brie had taken his head in her hands and kissed his lips. She licked his lips as she kissed him, pulling his tongue into her*

mouth, sucking on his tongue. He knew he responded, but this was so wrong for so many reasons.

"Brie..." He managed to say her name while she pressed her tongue deep into his mouth.

"Touch me..." She took his hands in her own and pressed them onto her full breasts. She felt good. Lord in heaven, she felt good.

"Use me, Sebastian. Love me, use me." She rose and knelt across his legs. She pulled his head to hers and kissed him again.

Sebastian put his arms around her and held her tight against his chest, her full breasts crushing into him. He loosened his hold and kissed her face, her neck. Brie put her arms around his head as he kissed her breasts. His hands found her full round ass. With fingers spread wide, he caressed her butt cheeks, pulling her closer to his body.

She kissed his face, holding his head between her hands, feeling his soft beard and grabbing his long hair in her fists. "Come with me, baby... Lie with me..." Brie lay back on the bed.

Sebastian lowered himself onto her body, nestling between her open legs, kissing her breasts, sucking on her large nipples. "Jesus, Brie..." and he lost himself in her full breasts. He kissed her lips, licked and kissed her throat, her chest, loving her breasts again.

He moved lower and kissed her belly. Sebastian kissed the inside of her thighs. He heard her moaning and felt her hips swaying. He wanted to make love to her, but he languished longer...

"Roll over, Brie." He rolled with her. She moved around and straddled his head, her legs spread wide – and taking his erection, held the shaft tight as she brought it deep into her mouth.

Sebastian pulled her hips down and held her close, tasting all of her, loving all of her, inhaling her dark musk. And he felt her hard pulsing orgasm.

She fell back onto the bed. Sebastian moved and lay between her open legs. He felt her breasts against his chest. He rose up and kissed her breasts again, sucking on her large areolas, drowning in her breasts – her large, soft, beautiful breasts.

"I'm going to make love to you..." And Sebastian pressed into her, thrusting and pushing. He raised one of her legs, locking it against his arm – and he made that bed rock. And he kept thrusting and pushing – breathing harsh in her ear until finally he was exhausted.

He rolled onto his side, bringing her with him. He touched her face, brushing her hair behind one ear and lightly kissed her cheek.

Brie got up out of the bed, put on her caftan and left the room – closing the door quietly behind her.

And Sebastian slept...

36

Nothing but the Truth

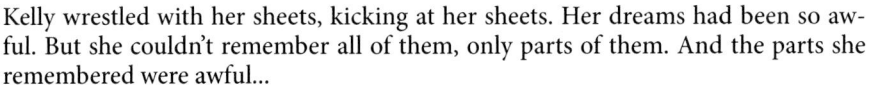

Kelly wrestled with her sheets, kicking at her sheets. Her dreams had been so awful. But she couldn't remember all of them, only parts of them. And the parts she remembered were awful...

> *Someone was hurting her – HE was hurting her, he was hitting her, pulling her around, pushing at her, hitting her... she remembered he was hitting her. Hard. Hitting her hard. She couldn't get away from him. She tried getting away. She remembered kicking at him – kicking so hard at him, trying to push him off with her legs. But he was too heavy. And he was hitting her. He was hurting her.*
>
> *She remembered the pain in her thighs, her legs, her bottom. He was hurting her. He was making love to her? No! He was hurting her. He was raping her? Is that what happened? He was raping her? He was raping her! It hurt so bad. The memory was awful. An awful memory. He was hurting her. Pushing into her. It hurt so bad, hurt so bad, hurt so bad. She was on her knees and he was hurting her. She couldn't get away. And he was hurting her. Hurting her. No! No! No! Stop! Stop! Stop! No! Get away from me!*

"Get away from me! Stop! You're hurting me!"

Sebastian heard her screams. He launched himself out of his chair and bounded up to the second floor, skipping every other stair. He practically stumbled over himself running down the hall. He entered their room – she wasn't in the bed!

He ran around to her side of the bed. Her legs had gotten tangled in the sheets, and her head and shoulders were on the floor. He knelt at her side and tenderly picked her up. He sat on the mattress and pulled her into his strong arms, crushing her body against his chest.

"Sebastian! I remember!" And she cried... her screams echoing throughout the house. And the tighter he held her, the louder she screamed. She pushed him away, pushing at his body with her fists, his chest absorbing the blows. He pulled her back close to his body, again holding her tight.

After what seemed like several minutes, she looked wildly into his eyes. ***"He raped me!"*** She shouted her words. ***"I was raped! I was raped!"*** Her breathing was harsh – her chest rose and fell with each breath.

"Yes, baby... He raped you." Sebastian drew her body tighter into his arms – rocking her, soothing her, holding her, comforting her, loving her. Though her breathing had calmed, she still gasped for each breath.

Again she pushed away from him. "Who was it?" Her tears had stopped, but her face was wet. Using the sheet, he wiped her cheeks.

"Does it matter?" He tried getting her mind from thinking about it, but in the end she would find out and blame him for not telling her. Sebastian took a deep breath. Was he ready for this? "Your ex husband Stevie had someone rape you." He waited for some kind of reaction from her.

"***Who!*** I asked you *who!*" She was pissed. What? At him? At Stevie?

"His name was Ronnie. Ronnie Wolff."

She looked into his eyes... then looked away. She was thinking. *Dear God, what was she thinking?* "I don't know him... Why did he hurt me? Why did he rape me?"

"Because Stevie wanted to get back at you and Roger." Sebastian knew this was going to open up an ugly can of worms, but he knew if he didn't tell her now she'd find out on her own. Here – with him – she was safe. "Honey, when Roger threw your ex out of the bar, Stevie planned on getting back at him."

The look on her face told him she still didn't understand. Kelly tried processing the pieces of information he fed her, but like a broken calculator it wasn't adding up. She needed to be told the whole story.

"Let's go downstairs and I'll tell you the whole story."

She gave him *that look.*

"Really, I promise. The whole story. Please."

"I have to go to the bathroom first. Help me, please."

Sebastian exhaled loudly and stood. He helped his wife walk to the bathroom. What the hell was he going to tell her? He'd better tell her the truth or she was going to figure it out. She was always too smart for her own good.

He helped her dress – she still wore his T-shirt. Her clothes hung on her. She needed to eat. He promised to tell her if she ate. She couldn't argue with that deal. Together they walked downstairs to the kitchen. The partially thawed chicken breasts were sitting out on the counter. He covered the plate and put them in the refrigerator.

Kelly noticed a wrapped ball of pasta dough on the counter. She liked it when Sebastian fixed her dinner. He was a fabulous cook – and now he cooked for her. How lucky was she?

"Sit at the counter and I'll fix you a sandwich. We won't eat dinner for a few hours."

While he made two sandwiches of sliced roasted turkey breast, she asked the question he didn't want to answer.

"How did he get into our house?"

Sebastian stopped spreading mayo on the Kaiser Rolls. "When you were in the hospital with your cancer, I asked Roger to get copies of our house key made so he and Cody could fix up the guest room for your mom."

"Yeah? That's no big deal." She looked at the turkey breast and felt her appetite growing. "So what happened?"

"Stevie was working at Mitchell's Hardware store. He's the one who made the copies of the house key."

"Um, excuse me while I plead stupid, but I still don't get it." She stealthily pinched a slice of turkey, devouring it in one bite. Sebastian smiled.

"Well, the way I heard it, when Stevie confessed..."

"He's in jail, right?" The look on her face was one of terror. He had never seen that look before.

"Yes, and he's not getting out. Ever. You don't have to worry." Sebastian reached across the butcher-block counter and caressed his wife's face, holding her face in his hand. "You don't have to worry."

"Thank you, Seb." She exhaled. She leaned into his hand and kissed his palm. After a few moments she was ready to hear more. "So... continue. Stevie was working at Mitchell's and Roger came in to get a copy made? But how does that equate to Ronnie what's-his-name coming into our home – and Stevie putting him up to it." She put her head in her hands. "This is making my head hurt."

"Okay, here's how I understood it. Ronnie was doing time for breaking into the New London Grille..."

"He broke into the restaurant? I heard he didn't get away with much cash, but caused lots of damage." She paused, letting her brain catch up with her mouth. "He did it... huh..."

"Yes. Apparently, Ronnie's cousin was a good friend of Stevie's. And when he got put away in county, his cousin asked Stevie if he'd take Ronnie's hours at the hardware store."

"Other than being terribly convoluted, keep going..." She munched on another piece of roast turkey breast.

"But I have to backtrack a little in the story..." He looked at Kelly. She playfully crossed her eyes. He laughed – it was good to laugh with his wife again. "From what the police gathered from Stevie, when he worked at the post office sorting outgoing mail, he discovered our wedding invitations. He recognized your name on the labels with my address."

"So he knew where I lived. But how did making keys... and Roger... Oh, God, Seb. Give me a bottom line here. Please." She had her head in her hands again.

He finished making the sandwiches. He put a toothpick with a large green olive on it through her Kaiser Roll, cut it in half and pushed the plate in front of her.

"Kelly, are you on any meds?"

"You know I'm not. Why?"

"Because wife, we're having Coronas with our sandwiches. That's why." He opened the refrigerator and took out two tall bottles. He opened them both and handed her one. They touched the necks in a toast – she drank the golden liquid.

"Oh this bullshit is worth a beer!" She smiled while she drank. Sebastian watched her, finally exhaling after so many weeks of not even knowing if she would survive.

"So do you want to hear the rest of it?" He put napkins at their plates.

"Sure, why not. Why didn't Stevie just do it himself? He tried it before – oh, yeah, I kicked him in his balls!" And she smirked. "But why did he get Ronnie to do it? Did he have something on him? Blackmail?"

"Nothing like that. Kelly, Stevie got Ronnie to do it because he was big like Roger."

"Um, I'm not connecting the key-making with Roger and Ronnie..."

"When Roger and Cody went into the hardware store to get the copies made, Stevie recognized Roger as the one who threw him out of the Harbor Pub. He wanted to get Roger's finger prints on our house key – that key would be the one the police would find after Ronnie..."

"Shit. That was years ago! I mean, I knew Stevie was a head case, but holding a grudge for how many years?"

"From what the detective said, Stevie planned this assault before he knew Ronnie was going to be in the county jail for a whole year. He waited one full year just sitting on his plan."

"So..." Kelly took another long drink. The ice-cold beer tasted so good. "Stevie got Roger to put his finger prints on the key that would tie Roger to the attack? Seriously?"

"That was the plan." He took another long drink. "And Stevie was supposed to wait around until Ronnie left our house, but he drove off. Do you remember calling 911?"

"No... I really don't." She licked mayo off her thumb.

"Thank goodness we have a good police force here, because when the 911 operator received your call she dispatched the police immediately. They found Ronnie standing outside of our house."

She put down the bottle and stared at her husband. "So they caught him red handed?"

"Um. You could say they caught him with his pants down."

"What the hell?"

"He did a job on you, Kelly." Sebastian closed his eyes, remembering that first week she was in the ICU. He drank more of his beer. "I was so worried I was going to lose you." He looked directly into her eyes and took a deep breath as he continued. "They said you bit his dick..."

The look on Kelly's face was sickening. "Why did I have his dick in my mouth? Oh God! He put his fucking dick in my mouth?" She took a long drink of the beer and gagged – and raised it again for another long drink. "This is too much. I don't think I want to hear any more. But that's not saying I don't want to hear the rest of it. Just not now."

Telling his wife about her assault was exhausting. Sebastian raised his bottle. "Whenever you're ready, I'll tell you what you want to know. But I agree. That's enough for one day." He winked at her. "Now, finish your sandwich."

Kelly gave him an exhausted smile, and resumed eating her wonderful roast turkey sandwich with a big green olive stuck in the middle.

That evening they dined on raspberry-glazed chicken breasts and his homemade fettuccine in a light butter sauce with parmesan and parsley. They sat in the dining room. Sebastian had set a formal table, even serving a chilled bottle of *Santa Margherita* Pino Grigio. Kelly played her favorite Lizz Wright CD. Everything was so nice, yet they weren't eating off his mother's china.

She drank from the crystal wine goblet. "Next time, let's invite Brie and Raffe. Then you can use your mom's china."

He looked at her and smiled – but it was a smile loaded with issues. *Oh boy...* What happened while she was out of commission? No, this wasn't the evening to delve into family matters. She was enjoying her husband too much.

"I like it like this." She raised her wine goblet in a silent toast. "Just you and me..."

After that delicious meal – and on top of all the mental stress – Kelly felt exhausted. Sebastian helped her shower. As she sat on the bed he dried her hair. She pulled one of his T-shirts over her head.

"I want to dye my hair again. I hate the silver."

"Whenever you want to make a hair appointment, tell me. I'll drive you down." He kissed the top of her head. Kelly looked up at him.

"I'll have to get my hair cut, too." She pulled at the short growth on the side of her head that had been shaved, touching the raised scar tissue. The new growth was short – and silver.

"Whatever you want to do..."

She lay on the mattress and yawned. "I'm so tired I can't keep my eyes open anymore." He kissed her forehead and covered her with both a blanket and a quilt, turned off her bedside lamp and left the room.

After cleaning up the kitchen, Sebastian showered and slipped into bed. He pulled her body to his – her back to his front, sharing one pillow like they had since that first night together so many years ago. In the quiet of their bedroom, he listened to her breathing. This had been a long day – telling her about the rape was the last thing he wanted to do. But she forced his hand.

They had been sleeping soundly for hours. Kelly rolled over, waking him. Sebastian heard her talking, but she was dreaming. In the soft early morning light of their bedroom he saw a smile play on her face. Hopefully it was a good memory running through her head...

> *"Daddy!" Her mom dropped her off at the train yard. Kelly's dad had left the house earlier that morning.*
>
> *"Hey there, Kelly-Belly! You ready?"*
>
> *"Yup. Let's go work the train!" Her father grinned broadly as he looked down at his daughter and held out his large calloused hand to her. She loved her daddy. They were going out on the D&RGW – his train.*

Kelly took his hand and together they walked across the tracks to the waiting engine. She skipped along, keeping up with her daddy's long strides – her red curls bursting out from beneath her blue-and-white engineer's cap.

"Is Nick the engineer today, Daddy?" Kelly knew all the engineers and other switchmen on the trains by name – but her favorite engineers were Nick and Max. They let Fred's daughter ride up front with them while he was throwing track switches and turning hand brakes.

"Yup." As they walked to the imposing black and orange locomotive, Nick blew the horn.

"We're late, young lady. You ride up front with Nick." He picked up his daughter, helping her climb the steep stairs to the cab and handed up her small metal lunch box. He waited until she waved down at him.

"Where we going today, Nick?" She sat next to the engineer in her dad's chair.

"We're dead-heading to Alamosa and returning with a load of rock. Think you can handle it all day, Kelly?" Nick knew she could handle it – she could ride the train 24-hours a day if her dad was with her.

"Yup!" Echoing her daddy's words. "Let's go!"

Kelly opened her eyes. "Is everything okay, Seb?" She touched his face, feeling his beard.

"I was watching you sleep, Love. You were dreaming." He closed his eyes, loving the feel of his wife's hands on his face – just the lightest touch of her fingers against his skin gave him permission to accept her comforting presence. Her face was close to his – he inhaled her sweet breath.

"My dad was in my dreams." Her hand stopped at his ear.

"You have good memories of your father?" According to Ruth, Kelly adored her father – the man who died when she needed him most.

"Some of my best memories are with my dad. It's funny, but I never called him Dad. I always called him Daddy." Kelly again felt Sebastian's beard. "My dad wore a beard... He died when I was twelve – if he had lived longer, he would have graduated to Dad." In the dim light she could barely make out her husband's face.

"Your mom showed me an old photo of you and your dad. I think you were about eight." He loved the feel of her hands on his face. "Your mom called you and your dad two peas in a pod."

And as expected, she began crying. "He was just the best person ever." Thinking about her dad was such an awful beautiful memory.

"Do you want to talk about it? About your dad?" He brushed the bangs out of her eyes.

"Yeah, if you want to hear it."

Sebastian kissed her forehead. "I want to hear your memories."

"My earliest memory of my dad was with him on the train. He was working on the trains when he met my mom. I guess you could say she had the best of both worlds."

"How do you mean?" He lightly rubbed her hip, feeling the bony protrusion of her pelvis.

"Well," Kelly looked up at her husband. "My mom married a man who she didn't have to see every day. What do you think about that, mister?"

"I'd say that would be sad. Don't forget, you were basically gone from my life for a month." He kissed her face.

"Sorry." She rolled over, her back to his front. "I'm cold."

Sebastian reached down and pulled up another quilt, and held her body with his arm on top of the quilt.

"That relationship worked for them. He was home most days, but there were times I remember he'd be gone for a couple days in a row. When he came home it was like Christmas and the Fourth of July all at once."

"Your mom and dad loved each other? They had a good relationship?"

"My mom was madly in love with my dad. I think that's why when he was gone for a few days it worked for them. When he came home, he literally swept my mom off her feet." Kelly lifted the blankets, making Sebastian hold her under the covers.

"There... That's better." Kelly snuggled into his warm body. "My dad was tall. I think that's where I got my height. My mom said I took after his side of the family – the tall side." And she laughed, but her laugh turned into a yawn.

"I miss you..." He nuzzled her hair. "I miss making love with you..."

When she didn't respond, he realized she was already sleeping. In the stillness of their bedroom, he listened as her breathing became shallow. And he held his wife... His wife. This was the woman he loved, the woman he married, the woman he almost lost. This woman who survived such a horrific attack...

And they slept, sharing one pillow...

37

Hurt

Kelly's recovery had been miraculous. Sebastian set her up with their friend Tom who was into cross training. He developed a training regimen that not only strengthened her muscles, but rebuilt her stamina as well. The first day Sebastian dropped her off at the gym, Tom met her at the front door. She was eager to get back to her old self.

Tom waved as Sebastian drove off and held the door open for Kelly. When she'd first entered the gym, she had seen the usual workout machines. But he brought her into another room. There she saw dumbbells, huge thick rubber tires, large rubber balls and kettle bells of various sizes.

"Don't worry, Kelly. We'll get to those eventually, but with you we have to start slow." Together they walked out through the back door of the building. "We'll begin by taking short walks and ease into longer walks. After your stamina increases, we'll get those muscles working. Are you with me?"

"Yes. I'm so tired of feeling tired."

Tom smiled. "Come on..." And they began their walk. But only after a few blocks she asked for his help.

"Tom, I can't do this..."

He put his arm around her waist and directed her to a bench. Kelly sat with her head down, breathing heavily. She looked up at her trainer.

"This is ridiculous..." And she cried. Kelly was so tired of lying around, not feeling strong – and now when she was beginning the new workout regimen, she already felt defeated.

Tom sat next to her. "Don't worry. Like I said, we're just getting started." He put his hand on her shoulder. "Baby steps, Kelly. Baby steps."

"Okay..." Kelly grinned through her tears. "So what are we waiting for?" She stood and began walking. Tom quickly caught up with her.

"Don't push it. Whenever you want to sit, tell me. We're not going to overdo it this first day."

Kelly trusted him, and they walked on for another half a mile before she had to sit again.

Over the next two months Kelly's strength increased. When Tom began working with her in the gym, he had her start off with some drop sets of leg extensions, including 5-by-5 squat lunges. He quickly realized Kelly was a fighter, not a milque-toast and soon increased her repetitions, including the over-head presses. But he held her back, cautioning her to ease into the more rigorous training. They hadn't started flipping tires or doing battle ropes yet, but he knew she would excel in those exercises too.

When they were done for the day, Tom drove her home – and waited until she climbed the porch steps and entered her house. Kelly locked the door and put her key in the bowl on the counter. She opened the refrigerator and took out a bottle of sparkling water, which she drank while leaning on the open door. She was tired. Her arm and thigh muscles were tired – she would take a shower first before laying down for a nap. Kelly knew Sebastian would be bringing home her favorite sub sandwich and chips for dinner.

She heard a knock at the door. She wasn't expecting anyone. Kelly unlocked and opened the door, and was pleased to see her brother-in-law. "Hi, Raffe. Won't you come in?"

"Thank you, Kelly. Is Sebastian home?"

"No... He doesn't get home until later. What's up?" She closed the door behind him.

"Can we talk?" Raffaele looked so serious.

"Sure, come on in. Do you want a sparkling water?"

"No thank you."

"Let's go in here. I just got back from working out and I need to sit." She opened the heavy swinging door that led to the dining room and told him to pull out a chair from the table.

"Kelly," he began. "How are you feeling?"

"Well, I'm getting there..."

But before she could say more, he cut her off. "I felt we should talk."

She sat at the table facing him, still not understanding why he was here, or what they had to talk about.

"Kelly, I thought after Gabrielle came over a while back and spoke with Sebastian... and since that ended badly..."

"Um, Raffe, I'm not sure what you're talking about. I didn't know Brie was here. How long ago did you say? Sebastian didn't mention anything about any conversation they had."

Raffaele's face paled. "You don't know anything about what happened between them?"

"Something happened between your wife and my husband? No, I knew nothing. But I sure am willing to listen now."

"I think... Kelly, this was a mistake." He stood and made an attempt to leave, but she held out her arm and stopped him.

"Raffaele. Sit." He had no alternative other than to sit back in his chair. "Talk to me. Brie was here, right? And she spoke with Sebastian, right? And I knew nothing about the conversation they had, right?"

He looked down at his lap. "Yes Kelly, that's right."

"So I take it if the conversation was innocent, Sebastian would have at least mentioned it to me."

"Yes Kelly... you are right."

"I hate playing twenty questions, Raffe. I think you should tell me exactly what happened between Brie and my husband – *Now*."

"It wasn't meant to hurt anyone..."

"*What* wasn't meant to hurt anyone? Obviously, it would be a non issue if it didn't hurt anyone. But why do I get the feeling I'm the only one here who's going to get hurt?"

"No one meant to hurt you, dear Kelly."

Now she was pissed. "Damn it, Raffe! What happened? What happened between your wife and my husband?" Kelly's dim light bulb again was slow to shine. "Oh dear God... Your wife and my husband slept together? They had sex? Am I getting warm?"

"Yes, dear Kelly."

"Damn it, Raffaele! Do not 'dear Kelly' me!" She stood too quickly and suddenly felt light-headed. She grabbed for the back of her chair but missed – and fell heavily onto the hardwood floor.

"Kelly!" He reached down and, taking her arm, helped her sit back in the chair.

"Thank you." That hurt. She could tell she injured her hip. "Now talk. And don't hold anything back." She rubbed her hip, hoping it wouldn't turn into a bruise.

Raffaele folded his hands in his lap. "When my Annalisa died so tragically I thought I would die. I wanted to die. I stayed in the apartment we had shared – not wanting to go out ever."

When Kelly didn't show any emotion, he continued.

"A dear friend came to me and helped me... She helped me want to live again."

"How pray tell did this friend help you, Raffe?" Her words were dripping with sarcasm.

He looked into her eyes. "She made love to me." The next words out of his mouth were spoken quickly. "But it didn't mean anything. She was just trying to help me."

"So after your wife died, you wanted to die. And a friend had sex with you. And because of that you found a reason to live? Do I have that part right?"

Raffaele nodded.

"So when I was in the hospital after some asshole raped and beat the crap out of me, Brie had sex with my husband so he'd have a reason to live?"

Again he nodded.

"Wow... So why did Brie feel compelled to come over to my home and talk to my husband about something that should never have happened? And obviously didn't think to inform me of their little tryst!"

"Kelly, it wasn't like that..."

"Really? Gabriella fucking my husband wasn't like *what*?"

"She was only trying to comfort him. All he could do was cry and I knew she could help."

"She... Tell me something, Raffe. Whose idea was it that my best friend, married to my brother-in-law, should go to my husband and have sex with him in order to comfort him?"

"It was my suggestion. I thought it would help Sebastian to have Gabriella bring him comfort."

Kelly stood and pulled her T-shirt off over her head, exposing her mastectomy scar and small breast.

"Look at me, Raffe! I *know* what Gabriella looks like! After being with her, do you really think Sebastian could go back to *this*?" Now Kelly cried. She cried out of anger, out of sadness, out of confusion – but mostly out of anger. "Do you?"

Kelly sat down in her chair, clutching her shirt to her chest. She couldn't help herself. She cried so hard she felt her heart pounding out of her chest.

"Kelly, my dear Kelly... My brother loves you." He sought to touch her, but she leaned back out of his reach.

"Raffe, I think you can leave now." She couldn't look at the man who sat in front of her. She heard him rise from the chair and push through the heavy swinging door.

"Oh dear God..." Kelly rose from her chair and slowly walked up the stairs to their bedroom. She removed her shoes and socks, kicking them into the corner of the closet, and stripped. She turned on the shower and stood under the rainforest showerhead. It felt so good to have that hot water wash off her sweat – if only it could erase the pictures in her head. What the hell was Brie thinking? What the hell was Raffaele thinking, asking his wife to fuck her husband? This is shit. And Sebastian never said anything. He never said anything.

After drying her hair, Kelly decided to take matters into her own hands. While she dressed, she mumbled under her breath, *"If he wants to have sex with someone, he can damn well have sex with his brother's wife. Damn him!"*

She reached to the upper closet shelf and pulled down her overnight bag, packing it with several changes of clothes. Returning downstairs to the kitchen, she yanked at the collection of canvas shopping bags from between the refrigerator and the lower cabinets, and mindlessly tossed food into one. From the cupboards, Kelly added a loaf of French bread. In another bag, she put several bottles of wine. This would be a long week.

She picked up Sebastian's keys from the bowl on the counter. Good – they were the keys for his Lincoln MKT. She stuffed them in her purse along with the key to their cabin.

Kelly took one last look at the kitchen – she loved this kitchen, but after today she might not see it again. She considered the ring on her finger, her beautiful emerald diamond halo ring. Without a moment's hesitation, she pulled it off her finger and put it in the bowl. Fuck him and his little whore.

Slamming the door behind her, she left the house without locking it and purposefully marched into the garage. She yanked open the SUV's door and climbed in, dropping the bags on the passenger floor mat. After starting it – and racing the engine – Kelly noticed the tank was full. Good. Before putting it into reverse, she took a deep breath – held it for a moment – and exhaled loudly. She backed out and pressed the remote, closing the garage door. Done.

Sebastian was in the middle of a business call when Carolyn knocked on his door. He looked up and shook his head *no*. But Carolyn entered his office and whispered that he needed to take this call. Appearing frustrated, he finished his call.

"Carolyn, what is so important?"

She handed him a piece of paper with 'call your brother' scribbled on it. "He said it's important." She left his office, closing the door behind her.

Sebastian pressed the speed dial number for his brother wondering as he did what the emergency could be. Raffaele answered on the first ring.

"Seb... I hope I didn't screw things up for you."

"What do you mean? How could you screw things up for me?" He grinned as he leaned back in his chair, wondering what his brother was up to.

"I thought you would have told Kelly about you and Gabriella."

"No, that was a matter between Brie and myself – and instigated by you, big brother. What happened?"

"I went over to your house and spoke with Kelly..."

Sebastian sat upright in his chair. "Raffe, what did you say to my wife?" A sense of panic came over him.

"I thought you had told your wife – I went over there to make her understand why Gabriella had sex with you."

He put his elbows on his desk, holding the phone to his ear with the palm of one hand. "Jesus Raffe. I never told Kelly. When Gabriella came over, I didn't even want to talk about it. Oh, God... Kelly knows."

"I'm sorry. I thought she knew."

Abruptly he stood, causing his chair to roll, slamming into his credenza. Several framed photos fell over, including their wedding picture. "Why in heaven's name would I tell my wife about that? Where is she now? Where is my wife now?"

"I left her alone in your home. That was about an hour ago."

"I need to go. Raffaele, don't you talk to her, don't go see her... Stay the hell out of this, do you hear me?" He had never been upset or mad or angry at his big brother – until now. Sebastian walked out of his office.

"Carolyn, I'm gone. If Kelly calls... Jesus. If Kelly calls, call me immediately, understand?"

"Sure..." Carolyn had never seen him so upset and out of sync. She immediately checked his calendar. He had an afternoon meeting scheduled – she promptly called the client and requested they reschedule.

He left the building and drove home. He could only think of Kelly – and how hurt she must be. He didn't even consider her anger. Sebastian pulled up to the closed garage door and pressed the remote. His SUV was not in the garage. *Shit.*

He raced up the porch steps – the front door wasn't locked. Upon entering his kitchen, he saw several canvas grocery bags littering the floor. He pushed through the heavy swinging door and ran upstairs to their bedroom. The closet door was wide open. Her damp towel was on the floor. Looking up on the shelf, he noticed her overnight bag was missing. *Shit.*

Sebastian tried calling her, but the call went directly to voicemail. *Shit.* He changed into jeans and a T-shirt, pushed his bare feet into tennis shoes, pulled on his worn leather jacket and ran back downstairs. He checked the wooden bowl on the counter – she had taken the key to the cabin.

And her wedding ring was in the bowl. He picked it up and held the ring between his fingers. Sebastian had chosen the stone because it matched her eyes – her beautiful emerald eyes. *Shit.* He put her ring on his pinky finger next to his own wedding ring. *Oh God Kelly...*

His phone rang. He looked at the caller ID. It was his brother. "What!"

"Have you found Kelly – I'm so worried..."

"Raffe, if you were really worried about my wife, you would not have told your wife to screw me!" He ran out of the house and into his Porsche. She had already gotten at least an hour head start – but he knew where she was going.

38

Truth and Consequences

Kelly drove down the private road, this narrow thoroughfare that had been carved through the woods. She parked the SUV and started the first of two trips up the field stone steps leading to the cabin. She couldn't carry everything in one trip – she was exhausted.

She took a goblet from the cupboard and opened a bottle of wine. Taking matches and newspapers from the sitting room, she exited the cabin, leaving her moccasins outside the door. As she walked down to her pond, she reveled in the feel of the mossy grass under her bare feet. This was her place – her refuge. She would stay here as long as she could.

The fire pit was just as they left it. She put down the wine and her goblet on the ledge. Pulling back the heavy tarp, she took logs from the cache of cut wood. It was dark – hardly any stars in the sky – but she knew this place like the back of her hand.

She built a teepee of logs in the fire pit, crushed newspapers under the logs and lit the paper. It didn't take long before a fire erupted. Standing close to this pit made of fieldstone, she welcomed the familiar flames – letting the heat warm her face, her body, but not her soul...

Kelly filled her goblet and, carrying the bottle, walked to the edge of her pond. The only sound she heard was a distant crappie leaping for its dinner. She sat on the edge, letting her feet sink into the cool water.

She loved the cabin. This place would remain hers. Sebastian bought it for her. If they separated, she wanted the cabin. He could have everything else. This was her cabin.

And she drank more wine. And she cried. Why? Why was she crying? Anger? Anger that her best friend fucked her husband – or as Raffe said, comforted her husband? Kelly muttered under her breath. *"I bet she comforted him..."*

It was so quiet out here. This was where she wanted to be – just her. No one else, especially not Sebastian. Christ, what the fuck did he do? And this was Raffe's idea? Brie could have said no. Hell, Sebastian could have said no. But no! No one said no.

Kelly drank more wine, feeling the effects of alcohol on an empty stomach. But she didn't care. And she drank more wine...

He had missed that damn county road turn-off, but didn't realize it until he had driven an additional thirty miles. He made a U-Turn in the middle of the highway and back-tracked. That took time, but now he was on the right road.

Sebastian hoped she was at the cabin. He hoped she would listen to him, hear him out. He really screwed up. He would ask for her forgiveness, but was this something for which she could forgive him? He had made love to Gabriella, his brother's wife,

Kelly's best friend. It all sounded so fucked up. How could she ever forgive him? Would she forgive him?

He drove down the narrow road and saw the SUV. He parked behind it. Because he didn't have a flashlight, he carefully made his way to the cabin. Looking down to the pond, he saw the low-glowing flames coming from the fire pit – and by the pond's edge, saw his wife lying on the ground. After saying a quick prayer, he took a deep breath and walked down the hill.

She was sleeping. A crystal goblet and an empty bottle of wine lay at her side. He sat on the grass near her. She was beautiful. He had always thought she was beautiful. And he was sure she was angry – and rightly so. He looked up to the cloudless sky. There were no stars in the heavens tonight. No North Star to follow. But he followed her because *she* was his North Star.

He looked out across the pond. He couldn't remember this place being so quiet... No loons calling. No mommy ducks swimming with their babies. It was too early in the season for giving birth. Sebastian knew that. His wife taught him that. Kelly taught him all she knew about nature. Now he realized his life might be over because she didn't want to be with him anymore. And she had every reason in the world not to want him in her life.

This was her place. She had wanted this cabin, this sanctuary. She had asked for a cabin so many times until he finally figured out what made her happy. He was a smart man – an educated man, but he could be so stupid. And he would lose her now because of his stupidity. If only he had told Brie no. If only he had stayed at a hotel instead of shacking up at his brother's home. If only he hadn't left town on that bogus business trip. If only...

His business was successful, but it was all about the next client, the next commission point. He had attained all he had hoped for. He knew the percentage of businesses that actually made a profit that first year, and he had achieved that and more. But without Kelly at his side it meant nothing. He would give it all away if she came back to him. All of it.

Sebastian felt a chill in the air. Rain had been forecast. He brushed the bangs from her eyes – but she didn't move. Carefully he took her body in his arms, stood and began the journey back up the hill to their cabin. He remembered the last time he carried Kelly up this hill from the pond. They had sat by the newly-built fire pit, and she had given him a truly astronomical science lesson. He so appreciated her knowledge of everything nature. And he wanted to learn more. He kissed her forehead – please don't let this be the end.

He pushed sideways through the door and, walking into their bedroom, laid her on the bed. He returned quickly to the kitchen and lit the water heater. Before locking the door, he remembered to bring in her moccasins. He carried them back to the bedroom.

She hadn't moved. Oh, she was drunk. Sebastian removed her shirt and jeans, and slid her into the middle of the bed. After using the bathroom, he removed his jeans and T-shirt and joined her in their bed. He pulled her body to his, kissed her head and slept.

Kelly woke. She had come out to her cabin alone, but now Sebastian was lying in bed with her, sharing her pillow, holding her close to his chest. She had been raped and Gabriella had made love with her husband. *Shit.* She still felt the effects of drinking an entire bottle of wine on an empty stomach – and she slept...

Sebastian woke, still holding his wife. He didn't have his phone or his watch, but it must be early. The sun hadn't made its appearance yet. And there hadn't been a moon either. It was dark in their bedroom. He moved slightly, repositioned his arm around his wife – and he slept...

He felt her crawling over him and heard her walk into the bathroom. Soon she returned and sat on the bed.

Sebastian rolled over and looked into her beautiful face. "Come back in bed. Please, Kelly." He held the quilt up for her. It was cool in the cabin. She got back into bed, but lay a few inches from him – facing him.

"Please Kelly..." She closed her eyes. Exhaling loudly, she rolled into his body, her back to his front. He enfolded her body with one arm, his other arm under her pillow.

"I'm sorry..."

It seemed minutes before she spoke. "Are you sorry for having sex with Brie? Or are you sorry you got caught?"

She was right in thinking that. If his brother had never come over to the house, Kelly would never have found out about her husband and her best friend.

"I'm sorry for breaking our marriage vows."

She didn't expect that answer. Kelly rolled her shoulder and looked into his face. "Yes you did." She closed her eyes and a single tear ran down her face. "I suppose I did too, getting fucked over by Ronnie what's-his-name."

He kissed her tear. "Kelly, please don't talk like that. It's not the same thing." He pulled her closer to his body. She felt his erection growing against her hip.

"Don't do that. If you want to screw someone... Leave and go back to Gabriella."

"I'm sorry..."

She pushed away from his body and brought the quilt down past her waist, exposing her small breast and scar. "Shit Sebastian! How can I compete with Gabriella like this?" Now her eyes drowned in tears and her chest heaved with her sobs. "I can't!"

"Oh Jesus, Kelly!" And Sebastian again wrapped her in his arms, pulling her tight against his chest. And he cried. "I am so sorry. I love you so much, Kelly. Jesus, you know that doesn't matter to me!"

She had never seen her husband cry. She put her hand on his face, feeling his beard, touching his beard, loving his beard, his face, his eyes. Sebastian opened his eyes and saw emeralds looking back at him.

"I am so sorry, Kelly... I am so sorry..." He kissed her lips.

She tasted his salty tears. She wiped the tears from his face. "You hurt me, Sebastian. He raped me and you made love to Gabriella. You hurt me."

Again Sebastian's eyes closed tight as he wept fresh tears. "I am so sorry. Kelly. God, I am so sorry..." He again enfolded her in his arms and clung to her, again pressing her tightly against him.

She felt the heaving of his chest, his body rocking with his sobs. "I love you... I really do. But for the life of me, I really don't know what to do."

"Don't leave me, Kelly. Please don't leave me."

She thought he would split her in half he held her so tight. Kelly pressed against his arms, but also let him know she didn't want him to let her go. "Hold me and just be here..."

She turned in his arms, her back to his front and held his arms tight in her hands. And again they slept, sharing one pillow.

The rising sun shone through the bedroom window, casting shadows of birch leaves on her face. Sebastian didn't know when or if he was ever this much in love with his wife. He had hurt her terribly and her anger was righteous. And no, he didn't know if she would or could ever forgive him. Soon she stirred. Kelly turned her head and looked at him.

"Would you make coffee?"

"Yes, Love..." He kissed her forehead. "I'll make you your coffee." He rolled out of their bed and walked into the kitchen. He must have been hurrying – she heard the clang of metal drop to the floor.

"Coffee will be ready in a few minutes." Sebastian peeked into the bedroom, but she wouldn't look at him. He returned to the kitchen and waited...

He poured coffee in her mug, adding the creamer – just how she liked it. He couldn't help but chuckle. Even in her hurry to leave town, she remembered to pack her creamer. Sebastian walked into the bedroom and sat on the bed, but did not touch her.

She opened her eyes and smelled the coffee. At least he had brought her coffee. That was something. She took the mug and sipped the steaming brew. "Thanks..."

The weather had turned and it had started raining. Usually when it rained at the cabin, she and Sebastian would lay in their bed, talking, reading, making love. She remembered when she helped him solve those literary clues in his crossword puzzles. They were easy for her and he was always amazed at her knowledge. She missed those days...

He returned to the kitchen. "Are you hungry, Love?"

"No..."

"I'll fix you something...You need to eat."

Kelly leaned up on one elbow while she finished drinking – the coffee was good. "I told you, I'm fine." She lay the empty mug on the bed.

He prepared a plate of apple slices and provolone. Sebastian poked his head back into the bedroom. "How are you feeling?" He seemed genuinely concerned.

She closed her eyes and mumbled something incoherent.

"Is there anything I can do?" Sebastian walked in the bedroom and put the plate on the bed near her. He picked up her empty mug and stood at the side of the bed – keeping his distance.

"Yes."

"Anything, Love. What can I do?"

"Leave. Leave me alone. Go home." She picked up one of the apple slices and held it to her mouth. She looked at him, her husband, her Ulysses. He had put on his jeans but not his T-shirt. God, she wanted him next to her but he had hurt her so badly – physically and mentally. Kelly tried so hard to hold back her tears, but failed miserably and the tears fell from her eyes.

Sebastian crawled up on the bed and moving the plate aside, collected her body in his arms. He whispered, *"Please don't cry..."* He tried comforting her, soothing her. Kelly pushed him away, but his arms held her too tight and she finally accepted the fact that he wasn't going to leave.

She pressed her face on his chest and wept. "I hate you for what you did. I hate you." Kelly allowed him to swallow her body in his arms. She loved the feel of his arms around her, the soft hair on his chest that she leaned against. "I hate you."

"I know you do. I'm so sorry." And he gently pulled a quilt over her. It seemed forever until her tears stopped, letting sleep and exhaustion finally consume her body, her heart, her mind... And he held her as she nestled against his chest – and slept.

When she woke, Sebastian was not with her – but there was a note on his pillow.

> *'Went to Aggie's. Look in the refrigerator. Love, Seb.'*

It was cool in the cabin. Kelly rose and used the bathroom. *Shit!* She needed a tampon! She put on jeans and a hoodie. And it was still raining. *Shit.* There went her plans of sitting down by the pond.

She called him. "Are you still at Aggie's?"

"Yes... What do you need?"

"Would you get me tampons?"

Kelly looked at her hand – why hadn't she noticed this earlier? Her wedding ring was on her finger. He must have found it in the bowl. She touched the band with her thumb, but had no further thought of it.

She opened the refrigerator and found a plate with a roast turkey sandwich made with the French bread – and a big green olive on a toothpick stuck into it. There were also beers in there from the last time they were at the cabin. Opening one, she brought the bottle and the plate into the sitting room.

She noticed crumpled newspapers pushed under the grate in the firebox, and several logs arranged on the andiron. Kelly walked to the stone hearth, picked up one of the long matches from the mantel and lit the newspapers. The dry logs caught, and soon the room warmed up.

The sandwich was so good! Except for the apple slices and cheese, it had been her first real meal in over twenty-four hours. She finished off the beer quickly, followed with that big green olive. Sebastian knew what she liked – he knew her so well...

She felt weak and tired. Kelly pulled a pillow from the bed and, taking one of the quilts, made herself comfortable on the loveseat. Sleep came immediately.

Sebastian unlocked the padlock and opened the cabin door. He carried in the canvas grocery bag in one hand and a case of Coronas on his shoulder. He looked into the sitting room – Kelly was sleeping on the loveseat and the logs were burning in the fireplace. The room felt warm and cozy.

He put away the groceries and took a quick shower. Dressed in his jeans and V-neck T-shirt, he walked back into the room where Kelly was sleeping. It was beginning to get chilly in the cabin. He picked up the wrought iron poker and stirred the logs, creating new flames, then brought her empty plate and bottle to the kitchen.

He busied himself by making more sandwiches – and added her obligatory large green olive and a handful of potato chips. Opening two beers, he arranged everything on a large tray and placed it on the coffee table. After dropping the tampons near him on the floor, he carefully lifted her feet and sat down, putting her feet on his lap. She stirred but didn't wake up.

He began massaging her feet. Sebastian remembered how much she liked her foot massage the last time they had come to the cabin. And if he had to kiss her feet or the ground she walked on he would, just as long as she forgave him. He raised one foot and kissed her toes. She grinned.

"Hi." Kelly looked up at him, turning slightly on the small couch. "Did you get what I asked for?"

"Yes."

"You took a shower?"

"Yes, Love. And there's plenty of hot water for you." He smiled and kissed her toes again.

"I think I'd better get cleaned up. Hand me the box, please."

Sebastian did as she asked and carefully put her feet on the floor.

"I'll be right back." She got up and walked into the bedroom. From his vantage point, he watched her strip. She was still so damn skinny – and she had a large bruise on her hip.

"Kelly, what happened to your hip?"

She looked back at him, then down at her hip. "I'll tell you after I shower."

Sebastian checked the messages on his phone. There were several texts from Raffaele. He glanced at the first text. "I hope Kelly is okay. Sorry." Yes Raffe, you are sorry, damn it. He deleted the rest. There were no other texts or messages from the office.

Kelly emerged from the shower and, dressed in just unders and his T-shirt, returned to the love seat.

"Come... You can sit under the quilt." After making herself comfortable, Sebastian covered her bare legs with the quilt and handed her a beer. They toasted bottle necks.

"Thank you for making the sandwiches." She picked up her plate, setting it on her lap. Kelly took a long drink of her beer and put it back on the coffee table. She looked sideways at him. "You know... I am glad you're here. I'm glad you didn't leave."

"I wouldn't have left. And if you had kicked me out, I would have slept in the SUV and tried again the next morning." Sebastian smiled his crooked smile. She loved that smile. "What do you think about that?"

"If you had left, I would have missed you. But that's not to say I'm not mad at you."

"Understood." And he did understand. He knew he was walking on thin ice the entire time he was with her at the cabin. And especially since it was raining, they were trapped in the cabin. Usually they could go out and explore the woods or sit by the pond. Tonight and most of the next couple days it was going to rain.

"Do you want to talk about your hip? How you got that bruise?" Sebastian wondered if it happened when she was working out with Tom.

"Do you really want to know?" She ate another potato chip.

"You know I do. I want to know everything about you." He frowned – she could be so maddening. "You know that."

She leaned back on the arm of the sofa and lifting her legs, put her feet on her husband's lap. He smiled and began massaging the bottoms of her feet.

"When I got back from working out with Tom, Raffaele came over and said he wanted to talk." She let Sebastian do his magic on her feet. "That feels so good. I love that..."

"Good. Continue, please."

"So, he thought you had told me about you and Brie. When he realized I was in the dark about it, he tried leaving. But I stopped him and made him spill."

Sebastian stopped rubbing her feet and just held them in his hands.

"Don't stop rubbing or I'll stop talking." And she meant it. Sebastian resumed massaging her feet.

"Good. Thank you. So I was asking him questions and he wasn't really answering them until I finally figured out what he was talking about. And I got angry and I stood, but I think I got up too fast because I dropped to the floor – hard."

"I'm sorry. Can I see the bruise again?" Kelly put her plate back on the coffee table and rolled toward the back of the sofa, exposing her left hip. She pulled the hem of her panties above the bruise. Sebastian touched it, softly rubbing across the blue and purple mark.

"Does it hurt? It looks like it hurts."

"Kind of. Since I don't have much meat on my bones – yeah, it hurts." She pulled the quilt back over her body as she lay back down.

"I'm sorry you had that conversation with my brother. I'm sorry for so many things." He looked at Kelly, but she wasn't looking back at him.

"I know. I'm sorry it happened, too. I mean... Really Sebastian, what were you thinking?" Now she looked directly at him. "I mean, when Brie – I don't know, how did – did she, um..."

"Kelly, I couldn't go home. Our home was a crime scene, and until the police were done with it, I couldn't go back." He lifted her foot and kissed her toes. "It was a mess. I'm glad you didn't see it."

"I didn't know that. I didn't know that part of what happened. Sorry."

"Don't be sorry." Sebastian concentrated on massaging her feet. "Raffe opened his home to me. I was in his basement spare bedroom. And one night after leaving you at the hospital, she came down to the room... I really don't want to talk about this."

Kelly looked at him. "But don't you think I deserve the truth? Don't you think I earned the right to hear the whole story?"

Sebastian held her feet close to his body and looked down. "Yes, you deserve the right – and you've probably earned the right to hear everything. But my God Kelly, I don't want to hurt you anymore."

"How could you possibly hurt me any more than you already have?"

"That's not fair!" As soon as he spoke those words he wished he could take them back. There was nothing fair about any of this. He had hurt her so badly, his wife, his Dulcinea. He betrayed their wedding vows, he betrayed her trust. While his wife battled for her life, he was having sex with another woman. He didn't even know if Kelly would survive, yet he had sex with his wife's best friend, his brother's wife...

"Jesus, Seb – 'that's not fair'?" She lifted her feet off his lap and pulled her legs up to her body, holding her knees tight against her chest. "That's not fair? I'll tell you what's not fair." She hated that her tears started again. "While I was lying in a hospital bed for how long you were having sex with my best friend!"

"I know. I shouldn't have said that. I'm sorry – again."

Kelly knew she should leave it alone, but she wanted to know. "I know you had sex with Brie. What else did you do?"

"What do you mean, what else did we do? It was only that one time..."

"You know what I'm talking about. What-did-you-do?"

"Please Kelly..." Sebastian hung his head and refused to look her in the face. But she pushed, and he knew she wouldn't let it go. She could be so tenacious. And this was probably the last night he would ever spend with his wife, if indeed she let him stay the night. When he told her the whole story, she would kick him out and never ask him to come back. Shit.

He looked into his wife's beautiful eyes brimming with tears. "We kissed."

"Where?"

"What do you mean 'where'?"

"You know what I mean. Where else did you kiss her? I know you kissed her face. Did you kiss her breasts? Her vagina? Where?"

"Jesus, Kelly... Yes. All of it."

"So, you just didn't have sex with her."

"No Kelly." He stared at her. "We did it all. Is that what you want to hear? We did it all." Sebastian slowly turned his head. He looked into the kitchen. That's the door he'd be leaving through in only a matter of minutes. His life was over. His marriage was over. She'd never let him touch her ever again. He hung his head and cried, his tears falling from his eyes onto his empty hands.

"I am so sorry. Kelly, I am so sorry..." Sebastian looked into glistening emeralds. "I love you always. Always and forever. No matter what ever happened I love you. And I am so sorry I hurt you. And I will spend the rest of my life asking you for your forgiveness, trying to make it up to you." He knew his words were spilling out of his mouth, but he didn't care. Right now, he'd do anything to come back into her good graces if not her arms.

But her expression hadn't changed. "Lock the door. I'm going to bed."

"Kelly... do you want me to leave?"

She stood. "You can stay out here." Leaving her pillow and quilt behind, she walked into the bedroom.

He brought the tray out to the kitchen. And as requested, he locked the door. Sebastian returned to the sitting room and, picking up her pillow and quilt from the loveseat, tried making himself comfortable on the small sofa. The fire was dying, but there was still warmth in the room. He heard Kelly wrapping herself under the blankets in the bed.

She let him stay. She let him stay one night. She could have kicked his cheating butt out – or she could have told him to go home and call his lawyer. But she let him stay in their cabin. Her cabin. This was her cabin. It would remain her cabin.

Sebastian propped himself up on one arm of the love seat and put his head on her pillow – her pillow – and smelled her scent. He rested his legs on the coffee table, and watched the fire as it died, leaving only glowing embers beneath the andiron. That's how his life would be now, only dying memories of their marriage, their life, their love. He knew he wouldn't sleep, but still he closed his eyes and folded his arms on his chest.

She couldn't sleep. Kelly looked up through the bedroom window – the moon was hidden behind clouds. She was cold. She was in their grand bed alone, waiting for him to come to her. But he wouldn't – she made it clear she didn't want him and he would respect her word.

She missed lying next to Sebastian... She didn't want him out of her life. She wanted him near her always. But she imagined him with Brie the way he was with her. Would the image of her husband making love with Brie torment her dreams forever?

She rolled over and, pulling the quilt over her face, closed her eyes. Again her own imagination haunted her. Kelly sat up in their bed, pulling her feet close to her and crossed her arms on her knees – and softly cried...

This was bullshit. She rose from the mattress and stepped onto the cold floor. She slowly crept into the sitting room where Sebastian slept. But he wasn't sleeping – he watched her as she walked toward him. He held out his hand to her. She took one more step and touched his hand with her own. Sebastian grasped her fingertips and wouldn't let go.

"Kelly..." He spoke her name softly and with as much love as he could put in one name – a name he loved, the name he knew. "Kelly, what do you want?"

She stood on the cold floor not knowing what to do. She didn't want to let him go – but he had hurt her so badly. She took a step closer to the loveseat. Sebastian pulled her the rest of the way and collected her in his arms. Kelly lay on his body on top of the quilt, her head pressed against his face. She held him tight around his neck.

"I heard you crying..." He kissed her temple.

"I want you... I want you to leave and never come back." She looked into his eyes. "I keep seeing you and Brie. I can't get the pictures out of my head."

There was nothing Sebastian could say to comfort her. She was right. What he and her best friend did was unforgivable. But the fact that she was in his arms said something – it said something about forgiveness? It said something about her love for him? It said something about second chances?

He didn't have to answer her when she questioned him about what he and Brie had done. But he had never lied to her, not even to save her heart from being broken. And it was because of his honesty that he was on the small sofa. And it was because of his stupidity that he was not in her bed. But she was with him now – she was with him now.

"I'm sorry, Kelly. I've never been more sorry about anything in my life." He kissed her forehead and brushed the bangs from her beautiful eyes. "I love you... always and forever." He felt her breath as she exhaled against his neck.

"I know you do." She raised her head and looked at him. She felt safe in his arms – she would always feel safe in his arms. And she knew he would never break her heart again. And she knew it wasn't his intention to hurt her when Brie came to him.

She took a deep breath. "I'm cold. Let's go to bed."

Sebastian sat up, gathered her body in his arms and stood. With the quilt hanging between them, he carried his wife back into the bedroom. He knelt on the bed and put her on the mattress. He kissed her mouth.

After using the bathroom, he quickly stripped and stood between the bed and the wall. Kelly held out her hand. He joined her – his wife, his heart, his life.

"Hold me."

Sebastian embraced his wife, pulling her close to his body.

"Seb..."

"Yes, Kelly..." He placed one leg across her legs, cocooning her body.

"I love you."

"Kelly, I didn't want to hurt you. I know I hurt you."

"Seb..."

"Yes, Love?"

"I love you..."

And they slept, sharing one pillow...

39

Second Chances

She felt the mattress strain as his body returned to the bed. Kelly moved close to him and pressed her face into his beard. "Did you make coffee?"

"Yes, Love." He felt her smile on his neck. He knew he was blessed – she had taken him back. Now the ball was in his court. He had better not screw up his second chance. He had an idea and hoped she would approve of the plan.

"Can I run something past you?" Sebastian brushed wisps of her auburn bangs from her eyes.

She raised her head and looked at him - studying his face. "I know that inflection in your voice, mister. You're planning something." Loving him was easy. Dealing with all the bullshit that came with it was something else entirely. But she also knew he was on his best behavior.

"I've been thinking about a change, but I need your approval."

Pushing her hand against his chest, she moved back to see his face better. A million thoughts passed through her brain. Change? Her world had been rocked by change. Over the last half year, she had been raped and assaulted – and almost died. Her husband had been with another woman, really been with another woman – and she had resolved to go on without Sebastian at her side. Now he wanted more change?

"Can we at least have coffee first before you rock my world... again?"

He leaned in and kissed her, his wife, his Dulcinea. "Yes Love. We can have coffee first. And I've already made a fire. It should be warm soon." He looked out the bedroom window. Not only was it raining but the wind had shifted. The birch tree branches were bending and thrashing wildly.

"Let's stay in bed until your fire does its job." She turned her back to his front and snuggled into her husband's hot body. She felt his erection wake against her hip, but she knew it was futile.

"You know, mister, we can't do anything about that – you do know that don't you." She smiled, knowing he would be frustrated – and thinking back to that first time she refused to make love. They had only been living together a week. Her reason was logical, but Sebastian had taken her refusal so personally...

> *"We're not having sex tonight..." She was sitting on the edge of the bed. Sebastian had showered and was very ready to make love with her.*
>
> *"You're joking, right?" He took hold of her arm and pulled her to him, making her lay next to him. But she put her hand on his chest and pushed away.*
>
> *"No. We're not. I started my period." She could tell he wasn't registering what she was saying.*

"I don't care." He was about to roll over on her body, but again she stopped him.

"But, Sebastian, I care!" She pressed on his chest, making him lie back on bed. This was not going to be easy. "I don't like the mess." She watched his eyes – he was considering what she was saying, digesting her words. She continued, supporting her decision.

"Look, we'd get the sheets all messed up – and it's not a lot of fun trying to wash blood out of these nice sheets."

"We'll buy new sheets!" Again he tried rolling on her.

"No!" She sat up with her knees at his chest. "And we're not making love tonight." Kelly cocked her head, hoping he wouldn't argue with her anymore. She took a big chance, turned out her bedside lamp and lay down next to him. "I love you, mister..."

"I know... I love you too, but I'm not happy..." He pulled her to him.

In the dim light of their bedroom, she saw a scowl on his lovely face. She smiled in his chest and pulled the quilt up over their bodies. Only after a few minutes did it dawn on her that he told her he loved her... too.

That entire night he tossed and turned, pulling her body against his, pushing into her body with his aching hard-on. They hadn't gotten any sleep that night, and it was hell for her in school the next day.

The next night was more of the same. Kelly just didn't want to deal with the mess of lovemaking while on her period. Sebastian still didn't understand, yet he respected her wishes – although that night was more of the same. He had held her, pulling her to him, pressing her body against an erection that refused to die.

At one point he cocooned her hips between his strong legs and practically crushed her against his groin. Though the feeling was extraordinary, the temptation great, she stood resolute and didn't give in.

After the third night, she woke early and took a quick shower. When she came back to bed, she put her hands on his rock hard cock and smiled her best smile. It was all Sebastian could do to not kill her with love as he climbed aboard her body.

"Are you sure, woman?" He was breathing heavy on her face, his beard pressing against her chin. "We're doing this?"

Kelly couldn't help but laugh. She loved this man, this man who she swore walked around with an erection. He was always ready to make love with her. And after three nights of not making love, he was definitely ready.

But first things first. This was Sebastian after all, and he so loved the feel of her thighs around his head. After kissing her eyes, her lips, her face, he began the hurried downward journey, stopping briefly to caress her breasts, kissing her sweet nipples, sucking on her sweet nipples. And he traveled lower...

She would never forget the feel of his soft beard against her body, his mustache lightly brushing across her sensitive clit... She could never get enough of him, her husband, her Ulysses. And he brought her quickly to an orgasm so deep it took her breath away.

But before they made love, he confessed his love for her. While he was lying on her, he chastely kissed her lips.

"Kelly, I love you..."

"I know... thank you."

"Thank you? Why are you thanking me, woman?"

Kelly pushed him off her and quickly crawled up on his body. She leaned down and holding his long hair in her hands, kissed his lips.

"Because. Now make love to me!" She kissed him again.

And his passion was unquenchable, culminating in another round of fierce lovemaking with this woman – his Dulcinea...

They hadn't made love since before her assault, since the night before he had left her alone – in their home alone. That would always be his biggest regret. And even if he wanted to make love with her, his wife had to be ready to make love with him. Lord, this was the biggest test of his patience – and he was not a patient man.

While Kelly was enjoying her first cup of coffee – he remembered to buy more of her favorite French Vanilla creamer from Aggie's – Sebastian worked in the kitchen. Today he prepared cheese omelets with sides of bacon – extra crisp for her.

The fire felt wonderful, and even though it was wet and raw outside, the cabin was warm and cozy. When Sebastian and his friends first came out to the cabin, they had taken inventory of the insulation – or lack thereof. That next weekend as Michael was updating the electrical, they installed rolls of insulation within the walls and above the rafters. Now even on this miserable wet day, the cabin was warm and inviting.

Sebastian carried in the large tray. He looked at his wife as he placed it on the coffee table. She was smiling. Check one for the chef! And he made screwdrivers, putting large green olives in her drink. His actions this morning really were nothing unusual. He always did more than she expected, he always made sure she was happy. Though the omelet may have had extra cheese or her bacon crispier, this was Sebastian. He loved her – and she knew it. And his love for her would only grow – and she knew it.

As she picked up bits of bacon from her plate, Kelly asked him about his plans.

"So..." he began, sounding very serious. "When I realized it was because of that bogus out of town meeting that you were raped..." He put his head down.

Kelly thought he would cry again. She leaned in and kissed his cheek, feeling his soft beard on her lips. "It wasn't your fault." But she knew he would feel guilty about that night for the rest of his life. It tore him apart knowing that she was alone when their home was invaded by that evil presence. And now he wanted to make a change. What? Move? He wouldn't sell their home. Oh what was this plan?

"I don't ever want to leave you alone again – ever." He looked so earnestly into her eyes. Whatever his plan was, it was important.

"I appreciate that." She picked up her screwdriver and took a sip.

"I'm going to quit my job."

She choked on her vodka-laced orange juice. "Say what?"

Sebastian chuckled and patted her back. "That is, I'm going to hand over the keys of the business to Phil. I'll retain ownership, but I won't be an active consultant anymore." He looked seriously at Kelly, seeing the proverbial wheels turning in her beautiful head.

"You'll remain the CEO, right? But you won't be physically in the office and you won't take meetings anymore." He had worked his whole adult life to attain his success. She knew enough about his business that this decision did not come lightly. But how long had he been considering this move?

"Basically. I'll retain majority ownership, but Phil is so damn smart. He deserves this chance."

"What about Carolyn?" She knew Carolyn ran that office and was working toward her master's in forensic accounting.

"Carolyn I'm sure will become a partner soon enough. She's smart! And between her and Phil, I'd just be in the way." He smiled his crooked smile. Kelly loved that smile.

"Okay, so what's your plan?" She assumed he wouldn't get another job. He had investments that would take him through retirement and beyond – he certainly didn't need the extra income.

"That's what I want to talk about – with you as my partner." Sebastian took her hand and kissed her fingers. "I want to buy the New London Grille."

"You want to buy a restaurant?" She looked into his hazel eyes and knew he was deadly serious. "Seb, I know you hated leaving your job as a chef. Is that what you want to do? Be a chef in your own restaurant?" This was not as absurd an idea as she thought it might be.

"Yes. And I want you as my partner." The inflection in his voice went from strong-assertive to almost pleading. Kelly couldn't hold back her smile.

"I have a feeling that whatever you do you will be successful." She kissed his lips again. "And yes, I would love to be your partner in a restaurant, although..."

"Although, what Love?" He loosened the grip he had on her hand.

"Well, what would I do in a restaurant?"

"My dear beautiful wife," Sebastian held her hand to his mouth. "You have managed to mold and inspire how many teenagers into becoming responsible members of society. I would love to have you be the manager."

"Manager?" Kelly looked into the fireplace. She had never imagined doing anything else other than teaching. She loved her job, even considering teaching college-level literature. She remembered that was part of their last conversation before her assault. She frowned.

"Kelly, what's wrong?" He misinterpreted her frown as a negative reaction to his idea. "You don't want to be the manager?" Now he was second-guessing his idea. Maybe he should have thought this through a little more.

"Oh, no!" She turned back to him. "I would love to be your manager!"

"So why the frown?"

"Do you remember our conversation the night before you went out of town? The night before I was attacked?" She knew this would bring up bad memories for them both, and quickly changed the subject – this was too nice of a morning to spoil it with bad memories. "Before we went to bed, I talked about teaching at the local university. Remember?" His face told her he didn't remember.

"Okay, here's the deal. I always thought I would teach in some capacity until I retired." She gathered her thoughts, making sure she said the right thing. "If you want to buy the New London Grille, then yes. I would love to work with you and be the manager. Like you said, if I can handle teenagers, I should be able to manage a restaurant, right?"

"Yes – right!" Sebastian pulled her to him and put his arms around his wonderful wife. "Yes Love, we can do this."

"Before we get ahead of ourselves, what plans have you made?"

First and foremost, he'd apply for a liquor license. Upon approval from the board he'd gut the restaurant. Roger would be in charge of the renovations. "And I thought maybe you and Gabriella would like to go on a buying trip..."

That was not the thing to say – that was not the name to mention. And as soon as he said her name, he knew he screwed up. Sebastian looked into the eyes of the woman he hurt so badly. "I'm sorry. It's just that you and Brie have been friends for so long."

"Don't worry about it. I don't think I'll be palling around with her for awhile, if ever." She took another sip of her screwdriver. "The one thing I regret – well, one of the things I regret I should say is that she had wanted us to be Finn's godparents. And since no one has said anything about that idea, I take it that's a moot point now."

"I think you're probably right. I haven't talked to Raffe since that day..."

"Did he call you or what?" Kelly knew nothing about the circumstances leading to Sebastian's decision to drive out to the cabin and find her.

"I was at my office – he called me after he had talked with you. He was concerned that what he said to you might have screwed things up between us – you and me."

"Wow. How perceptive of him." Kelly played with Sebastian's knee. "Yeah, I think he screwed things up, but I have a feeling he and Brie might have a bigger falling out. You know he convinced Brie to go to you."

"That's what Brie said when she came over to talk. I know I didn't tell you about it. That was the same day you had that nightmare, when you realized you had been raped..."

"What exactly did Brie tell you?"

"She said Raffaele asked her to come to me, to have sex with me." Sebastian knew this was going to open up freshly healed wounds. "I told her that was one hell of a way for my brother to show his love for me."

"You were right. I guess I understand his reasoning, since it helped him get over the loss of Annalisa. But for crying out loud, Brie could have told him no – and you could have told her no too."

"Please don't rehash this. We've come so far in such a little while. Please." Again he was pleading for his life.

She took his arm into her hands and leaned against him. "No, we're not rehashing this. And we're not talking about it. Bottom line is that Raffaele put Brie up to it – it wasn't your idea to go looking for comfort."

"Thank you, Love." He kissed her forehead. In response, she yawned.

"I think someone needs a nap. I'll get more logs for the fire." Sebastian rose from the loveseat, pulled on his jacket and walked down near the fire pit. He lifted the heavy tarp and from the cache of cut logs, took enough dry wood to keep the cabin warm for the rest of the day.

While he was getting the fuel, Kelly rummaged around in the pile of newspapers for kindling, and happened upon old NYT Sunday crossword puzzle pages.

And as they did in the beginning, they lay in the big bed solving the lengthy puzzles.

And as in the beginning, Kelly helped him with the literary clues.

And as in the beginning, he was amazed at her knowledge of the written word.

And as in the beginning, she fell asleep with her head on his shoulder.

And as in the beginning, he whispered *I love you* – and laying the half-finished puzzle on his chest, closed his eyes and slept.

And together they slept for the remainder of that rainy, dreary day into the late afternoon – sharing one pillow, as they did in the beginning...

He woke and inhaled her sweet breath... and softly kissed her forehead.

She lazily opened her eyes and looked at her husband, her Ulysses. Of all the men in the world, she fell in love with a hot man – a hot hairy man. She turned onto her front and pushed her face against his beard.

"I love you, Sebastian."

"I know. Thank God..." He put his finger under her chin and raised her face to his. "Thank God." And he kissed her, his wife, his Dulcinea.

"Should we eat?"

Again she snuggled into his warm body. "I'm not that hungry."

"You need to eat. I'll make sandwiches." He kissed her forehead and crawled over her. He wanted to stop – he wanted to lie on her body, pull at the tangle of auburn curls... He wanted to make love to his wife. But he got out of bed.

In a few minutes he called to her. "Come on, Kelly."

She walked into the room. He looked critically at her body.

"You need to get healthy. Sit. Eat. Please."

She sat next to him on the loveseat. "Yes Sir!"

The sandwiches were wonderful and they had chips left over. And the beer was cold.

"This is perfect, Seb. Thank you."

He leaned into her and kissed her face. "Yes, it is..."

She woke early and began to get out of bed – she knew her movements woke her husband. Kelly leaned over the bed and kissed the man who would love her always and forever. "I want to check something – keep the bed warm." She kissed his lips again and walked into the bathroom. Soon he heard the sounds of the shower.

He assumed he knew what she was up to, but if history served him well he would never again assume anything about her or anything she might be up to. The bathroom door opened – she came out wrapped in a large fluffy blue towel.

"Sebastian – you have to promise something." The fact that she was standing at the bedside in just a towel gave him hope for activities to come. And yes, he would promise her anything.

"We have to go slow – you have to promise. You have to go easy on me, okay?"

"Promise..." He watched as she climbed onto the grand bed, still with the towel wrapped around her. He raised himself on one elbow. "May I help?" He slowly pulled at the towel. She held onto the towel, then giving him her best smile, let it go.

"Kelly, whatever you want me to promise – I promise." He smiled his crooked smile.

She loved that smile – but she needed him to really hear her. "We have to go slow. Please." She sat back on her ankles and tried putting on her stern face.

"Slow. I can go slow – and I can be gentle..." He looked at her body. She was so damn skinny. She needed to eat more, but he knew she already felt so much better. And with Tom's help and encouragement, she would soon be healthy and strong again.

"Seb... I want to make love with you..."

He reached out to her and pulled her to him. She lay across his chest. He held her face in his hands, kissing her, making love to her with his tongue. "I love you, woman."

Kelly kissed his shoulder, softly finding his nipples with her fingers. She loved the thick hair on his chest and belly – she always had, from the first night she had stayed with him. She had gotten used to sleeping in his bed, his dark muscular body lying next to her... running her fingers through the thick black hair that covered his chest and belly. She kissed him, playfully pulling on his bottom lip with her teeth.

Sebastian held her in his arms and rolled over. "I'll be gentle... I promise." He kissed her lips as he nestled between her open legs. "I'll be gentle. I love you so much, Kelly. I'll be gentle."

He moved lower on her body, kissing his wife as he traveled toward the foot of the large bed. He kissed her breast and her sweet nipple – and pictures of Brie's large breasts entered his mind. He couldn't help but think of her full breasts, the feel of her breasts around his head, sinking into the cleavage of her full, beautiful breasts.

He closed his eyes tight, determined to erase those memories...

Kelly noticed the face he made. "Seb... What's wrong?"

Her question caught him off guard. He was with his wife. He shouldn't be thinking about anyone or anything else. He loved Kelly, he loved her breasts – breast. He loved his wife.

"Nothing Love..." He looked up into emerald eyes. He was here with his wife, loving his wife. There was no place he'd rather be than with his wife. He lowered himself and lay between her legs, licking her thighs... He pushed her legs further apart and inhaled her sweet musk.

She lightly touched his head as he tasted her silky skin... and thought of Brie's dark pubic hair. It had felt so erotic, the smell of her body – so foreign to him but so exotic...

He stopped. What the hell was he doing? This was his wife. He was loving his wife...

Sebastian cradled her thighs in his arms, loving every part of her, kissing every part of her. And he brought her quickly to a hard orgasm. And he lingered where he could push her body over the moon.

But she was impatient. Kelly grabbed his long hair in her fists and brought him up to her, holding his face to her lips, inhaling her scent on his mustache. She loved his weight on her, smothering her with his love. He pressed into her, making small, deep thrusts. He held himself deep inside her.

"Are you okay?" She knew he wanted to push hard into her, to thrust so deep, so hard it would rock the bed.

"Kelly..." His breath hot on her face. "I'm making love to my wife..." And he kissed her again, making love to her with his tongue. "I can't get enough of you, woman!"

Again he pressed into her, pulled out slightly and slowly pressed deeper into her. He repeated these small thrusts for as long as she wanted, always pressing deeper into her body. His hands caressed her face, loving her face, kissing her face.

"Love, are you okay?"

"I'm almost there... I'm almost there." She closed her eyes. "Love me..."

And he did as she asked, but gently – oh so gently, pressing hard into her, barely rocking the bed. And he brought her to an amazing orgasm – gently. And he followed with his own.

Sebastian kissed her lips, her eyes, her face. "God, I love you woman." He rolled on his back, bringing her with him, and covering her body with a quilt, they slept the rest of the morning.

"Come on, sleepy head... Wake up... It's stopped raining..."

She opened her eyes and looking up through their bedroom window, saw a cloudless sky. "I thought it was supposed to rain all week." Kelly lay her head back down on his shoulder. She had slept on his body.

"Evidently the weatherman was wrong." Sebastian caressed her back from her shoulders to her butt and, following her spine, slowly brought his hands back to her shoulders. She felt his erection push between her thighs.

"What a way to wake up..." Kelly kissed his shoulder, and looked up into the eyes of the man who was so unbelievably gentle when they made love. So gentle. And she needed to use the bathroom. She rolled out of the bed.

While she was gone, Sebastian checked his text messages. Nothing of concern came from the office. Good. He knew Phil and Carolyn were taking care of everything. For a minute, he felt like an outsider looking in but thought better of it. His business was in excellent hands – and now he and Kelly could start their new life.

"What are you doing?" She saw him holding his phone. "You're not wondering what's going on back at your office are you?" She climbed into the big bed and rolled next to his warm body.

"No, in fact I was thinking... My office is in good hands." He put his arm out so she could cuddle next to him. "Everything is good."

"I love you, Seb."

He looked at her, his wife, his Dulcinea. "I love you, too. And I would certainly love to show you how much I love you... again..."

Kelly lazily climbed back on his body. And after making love – after slowly making love, again they slept.

After taking his shower Sebastian made French toast and bacon for breakfast. He carried their plates on a large tray down to the edge of the pond. Kelly carried the syrup and the screwdrivers – hers with a big green olive in it. He set the tray on the fieldstone ledge.

"This fire pit sure has come in handy." She picked up her plate. "I think it's one of my favorite things about coming out here." Kelly sat on the ledge balancing her plate on her legs. She looked out over the pond – lost in thought. "Sebastian..."

"Yes, Love?" He leaned the tray against the wall of field stone.

"You're my favorite thing about coming out to the cabin." And of course she shed tears.

He walked over and sat next to her. "I love you, Kelly." She pressed her forehead into his chest. He kissed her hair "I love you so much." And with his fingertips, he traced the raised half-moon scar on her scalp. "I almost lost you, my Dulcinea. I'll never leave you alone again."

"I know..." She looked up at him and smiled her best smile.

He rose from her side and walked back to his plate – and watched her while he ate. Her hair had finally grown out long enough to cover that scar. But he knew where it was. He knew where all her scars were – even the one that almost broke her heart.

She had been through so much in her life, and every tragedy – the death of her father, her breast cancer, and the rape and assault seemed to make her stronger. He was so proud of her... So proud of his wife.

Kelly had missed Christmas last year and her birthday this year. Sebastian would make a plan. He was going to help her celebrate those lost occasions. He thought of the short list of people who could help him make the celebration special. Now he was eager to get started – but first he had to make sure these days at the cabin were special.

"I'm full." She drank the rest of her screwdriver. And after sucking out the sweet pimento, she ate the olive in two bites. "This was good, baby." She wiped her mouth with a napkin and again she looked out over the pond. "It's too early for any babies. It's so quiet out here."

"I know Love, but I have an idea."

"Oh Lord, what's up your sleeve now?" She laughed. He loved her laugh.

"We haven't taken pictures for so long. All those photos on the bookshelves are old..."

"All those photos remind me of happier times. And if you're thinking of taking pictures of me with this skinny body and this damn silver hair, you've got another think coming!" Kelly tried looking angry – and knew she wasn't doing a good job.

"I've seen you at your worst and I've definitely seen you at your best. And guess what?"

Kelly stood, walked over to him and sat on his lap. She put her arms around his neck and kissed his face. "What?" She looked into hazel eyes. "Tell me."

"I love you. Always and forever."

"I know that, silly. I wouldn't have married you if you didn't!"

"Come on. Let's go exploring. And I promise – no pictures." Sebastian eased her off his lap and stood. He took her hand and kissed her knuckles.

They walked across their property, stepping over the little frozen streams behind the cottage – the ones that gradually opened, allowing the frigid spring-fed water to splash over stubborn ice shelves. Though it was too early in the year, Kelly could see the beginnings of life. The lilac bushes that grew outside the dooryard were budding out and soon their intoxicating perfume would fill the air.

They held hands while they walked down the narrow winding road. Their road. Even though it wasn't marked private no one ever used this road. The thick growth of tall old sugar maples bordering the length of the road hadn't budded out – the uppermost branches resembled intertwining skeletal fingers. And because of the lack of foliage she was able to point out several porcupine nests built high up in the forks of trees.

"There are porcupines around here? Do they attack?" All Sebastian knew about porcupines was what he saw in cartoons as a child.

"No silly. They're very docile creatures. Do you know they're actually large rodents?"

Sebastian knew he was about to get a primer on porcupines and, unlike when he first met this redhead, he was eager to learn. "Tell me more."

They held hands as they walked along the road, many times Kelly pointing out the more interesting aspects of the woods.

"Well, beavers are the only rodents larger than the porcupine."

"I've never seen beavers out in our pond."

"I bet if we brought two kayaks next time we could find a beaver dam further down the pond toward the lake." She looked at Sebastian. "Would you like to do that? Go kayaking with me?"

"Yeah, I think I'd like that." He brought her hand to his mouth and kissed her fingers. "Tell me more about porcupines."

"I can't believe you! Do you remember when we met you didn't want to go out into nature? You did everything you could to avoid walking in the park. You remember that?" She was smiling at him – but she'd never laugh at him. He was her student, and she knew never to laugh at her students.

"I would never have gotten anywhere near this close to learning about nature if it were not for you. I love you – therefore, I love nature."

"Oh, how Cartesian of you!" She laughed and continued teaching her eager student. Kelly held his arm as they walked, pointing to the nests. "You can't get too close to a porcupine..."

"Because they'll shoot their quills at you, right?"

"No Seb, they don't shoot their quills." She smirked, but did not laugh. "When they're threatened, their quills stand up, especially in their tails. That's their main defense – their tails. If a porcupine hits you with its tail, the barbs will detach and stick into whomever or whatever had gotten too close."

"How do I know if I'm getting close to a porcupine? I mean, when I'm walking in the woods, how would I know if I'm too close?"

"Because you'll smell them... kind of like stinky goat cheese. When predators smell that odor, they know to back off. Got it?"

"Got it." They continued walking – but he wanted more. "Do they ever fall out of the trees? Their nests?"

"Actually, yes. Porcupines aren't very smart and they'll reach out of their nests for a tasty leaf and whoops! Down goes the porcupine!" She smacked her hands together, mimicking for him the sound of a splat.

"Ouch." He pointed up to a smaller nest. "Is that a porcupine nest?"

"No. That looks more like a squirrel nest..." As they walked, Sebastian continued to be amazed by how much Kelly knew about nature, and never tired of her knowledge of the trees and animals around their property. He knew he was blessed that she forgave him – he would never dishonor her again with his words or actions. Yes, he was blessed.

They took their time walking back, but as they neared the cottage the skies darkened again. At least they had been able to get out for a few hours.

They stayed at their cabin for another day. Kelly couldn't wait to get home and get back to their normal lives. However, normal now meant the beginning of a new life – opening their new restaurant. She was ready. After all the shit she went through, she was more than ready to begin their new life together.

40

Enlightenment

Life would go on, but there were too many unanswered questions for which she needed answers. So many things about the assault and rape, her attacker, her hospitalization – and it seemed everyone knew the details except her. She wasn't sure where to start, but she knew exactly who could help. While Sebastian took his shower she made the call.

"Hey gal. What's up?"

"I need your help." If anyone could help her find the answers to her questions, it would be Roger. She hoped he wouldn't try to protect her from the truth.

"Anything Kelly – you know that."

She took a deep breath. "Roger, I want to know more about the attack, my rapist... What happened, how it happened... What happened to me..."

A long pause followed. She knew he was weighing his options... Give her the information she needed and feel Sebastian's anger – or not help her, thereby keeping her in the dark. She heard him exhaling.

"What do you want to know?" This was big! He might actually help her.

"I don't know where to start. I want to know what happened in my home, in my bedroom. What Ronnie did to me, all my injuries... I mean, I know he did bad things to me..." Now she was rambling, trying to say so much in just those few minutes.

"How can I help? What do you need?"

Yes! He was coming through for her. Kelly felt great affection toward Roger, and she knew whatever information he could produce would be because she asked to see it. And he would be at her side supporting her.

"I want to see the crime scene photos. I want to read the medical report of my injuries. Can you do that for me? Can you get that information for me?" She looked over at the door to the bathroom, hoping Sebastian wouldn't come out before she was done with this conversation. If he knew what she was asking of Roger, he might put a stop to it before she could find her answers.

"Kelly, I wish you didn't want to see that stuff."

"But Roger – *you* did! And so did everyone else! He attacked *me*! He raped *me*! In my home – in my bedroom!" Again there was a long pause. She could hear her friend breathing into his phone. *Please Roger...*

He audibly exhaled... "Let me make a few phone calls. I'll call you back."

"Thank you, Roger. I knew you'd come through for me.

"Don't thank me yet, gal. You may not like what you see."

She hung up from the call just as Sebastian appeared, wearing a towel around his waist. His long hair was wet, his beard was wet – he looked fantastic.

"Who was that on the phone?"

She could never get anything past him. And she wasn't about to lie to him, but a white lie that didn't contain all the information was okay.

"I was asking a friend for a favor. No big deal." She stood and walked toward her husband. He looked like a Christmas present wrapped in a fluffy white towel.

He looked at an imaginary watch. "I wish I didn't have that breakfast meeting..."

"You'd better reserve some time later, mister."

"What? Tonight?"

"Yes, Seb. Tonight." But she couldn't interpret his mood. Was he going back on his word about starting over? What was it...? She stood her ground, the palms of her hands flat on his chest. "What aren't you telling me?"

He smiled his crooked smile. She loved that smile. "This..." Sebastian dropped the towel and made her walk backwards, pushing her onto the bed. He pressed her body into the mattress and nestled between her open legs. "This..." He pushed into her, hard into her, thrusting with all his might into her. And he didn't stop, pushing, thrusting, grunting as he made love with his wife.

She wrapped her legs around his waist and holding his long wet hair in her fists, kissed his lips. She found his tongue and made love to his tongue as he continued thrusting into her.

"Are you there Love...?" His words came out in staccato breaths.

"Give me – all of you Sebastian!"

And he gave his wife all he had – he gave her his body, he gave her his love, he gave her his heart – and they came together as one. He collapsed onto her body, almost smothering her, his breath hot on her face.

He looked into emerald eyes. "I can never get enough of you, woman..."

After Kelly took her shower and ate a quick breakfast, she met Roger down at the police station. They were escorted to a room with no windows. Roger and Kelly sat on the same side of a long metal table. At Roger's request, Lt. Rafferty had agreed to meet with them privately.

"You know... we can still leave." Kelly had never seen Roger so upset. His eyes were raw – had he been crying?

"No. Everyone else in my life knows what happened to me. In the last couple months, I've finally learned to cope with the attack. Now, I want to see..." She looked down at her hands. "I want to see..."

A knock on the door announced Lt. Rafferty's arrival. He entered the room carrying a large file folder. Roger stood and shook his hand – and introduced Kelly.

"Mrs. Bonsignore, it's a pleasure to finally meet you. The last time I saw you ma'am, you were not doing very well." His smile was genuine. "May I sit?"

"Please. Thank you for agreeing to meet with me, Officer Rafferty." Kelly nervously looked at the thick file folder the officer held.

"Before we get started, please call me Joe." He looked at Roger, and again back at Kelly. He opened the folder he had placed on the table and pulled out several thinner folders, each labeled with her initial and last name.

"Thank you, Joe. Did Roger tell you what I wanted to know? What I wanted to see?" Her voice wavered. She swallowed hard, wanting to impress upon the officer the urgency of her inquiries.

"Yes Kelly. He said you wanted to know more about the attack, what happened..."

"And I want to see pictures! I've seen enough TV dramas that I know you've got crime scene photos of, well, everything. Even me." She looked at Roger. "I want to see everything." She turned her attention back to the files spread out on the table and addressed Lt. Rafferty. "Where do we start?"

Roger opened the file labeled 'HOME INVASION.' He pulled out 8x10 photos. While some were in color, many others were black and white. Kelly took the stack of photos and began paging through them. The top three photos were taken with a wide angle lens, illustrating the layout of the bedroom. The next photo showed a close-up of her body, but she didn't immediately recognize herself as the body lying on the bed.

"Oh God..." She looked at her friend. "That's me?" She inspected the photo. The body lay on its back. Its head and the pillow under it were covered with blood, the eyes swollen shut, the face unrecognizable – so much blood. And there was blood on the groin and thighs and on the sheets under the body. She couldn't look away. The body had been photographed from several angles, and some of the close-ups included a small white plastic ruler.

She paged through the next few photographs. The EMTs had begun their work on the body – checking for a pulse, an IV in its hand, a stethoscope on its chest, a blood pressure cuff on its arm, a cervical collar around its neck and thick wound dressings between its legs. The final photograph was of the bed only. Where the body had been was now a large pool of blood – so much blood.

"I never knew..." And she continued flipping to subsequent photos. The next photographs captured the blood on the head board, more close-ups of the pillow and several photographs of the carpet. She could make out bloody footprints going from her side of the bed around and out the doorway. Kelly looked at Roger before turning to the next photo – a close-up of her dining room door.

"Are these his hand prints on the door? Ronnie's?"

Lt. Rafferty answered. "Yes, ma'am."

"Okay," she took a deep breath... "I've seen enough." She handed the stack of photographs back to Roger. "What about the hospital? I was taken to the ER, right?" Kelly looked at Lt. Rafferty. "Are there hospital photos?"

Lt. Rafferty glanced in Roger's direction before answering her. "Yes Kelly. But I wish you wouldn't look at them."

Now she was mad. "Why not? That was me! And how many other people saw me like that? EMTs? Obviously. Doctors and nurses, right? Police? How many police officers saw me like that?" She was determined not to cry. "I want to see everything! I want to see them all!"

Roger collected the crime scene photographs and opened another file labeled 'K. BONSIGNORE VICTIM.' He passed them to her.

Kelly whispered, *"Thank you Roger."* She opened the file and let out an audible gasp. The first full color photograph held nothing back. She was bloody and naked and lying on a gurney in the ER. There were many medical personnel around her, all wearing colorful scrubs, booties and masks. The next few photographs were also in color and incredibly explicit – she noticed that both Lt. Rafferty and Roger had averted their eyes.

In one photo, her legs were raised and spread and secured in sheet-covered supports. Kelly guessed this was her gynecologist's perspective. There were close-up photographs of her rectum with a deep tear across her perineum. In another photo, a gloved hand held a little white 90° ruler against her private parts. There was nothing left to the imagination – and it looked horrible. The thick wound dressing that she saw in the home crime scene photo had been removed. On the sheet under her butt was lots of blood – lots of blood. So much blood. She turned to the next page.

This was a close-up of her face. Her face? She guessed it was her face, but she didn't recognize anything about her face. The eyes were black and swollen shut, and her jaw hung hideously off center. Kelly looked up at Lt. Rafferty.

Roger spoke softly. "I don't know if you remember or if anyone told you, Kelly, but he dislocated your jaw."

She looked at Roger. "No. No one told me. No one told me anything..." She paged through more photographs, some of them she paused, looking closely at the injuries – others she quickly scanned and went to the next photograph. "I don't remember anything and no one cared enough to tell me anything."

Lt. Rafferty answered her. "Mrs. Bonsignore, you're wrong. Everybody cared too much to tell you."

She looked at the officer and pointed to her head in the photo. "Do you know why they shaved my head? I have a scar on my scalp." She raised her hand and pushed her fingers through the new silver growth that covered the scar.

"Yes, ma'am. He gave you a concussion, and after they got you into surgery the doctors realized your brain was swelling."

She questioned Roger. "Did you know this?"

"Yes, Kelly. I knew that." He avoided her eyes, lowering his head. "If the surgeons hadn't relieved the pressure, you would have died..." He looked back at her – his brown eyes glistening. "You would have died..."

Kelly had no words – she had never seen her friend so affected. She looked back at the officer. "Please continue, Joe."

"Like Roger said, they had to relieve the swelling of your brain so you wouldn't have a stroke." He looked at Roger and then back at Kelly before continuing. "The surgeons had to shave your head, remove part of your skull..."

She held up her hand. "Okay I get it. Thank you, Joe." Again, she felt the thick half-moon shaped scar. "I know you saw these photos... You saw what that son-of-a-bitch did to me..." Kelly tried hard to hold back her tears. "Everybody saw what he did to me but me!" She turned to Roger and gripping his arm, pressed her forehead against his shoulder – and cried.

He put a comforting hand on her head, smoothing her hair back from her face. "Come on, gal. We're done here." Roger attempted to end the meeting, but she resisted.

"No." Kelly sat up and addressed Lt. Rafferty. "I want to see photos of Ronnie. I want to see pictures of the man who fucked me over."

When he didn't immediately answer her, she looked at Roger. "Don't I have that right? Don't I have a right to confront my rapist?"

"Yes, Kelly." Lt. Rafferty exhaled. "You have that right." He put away the hospital photos and opened another file labeled 'R. WOLFF.' He hesitantly pushed the file in front of her.

She opened it and pulled out the photos. On the top was Ronnie's booking photo. According to the measurement behind him, he stood six feet and five inches tall. And he was a large man.

Kelly turned to Roger. "They said Stevie tried pinning the attack on you. Did you know that?"

"Yes... I knew that right after I arrived at the hospital."

She continued paging through the police photos. "Oh my..." She looked up at Lt. Rafferty. "This is how the police found him, right? Sebastian said they found him with his, um, pants down." She scrutinized the photograph. "He looks scared, doesn't he?"

"He tore you apart." Roger looked from the officer back to Kelly. "I don't think you want to feel too badly for him."

"I know, but he looks scared." Again she searched for answers. "Seb said Stevie put Ronnie up to this, raping me. Do you think Ronnie knew what he was doing?"

"Mrs. Bonsignore... Kelly," Lt. Rafferty's voice was soft but stern. "Ronnie had a long rap sheet, mostly breaking and entering, misdemeanor property offenses. He was never brought up on any personal crimes." He leaned into the table, emphasizing his next words. "This was an assault and battery, a felony, a rape. Stevie may have put him up to it, but Ronnie was the one who took it upon himself to practically kill you. Do you understand?"

"Yes, Lt. Rafferty. Thank you." She turned to the next photo and cringed. "Really? Why would they have a closeup of his dick?"

She looked up at Lt. Rafferty, then turned her attention back to the photograph, inspecting the image – and noticed the imprint of a perfect set of incisors across the shaft. The little white 90° ruler was in the photo.

"Sebastian said I bit him... Are those my teeth marks?"

A sad smile crossed Lt. Rafferty's face. "Yes. We were all proud of you for fighting back. You must have fought like a wildcat..."

"I honestly don't remember... I don't remember any of this..." Kelly placed the photo face down on the table. She leaned back in her chair, and quietly exhaled. "When did Seb get here? I know he had gone out of town..."

Roger brought her up to date on the series of events that lead Sebastian to the hospital. Kelly hadn't realized how deeply her attack had affected her husband. And Lt. Rafferty filled in the blanks, including telling her how much Sebastian wept when he learned of her injuries.

She had never heard that story. This knowledge was overwhelming – she leaned forward, resting her elbows on the table.

"Gal, that man would have spent every minute of the day with you if he could. He was out of his mind with grief. I've never seen a man cry as much as he did." Roger waited for her to comprehend the impact Sebastian's despair had on him and everyone around him. "We didn't know if you would live. I swear if anything happened to you, he would have died."

"I didn't know... I really didn't know."

Roger put a big callused hand on her arm. "Did you know he took care of you while you were in the rehab ward?"

"I know he visited me. I heard him talking... I guess I didn't understand all that went on, but I remember he talked to me..." She wanted to go to Sebastian. That's all she wanted right now – go to her husband.

"He bathed you, he massaged your muscles. He turned you so you wouldn't get bed sores. He set up an office in your room." Roger looked at Lt. Rafferty, then turned back to Kelly. "I've never seen a man so devoted, so much in love with his wife."

The meeting with Lt. Rafferty and Roger made quite an impression on her – and had made her see Sebastian in a new light. How could she have been so stupid... How could she have not seen or felt his love for her. But before she could go home, there was a stop she had to make.

She pulled up to the house and saw the jogging stroller outside. Kelly took a deep breath and walked up the porch steps. The door was ajar – she pushed the door open and called out for Gabriella.

"In the kitchen!" Kelly walked across the expanse of the foyer and into the kitchen. Brie sat at the table while Finn ate goldfish crackers in his high chair. When she looked up at Kelly, she started crying.

"Brie, what's wrong?" She sat next to her friend.

"Kelly, he left me." And she cried harder, clutching a dish towel to her face.

"Raffaele left you? What the hell? What happened?" Of course she knew what happened. She figured after Brie had her night with Sebastian, there was going to be fallout.

"You know what happened..." Brie could hardly look at her friend. "That was such a stupid thing to do – and Raffaele asked me – and I did – and he was jealous!"

"You are kidding me!? But it was his idea!"

"I know. It's all so stupid. He said it was my fault... my fault because I agreed to it."

"Oh, hell. That's bullshit! Where is he now?"

"I don't know. I heard him on the phone with his manager talking about going back on the concert tour. Kelly, he could be gone for months at a time. He's going to miss out on his son!"

"You're sure you don't know where he is?"

"Um, I thought he was in the recording studio, but when I walked down there the studio was empty. He's gone. Oh God, I am so stupid!"

"Look, I don't appreciate what you did with my husband, but it was Raffe's idea. That's bullshit." Kelly moved her chair closer to her friend and hugged her tight. "That's bullshit."

Brie wiped her eyes with the dish cloth. "I wanted to call you, but I didn't think you wanted to hear from me." She blew her nose in the towel. "Kelly, I'm so sorry for what I did. You know I'm sorry."

"I know. I won't lie – When I heard about it, I wanted to leave Sebastian. I packed up what I needed and left for our cabin. But he followed me. And I'm glad he did."

"You and Sebastian are good now?"

"He is my life. I love him more today than I ever have. And that's why I came over."

Brie composed herself, sniffing back more tears and remembered her manners. "Do you want coffee? I think there's some left in the air pot."

"Thanks." Kelly stood and poured herself a cup. She looked down at Brie and little Finn. Yes, she was angry that her best friend had sex with her husband, but she also felt compassion for Brie. They were so happy. She knew Brie gave Raffaele back his life. With the birth of Finn, he finally put an end to the nightmare that had haunted him for twenty years. And now he was willing to throw that life away? She returned to the table.

"Brie, I went to the police station and saw the crime scene photos of... well, everything. Me, my home, the emergency room..." Kelly related her meeting with Roger and Lt. Rafferty. "I was surprised. I never knew the assault was that violent."

Brie looked incredulously at her friend. "What are you talking about not thinking it was that violent? Kelly, that son-of-a-bitch broke your skull! He almost killed you!" She looked back at her son, who was slowly nodding his head.

"Stay here. I'm putting Finn down for a nap." Brie stood and picking up her sleepy son, left the room. When she returned, she sat at the kitchen table across from Kelly, placing the baby monitor between them.

"Why did you put yourself through that?"

"Because I had to know. Everyone else knew but me. And now I know."

"When your mom saw you that first time, she fainted."

"I didn't know any of this... No one told me anything." She took a sip of coffee. "You went into the ICU with my mom?"

"Yes. No one thought you would live, least of all your mom. She prayed that God would show mercy on you."

"Jeeze, Brie." Kelly held her coffee mug and her tears started. "I never knew! No one fucking told me!"

"Sorry..." Brie turned up the baby monitor, listening for any noise coming from the nursery. "We were just so worried about you – about Sebastian."

Kelly wiped her face with a napkin. "Tell me about Sebastian. Please."

"He cried... He cried all the time. And Raffe said he had a terrible nightmare about you. He told me Sebastian thought he was making love to you, but it was just a terrible dream... As much as I hate what my husband asked me to do, he really was trying to comfort his brother. I saw how much grief Sebastian was going through – and to tell you the truth, the only person who could really comfort him was you."

"When we were at the cabin, Seb and I talked. He told me everything... I know it wasn't your idea."

"Thank you... But I will be sorry for the rest of my life." Brie sniffed back more tears. "Because of what Raffaele asked me to do, you and Sebastian almost split – and now he's left me. It's all so fucked up!"

"I know, Brie." Kelly reached across the table and took her best friend's hand in her own. "I know."

41

Rough New Prizes

Sebastian stood at the butcher-block counter waiting for her.

"You're home!" Kelly went to hug him, but he stopped her – holding her at arm's length.

"Why did you go behind my back?"

His anger surprised her. "What do you mean? I didn't go behind your back." She assumed he found out about her meeting with Brie.

"Roger called. He was worried about you – after you saw the crime scene photos. If I had known you were going to do that, I would have tied you to a chair!"

Oh, he was pissed. "Sebastian, if I had asked you to go with me, would you have?"

"No!" He put his hands on her again, but in a gentler manner, caressing her shoulders. "And I would not have allowed you to see them either." He pulled her to his chest.

She held him around his waist, resting her head on his shoulder. "I had to see for myself. I had to see what he did to me... I needed to see what happened to me. I had to know the whole story."

"So? Now that you've seen those pictures, how do you feel?"

"How do I feel?" Kelly leaned back and caressed Sebastian's handsome face, feeling his soft beard. "I feel more in love with my husband than I ever have been in my life." She kissed his lips. "Roger told me how you cared for me in the ICU and while I was in rehab. I never knew... Please don't be mad..." And again she held him tight, her face pressed into his neck.

He couldn't speak. What he had done for his wife was out of love – never thinking he should or would have done anything else *except* care for her. He never thought of telling her what he had done for her – bathing her, massaging her muscles, talking to her, spending entire days in her room looking for any sign of life.

Though there had been many frustrating days wanting her to open those beautiful eyes, he did what any husband who loved his wife would have done. He didn't know how to do anything else. And now she knew – and now she knew.

And now she said she loved him so much more because she knew. He never expected any thanks or gratitude for what he had done for her. He just wanted her back. She was his world – his life, his wife, his Dulcinea. And now she knew...

"I love you... always and forever." Sebastian held her face in his hands and kissed her mouth, making love to her with his tongue... He took a step back and couldn't help smiling. He had incredible news to tell her. They were about to embark on their new lives.

He fished in the inside pocket of his suit coat, pulled out a folded document and handed it to her – he was grinning like a kid. "We are the proud owners of the New London Grille. How do you like that, Mrs. Bonsignore?"

"Oh my God! I love it! And I love you!" She kissed him hard, pulling on his shoulders and hugging him. "I am so proud of you!"

"Do you know what this means?" So many things had already transpired today – now she was wondering what was next. He sat on the stool and pulled her to him, making her stand between his legs. "We have to find a name... We have to name our restaurant." He brushed the bangs from her eyes, softly rubbing stray tears from her cheeks.

Kelly closed her eyes, loving the feel of her husband's touch. She took his hand and held it to her chest. "I have an idea..." She opened her eyes and stared at him. "I thought of it when you first mentioned you wanted to buy the restaurant."

"Okay, I'm listening."

"Bella's. Your mom's name was Rosabella. She taught you how to cook. So shorten it and call your new restaurant Bella's."

She hadn't seen Sebastian shed many tears – except the copious amount at the cabin when they were healing. But now he was crying and he was smiling. Again he held her shoulders.

"I love you, Kelly. God, woman, I love you!"

Before Sebastian returned to his office for the afternoon, he made sure there were no more surprises. After fixing lunch for them, he escorted Kelly up to their bedroom. He was still not happy she had seen those terrible photos. Even he hadn't seen them, but he had a front-row seat as he watched her struggle for her life. And he was with her through her recovery – her miraculous recovery.

"I'm tired, and I think I'll take a nap." She leaned into him. "But I wish you'd come to bed with me. I'd sleep better..." Kelly pulled his face to hers and planted a big kiss on his lips – but her kiss turned into a yawn.

"That's my girl!" Sebastian laughed. "Come on. Lie down."

Kelly did as she was told. He covered her body with a light quilt, leaned over and kissed her forehead.

"I'm locking the door." Sebastian closed his eyes, knowing a spare key was the way Ronnie had entered their home. "Only you and I have the keys. Understand? You're safe."

"Thank you, baby. I love you." Kelly closed her eyes. She was exhausted.

> *He was hurting her. He was hurting her. Stop! Stop! You're hurting me! He was so heavy – she couldn't get up. He was hurting her. She saw his face – and he was hurting her. There was so much blood – blood on the sheets, on the pillow case – his bloody hand prints were on the door. There was so much blood – on her face, on her body, on the floor. Doctors and nurses in colorful scrubs were stepping in the blood. There was blood everywhere – he was hurting her and the doctors and nurses were gathered around watching him rape her.*

"Sebastian!!!" She bolted upright. The house was quiet. She was alone in their bedroom. There was no blood. God, what an awful nightmare. Between dreams of Ronnie raping her, and images of Brie making love to her husband, she would never get any rest again.

It was time to put in her resignation. And telling her principal was going to be hard. But if she was going to be a partner in her husband's life – in their restaurant – she needed to be with him full time. Kelly took her phone and pressed the speed dial key for the school. Claudia answered on the first ring.

"Hi, Kelly. What's up?"

"I have to see you and Mr. Jorgenson about my resignation. Can I come in this afternoon after school?"

Claudia's voice quickly went from cheery to somber. "Kelly, that's fine. Why don't you come in around four o'clock?"

"Thank you, Claudia. I'll see you then." She knew from the concerned tone of Claudia's voice that they had been expecting this. She had lost so much time. Her medical leave of absence lasted half a year, and she hadn't been back at all since her recovery from the assault. She really loved teaching, but it was time. She was beginning her new life. It was time.

Kelly looked at her watch – there were almost two hours before the meeting. She lay back on the bed and rolled on her side, facing *his* side of the bed. She could smell *his* scent on her pillow – their pillow. She dozed...

Rarely was the school this quiet. Even when classes were in session, the halls held the echoes of laughter and bustling students. But now, she only heard her footsteps as she walked down to Mr. Jorgenson's office. Her life was changing – who knew that a chance meeting in a bar would have changed her life forever...

Mr. Jorgenson was in his office with Claudia. Kelly walked in and sat. Claudia had been crying. She composed herself.

"If you're sure you want to put in your resignation, we have your paperwork ready for your signature."

"Yes, Claudia, I'm sure."

"Kelly," Mr. Jorgenson cleared his throat. "I think I speak for everyone here when I say you will be missed."

He was so kind. She would miss him more than anyone else. If she could have wished for a father figure, he would have fulfilled that role. His door was always open and he always had a kind word for everyone – even the students who had been sent to his office felt better after talking with him.

"First I lost Gabriella..." He winked at her. "And now I'm losing my best teacher.."

"I'm sorry, Mr. Jorgenson. But honestly, I can't wait to begin this new chapter in my life – running our own restaurant." She attempted a smile, but it came out as tears. "I didn't mean to cry." Kelly pulled a tissue from the box on his desk.

Claudia handed her a pen and whispered through her own tears, *"Don't be a stranger."*

Kelly signed the paperwork, then leaned back and exhaled. "You know, I thought I'd teach until I retired." She smiled at her former principal. "I really did. I always wanted to teach. And you know I love my students. But now, I'll be managing a restaurant!"

After hugging Mr. Jorgenson and Claudia one last time, she walked out of the office, closing the door softly behind her. The tranquility of the school still amazed her as she walked down the empty hallway. It felt like she was leaving a funeral – a funeral for a teaching career she loved. But instead of that crushing pain in her heart, she almost felt reborn. She was going to begin a life working alongside her husband.

She checked her phone. There was a missed call from Sebastian. But when she tried calling him, it went to voice mail. She called his office. Carolyn answered.

"Hi, Kelly. What can I do for you?"

"I'm looking for the tall guy? Beard? Good dancer?"

Carolyn laughed. "He wants you to meet him at the Harbor Pub at six o'clock. And he said to put on your dancing shoes."

Kelly loved his surprises. She had enough time to go home and change.

So many of her clothes still hung on her thin frame, but she finally chose a pretty dress with a wrap-around waist. She sprayed his favorite perfume, *Ange ou Démon Le Secret*, on her wrists and neck, and put on her necklace – the banded chert in the shape of a heart, positioning the stone over her trachea scar. Then slipping on her heels and, while looking in the full-length closet mirror, she took a model's stance and whispered, *"It's showtime!"*

Kelly drove directly to the pub. The parking lot was full. There must be a private party going on. Eventually, she found an empty spot and walked down to the pub.

She opened the door. If it hadn't been the middle of May, the Harbor Pub would really have outdone themselves with their Christmas decorations. She was confused – and even more so when a very tall Santa approached her. Kelly looked up into the familiar face, partially hidden by a fluffy fake beard.

In his rich deep voice, Roger greeted her. "Ho! Ho! Ho!"

"Ho Ho Ho yourself, Santa." She was going along with the joke, knowing her friend was definitely multitasking out of his comfort zone. Santa put his gloved hand out and, taking her hand, led her into the private party room.

Kelly thought she had entered a winter wonderland. To the left was a large fully decorated and flocked Christmas tree – from above hung strings of blinking red, green and yellow lights. In the middle of the room, Sebastian stood holding a plastic mistletoe branch over his head. Santa escorted her to her husband.

"What's all this?" She hugged him, then turned and looked around. She couldn't believe how magical everything appeared. As her eyes became accustomed to the dim light, she made out the faces of her friends, fellow teachers – and her mom!

"This, my wife, is what you missed out on these last months." He glanced up at the plastic mistletoe, then back to her. Kelly laughed and understood his silent message. She wrapped her arms around her husband's neck and kissed him hard – and was surprised when the small gathering of friends applauded.

"Merry Christmas, Love." And she cried. Sebastian wrapped his wife in his arms and, holding her against his chest, cried along with her. He was so grateful that she was still in his life.

She whispered in his ear, *"When did you arrange all this? It's all so beautiful!"*

"Connections, my dear wife." And he gave her his crooked smile.

She left his side and walked over to her mom, hugging her so tight. "Mama? When did you get here?" Now her mom was crying, too.

"I came in this afternoon. Your husband can be very persuasive, my girl."

"Don't I know it, Mama." Kelly looked back at Sebastian through fresh tears. "Don't I know it."

She noticed Tom and Cody standing in line for their hugs. "I'm never going to stop crying!" Kelly's friends laughed. Her tears were something of legend, and those who loved her accepted her tears as a fact of life.

Sebastian walked up to his wife and pointed to the corner of the room. "Go see your friend."

Kelly spotted Gabriella standing off from the group. She quickly walked over to her and hugged her tight. "I'm so glad you're here, Brie. Thank you for coming."

"I'm not staying. I just wanted to wish you a Merry Christmas." Kelly knew why she couldn't stay. She hugged her best friend. "We'll get together soon!" Brie turned and left the room. Kelly walked back to Sebastian who was speaking to the little group.

"We're going to enjoy dinner soon. Everyone please take your seats." Sebastian and Kelly joined her mom at one of the tables.

"Seb, this is the best. Really. Thank you..."

He pointed over to the Christmas tree. "I think there's a hidden envelope with your name on it..."

Kelly stood and peered between the branches. Among the twinkling lights she found the small sealed envelope. She tore it open, pulled out a card and silently read the message.

"I'm a star?" She looked at her husband in astonishment. "You've named a star for me?"

Sebastian rose from the table and walked up to her. She hugged him around his neck. "Oh, Seb, this is so perfect!"

"You share your name with Denebola, the blue star in the Leo the Lion's tail." He hugged her back. "Do you remember my science lesson under the stars?"

"Yes... I remember. It was a night I shall never forget." Kelly kissed her husband's lips. "It was unforgettable... because of you."

He put his arm around his wife's waist and escorted her back to the table. Phil, his wife Emily and Carolyn had also joined Ruth.

Santa walked to the middle of the room and, in a deep voice resonating with authority, announced it was time to eat dinner! Sebastian held out his elbows to Kelly and her mom, and escorted the women to the buffet tables. Kelly filled her plate – it had been a while since she had consumed this much food.

The conversations at the table covered everything from Sebastian leaving his business to the exciting prospects of opening his own restaurant. Kelly felt full and sat back in her chair, but she wanted to know the future plans for the office.

"What are you and Phil going to do now without Sebastian hanging around?"

Carolyn sipped her wine and looked over at Sebastian. "Did you know Phil and Emily are expecting?"

"No! I didn't know!" He raised a toast to his business partner and his wife. "Congratulations you two!"

"Thank you, Sebastian." Phil winked at Kelly. "Well, because our family is growing, we're going to convert your office into a daycare!"

"Say what?" Sebastian almost choked on his wine. Kelly laughed, and the friends around the table joined in the laughter. She looked up at the familiar person who approached their table.

"Chef Tony!" Kelly stood and held out her hands to him. "Chef Tony! I'm so glad you could join us! Can you sit with us?" Behind her, Sebastian laughed. *What?*

"I prepared this celebration for you, Kelly. Your husband can be a very convincing man." Chef Tony leaned down and shook hands with his new employer.

"You came all this way to prepare my Christmas dinner?" Kelly's dim light bulb took longer than normal to shine. "Oh my goodness! You're going to work with my husband in our restaurant!"

Sebastian couldn't help but laugh. "Did you really think I could make all that food on my own?" He stood and pulled her to his side. "If I'm going to make Bella's a success, I need to surround myself with the very best. And with my wife as manager and Tony as executive chef, it will be."

He turned to Tony and whispered, *"It's time..."*

Chef Tony walked off. Sebastian asked Kelly if she'd please accompany him to the middle of the room. He turned her attention to the back of the room. Chef Tony and Roger, sans the Santa suit, wheeled out a cart with a birthday cake decorated with too many wildly flickering candles. The many voices in the room erupted in a loud chorus of *Happy Birthday.*

Kelly's tears flowed. She put her hands to her face, watching as the beautiful cake stopped in front of her. The birthday song refrain culminated in a rousing applause.

"Come on, gal. Blow these suckers out!" Kelly smiled at Roger. She closed her eyes and with all her might – blew! Only a few candles remained lit. Sebastian helped her blow out the stubborn flames.

"But it's not my birthday, Seb!" Her tears would not stop.

"Love, you missed your birthday." He kissed her cheek, tasting the salty tears. "Happy birthday, baby."

She couldn't speak – she could hardly breath. Her husband, the love of her life was making up for her lost celebrations. She hugged him around his waist, not ever wanting to let him go.

As if on cue, her friends voiced a collective sigh. Kelly laughed and looked into Sebastian's hazel eyes. She whispered, *"Thank you... I love you so much."*

But he wasn't done with her celebration. Sebastian reached into his suit coat pocket. "Happy Birthday, Love..." He handed her a small ring box.

"Oh Seb! I love it."

"You haven't opened it yet, silly." He looked over at Ruth and winked as his wife pulled at the colorful bow and opened the box.

"Oh!" Kelly stopped breathing – the room swirled around her. Roger, who stood at her side, caught her with one arm before she collapsed. He made sure she was all right before returning to their table.

"Before you pass out on me..." Sebastian pulled out the ring, which of course was exquisite. An eternity ring in a rose gold band with diamonds and a single garnet – her birthstone. He placed the ring on her right hand ring finger. Kelly held up her hand, and watched as the twinkling lights above made the dark red gemstone sparkle.

"It's just the best!" She held his face close to hers. "It's just the best. You're just the best. I love you!"

"I love you – thank you." He kissed her on her forehead.

"Sebastian, thank you for what?"

"For loving me, for not leaving me... For loving me..."

He escorted his wife back to the table where the women took turns admiring the beautiful ring. As Chef Tony cut and portioned the pieces of cake, the Harbor Pub's wait staff distributed them to the guests. Soon they were all dining on the most delicious cake ever. Kelly was having the time of her life.

The theme from *Dirty Dancing* began. Sebastian stood and held out his hand to his wife. "Would you dance with me?"

He led her to the center of the room. Putting his arms around his beautiful wife, he spoke softly in her ear. "Kelly, you *are* the time of my life..."

When they danced, the guests who had gathered around the impromptu dance floor applauded. This was a magical night, and it was because of Sebastian's love that it was magical. He adored her, and she knew it. He loved her, and she knew his love for her would never end.

Kelly closed her eyes and let her husband embrace her, holding her close to his chest, his body, his heart. She felt more in love with this man, her husband, her Ulysses than she ever had. And he would never leave her – ever. And she knew it. Kelly kissed his lips, feeling his mustache on her face. This absolutely was the time of her – their – life. Always and forever...

The music still played in her head as Kelly crawled into their grand bed. She was exhausted. And after a night of dancing and a huge meal, she couldn't keep her eyes open. She laid her head on her husband's shoulder, kissed his chest – and slept.

And like he had since the first night they stayed together, he held her, his wife, his Dulcinea throughout the night, never letting her go...

The early morning sunlight woke Sebastian first, his arm still around his wife's body, his head on her pillow. He listened to her breathing. For so many weeks the only sound of her breathing had come from a noisy ventilator. Now he listened to her soft breathing – and he dozed...

She moved her head. Sebastian shared her pillow just as he had shared her pillow since that first night together. Kelly opened her eyes and looked at the man who slept next to her. His long hair wild on the pillow, his beard and mustache framing the lips she loved to kiss. His eyes slowly opened. She smiled.

"Good morning, Love." He inhaled her sweet breath. "How are you feeling?"

"I could have danced all night..." She kissed his lips and mouthed *Love you...*

"I couldn't make love with you last night, Love. You fell asleep." He smiled and pulled her closer. "I want to make love with my wife. I want to make love with my best friend." His tears started. "I want to make love with the woman who saved my life."

He didn't mean to cry – but his tears came and he couldn't stop them. Kelly rose up and straddled his body, holding his hips tight between her knees. She held his head, pulling his long hair in her hands and kissed his lips – kissed his eyes, tasting his tears.

"Don't cry, Seb... don't cry..." She loved him quietly, not making the bed move, not making his body move. Just slowly making love to the love of her life.

The week had been busy. Kelly and her mom had invited Brie to have lunch with them. Though their talk didn't touch on Raffaele's abandonment of his marriage, they found many topics of conversation that lasted them through dessert. This would be a short trip for Ruth. After joining her daughter and son-in-law for a wonderful dinner in their home, she left on the late night flight back to Colorado.

The couple finally had a morning where they could both sleep in. After leisurely making love, they took their time like they used to back in the beginning... re-connecting, catching up on missed opportunities to talk, listen, feel, touch, sense. Kelly took advantage of this time to bring Sebastian up to date on Brie and Raffaele, certain that he didn't know anything about their split.

"I never thanked you for inviting Brie to my party."

"Kelly, I didn't talk to her. I asked Carolyn to call her." He felt uncomfortable even saying the name of the woman who had helped him through his grief – and almost ended his marriage. "I left it up to her whether she wanted to attend or not." He raised his heavy eyebrows to emphasize his words.

"I understand..." Kelly combed her fingers through his thick chest hair and took a deep breath. "Everything's not good with them..." She wondered if this would be the best time to relate the conversation she had with Brie. No time like the present.

"What do you mean?" He kissed her forehead and rolled onto his side, pulling her legs closer to his with his feet.

"After I left the police station, I went to see Brie." She looked into his eyes. He was frowning.

"What did you two talk about?" He brushed the auburn curls from her eyes, following the curve of her beautiful face.

"Raffe left Brie."

Sebastian's hand stopped. "He did not!" He rolled onto his back.

"Yes, he did. And she knew why, too." Kelly rose up on one elbow, not taking her hand from his chest.

"I have a feeling I know the answer." He looked up at the ceiling, not sure where this conversation was going. But Kelly put her hand on his face and made him look at her.

"Seb – that's in the past. Understand? Ancient history. No looking back. Understand?"

"Understood. So tell me what you know about my brother."

"Raffe was jealous that Brie agreed to go to you." Kelly raised one eyebrow. "Can you imagine that? He was jealous, and he had asked her to do it."

"I'm surprised my brother..." His gaze returned to the ceiling. "I'm surprised my brother would kick her to the curb after he asked her... you know..."

"Brie was so sad. She overheard Raffe talking to his manager, and apparently he's gone back out on tour." Kelly cuddled into Sebastian's warm body, her hand traveled down to his soft belly hair.

"What about Finn? He told me that Finn..." He swallowed hard. "He told me that Finn was his second chance. He adored that little boy. I don't get it." Sebastian hugged his wife harder. "I just don't get it."

Kelly loved lying in her husband's arms. Even talking about something as uncomfortable as Brie and Raffaele, she felt safe from the problems of the world as long as he held her close.

"Do you think I should call my brother?"

"I think we should stay out of it." Kelly kissed his chest, nosing through the thick hair. "Besides, we'll have enough to do getting our restaurant going without worrying about them." She found her husband's nipple and sucked on it. Her hand traveled south and discovered his growing erection.

Sebastian closed his eyes and exhaled loudly. "Lord woman, what are you doing to me..."

"Shush, man..." And she climbed on his warm, hard body.

"We have a lot to do today." He stood at the butcher-block counter.

Kelly poured her second cup of coffee. She brought her creamer and sat across from him. "Are you meeting with your lawyer this morning?" Sebastian had entrusted the application for his liquor license in the capable hands of his attorney.

"Nope. I already talked with her. We're just waiting to hear back from the board." He put his coffee mug down. "I want you to stop by the office today. Bring your teacher retirement fund paperwork with you."

"I've got it all organized in my folder. Will you roll it over for me?"

"No. Phil will handle it. I need to see Roger and meet Lee Shipman, his architect. I've never heard of this guy..."

"Look, you know what you want – stick to your guns." Kelly emphasized her words by tapping her finger on his hand. "If you don't like it, don't go with him. This is your restaurant."

"Yes ma'am." Sebastian smiled at his wife. He walked around the counter and, pulling her into his arms, kissed her. "I'm out of here. I love you."

"I love you, too." She returned his kiss. "I want these lips on me this evening... Understand?"

"Understand." He picked up his keys from the bowl and left the house.

Kelly tried calling Brie. She hadn't heard from her friend since they had lunch with her mom. But the call went to voicemail. She left a quick message, then brought her coffee into the living room. She didn't have anything to do for a few hours – and Sebastian's leather chair was calling her name.

He pulled up in front of what would soon be his restaurant. The building had already been gutted, and the full roll-off dumpster sat out in the parking lot. Roger met him in the doorway, holding back the heavy plastic zippered door. Sebastian ducked as he walked in and stood in the cavernous space.

"This is incredible. Where's our architect?"

He heard the rustling of plastic and was surprised to see his friend Cody walk into the building followed by a woman.

"Seb! May I introduce Leigh Shipman – my little sister."

Sebastian laughed, then shook Leigh's hand. "Ms. Shipman, it's a sincere pleasure to meet you." He winked at Cody. "But are you sure you want to be associated with this character?"

"Please call me Leigh. And who do you think keeps my big brother in line?"

"Thank you, Leigh. And please call me Sebastian." He took a step back and waved his arms at the empty shell. "This space will hopefully be Bella's Italian Restaurant by August. You've had time to assess the interior?"

"Yes. And Roger has been very helpful. If you're ready, I'd like to show you the preliminary plans." They walked over to a large piece of plywood that had been laid across two sawhorses. She opened the first roll, illustrating her plans for the kitchen. As Sebastian looked over the plans, he made a few suggestions. Overall, he liked the basic layout – and gave an approving nod to his new architect.

Kelly brought her paperwork into the office. Carolyn was talking with Michael – and looking very cozy. She knew Michael wasn't dating anyone, and Sebastian never said anything about Carolyn having a boyfriend. It didn't take her long to figure out these two lonely people had found each other. She smiled at the couple, then walked into Phil's office.

When he saw her, he stood. "Good morning, Kelly. Hope you don't mind if I help you with your retirement."

"No, that's fine. Seb's having fun today talking with his new architect."

"As I understand it, we're rolling over your teacher retirement into an IRA. Shall we go into the conference room?"

She followed him and sat at the table – and looking at Phil, took a deep breath. "Phew."

42

Changes

"So?" Sebastian waited for her response. He was trying out new recipes with Kelly as the official guinea pig. He waited patiently for her expert analysis.

"Okay, so I've had your chicken piccata before – but the way you prepared it this time is better. I think I like the thicker sauce."

Sebastian was taking notes in his ever-growing spiral notebook. He had begun carrying it around months ago. Though it appeared cumbersome to those who relied on their electronic tablets, to him it had become an integral part of his life – taking notes in his personalized shorthand.

"But..." Kelly paused, waiting for him to stop writing.

"But what?" Now Sebastian's heavy brows frowned.

"Oh, there are no 'buts' about the meal... But I think the salad is the star of this show."

"Really? You liked the Romaine and baby arugula mix with the grilled peaches and candied pecans?"

"Yes, but I really like the dressing. What's in that dressing?" She retrieved her salad plate. Kelly swirled her finger in the remnants of the creamy liquid and, putting her finger into her mouth, sensually sucked on her finger. She knew exactly what she was doing.

"Don't do that... we have too much work to do this evening."

"As if work ever stopped you, mister!" She smiled her best smile, knowing exactly what he was thinking.

"It's... the dressing..." His mind battled between explaining the ingredients in a salad dressing, or planning the strategies of undressing his wife. "Lord, woman... okay, it's a honey and goat cheese base with olive oil and vinegar."

"Well I love it!" She put her finger deeper into her mouth, sucking on her finger. She smiled. Yes, she knew exactly what she was doing – and she knew exactly how he would react.

Sebastian stood. "You can't do this to me." He moved his place setting off to the side, careful not to spill his wine. "We have too much work to do... I haven't seen you all day, woman. I've been holed up in that shell of a restaurant – and I haven't seen you all day..."

He pulled Kelly to her feet and held her in his arms, kissing her face, her lips, making love to her with his tongue. "I haven't seen you all day..."

Kelly untied the leather cord that held his hair. Though the ends of his hair were black, the new growth around his face was graying. She pulled his hair forward, clutching handfuls in her fists while she kissed him.

"Take your shoes off, woman..." He breathed the words on her face. He could never control himself around her. Never. And she did as he requested, kicking off her moccasins. Sebastian held her by her waist and eased her body up on the table.

"Lie back... Please..." Again she did as he asked and opened her jeans. He reached under her and tugged her jeans and panties off her legs.

Kelly raised herself up on her elbows and watched as he stepped out of his trousers and boxers, kicking them away. She moved toward the edge of the table. He leaned down and lifted her, collecting her in his arms.

"Put your legs around me." Again she did as he asked, holding on to his neck as he slipped into her. And he held her – just held her so tight, crushing her against his chest, almost constricting her breathing. The feeling was incredible. He just held her, not moving – just held her. And she felt his cock throbbing.

He took a few shuffling steps back and sat heavily on his chair, still holding his wife's body around him. "Sorry, Love..." He bowed his head, his forehead resting against her chest – trying to catch his breath.

"Seb... What? Why are you sorry?" Kelly touched his head, loving his long hair, his beard, forcing him to look up at her. His hazel eyes glistened. "Why are you sorry?"

But she knew why he said that – he thought he hadn't satisfied her. "Sebastian, are you kidding me? I love you! You touch me and I explode. You look at me and I explode. I dream of you and I explode." She kissed his eyes. "I love you, silly."

That's all he had to hear – that she loved him anyway. But he knew that – he always knew that. From the moment he met her, he knew she would love him... always and forever. "I love you, woman." And again he pressed his forehead on her chest – she combed her fingers through his long hair, loving him, her husband.

Whatever would she do without this man...

This would be another busy week. In fact, the last two months had been full of busy weeks. The restaurant was finally coming together under the watchful eye of his architect. Roger and his crew had been on site every day, ensuring Sebastian's vision became a reality. And Michael's sister Connie, who was also an interior designer, created the color palate.

The conference room became the official repository for boxes filled with bar and restaurant fixtures, piles of material swatches for the chairs, and paint and wallpaper samples. Everyone involved wanted Bella's to be the premier Italian restaurant in the five-state area.

He poured more coffee into Kelly's mug. "When are you meeting with Michael and Carolyn? Weren't you three going on a road trip to check out more lighting fixtures?"

"Um, I think I'd be in the way."

"Why would you be in the way? I thought you and Carolyn got along. What's wrong?"

"Seb, are you really that thick?"

His concerned frown slowly morphed into one of surprise. "Michael and Carolyn? Really?"

"Yes, silly. Really."

"When did this happen?"

"You've got so many irons in your fire right now, I'm surprised you remember to come home every night and make love to your wife."

"I will always remember to make love to my wife." He leaned across the butcher-block counter and kissed her lips.

"What about tonight?" But he was already engrossed in reading his latest text messages. She took a sip of her coffee and softly added, "Or maybe I'll just hit on Roger..."

Without looking up, Sebastian mumbled, "Okay..." and replied to one of the many texts. He looked up at Kelly. "What? What about Roger?"

She laughed. "I said... I love you and I'll see you tonight." Kelly walked around the counter and hugged her husband around his waist. She kissed his lips, loving the feel of his mustache and beard against her face.

"I love you, too." He put his arms around her. "Tonight."

After an exceptionally long day, Sebastian was ready for an evening in the hot tub. He had brought a bucket of ice and several Coronas down to the tub where Kelly waited. The hard jets massaged their bodies, relaxing them, sending them into a state of unabashed lethargy. They leaned into each other, her head on his shoulder, his head against hers. Neither wanting to move, feeling content just being with each other – touching arms, hips, thighs, feet...

"Tom brought something to my attention – I think you might want to consider it."

"What is it, baby?" She took a long drink of the golden beer.

"He told me about a week-long immersion seminar in hotel and restaurant management. He's attending, and said he'd bring you with him – if you want."

"Where? Here?"

"No. In Chicago." Sebastian kissed the top of her head. She looked at him. Kelly knew Sebastian wouldn't let her travel alone – and she knew he was too busy with his restaurant to leave. What was his plan?

"Seb, I think that would be a good thing for me. I've never been a manager and there's so much about the restaurant business that I don't know." He was frowning again. "Why are you frowning? If you don't want me going to the seminar, why did you bring it up?" She could see he was arguing with himself. Let her attend and be out of his sight for five long days? Or keep her here and let her be a manager without any training. She wanted to be his right arm – not a millstone around his neck.

"Did Tom give you any information about the seminar?"

"Yes. The pamphlet's in the house. I thought I'd bring it up first to see if you'd be interested..."

She knew this discussion was killing him. He obviously wanted her to attend, and if she was with Tom she would be safe. "I'd at least like to look at the literature." She kissed his shoulder. "And I think I'm a prune..."

He laughed – it was time to get out. He rose and pulled his wife up and into his arms. "I love you, woman." He kissed her chastely on her lips.

She kissed him back, pulling his long wet hair in her hands. "Show me, mister..."

Sebastian left the folded pamphlet on the butcher-block counter. Kelly looked it over while they had their morning coffee.

"There's a lot of very useful information here. I think this would be such a good seminar for me. You said Tom is going, too?"

"Yes. He's expanding – he's adding a coffee and pastries bar within his florist shop. This seminar would give him the tools he needs." He watched her intensely as she perused through the information contained in the pamphlet.

"Wow... managing the staff... allocating duties... motivating the staff..." She looked at her husband. "Would I be able to use a big stick for motivation?"

She finally got a smile out of him. This whole going out-of-town business was really weighing on him. She knew he was worried about her safety. Now she would be out of his sight for five, maybe six days? This was going to drive him nuts.

"Seb, this is information I need. I mean, how do I know how to hire a bartender? How to manage a staff? And the service standards? The health and safety regulations?" She took a long drink of her coffee. "I think this crash course in restaurant management is perfect."

She could tell he was feeling more comfortable knowing she'd be busy and in safe hands. The seminar would also be conducted in the same hotel where she and Tom would stay.

"So how do we make reservations?" And why did he have that crooked grin on his face?

"I've already registered you." He looked sheepishly at his wife.

"When?" Kelly didn't know if she should be alarmed, or if this was just business as usual with Sebastian.

"When Tom first told me about the immersion classes last month."

"And you're just telling me now? What if I had made plans to visit my mom in Colorado?!"

"But you wouldn't have gone there without me." He had that look about him. The same look he had when he found out she had gone to the police station and saw the crime scene photos.

"Okay, mister. Tell me when I'm leaving..." She couldn't keep the humor out of her cross look.

"You and Tom leave Sunday afternoon. You fly directly to Chicago."

"This Sunday? The day after tomorrow Sunday?" Wow, when he made up his mind, there was no getting past him. He had never been a control freak – not until she had been assaulted. But she couldn't fault him, not for this.

She stood and put her arms around his shoulders. "Will I be surprised if I find you in bed with me in that hotel?"

"No, you won't be surprised." He smiled his crooked smile. "There's a restaurant supply vender in Chicago I want to check out. I'll be down there on Wednesday through the end of the week."

She pressed her lips into his beard. "I thought as much..."

43

Chicago

The seminars in restaurant management began at 6:30 in the morning, and didn't conclude until after 5:30. Monday morning was spent registering and having an informal meet-and-greet while enjoying a Continental-style breakfast. A very elegant speaker made the opening address, and introduced the courses that would be presented throughout the week.

Kelly wore a badge with her name and business typed in large letters. She had never seen the name **Bella's Italian Restaurant** written in bold lettering. It was almost surreal, feeling the embossed words under her fingers. She was proud introducing Sebastian's restaurant to the rest of the world, even if it was only 150 people.

After Wednesday's seminar concluded, Kelly made a beeline for her room. She showered and donned the hotel bathrobe. He had told her not to open the door – he would text her when he arrived. While she waited for his text, she lay on the bed and napped – but not for long. Her phone vibrated. It was him. She quickly walked to the door.

God, he looked good! She hadn't seen him in three days and honestly, it felt like an eternity. He walked in carrying a large bag of Chinese take-out and a six-pack of beer. He gathered her in one arm, crushing her to his chest, kissing her, breathing on her face, telling her in exhaled breaths how much he loved her. She let him walk her into the bed – Oh, she loved this man.

He stopped – and just looked at her. "Do you know how much I missed you, woman?" His words were so sincere, his look so Sebastian. He kissed his wife, softly at first, almost chastely until his passion for her took over and he couldn't help himself. He forced his tongue into her mouth, tasting her, loving her, making love to her with his tongue, consuming her mouth with his own.

She untied the leather string, freeing his long hair. Kelly touched his face, placing both hands on his beard and drowning in her husband's kisses. She unbuttoned his shirt, revealing the thick hair she loved so much.

"Stop. You need to eat first or..." He gave her his crooked smile. "Or I'm going to climb on your body and this food will go to waste..." Sebastian placed the cans of locally brewed Pegasus IPA on the bedside table. Kelly helped him open the take-out bag, pulling out containers of the most heavenly-smelling oriental indulgences.

"Here – I got your sesame chicken and a side of fried rice." He handed her the containers. "And I also brought a cup of your favorite pork wonton soup."

"Thank you, baby..." Kelly sat on the bed cross-legged near the head, smoothing the blankets and spreading the delicious dinner in front of her. She watched as Sebastian took out his food.

"General Tso's Chicken?"

He looked at her. "What else?" Sebastian grinned, kicked off his shoes and eased his body up on the mattress. He also had brought fried rice for himself.

She handed him a beer. "Did you remember the fortune cookies?" Kelly licked her fingers, savoring the rich flavor.

"Kelly..." He carefully leaned forward and kissed his wife's face. "You are my fortune cookie. You are my four-leaf clover..." He kissed her lips. "Kelly, you are my North Star..."

After they ate their dinner, Kelly moved closer to her husband. She pushed his shirt off his shoulders and made him lie back on the bed. She caressed his chest, silently telling him she wanted to love him – nuzzling his chest hair, finding his nipples, sucking on his nipples...

Sebastian reveled in his wife's touch – her fingers, her lips, her tongue. He pulled her body to his and kissed her, holding on to her as if his life depended on it – because it did. Her life made his life complete.

"I'm going to shower... don't go anywhere!" He rose and, as he walked into the bathroom, stepped out of his trousers and boxers. She loved watching her husband as he stripped. His chest and belly were covered with thick black hair, and except for a triangle of fuzzy black hair at the base of his spine his well-muscled back and butt were smooth. She lay back on the bed, waiting for the man who would make her body sing.

She must have been tired – she woke to her husband lying next to her on the bed, facing her. Why didn't he wake her?

"Why didn't you wake me?" She touched his temple, combing her fingers through his long hair, touching his shoulder, touching his chest. "What time is it?"

"It's after midnight." In the dusk of their room he could barely make out her beautiful emerald eyes. "Love, you were so tired."

He brushed her hair from her forehead and continued down her face. He touched her neck and slowly pulled the bathrobe from her shoulder. He rose up on one elbow and kissed her shoulder... and slowly pushed her onto her back, kissing her breast. He loved her breast, kissing her sweet nipple, loving her sweet nipple.

"Sebastian – I love you so much..." Kelly closed her eyes and enjoyed the feel of her husband's hands on her body, across her breast, down her belly, touching her thighs and reaching between her legs. He pressed his fingers into her while he kissed her face, making love to her with his tongue.

"I want you – now." She held his face between her hands – the face of the man who loved her beyond words. "I want you now... always and forever!" His beautiful hazel eyes glistened – he was crying.

"Seb?" He was really crying. She rose up from the mattress and gently pushing him onto his back, climbed on his body, holding him close between her thighs. "Sebastian, what's wrong?"

"I was so afraid I'd lose you..."

Oh my. She kissed his eyes, tasting his tears. She kissed his soft lips, making love to him with her tongue. "Baby, I'm not going anywhere. Is that what you're worried about? Me alone down here?" She smoothed her hands over his beard.

"Yes. I've been so worried." And he held her tighter to his chest. He released his grip and placed his hands under her robe, touching her bare skin. His fingers following her spine down to her hips and heard her moan as he found her hot spots.

"I'm right here." Again she kissed his face, touching his beard, enjoying the feeling of his hands on her, caressing her. "What do you want, baby?" She kissed his lips. "You tell me what you want."

Sebastian enveloped her body in his strong arms and holding her close to his chest, rolled over and nestled between her open legs. He kissed her lips, her eyes and breathed her name as he pressed into her, not moving, just holding himself deep within her, his wife, his Dulcinea.

Kelly held on to his long hair, pulling handfuls in her fists, keeping his face close to hers. She surrounded his body with her legs, locking her ankles on his back. And she kissed him, her husband, her Ulysses – the man who would never leave her. She felt secure in his love for her, a love that would remain with her – always and forever.

"Sebastian... I'm there... Love me... Please love me..."

He obeyed her command and thrust harder, making the bed rock, making her body climb higher, giving her all he had – and continued driving and thrusting until he had no more to give. And he gave her more... He collapsed on her, breathing so hard in her ear. "Love...?"

She knew what he was asking and stared into his eyes, his beautiful hazel eyes shrouded beneath heavy brows. "You satisfy me every day, mister..." Kelly combed through his hair with her fingers. "I love you, Sebastian... always and forever..."

She held him as he rolled off her body, her leg still under him. In the dark of their room, with her husband's warm breath on her face, Kelly came to a stunning realization. She would die without this man – literally die without him.

"How did you do it? All those weeks I was in a coma? How did you manage it?" But before he could speak, she knew the answer – and understood why Raffaele had sent his wife in the guise of comfort to her husband's bed. She answered her own question. "Sebastian, I finally get it – I finally get it..."

"What do you get, Love?" He smelled her sweet breath on his face.

"I get why your brother asked Gabriella to go to you – to comfort you." She put her hand on his face, caressing his beard, smoothing his hair behind his ear. "I get it because I know I would die without you – without you at my side." She kissed his lips. "I would die..." And she cried.

"I'm not going anywhere." He kissed her tears. "But are you telling me you forgive Gabriella? You forgive Raffe?" And just the mere fact he was saying Gabriella's name, the woman who gave herself to him – or did he give himself to her – while his beautiful wife struggled to survive was monumental.

"Let's just say I understand. I know Gabriella gave you comfort. I'm not stupid. I also know you love *me*." She kissed his nose. "I'm too smart for my own good, you know." She touched his face, the face of the man who would never abandon her – who would never go to work and not come home. Sebastian would be with her forever – always and forever...

He kissed her lips. "We should sleep or you're going to be tired all day tomorrow... this morning." He raised his body – she pulled her leg out from under him.

"Roll over, Love." And she turned, her back to his front, and he enveloped her body in his arm. "I love you, Kelly." And they slept, sharing one pillow...

The final full day of the seminar passed quickly. Thursday night, they joined Tom for dinner. He and Kelly spoke highly of the seminars they attended throughout the week, and Sebastian enjoyed listening to the animated banter. It had been so long since she exuded this much excitement about anything. She was back – his wife was back.

Kelly and Sebastian returned to her hotel room. After showering, they lay in the grand bed. He knew she was exhausted, so he volunteered to give his wife a full body massage.

"Lay on your front, Love." Kelly didn't need much encouragement – her body ached. She felt exhilarated being back in a classroom setting, but the long hours were taking their toll. It hadn't even been a year since she had been assaulted. And after another long day, just having his hands on her would be wonderful. While she was in class that day, he had stopped by a specialty shop that sold massage oil. Sebastian knelt across her legs.

"Are you ready, Love?" He squirted some of the oil on his hands and could feel it warming in his palms already. "I think you're gonna like this..." And he began on her neck, using his fingertips to spread the oil around her throat, on her shoulders, between her shoulder blades.

"Oh... Seb..." She was purring, almost whispering her words. *"I think you have created a monster..."* And that's the last thing she said for awhile. The only thing he heard from her was an occasional moan as he added more oil to his palms and followed her spine, pushing on her back muscles, gradually moving down to her hips. He asked her to spread her legs and repositioned himself between her open thighs. His hands – his warm hands – followed the curve of her ass, her hips, and between her legs.

He took his time, massaging her legs from her hips to her feet. He began slowly, putting more pressure on her muscles, his hands covering her thighs, pulling on her legs, kneading her calf muscles. He could hear her faint moans as he raised her feet, massaging her toes... and gradually worked his way back up to her spine.

He turned her onto her back. The massage continued – her shoulders, her arms, her chest... He eased her legs wide apart and leaning down, inhaled her sweet musk. He tasted her silky skin, taking his time, kissing all of her, loving all of her and bringing her to an incredible orgasm. But he wasn't done and he continued licking and sucking until she called out his name – or something sounding like his name...

She rose up and, grabbing a fistful of his hair, made him lay on her. He pressed his full length into her. A loud groan escaped from deep within her body. She wrapped her legs around him and pulling his face down to her own, kissed him – exhaling his name between each kiss.

Her breathing was all he heard – her sensuous breathing, whispering his name in long breaths. Just hearing her breathe his name enflamed his passion – and he couldn't help himself. He thrust into her so hard, not holding back, giving her everything he had. He kissed her face, sweat dripping onto her face – and as he found his release, he brought her, his wife, his Dulcinea to another hard orgasm.

He collapsed on her, crushing her into the mattress. And she held him close, not ever wanting to let him go – and they both slipped into a sound sleep...

44

Never Want To Leave

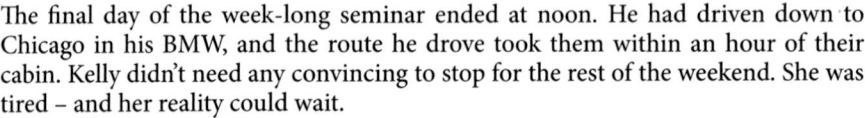

The final day of the week-long seminar ended at noon. He had driven down to Chicago in his BMW, and the route he drove took them within an hour of their cabin. Kelly didn't need any convincing to stop for the rest of the weekend. She was tired – and her reality could wait.

They arrived as the sun was setting. Sebastian knew she wanted to watch the evening colors of the sky down by the pond. He let her go ahead of him while he brought two days of provisions into the cabin. He joined her at the water's edge, and together they drank ice-cold Coronas.

Kelly leaned into her husband's arm. "I wish we could stay here... I would give up everything to be here with you forever."

"Would you give up our restaurant?" He looked hard at her, his wife, his Dulcinea. "Would you give up our home?"

"If it meant I would be with you every day for the rest of our lives – yes. I would give up everything." And the tears started.

"Woman, what's wrong?" Sebastian remembered a similar conversation they had at the cabin when she contemplated giving up her teaching career. He put his arm around her and pulled her nearer to his chest. "What's wrong, Love?"

"Sometimes I'm afraid that, you know, we won't have all this time. I mean, I had cancer and was assaulted and almost died..."

"You know I'd give up everything to be with you." He kissed her temple. "If you wanted to never leave this cabin and live here for the rest of our lives... Kelly, if that's what you wanted, I would give up my business – I would give up our restaurant."

She looked at him, her husband, her Ulysses. "But I would be taking away your dream, your dream of owning your own restaurant. And no matter what I would want – and no matter what sacrifice you would make for me – that restaurant is your dream. And I'd never take that dream away from you." She looked out over her pond. "I would never take your dream away from you."

And they sat by the edge of her pond, watching the brilliant red sun say its last farewell as it slipped beyond the horizon, behind the tall tamarack larch on the distant shore...

45

Always and Forever

"Connie, where did you find these photographs of Sebastian's parents?" Kelly had been walking through the almost completed restaurant. The enlarged and framed sepia photographs that hung on the walls above the booths were stunning. Connie really knew her stuff.

"Sebastian let me go through a box of photographs he had stored away. I don't think he even knew what was in there." She looked up again at her handiwork, happy that Kelly approved.

"Did you find any of him and his brother as children?" Now Kelly was more than interested in the answer. She had never seen any pictures of Sebastian as a child.

"There were some albums I didn't go through." Connie straightened one of the heavy frames. "But I'm willing to bet that's where you'd find them."

The two women continued walking through the spacious and very vacant building. Everything had been meticulously chosen. The tin oiled-bronzed ceiling tiles, special-ordered from Italy, and the heavy flocked wallpaper above the natural wood wainscoting reflected the old world integrity. Connie's background in design helped Sebastian make the decisions that brought his dream of a true old world Italian restaurant to reality.

Kelly put an affectionate arm around Connie's shoulder and gave her a hug. "The atmosphere is so comfortable. I know this is what Seb wanted."

"Thanks, Kelly. I think so too." She looked at her watch. "I have to leave and check on the tables and chairs. They should be delivered by the end of the week."

"Thanks, Connie. I'll see you later. Everything looks perfect."

"Kelly!" Chef Tony called to her from in the kitchen. As she made her way through the empty restaurant, she stopped by the large bar made from reclaimed wood. She knelt up on a bar stool and peered over the edge.

"Hi Kevin!" Kevin was the bartender at the tavern near the college, and when he heard Kelly was interviewing for restaurant staff positions he was the first to apply.

He looked up her "Hey Kell! What's happening!"

"Just managing..." And she laughed as she stepped down from the stool and continued walking back to the kitchen. She pushed through the swinging batwing doors.

"It's beautiful, Chef Tony." Sebastian had given Tony *carte blanche* when it came to stocking his kitchen. Kelly was truly impressed, and silently watched as the executive chef moved the biggest stand mixer she had ever seen into place.

"Like it?" He wiped his hands on his black floor-length apron and put his hands on his hips. "I love it!" He walked up to Kelly, grabbed her shoulders and put a big kiss right on her lips. He took a step back and with his arms outspread, turned in a circle. "I love it!"

She knew Sebastian loved working with Chef Tony when he attended Macalester College. Now her husband had his mentor back in his own kitchen – in his own restaurant. She touched the gleaming steel work station and looked at the chef with great affection. "I'm so glad you're here..."

She left the kitchen, walked back to the bar and sat on one of the stools. Kevin looked up from his toils, cleaning and putting away the new glassware Sebastian had ordered. Only the best – and the best was expensive.

"What's next, Kelly?" Kevin's heritage was African American and Irish – which gave him a distinctive look and an infectious smile.

"I'm waiting for the menus to arrive. Do you have a list of the brand-name liquor you want? I know Seb likes Jameson."

"That he does, Kelly." Kevin winked at her. "And I've got the list right here, both brand and rail." He pulled a notepad from under the bar and tore off the top sheet. "This should be it."

Again, he gave her his award-winning smile. Kelly couldn't help but smile as she got down off the stool – and was grabbed from behind around her waist.

"Hello wife!" Sebastian scared her – when she realized it was him, Kelly playfully slapped his arm.

"Hello yourself!" She kissed his mouth. "What have you been up to?"

Sebastian put his phone on the bar and placed a large package next to it. "Open it."

Kelly loved his surprises. She pulled at the brown wrapping paper. "Our menus!"

She lifted the first one – the weekly dinner menu. It was only two pages, and held the best of the best that Chef Tony could offer. Bella's Italian Restaurant would serve lunch and dinner meals only, offering the freshest proteins: chicken, scallops, shrimp and select cuts of beef and pork.

A special Friday menu, featuring halibut and salmon, would be available for the elderly and retired population in the area. Though the Church had long ago changed its rules for Friday abstinence, many older diners appreciated the effort the better restaurants made in satisfying their religious traditions.

Kelly picked up the weekend lunch menu. One of the options caught her eye. "When did Terese give you her recipe for jerk chicken with butter beans?"

"The night of your Christmas Birthday party I asked her if we could use it." Hoping for his wife's approval, he quickly added, "You know I love the spice, and offering it on Saturdays seemed like a good idea."

"You made a good decision. I don't think anyone else serves that around here." She looked back at him and noticed a frown. "What?"

"I'm expecting the linens guy any minute."

She laughed. "The linens guy?"

"The guy who's going to deliver clean and ironed napkins every morning." He gave her his crooked smile.

She loved that smile. "I'll watch for him. But right now you need to go see what Chef Tony has done to the kitchen."

As he walked to the kitchen, Kelly called to him. "Kevin has the liquor names here."

Sebastian pivoted around and faced her as he continued walking in reverse. "I'm going to the liquor store later this afternoon." He turned and pushed through the twin doors.

Michael entered the restaurant, carrying coils of additional wiring for the wall sconces. Since he was in charge of everything electrical, he was on site nearly every day. This morning he had more bounce to his step – he must have had 'breakfast' with Carolyn. Kelly hid a knowing grin.

She turned back to Kevin. "Anything else I need to know here?"

"Nope. Everything's under control."

Sebastian came out from the kitchen and stopped at the bar. Kelly gave him Kevin's list.

"Roger's meeting me at the liquor store with his pickup truck." He folded the paper and stuffed it in his back pocket. "Then I'm going to stop off at Tom's florist shop and order the bouquets for the tables." He pulled Kelly into his arms and kissed her passionately, even surprising his wife with the sudden public show of affection.

"Sebastian, is everything okay?" She looked into his hazel eyes – the eyes of the man who would love her always and forever...

"Everything is perfect." He hugged her tight against his chest. "Everything is perfect."

She watched her husband leave the restaurant – and felt a heaviness she didn't understand. Must just be the magnitude of preparing for opening night in just one more week. She dismissed the feeling.

Immediately after Sebastian left, the food vendors arrived. Kelly escorted them into the kitchen where Chef Tony would review the menus and put in his first order. He had already hired his kitchen staff, including the prep cooks and sous chefs.

When word spread that she was the manager of Bella's, some of her former high school students applied, many of whom were enrolled at the local college. Both the front and the back of the restaurant staff were going to meet with her later in the week. Kelly wanted everything to run smoothly opening day.

Sebastian's phone rang. He had forgotten to take it with him and had left it on the bar. Kevin called to Kelly. "Can you take this?"

She quickly walked back to the bar and taking her husband's phone, answered with a cheery hello.

"Hey, is Sebastian Bonsignore there?" For a heartbeat Kelly thought she recognized the voice, but again dismissed it as just another vendor. She had met so many people in the last week it was easy to get one voice confused with another.

"No, he made a trip to the liquor store but he should be back within the hour. Can I help you?" There was an uneasy silence on the other end. *Why were the hairs on the back of her neck standing up?*

"Do you know which liquor store?"

Now that was an odd question. Obviously, he would have gone to the locally owned store a few blocks away, not the larger box store near the mall.

"Yes, he's at Macmillan's – two blocks up on 4th Street." Again she felt uneasy. *Why?* Sebastian was dealing with so many people right now. And because he didn't have his phone, the folks wanting to speak with him were left in the lurch. But she was trying to help. "I think if you called there you'd find him."

Again that uneasy feeling swept over her. *Why?*

"Okay, thanks for your help." And the caller hung up.

What was familiar about that voice? She put Sebastian's phone in her back pocket – she couldn't spend any more time on that question.

While she was deliberating with Michael regarding the sconces Connie had chosen for the booths, Sebastian's phone rang again. She looked at the caller ID. Lt. Joe Rafferty. Why was he calling Sebastian?

When she answered the phone, that sense of dread enveloped her – again.

"Kelly, where's Sebastian?!"

Oh God... that voice... that other voice... it was Stevie... Oh God!

"Joe, he's at the liquor store. What's going on?"

"Stevie appealed his conviction and got his sentence reduced to time served..."

Oh God...

"His mother called 911 and said he took a gun from her house!" When his words were met by silence, he continued. "Kelly, he shot Roger..."

> *Roger had just gotten out of his pickup truck when Stevie confronted him – from behind, like the cowardly shit he was. "Hey you! Marine!"*
>
> *He turned around – and felt the bullet burn into his chest. Roger lost consciousness before his body hit the pavement.*

"... and now I'm afraid he's after Sebastian."

Oh God...

"Sebastian doesn't have his phone – he's at Macmillan's!"

"Thanks!"

Oh God...

"Michael! Kevin!!" Both men looked at her. "Find Sebastian! I think he's at Macmillan's! ***Find Sebastian now!***"

Without hesitation, the two men hurried out through the front doors leaving Kelly standing alone in the middle of the empty restaurant.

Oh God...

Time stopped. She could hear the voices of the vendors in the kitchen talking to Chef Tony.

Oh God...

Her phone rang. "Sebastian!?"

"No Kelly... this is Lt. Rafferty."

Oh God...

> *Sebastian had filled two shopping carts with liquor bottles and mixes from Kevin's list. As he stood at the counter waiting to pay, he heard an unusual sound behind him.*
>
> *But the store clerk who held a concealed carry permit knew that sound... the sound of the cocking of a gun.*

"I'm sending a squad to pick you up. You need to get to Mercy Hospital immediately."

Oh God...

"Chef Tony!"

Tony busted through the swinging doors.

"I'm going to the hospital. Something terrible has happened to Sebastian..."

Oh God...

A state trooper picked up Kelly at the door of her – of Sebastian's restaurant, and with sirens blaring, drove at break-neck speed to the emergency entrance of Mercy. The cruiser pulled up to the door. Kelly jumped out before the car stopped. Lt. Rafferty took her by the arm and hustled her into the ER.

Oh God...

"Joe... is Sebastian..."

"Kelly, he's alive. But we need to hurry." Lt. Rafferty gripped Kelly's hand as they ran down the narrow corridor.

Oh God...

They stopped outside an emergency room. There was so many medical staff surrounding a gurney – she couldn't see who was on the gurney... *but she knew who was on the gurney...*

"SEBASTIAN!" She shrieked his name and tried getting past the officers who were guarding the room. Lt. Rafferty held her against his chest. She felt his badge digging into her shoulder.

A plain-clothed detective approached them and addressed Lt. Rafferty. "Joe, the liquor store clerk shot Ward. He's dead." He nodded and wordlessly dismissed the woman.

Kelly could only breathe the words. "Stevie shot my husband?"

"I'm so sorry, Kelly."

Oh God...

A member of the medical team – his scrubs stained with blood – came out of the room. He slowly pulled down his surgical mask. "Mrs. Bonsignore..."

> If Kelly spoke, she knew it would be over – she knew her life would be over.
>
> And if she didn't say anything, then it would be fine.
>
> She and Sebastian would go home.
>
> And she would make love with her husband – because he was her husband, always and forever.
>
> And they would sleep and they would wake up and they would open their restaurant.
>
> And they would be happy...

"Mrs. Bonsignore, I am so sorry..."

NO NO NO NO NO NO NO!

"Mrs. Bonsignore... please... come with me..."

Kelly looked up at Lt. Rafferty, her eyes pleading with him that he could make this all go away. This was not reality. This was a cruel joke. Someone was making a cruel joke at her expense. But he had tears in his eyes.

Lt. Rafferty slowly walked with her into the ER where her husband's body lay. The medical team that had been working on him backed away, letting Kelly approach the gurney.

She looked at his face – his face appeared so peaceful. His eyes – his beautiful hazel eyes shrouded beneath heavy brows – were closed. His lips – his soft lips that she loved to kiss – that she had kissed only minutes before – were closed. His shirt had been ripped open and his chest – his wonderful chest with the dark hair that she loved touching – his chest had been cracked open.

She touched his arm. It was still warm. Kelly leaned down and kissed his lips – those lips she loved, those lips she loved...

46

Reunion

Ruth came as soon as Gabriella called her...

> "Ruth, this is Gabriella."
>
> "Well hello, honey. How's that pretty little baby of yours?"
>
> "Ruth, Kelly needs you..." Brie started crying and couldn't take a breath. She desperately tried composing herself. Before she could say anything more, Ruth knew something terrible had happened.
>
> "Brie, honey... what happened?" Silently Ruth prayed – she wasn't sure why but she prayed.
>
> "God, Ruth..." Gabriella sniffed hard. "Sebastian was killed."
>
> "Oh my sweet Jesus in heaven!" Ruth sat down hard on the bench near her desk. "Oh my sweet Jesus in heaven..."
>
> "Kelly needs you..." Brie held Finn while she spoke with Ruth. He was squirming and she had no one to pass him off to. Where the hell was Raffaele when she needed him – when she really needed him?
>
> "Brie, I'm coming right now. I'm taking the first flight out of here and I'm coming right now." Ruth motioned to her secretary to remain in her office until she was done with this call. "Tell Kelly I'm coming. Oh dear God, Brie. How does this happen?"
>
> Ruth hung up the phone and opened her computer. While making reservations for her flight out of Grand Junction, she whispered a prayer...

After she left her husband – her Ulysses – at the hospital, Lt. Rafferty drove her home. Vehicles were parked in the driveway and on the street. Lt. Rafferty escorted Kelly up to her house.

So many people stood on the porch. Carolyn greeted her with a warm hug. Kelly felt she couldn't cry any more – but her tears came again. "I can't do this!!" Carolyn took her keys and opened the door for the many friends gathered.

Michael enveloped Kelly in his arms, trying to comfort the woman who just lost her whole world. She hung on to him, her fingernails pressing into his back. He whispered, *"I am so sorry..."* And her crying only got louder, knowing that anything her friends said wouldn't make a bit of difference. She wanted her husband.

She looked up from his shoulder and saw Brie. Michael released her into the arms of her best friend. Now both women cried. Kelly eventually let go of Brie and looked around the kitchen – and realized the number of people who surrounded her – the people who loved Sebastian – who knew Sebastian before he had met her.

"Seb loved every one of you..." Brie kept an arm around Kelly's waist. "And I love you, too..." Kelly wiped the tears from her face. "Thank you for coming... thank you..."

Kelly reached out and embraced each one of Sebastian's friends, softly thanking them for their love and support. She turned to Lt. Rafferty. "Joe, thank you for bringing me home..."

He wanted to express his sadness – but he had no words of comfort. Lt. Rafferty affectionately grasped her hand and left the house.

"Kelly..." She slowly acknowledged Cody's voice and turned to him. "There's a sub sandwich for you – tuna and provolone. It's in the fridge. And I've made a pot of coffee... for later, if you want any."

"Thank you... thank you all." Kelly touched the wooden butcher-block counter – the first thing she saw when entering the kitchen on their first date... "I think I'll go lie down for awhile."

The many friends of Sebastian's took their turn and hugged Kelly again before leaving. Only Brie stayed behind.

"Brie, you can go..."

"I've got a sitter with Finn. I'm staying."

Kelly gave her a half smile and walked out of the kitchen. She ascended the stairs and walked into their bedroom. From down in the kitchen, Brie heard Kelly's cry. She ran up the stairs.

Sebastian had showered that morning and had left his towel on the floor. Kelly sat on the bed holding his towel to her face, inhaling his scent...

"Kell... come on..." Brie tried taking it from her, but Kelly fought her, finally lying on the bed with the damp towel held tightly against her body. Brie pulled a quilt over her friend and left the room.

Ruth arrived early the next morning. Though Kelly was grateful her mom was with her, no words were spoken. Ruth could not bring solace to her daughter. All she could do was hold her close, listening to her sobbing.

Lt. Rafferty came to the house, offering words of comfort, telling her Sebastian never knew what hit him – he felt no pain. He also tried explaining why the court system failed her. But Kelly didn't want to hear any reasons why her husband wasn't at her side, why he wasn't here with her, next to her, the way he had promised he would be – always and forever...

That night Ruth offered to babysit Finn while Gabriella stayed with Kelly. She slept in the guest room down the hall from Kelly's bedroom...

It was such a perfect evening. The stars in the heavens were so bright. Sebastian pushed off with both feet and lay on his back. Kelly lay on her husband's body, her hands on his chest supporting her head. He swam a back stroke. Soon she looked up and noticed their fire pit fading in the darkness...

We should start back, Sebastian... But he didn't hear her. She lay her head on his chest, feeling his muscles as he stroked through the water. She raised her head again – their fire pit grew faint. They were too far from shore.

His body began sinking – taking her with him. She let go and tread water – and watched as his body slowly disappeared. She screamed at him... Wake up! Wake up! Sebastian! But his body sank deeper in the black water until she couldn't see him anymore.

She couldn't tread water any longer and she began sinking. She screamed for him...

Brie heard Kelly's howls. She ran out of the guest room into the bedroom. Kelly was thrashing in her sheets. Brie got into bed with her and held her tight until she gradually heard Kelly's cries lessen, her breathing become more even. And Brie slept next to her best friend in Sebastian's bed for the rest of the night.

Caleb returned his phone to his pocket and let out a long, wavering breath. He composed himself and headed for the dressing room.

"Raffe, I have news from home."

Raffaele was preparing for his concert and was only half listening to his manager. Hearing news from home meant his son was growing up without him, or his beautiful wife had filed for divorce. He missed them terribly. Admittedly, he was the one who left his family – he was the one who had sex so brutally with his wife, the woman who gave him back his life. They just never got back on track after that horrible night. And now he was receiving word from home.

Caleb stood behind Raffaele's chair, both hands resting on his client's shoulders. "There's no easy way to say this... I am so sorry... Your brother was killed..."

Raffe turned in his chair and looked up at his manager's tear-stained face, not understanding what he was being told.

"I'm cancelling everything. We'll figure it out."

Dominicci, the world renowned tenor, slowly turned back to his reflection in the large ornate mirror – still not comprehending the words.

"I'm making flight plans for you."

Raffe stared into his own eyes – so similar to his brother's... His brother... This could not be. How could this happen? Sebastian was the smart one, the level-headed one, the one who found the love of his life in a dark bar.

"You need to go now."

And his world stopped. The sun died and the moon crashed into the sea... *Oh God... his brother... his little brother...*

And he bowed his head and wept.

Raffaele arrived early in the morning. He leased a car and drove into town. Pulling up in front of his house, he noticed another car in the driveway – he didn't recognize the car. Had his wife moved on? Already? He slowly walked up the porch steps and took out his house key – had she changed the locks? His key worked, and he pushed opened the heavy door.

The house was quiet. Surely Finn should have been up by now. Raffe slipped off his shoes and walked across the foyer into the kitchen. There was coffee in the pot. He felt it – it was cold. He poured out the old coffee and made a new pot.

While the coffee brewed, he took off his coat and walked up the carpeted grand staircase. He still heard no sounds. Raffe walked down the hallway – he was apprehensive about looking into his wife's bedroom. His wife hadn't slept in their bed since that awful night. He was so stupid.

He stopped before the doorway and leaned in. There was someone in his bed, but it wasn't his wife. He softly rapped on the door. A head poked out from under the sheet.

"Ruth!" He walked into the room. "Oh goodness! Ruth!"

"Raffaele!" Ruth looked up at him apologetically. "Raffe, I'm so sorry. Gabriella is with Kelly at her house." She pulled on her robe and pushing back the covers, swung her legs onto the side of the bed. She modestly smoothed her flannel nightgown across her legs and stood.

"I just found out about my brother... I guess she didn't know I'd come home..."

Ruth walked to him and put her arms around his waist. "Honey, I am so sorry." She looked up at Sebastian's brother. "I am so sorry..."

"Thank you, Ruth." He hugged her back, then walked out of the room and looked down the hall toward the nursery. "Does my wife have our son?"

"No, he's here. He should be getting up."

"Okay... I'll get my boy. Thank you, Ruth." He walked down the hall to the nursery and heard Finn humming and burbling a familiar aria.

Ruth walked downstairs and into the kitchen. She smelled the freshly brewed coffee. Yesterday was a long day, and the coffee was a welcome friend. As she poured her first cup, her cell phone rang. She checked the caller ID.

"Hello, Brie. How is my daughter?"

"She had a nightmare, Ruth." Brie exhaled, remembering her best friend's torturous dreams. "But she finally slept... I think she had a good night."

"Honey, Raffe is in town." There was silence on the other end. She knew Brie was mulling over that news. Ruth waited patiently.

"I'm glad he's here. I guess I knew I'd see him again some time, I just wish it was for other reasons – not for his brother's funeral."

"Can I talk to Kelly?"

"She's still sleeping. I don't want to wake her until absolutely necessary, if you don't mind."

"That's fine, Brie. Why don't I head out to the house and you come home... Raffe made coffee." Her suggestion was more of a nudge than a question. Brie and Raffe needed to talk.

"I'll wait until you come over, Ruth. Thanks."

Ruth put down her phone and taking her coffee, returned to her room to dress.

"Who was that?" From her bedroom upstairs, Kelly had heard Brie's voice and came down to the kitchen.

"Sorry, Kell... that was your mom. She's going to come over here and be with you. Raffe's in town." Gabriella and Kelly looked at each other. Kelly had just lost her husband – and now Gabriella's husband had returned.

"Brie, go... I'm fine. I have to shower and get ready anyway." Kelly hadn't cried yet this morning. Granted, she had only been awake a few minutes...

"If you're sure. I'd really like to see Raffe." Brie hugged Kelly – and felt her dam burst. Brie held her friend, soothing her, rocking her in her arms. And that's how Ruth found them when she arrived at the house.

Kelly backed away and laughed. "I'm hopeless – I know I am. Thanks Brie. Go see your husband." She wiped the tears from her face. "And Brie, welcome him home. Please." Gabriella nodded and left the house.

She turned to her mom. "Brie made coffee. Have you had yours yet?"

"Yes, my girl. But I'll sit and have more with you." Kelly took the French Vanilla creamer out of the refrigerator, and together they sat at the butcher-block counter, silently drinking the warm brew.

While the medical examiner concluded the autopsy on her husband's body – the bullet had shattered Sebastian's spine – Kelly began the task of arranging the funeral. She was never involved in planning her father's funeral. After he died – after her daddy so tragically died – she had retreated into her bedroom, coming out only to go to school and maybe eat a meal. But now with her mother's guidance, Kelly planned her husband's funeral.

The funeral home asked for one of his suits. Even though in his will he had requested cremation, Kelly insisted on an open-casket viewing. She stood in his closet and inhaled the smell of *him*. All his clothes, his suits – his beautiful suits carried his scent. Her hand floated across the expensive material of his suit coats before choosing one – the one he wore at their wedding.

She pulled the coat off its hanger – the tiny burgundy boutonnière still pinned on the lapel exploded into dust. The irony was not lost on her that his body would also become dust. Kelly held the coat to her face and wept.

After bringing the suit to the funeral home, Kelly drove to the hospital. She had to see Roger. Stevie shot Roger – she didn't know the extent of his injuries. As she approached his hospital room she was met by a dozen police officers sitting and standing around the open door. Those who sat stood when they saw Kelly – silently making room for her as she walked into Roger's room.

The head of his bed was partially raised. A thick white bandage covered his chest, his right arm cradled in a sling. When he saw her he smiled – then closing his eyes, he cried. Kelly walked up to the right side of the bed and touched his shoulder.

"Gal, I am so sorry..." With his left hand Roger held her hand. He knew her tears – and this was one time no one could have fixed those awful tears.

He looked up at the wife – the widow – of his best friend. He had seen death. He had been around fellow Marines killed in battle. But knowing Kelly's husband died crushed his heart. And he felt so helpless because he couldn't do anything about it. All he and Kelly could do is mourn and grieve and scream and cry for the loss of the man they both loved.

She looked into Roger's glistening brown eyes. "Are you going to be okay? Are you okay?" With tender fingers, she touched the bandage on his chest.

"Kelly, I'm going to be fine." Roger softly rubbed her hand – and had the good sense not to ask how she was feeling. He knew her – and he knew the woman standing at his bedside was just this side of exploding with grief.

She leaned in and kissed his cheek – the former Marine choked back his tears... Kelly affectionately touched his shoulder again, turned and walked out of the room.

Before the visitation began, before anyone else arrived at the funeral home, she had to see her husband, her Ulysses in private for the last time. Ruth escorted her daughter into the parlour but stayed a few steps behind.

Oh God. Kelly didn't know how she could do this! She touched his tie – the tie she bought him, the tie he wore to their wedding. She reached under his head and pulled at the leather string, releasing his long hair. As she smoothed his hair around his shoulders her hand rubbed against his neck – it felt cold and hard.

He appeared so peaceful – as if he were sleeping in their bed. She wanted to lie next to him, hold him close to her...

> *It was still dark when she woke. Through the bedroom window, the full moon played hide and seek behind the stand of birch trees. Kelly looked*

at the man who slept next to her – his arm and one leg lay across her body, his face next to hers on one pillow, his warm breath on her face. The flickering moonlight splashed its glow on them... Just the thought of his warm body on her, under her, around her made her body yearn for him again. But he was right here. All she had to do was touch his face, his shoulder, his hip and she could have it all again... She stayed where she was, cocooned around this man...

"Come on, Kelly." Ruth touched her daughter's arm. "Everything is ready."

"Aren't the flower arrangements beautiful, Mama?"

"Yes, my girl. Everything is lovely..."

Kelly turned to her mom. "Sebastian's attorney told me that he had set up a scholarship at the college."

"Did you know that before the obituary was written?"

"Yes. Phil from the office helped me write it. It's short, but it's what he would have wanted. I kept a copy." Kelly pulled the newspaper clipping out of her bag. "Phil took care of everything. You know he's running Sebastian's business now... He and Carolyn."

Kelly gave the notice to her mom. Ruth opened the folded newspaper clipping and silently read...

Sebastian Giordano Bonsignore, 43, tragically left this earth for his heavenly home on August 23rd. He was preceded in death by his parents Rosabella and Vicenzo Bonsignore and sister-in-law Annalisa Bonsignore. He is survived by his beloved wife Kelly Isabella Cameron Bonsignore, his brother Raffaele Dominicci Bonsignore (Gabriella), and nephew Tommaso Finnean.

Visitation will be at Richardson Brothers' Funeral Home Tuesday, August 27th from 5:30-8:00. The funeral service will be held at St. Catherine's Chapel on Wednesday, August 28th at 10:00.

In lieu of flowers, the family has requested donations be made to the SGB Scholarship Fund at the Lakeview Community College.

Ruth refolded it and handed it back to her daughter. "This is nice, honey. Phil did a good job."

Brie and Raffaele came into the room. His homecoming had been so sad – and at the same time so happy. Brie had accepted him back into their little family. Kelly could tell Raffe had been weeping. His eyes were bloodshot and swollen.

Brie left his side and hugged Kelly. "I think they want to open the doors."

Kelly looked at Brie and then her mom. "Okay..." But she wanted one last look at Sebastian, her husband, her Ulysses. Kelly turned back to the casket and touched his beard, his hair, the heavy brows that shrouded his beautiful hazel eyes...

She whispered, "*I love you, always and forever...*"

Michael and Carolyn were the first to sign the register. Carolyn walked over and hugged Kelly.

"Sebastian was responsible for making my life so much better. I'll never forget him." She kissed Kelly on her cheek and waited for Michael to pay his respects.

"You know how I felt about Sebastian... My local IBEW made a generous gift to his scholarship fund."

Kelly only nodded and whispered, "*Thank you, Michael...*"

He hugged Kelly, then took Carolyn's hand as they both walked over to the casket.

Phil and Emily came in with their twins. "Kelly – Brody and Jase wanted to say goodbye. They remembered how kind Sebastian was when they watched the fireworks from the office." The boys, now thirteen years old took turns hugging Kelly.

"You're getting to be young men!"

They smiled at her, then backed up and let their dad talk to Kelly.

"Sebastian saw abilities and talents in me I didn't know I had." Phil took a composed breath, but his voice still wavered. "You know I will take very good care of his business." He left to join his wife and sons who waited patiently to pay their respects to the man so many people loved.

The line of friends and former coworkers seemed to go on forever.

"Kelly," her mom spoke softly. "How are you doing? Would you like to sit?"

Kelly refused to sit – she wanted Sebastian to be proud of her. After what seemed hours – and it probably was – the line gradually ended. She was exhausted, and finally reaching for a chair, sat heavily on the soft cushion. She leaned her head back – she was even too tired to cry.

Ruth pulled a chair up next to her and patted her daughter's hands. "Let's get you home, my girl."

With half-opened eyes, Kelly turned to her mom. "How did you do it, Mama? Greeting all of daddy's friends..."

"I don't know. I really don't know..." Ruth glanced down at her lap, caressing the thin gold wedding band she still wore – and exhaled loudly. "Honey, do you remember the engineers? Max and Nick?"

"Of course. They worked with daddy."

Ruth's blue-hazel eyes glistened. "When your daddy died there was no consoling them at the funeral. Those big men just sobbed. I've never seen grown men cry like that." She took her daughter's hands into her own, remembering...

"They weren't only sad that Fred had been killed in that awful way – they mourned your loss, too. You and your daddy were inseparable on that train. Both men were so worried for you. They worried how you would get by without your daddy." Ruth wiped a tear from her daughter's face. "The sun and the moon rose and set with your daddy. Everyone knew that. And when he died, we knew your world would never be the same – and it wasn't, my girl."

Kelly had no words. When he died she didn't think she could live, much less breathe without her daddy. Her grief was unspeakable – her heart bursting out of her chest. And now with the death of her beloved husband, her Ulysses, she remembered that suffocating feeling...

Ruth caressed her daughter's shoulder. "I think Tom has fixed something for you to eat at the house."

"Oh, Mama – I'm not hungry."

"You will eat or you'll never get through tomorrow." She took her daughter's hand and helped her stand.

Kelly took a last look at Sebastian, her husband. "Will he be okay here? All alone?" Again, she felt that crushing feeling rise in her chest.

A man's voice from behind startled her. She turned.

"Ma'am, it's our honor to stand vigil."

Lt. Joseph Rafferty and two of his officers, all in full uniform, stood before her. And finally her tears fell. Lt. Rafferty gathered her in his arms.

"We'll watch over your husband. You go home."

"Thank you, Joe..." Ruth took Kelly by her arm, and together they walked out of the room where Sebastian's body lay.

47

The End

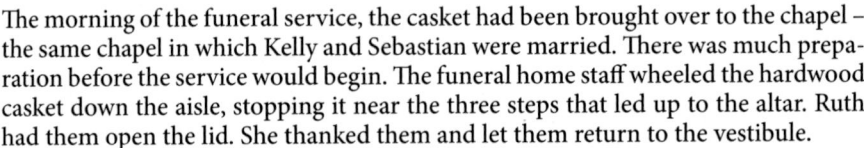

The morning of the funeral service, the casket had been brought over to the chapel – the same chapel in which Kelly and Sebastian were married. There was much preparation before the service would begin. The funeral home staff wheeled the hardwood casket down the aisle, stopping it near the three steps that led up to the altar. Ruth had them open the lid. She thanked them and let them return to the vestibule.

Ruth looked at the body of her son-in-law. She only now recognized the suit – it was the one he wore when he married her daughter. She softly touched the tie – and said a brief prayer – a prayer for his soul, a prayer for her daughter, a prayer for the world that was now without this wonderful man in it. She heard someone coming up behind her.

"Hi Mama." Kelly touched her mom's shoulder. Ruth turned – and tried very hard not to cry. But she broke down as she pulled her daughter into her arms.

"I am so sorry, my girl."

Kelly knew her mom had great affection for Sebastian. It was only months earlier that he had flown her in from Colorado for her Christmas Birthday party. Ruth wiped her face and quickly composed herself.

"Honey, your guests will be here soon." She paused. "And I want to share something with you before they come." Ruth opened her bag and pulled out a folded lace cloth. "This was the pall that was placed on your father's casket. Now, I'll place it on Sebastian's."

Kelly felt the soft, delicate cloth. "I never knew... I guess I wasn't paying attention."

"Honey, you were just a kid. You were twelve – and you were so angry."

"Mama, I hated you when daddy died..." Kelly felt new tears. She remembered how awful she treated her mom after her father died.

"I know, my girl... I know."

"Mama, I am so sorry. I love you, Mama..." Kelly looked around and saw Roger standing behind her – his right arm in a sling.

"Roger, what are you doing here? Why aren't you in the hospital?" She left her mom's side and hugged him around his waist. He hugged her back with his left arm and kissed her forehead.

"Kelly," his deep baritone voice almost a whisper. "I'm one of the pall bearers. No one could keep me from being here for Sebastian – and for you." He hugged her again. "I loved him too, Kelly..."

"I know Roger..." She pressed her face into his chest.

Ruth touched her daughter's shoulder. "Kelly, you need to go back and greet your guests – your friends – Sebastian's friends."

"I'll walk with you." Roger held out his left hand and, taking her hand, escorted her back to the vestibule. Ruth watched her daughter walk with a man who could never take Sebastian's place – but who she knew cared deeply for her daughter...

The funeral staff brought the last of the many floral arrangements into the chapel. Tom had backed his florist van to the side door, orchestrating the delivery.

"Hi, Kelly." Tom hugged her and kissed her cheek. "I know this is hard... You have so many friends here today..." He looked up at Roger and nodded. "And we're going to be there for you after today too. You're not alone..."

"Thank you, Tom." She looked at the procession of colorful arrangements in vases and baskets that had been brought into the chapel, many she recognized from the viewing the night before. "The flowers are so beautiful..."

Emily and Phil arrived. Emily would sing *He Walks With Me* while the family entered the chapel before the service began. Phil not only prepared a reading from the Old Testament but would also serve as a pallbearer.

She hugged Phil. "Thank you for doing this for me... for Sebastian..."

He put his arm around Kelly. "It's the least we can do for your husband."

She turned to Emily. "How are you feeling? I never asked you yesterday."

"I've never felt better." Emily looked at her husband and touched her growing belly. "We're having a boy."

Kelly leaned in and kissed her cheek. "I am very happy for you both."

Emily's tears started – Phil took his wife by her elbow, and together they walked into the chapel.

Kelly turned to Roger. "I know you want to be a pallbearer – but with your arm, your injury. Are you sure?"

"Don't worry about it." Again, he put his arm around her shoulder – she leaned into his tall frame.

Raffaele and Brie entered the vestibule holding hands. Even in her grief, Kelly was happy for them. "Thank you Raffe for singing at Sebastian's... at your brother's..."

"My dear Kelly... when your mom asked me I didn't hesitate for a minute. I told her it would be my honor to sing for my little brother." He enfolded his sister-in-law in his arms – she felt his tears on her face.

Brie touched her husband's shoulder. "Kelly, we'll see you in a few minutes." She and Raffe walked into the chapel.

More pall bearers arrived. Chef Tony and Kevin walked up to Kelly. When she hugged the chef, her tears started again. "Chef Tony, I am so sorry..." She tried comforting him.

Chef Tony held her shoulders. "Bella's is still Sebastian's restaurant. It will always be his restaurant – and I am proud to be the Executive Chef in my friend's kitchen!"

Kelly kissed his cheek and whispered her thanks. He put his hand on her face and moved to the side.

Kevin hugged Kelly. "I feel such guilt – it should have been me who went out that day." He looked at her through his own tears. "Sebastian would be here if he stayed with you."

"Please don't think like that!" She hugged him tight. "Please..."

He smiled, though it wasn't his usual award-winning smile. Kevin left her side and followed Chef Tony down the aisle.

Cody came in carrying a bible. He would read a passage out of the New Testament. Kelly hugged him tight and whispered, "*Thank you, my friend.*"

Michael and Carolyn were the last to come in. When Kelly saw them, her tears started – again. "Thank you, Michael for being a pallbearer. Sebastian..."

"It's okay, Kelly..." Michael looked up at Roger and nodded his approval. He and Carolyn left to go to their seats.

There was an unending procession of people – so many came to say goodbye to Sebastian. Friends of theirs, his clients, his former chef – they all came to see her husband... they all came to say goodbye...

Kelly's knees buckled. Roger held her closer to his body. She was grateful for his support. It suddenly dawned on her that he loved her – and yet he had stood by her all these years and watched her fall in love and marry another man.

She looked up at Roger and mouthed *thank you*. Roger could only assume she was grateful for supporting her. In his wildest dreams, he never imagined she knew his secret.

It was time. Emily took her place on the altar and began singing...

> *"I come to the garden alone, while the dew is still on roses, and the voice I hear falling on my ear the son of God discloses.*
>
> *And He walks with me and He talks with me, and He tells me I am His own..."*

Roger escorted Kelly and her mom down the aisle to the front pew. He sat with Kelly, who sat next to Brie and Raffe. Ruth walked up to the casket carrying the lace pall.

Kelly watched as the funeral staff slowly closed the lid on the coffin. *Oh God!* Her mournful cry echoed throughout the little chapel. She pressed her face into Roger's arm.

Ruth held back her own tears as she began the invocation.

> "We have gathered here to say goodbye to Sebastian Giordano Bonsignore. It was in this very chapel where I married Sebastian and my daughter Kelly. Now we are saying goodbye to this wonderful man. My sadness is too much. I cannot bear to say goodbye to my

> son-in-law. But as a minister of the church it is my duty to help you, his widow and his friends to say goodbye."

Phil rose from where he sat and helped Ruth place the delicate lace material on the casket. She quietly thanked him. Ruth turned, and addressed the mourners.

> "As in baptism, Sebastian Giordano Bonsignore put on Christ – so in Christ, may Sebastian be clothed in glory. Let us pray... Dying, Christ destroyed our death. Rising, Christ restored our life. Christ will come again in glory..."

The congregation responded, "Amen."

Cody and Phil walked up the three steps to the altar and stood at the podium. Cody read Psalm 23 from the Old Testament...

> "The Lord is my shepherd, I shall not want. He maketh me to lie down in green pastures: He leadeth me beside the still waters. He restoreth my soul: He leadeth me in the paths of righteousness for His name's sake... Surely goodness and mercy shall follow me all the days of my life: and I will dwell in the house of the Lord forever."

Phil read from the New Testament...

> "Dear friends, now we are children of God, and what we will be has not yet been made known. But we know that when Christ appears, we shall be like Him, for we shall see Him as He is."

Ruth joined the men at the podium and thanked them both. They walked back and took their places behind where Sebastian's family sat. She asked the congregation to stand and opened her bible. She read a gospel from the Book of John.

> "Do not let your hearts be troubled. You believe in God, believe also in Me... And if I go and prepare a place for you, I will come back and take you to be with Me... I am the way and the truth and the life. No one comes to the Father except through Me."

Ruth closed her bible and asked the mourners to sit. She walked out from the podium – and spoke to the many people gathered in the small chapel.

"My daughter called me one day and said she was getting married. Of course, I was happy for her. She said *he* was the one. In the same breath, she asked if I'd officiate at the wedding." Ruth winked at Kelly. "The day I arrived, Sebastian put me to work in his kitchen. He and I made fettuccine for dinner that evening. I enjoyed his company so much. He was smart and funny – and very patient with me as I fumbled with that first batch of pasta."

Ruth took a couple steps, and continued. "My daughter called me one day and said she had been diagnosed with breast cancer. Of course, I came in from Colorado immediately. Sebastian doted on Kelly, and it was then that I witnessed first-hand the love between husband and wife." Ruth took a tissue from her sleeve and wiped her eyes.

"And Sebastian was at my daughter's side during a terribly painful period in her life. He cared for her, never losing hope that she would survive. And it was because of his love and attention that my daughter recovered. And they had made plans to open a restaurant..."

Ruth exhaled loudly. "My daughter's friend Gabriella called me just the other day, telling me Sebastian had been taken from this earth." Ruth looked at her daughter, then again at those who sat in the pews.

"I will remember Sebastian as a man who succeeded in business, who laughed out loud, who lived life to its fullest... I will remember Sebastian as the man who fiercely loved my daughter. And I will never forget him..."

Ruth took a moment and composed herself. She then requested the countless number of friends gathered to share their own reflections and memories.

Many people stood and shared their experiences with Sebastian. The stories were often full of humor – it was good to laugh. And there were other stories. Stories of love – love for the man who touched so many lives.

Kelly heard many of the stories, but soon tuned out the voices. Her mind was on her husband... her husband who would not be with her any more... her husband who would not be waiting for her at home. She leaned into Roger's arm and softly cried.

The stories concluded. Ruth again addressed the congregation. "I will now give you my final blessing...

> "Lord, grant eternal rest onto your son Sebastian Giordano Bonsignore, and let perpetual light shine upon him. May the souls of the faithful departed, through the mercy of God, rest in peace. Amen."

Raffaele walked up to the altar and began singing the beautiful *Time to Say Goodbye*, but he couldn't hold his emotions. And he wept. Gabriella left her place at Kelly's side and walking up to her husband, held him tight, and together they sang...

> *Time to say goodbye.*
> *Paesi che non ho mai...*

Raffe kissed his wife and returned to the pew where Kelly sat. She kissed his lips and whispered, *"That was beautiful. Thank you."*

Brie walked down from the altar and stood near Emily by the closed casket.

"As Sebastian's friends bring him on his final journey," Ruth began, "Emily and Gabriella have chosen to sing *On Eagle's Wings*. I feel this hymn is so appropriate. Sebastian was introduced to nature through the wise and patient teaching of his wife. Now we pray that God will raise his soul on eagles' wings and hold Sebastian in the palm of His hand. Amen."

In perfect harmony, Emily and Brie began singing... *"You who dwell in the shelter of the Lord..."*

The pall bearers – Michael, Chef Tony, Phil, Kevin, Cody and Roger – took their positions around the coffin that held Kelly's heart.

> *And He will raise you up on eagles' wings*
> *Bear you on the breath of dawn…*

As one, they lifted and carried the heavy coffin down the aisle and out of the chapel into the waiting hearse. His body was to be cremated.

> *Make you to shine like the sun*
> *And hold you in the palm of His hand...*

Roger walked up the aisle and held out his hand to Sebastian's widow. She had been waiting in the pew until the hearse drove away. He escorted her back to the vestibule, where more words of comfort and condolence were offered. Kelly didn't hear the words. She saw their mouths move, but she never really heard the words. She shook so many hands – she received hugs from so many arms.

Eventually she was alone.

"My girl," Ruth was at her side. "Gabriella and Raffe are hosting a reception in their home..." She knew this was Kelly's time – and she had to honor how her daughter wanted to deal with it.

"Mama, I just want to go back to the house. But can I call you... later?"

Ruth was very concerned for her daughter, remembering in the days following her father's death how she had hidden from the world in her bedroom. "Kelly, you will call me."

"Yes, Mama..."

Ruth also knew she would only agree to mollify her concern. "You call me. I am so worried about you..." She hugged her daughter tight.

Kelly held her mom close and whispered, *"Promise..."* She kissed her mom's cheek and left the chapel on Roger's arm. He would drive her home in his pickup truck.

They rode in silence. After Roger pulled up to the garage and parked, he offered to come in. She looked at the porch steps – and spoke as if in a dream.

"Thank you. But I think I'm tired..." She was exhausted and just wanted to cry.

Before she got out of the truck, he reached into his left suit coat pocket and took out Sebastian's tie. He handed it to her. "I knew you wanted this, gal."

Kelly looked at him and whispered, "Thank you..." It was obvious he cared for her, but she needed to be alone with her memories.

He got out of the truck, walked around to the passenger side and opened her door. With Sebastian's tie in one hand, she let him assist her – stepping on the running board first. He watched as she walked up the porch steps to the front door.

Roger started his truck and waited, making sure the door closed before backing out and driving away...

Kelly locked the door behind her. She stood at the butcher block counter – the first thing she saw when she came into the house. There were too many memories. His kitchen, the dining room, their bedroom – every room had a memory...

She put his favorite Boney James CD into the stereo and sat in his leather recliner. Kelly held the tie to her heart – the tie he had worn at their wedding, the one he wore at his funeral. She pressed her face into the back of the chair – and smelled *him*. She dozed...

After a brief nap, she called her mom and let her know she was okay – that she was fine and not to come over. Of course, Ruth was concerned, but she wouldn't push her daughter. They agreed to meet for breakfast.

That evening, Kelly stood at the open refrigerator door. Though it was stocked with the offerings of well-meaning friends, she had no appetite. She closed the door and walked zombie-like upstairs to their bedroom – her bedroom.

She entered their closet – her closet – and inhaled *him*. She began going through his wardrobe, touching his clothes, smelling his clothes. She opened a drawer and found his latigo ties – the ones that held back his beautiful long hair. And Kelly finally broke down. Clutching the soft suede strips in her fist, she slowly collapsed on the closet floor and wept...

She looked at the time. It was almost midnight. She crawled into their great bed and waited for her husband. He must be late coming home from a meeting. But he never came home – and Kelly finally slept, holding his pillow as she would have held his body...

Later that week, she met with Sebastian's lawyer at his office – Phil's office. There was so much paperwork to go through – signatures and initials on everything. While they sat in the conference room reviewing her husband's final wishes, Kelly again realized the enormity of his love for her. Sebastian had ensured she would be financially comfortable for the rest of her life. His estate also covered all taxes and insurance for their home and the cabin property. For the rest of her life she would want for nothing... She would want for nothing.

She wanted her husband...

He had also requested his ashes be spread around their cabin property. She didn't know he had put that in his will! *No!* How could she do that?

Taking what was left of her husband – her Ulysses – in a ceramic jar...

Taking what was left of her husband and throwing it away...

Taking what was left of her husband and discarding it like yesterday's memories...

This was too much. He had asked too much. She hadn't the strength. She couldn't do it. She wouldn't do it. But she had to. He wanted her to do it. Through his written word he commanded she do it. *Oh God.* But she couldn't do it alone...

She sat in the conference room – feeling so small sitting at that large polished wooden table... She couldn't do it alone... *Oh God...*

Carolyn met her as she walked out of the room. She had packed a box of Sebastian's personal items including their framed wedding photo. As if in a dream, Kelly thanked her and walked out, carrying one lousy banker's box filled with memories. She never wanted to be in his office again.

She left the converted library building and walked down the granite steps, counting each step... Twelve steps – the quartz bits in each step sparkling against the early morning sunlight.

She was physically and mentally exhausted. These last days were too much. Just too much. She had never felt so tired, so beaten down. Just too much...

Roger was waiting, standing beside his truck. He had become her personal assistant, driving her wherever she needed to go, listening to her as she talked – and listening to her tears. She knew he cared for her... And she was grateful for his friendship.

He opened the passenger door for her and waited until she was settled. He returned to the driver's seat.

"That's it, Roger. I'm done here." Kelly placed the box between them and stared out the window, looking for the last time at that old sandstone building. The last time...

"Gal... Carolyn and Mike are getting married." Roger watched for her reaction. She slowly turned her head and looked at him, but had no response. "They didn't want to wait. They wanted you to know. That's all."

"Um... Carolyn didn't say anything. Of course I'm happy for them. I'm glad they're not waiting." Again looking out the window at nothing, she spoke as if in a dream. "It's not good to be alone..."

The opening of Bella's Italian Restaurant had been delayed by ten days. Kelly was bound and determined that Sebastian's vision became a reality. Everyone, including Kevin and Chef Tony and all the servers and staff were committed to following Sebastian's dream.

Epilogue

Kelly had come into the restaurant early – hers was always the first vehicle in the parking lot. Brie arrived a few minutes later followed by the noon prep cooks. While Kelly stood at the servers' station folding the freshly laundered and ironed linen napkins, a man she didn't recognize entered through the unlocked door. She looked around for Brie, but she had apparently walked back into the kitchen.

"We're not open yet." Kelly hoped this man would leave. This was her time – her alone time before the noon rush. She could hear Brie's voice laughing with the prep staff.

"Excuse me, Mrs. Bonsignore – I'm not here to eat."

Kelly stopped folding. This man looked so serious. What now?

"Kelly... Mrs. Bonsignore, I'm Matt English. I was your husband's urologist."

"Um, how can I help you... Dr. English?"

"I don't know how else to say this – while your late husband was under my care, he made a deposit with our sperm bank."

Kelly knew Sebastian had gone to his doctor's office to check his swimmers. But she didn't know anything else he had been doing there – or planning.

"I don't understand... Why are you telling me this...?"

"Mrs. Bonsignore, your husband donated his sperm if you decided to have his child."

The last thing Kelly remembered was a pair of strong hands catching her as she fell to the hardwood floor.

Acknowledgments

My first name – the name my mother gave me – was Mercedes-Mary McPherson. I was named after my mother's aunt, my great aunt. Until I was born, my mother lived at a home for unwed mothers, run by the Carmelite nuns.

A few weeks later, I was adopted and my name changed to Carol Jean. When I set to publish this trilogy, I wanted to use my birth name as my pen name. I mean, it really is a neat name, kind of rolls off your tongue. So now you know.

After my two youngest started grade school, I returned to college as a non-traditional student. The late Prof. Joseph Maiolo taught writing. It was for his class that I penned a short story entitled Rough New Prizes. (Yes, he gave me an A.) Years later after I retired, I discovered my little story and realized I now had the time make Kelly and Sebastian's life into a novel.

With a legal-size tablet and fountain pen, I sat on my lovely front porch and wrote what would become the first book in a trilogy. Lisa, my friend and former college classmate was the first to believe in me and became my editor. I've dedicated the first book in her name.

During the Northern Minnesota winters, I work at a cross-country ski chalet. Between serving mugs of hot chocolate to chilled families, I furiously penned the stories that would complete the trilogy. The ambiance of a roaring fire in the stone hearth was my muse...

Then, there are the railroaders in my life. You see, the main female character who's present in all three novels grew up in Colorado. At age 12, her father was killed in a train accident – the repercussions of which would follow her throughout her life. But I didn't know much about the trainline in that part of the country. Providence again was in my corner because, since my retirement, I've worked part time at the Lake Superior Railroad Museum. I consulted with Nick T., my favorite engineer. He introduced me to the Denver and Rio Grande Western railroad line. And he thankfully added that the engine should be the Tunnel Motor.

Rick M., a railroader and admitted train addict living in Texas, offered to do a final edit on the stories of the D&RGW Tunnel Motor. His suggestions and candid remarks helped to bring that hulking locomotive to life.

The beautiful covers for all three books were created by Julie M., an amazing graphic artist. I found her by accident on Google. Sometimes in life, there are no real accidents, because she is a remarkable artist! Before you read any novel, the cover must draw you in, and her designs compel you to open the book and read that first chapter – then it's up to me to keep you captivated with the stories. But I couldn't have done it alone.

I am surrounded by incredibly talented women, among them, my proof reader Sandra U., and my editors, Judy K. and Aurora W., who throughout this process knew how far to push me to become a better writer. I cannot thank them enough.

And to my Facebook friends and neighbors who read numerous drafts of the novels – their honest criticisms helped make the stories real. It is because of them that I am successful. I could not have published these novels without them.

A special thank you goes out to my neighbor Tracy L. Many evenings as we sat on my front porch, I would toss out ideas and story lines with her. Our conversations became the catalyst to some pretty spectacular twists, ensuring that my readers, once they began that first book, could not put down the Trilogy until reading the final pages of the third book.

Since I was just a little girl, I've had this obsession of putting my thoughts on paper – but never understood why. Within the last year, I discovered the identity of my biological father. (Don't you love how a story comes full circle?) He had met my mother while they attended college in Louisiana. At the time, he worked as a sports column writer for the college newspaper. When his girlfriend became pregnant, so I've been told, he offered marriage, but she declined and moved to Minnesota.

And he went on with his life. For over 60 years, he was a newspaper columnist, writing for newspapers in Tennessee and Pennsylvania. I've done the research and read some of his work. Ironically his writing style is similar to mine – or is my style similar to his? Writing was literally in my soul! Thank you, Ed G. for giving me such a talent! I am eternally grateful.

One character that is present in all three novels is based on a factual person. My father and his best friend Joe Rafferty were members of the Army Rangers, 2nd Battalion, Co. C. In preparation for D-Day, he and my dad trained in Bude in Cornwall, whose cliffs most resembled those in Normandy. At the landing on Omaha Beach, on that brave and terrible day in 1944, Capt. Joseph A. Rafferty was killed. His body was buried in Normandy. The character of Joe Rafferty is portrayed an honorable individual.